Jack At Sea
All Work And No Play
Made Him A Dull Boy

By

George Manville Fenn

Double 9
BOOKS

Jack At Sea
All Work And No Play Made Him A Dull Boy
by George Manville Fenn

Copyright © 2023

ISBN: 978-93-61425-21-9
Published by

DOUBLE 9 BOOKS

2/13-B, Ansari Road
Daryaganj, New Delhi – 110002
info@double9books.com
www.double9books.com
Tel. 011-40042856

ABOUT THE AUTHOR

George Manville Fenn was a very productive author of novels, a writer, an editor, and an educator from England. He was born on January 3, 1831, in Pimlico, London. He mostly learned on his own; he taught himself Italian, French, and German. During the years 1851–1854, he went to Battersea Training College for Teachers and then became the head of a state school in Alford, Lincolnshire. In the early 1850s, Fenn started to write short stories and pieces for newspapers and magazines. The Old Forest Ranger, his first book, came out in 1856. Afterward, he wrote more than 100 books, many of them for teenagers and young adults. He was one of the most famous writers of his time, and his books were well-liked and read by many people. He also worked as a reporter and writer for Fenn. Among the newspapers and magazines, he worked for was The Boy's Own Paper, which he ran from 1866 to 1874. He worked hard to make children's books better and was a strong supporter of education and reading. The Englishman Fenn passed away on August 26, 1909, in Isleworth.

CONTENTS

Chapter One
When a boy is not a boy

"Fine morning, Jack; why don't you go and have a run?"

John Meadows—always "Jack," because his father's name was John—upon hearing that father's voice, raised his dull, dreamy eyes slowly from the perusal of the old Latin author over which he was bending, and looked in Sir John's face, gazing at him inquiringly as if he had been walking with Cicero in Rome—too far away to hear the question which had fallen upon his ears like a sound which conveyed no meaning.

Father and son were as much alike as a sturdy sun-browned man of forty can resemble a thin, pale youth of sixteen or so. In other words, they possessed the same features, but the elder suggested an outdoor plant, sturdy and well-grown, the younger a sickly exotic, raised in the hot steaming air of the building which gardeners call a stove, a place in which air is only admitted to pass over hot-water pipes, for fear the plants within should shiver and begin to droop.

Sir John had just entered the handsome library, bringing with him a good breezy, manly suggestion of having been tramping through woods and over downs; and as soon as he had closed the door, he glanced at the large fire near to which his son had drawn a small writing-table, said "Pff!" unbuttoned his rough heather-coloured Norfolk jacket, raised his eyes to the window as if he would like to throw it open, and then lowered them and wrinkled up his forehead as he gazed at his son, carefully dressed in dark-brown velvet, and wearing correctly fitting trousers and patent leather shoes, a strong contrast to his own knickerbockers, coarse brown knitted stockings, and broad-soled shooting-boots.

Sir John looked anxious and worried, and he stretched out a strong brown hand to lay upon his son's shoulder, but he let it fall again, drew a deep breath, and then very gently asked him the question about the walk.

"Did you speak to me, father?" said the lad vacantly.

"Speak to you!" cried Sir John, in an impatient, angry tone, "of course I spoke to you. It worries me to see you so constantly sitting over the fire reading."

"Does it, father?" said the lad, wincing at the tone in which these words were spoken, and looking up in an apologetic way.

"I didn't mean to speak to you so sharply, my boy," continued Sir John, "but I don't like to see you neglecting your health so. Study's right enough, but too much of a good thing is bad for any one. Now, on a fine morning like this—"

"Is it fine, father? I thought it was cold."

"Cold! Tut—tut—tut! The weather is never cold to a healthy, manly boy."

"I'm afraid I'm not manly, father," said the lad.

"No, Jack, nor healthy neither; you are troubling me a great deal."

"Am I, father?" said the lad softly. "I'm very sorry. But I really am quite well."

"You are not, sir," cried Sir John, "and never will be if you spend all your time over books."

The lad gave him a sad, weary look.

"I thought you wanted me to study hard, father," he said reproachfully.

"Yes, yes, my boy, I do, and I should like to see you grow up into a distinguished man, but you are trying to make yourself into the proverbial dull boy."

"Am I? And I have worked so hard," said the lad in a weary, spiritless way.

"Yes; it's all work and no play with you, Jack, and it will not do, boy. When I was your age I was captain of our football club."

Jack shuddered.

"I often carried out my bat at cricket."

The lad sighed.

"I could stick on anything, from a donkey up to an unbroken colt; throw a ball as far as any of my age, and come in smiling and ready for a good meal after a long paper-chase."

Jack's pitiable look of despair was almost comical.

"While you, sir," cried Sir John angrily, "you're a regular molly, and do nothing but coddle yourself over the fire and read. It's read, read, read, from morning till night, and when you do go out, it's warm wrappers and flannel and mackintoshes. Why, hang it all, boy! you go about as if you were afraid of being blown over, or that the rain would make you melt away."

"I am very sorry, father," said the youth piteously; "I'm afraid I am not like other boys."

"Not a bit."

"I can't help it."

"You don't try, Jack. You don't try, my boy. I always had the best of accounts about you from Daneborough. The reports are splendid. And, there, my dear boy, I am not angry with you, but it is very worrying to see you going about with lines in your forehead and this white face, when I want to see you sturdy and—well, as well and hearty as I am. Why, Jack, you young dog!" he cried, slapping him on the shoulder, and making the lad wince, "I feel quite ashamed of myself. It isn't right for an old man like I am."

"You old, father!" said the lad, with more animation, and a faint flush came in his cheeks. "Why you look as well and young and strong as—"

"As you ought to be, sir. Why, Jack, boy, I could beat you at anything except books—walk you down, run you down, ride, jump, row, play cricket, shoot, or swim."

"Yes, father, I know," sighed the lad.

"But I'm ashamed to do anything of the kind when I see you moping like a sick bird in a cage."

"But I'm quite well, father, and happy—at least I should be if you were only satisfied with me."

"And I do want to see you happy, my boy, and I try to be satisfied with you. Now look here: come out with me more. I want to finish my collection of the *diptera*. Suppose you help me, and then we'll make another collection—birds say, or—no, I know: we'll take up the British fishes, and work them all. There's room there. It has never been half done. Why, what they call roach vary wonderfully. Even in two ponds close together the fish are as different as can be, and yet they call them all roach. Look here—we'll fish and net, and preserve in spirits, and you'll be surprised how much interest you will find in it combined with healthy exercise."

"I'll come with you, father, if you wish it," said the lad.

"Bah! That's of no use. I don't want you to come because I wish it. I want you to take a good healthy interest in the work, my boy. But it's of no use. I am right; you have worked too hard, and have read till your brain's getting worn out. There, I am right, Jack. You are not well."

"Doctor Instow, Sir John," said a servant, entering.

"Humph! lost no time," muttered the baronet. "Where is he, Edward?"

"In the drawing-room, Sir John."

"I'll come. No; show him in here."

"Father," whispered the lad excitedly, and a hectic spot showed in each cheek, "why has Doctor Instow come here?"

"Because I sent for him, my boy."

"But not to see me?" said the lad excitedly. "Indeed I am quite well."

"No, you are not, boy. Yes, he has come to see you, and try to set you right, so speak out to him like a man."

At that moment steps were heard crossing the polished oak floor of the great hall, and directly after a keen-eyed, vigorous-looking man of about six-and-thirty entered the room in a quick, eager way.

Chapter Two
Doctor Instow's prescription

"How are you?" he cried, rather boisterously, to Sir John, shaking hands warmly. "Well! no need to ask. And how are you, my Admirable Crichton?" he said, turning to Jack to continue the hand-shaking. "Well, no need to ask here either."

"No; I'm quite well, Doctor Instow."

"What! didn't they teach you to tell the truth at Daneborough, Jack Meadows?"

"Yes, of course," said the lad sharply.

"Then why don't you tell it?" said the doctor.

"There, Jack, you see," said Sir John quickly.

"What! has he been saying that he is quite well?" cried the doctor.

"Yes; he persists in it, when—"

"Any one can see with half an eye that he is completely out of order."

"You hear, Jack?"

"Yes, father, I hear," said the boy; "but really I am quite, quite well."

"'Quite, quite well,'" said the doctor, laughing merrily, as he sank back in his chair. "Never felt better in your life, eh, Jack? Haven't been so well since I doctored you for measles, ten years ago, when I was a young man, just come to Fernleigh, eh?"

"I do not see anything to laugh at, Doctor Instow," said the lad gravely.

"No? Well, I do, my dear boy—at the way in which you tell your anxious father and his old friend that there is nothing the matter with you, when the nature in you is literally shouting to every one who sees you, 'See how ill I am.'"

"Doctor Instow, what nonsense!" cried the lad.

"Indeed? Why, not ten minutes ago, as I drove towards the Hall, I met the Rector, and what do you think he said?"

"I don't know," said Jack, fidgeting in his chair.

"Then I'll tell you, my lad. 'Going to see young Jack?' he said. 'I don't know, but I expect so,' says your humble servant. 'Well, I hope you are, for I've felt quite concerned about his looks.'"

"But I can't help looking pale and delicate," cried Jack hurriedly. "Plenty of other boys do."

"Of course they do; but in your case you can help it."

"But how?" said Jack fretfully.

"I'll tell you directly," said the doctor. "Look here, Meadows, am I to speak out straight?"

"I beg that you will," said Sir John quickly. "I have sent for you because I cannot go on like this. No disrespect to you, my dear Instow, but I was thinking seriously of taking him up to some great specialist in town."

"I'm very glad to hear you say so," cried the doctor. "If you had not, before many days were over I should have sounded the alarm myself."

"Indeed!" cried Sir John.

"Yes; I should have presumed on our old intimacy, and told you what I thought, and that it was time something was done. We'll take him up to Doctor Lorimer, or Sir Humphrey Dean, or one of the other medical big-wigs. You sent for me, then, to give you my opinion. Here it is straight. It is the right thing to do, and before you start, I'll write down my idea of the proper course of treatment, and I guarantee that either of the fashionable physicians will prescribe the same remedies."

"Then," said Sir John eagerly, "you think you can see what is the matter with him?"

"Think? I'm sure, sir."

"I am glad of it, for I had decided not to take him up to a physician."

"Thank you, father," said Jack, giving him a grateful look. "There really is no need."

"Because," continued Sir John firmly, "I thought the matter over,"—and he talked at his son—"and I said to myself that it is impossible that a London doctor can in a visit or two understand the case half so well as the medical man who has known and attended him from a child."

"Thank you, Meadows," said the doctor warmly. "I thank you for your confidence. I do not want to boast of my knowledge, but, as I said before, I am perfectly sure of what is the matter with Jack here."

"Yes? What is it?—or no, I ought not to ask you that," said the father, with a hasty glance at his son.

"Oh yes, you ought. Why not? In this case it is quite right that he should know. I am going to convince him that he is in a very bad way."

"You think so?" cried Sir John, leaning forward anxiously.

"Yes, sir, a very bad way, though the conceited young rascal is laughing in his sleeve and mentally calling me a pretender."

"Indeed, no, Doctor Instow," cried Jack indignantly.

"What? Why you are saying to yourself all the time that you know better than I."

"I only felt that I was right and you were wrong, doctor," said the lad frankly.

"Same thing, my boy," cried the doctor, smiling. "Not the first time two people have been of different opinions, and we shan't quarrel, Jack. Know one another too well."

"Yes, yes," said Sir John impatiently. "But you said you thought he was in a bad way."

"I said I was sure."

"Yes, yes; then what is to be done? We must get him out of the bad way."

"The right treatment to a T," said the doctor.

"Then be frank, Instow," said Sir John; "what is the matter?"

Page missing, to be inserted when found.

Page missing, to be inserted when found.

fight again, but it has been fostered too much. Dad here, in his pride of your attainments, has allowed you to go too far. He has thought it was a natural weakness and tendency to bad health which kept you from taking to outdoor life more, but neither he nor I had the least idea that you carried it to such an extent, and it did not show so much till you came home after this last half."

"No, not till now, my boy," said Sir John.

"The result of the grinding of the past four years is just coming out with a rush," continued the doctor, "and if you went back to the school you would break down by the next holidays."

"If I went back?" cried the boy. "If? Oh, I must go back. I am expected to take some of the principal prizes next year."

"And lose the greatest prize that can be gained by a young man, my lad—health."

"Hah!" sighed Sir John; "he is quite right, Jack, I am afraid."

"Right as right, my boy. Here in four years you have done the work of about eight. It's very grand, no doubt, but it won't do."

"But what is to be done?" cried Sir John.

"Let the brain run fallow for the other four years, and give the body a chance," said the doctor bluntly.

"What! do nothing for four years?" cried the lad indignantly.

"Who said do nothing?" said the doctor testily.

"Do something else. Rest your brain with change, and give your body a fair chance of recovering its tone."

"Yes, Jack, my boy; he is quite right," cried Sir John.

"But, father, I should be wretched."

"How do you know?" said the doctor. "You have tried nothing else but books. There is something else in the world besides books, my lad. Ask your father if there is not. What's that about sermons in insects and running stones in the brooks, Meadows? I never can recollect quotations. Don't you imagine, my conceited young scholiast, that there is nothing to be seen or studied that does not exist in books. But I'm growing hoarse with talking and telling you the simple truth."

"Yes, Jack, my boy, it is the simple truth," said Sir John. "I was saying something of the kind to you, as you know, when Doctor Instow came; but all the time I was sure that you were ill—and you are."

"Oh yes, he's ill, and getting worse. Any one can see that."

"But I do not feel ill, father."

"Don't feel languid, I suppose?" said the doctor.

"Well, yes, I do often feel languid," said Jack, "when the weather is—"

"Bother the weather!" roared the doctor. "What business has a boy like you to know anything about the weather? Your father and I at your age would have played football, or cricket, or gone fishing in any weather—eh, Meadows?"

"Yes, in any weather," said Sir John, smiling. "A British boy knowing anything about the weather! Bosh! Do you think any of our old heroes ever bothered their brains about the weather when they wanted to do something? Look here! another word or two. You always go to sleep of course directly you lay your head on the pillow, and want another snooze when it's time to get up, eh?"

"No," said the lad sadly, "I often lie awake a long time thinking."

"Thinking!" cried the doctor in tones of disgust. "The idea of a healthy boy thinking when he goes to bed! It's monstrous. An overstrained brain, my lad. You are thoroughly out of order, my boy, and it was quite time that you were pulled up short. Frankly, you've been over-crammed with food to nourish the brain, while the body has been starved."

"And now, my boy, we're going to turn over a new leaf, and make a fresh start. Come, doctor, you will prescribe for him at once."

"What! jalap and senna, and *Pil. Hydrargerum*, and that sort of stuff, to make him pull wry faces?"

"I do not profess to understand much of such matters; but I should presume that you would give him tonics. What will you give him to take— bark?"

"No: something to make him bite."

"Well, what?"

"Nothing!"

"Nothing?"

"Ah, you are like the rest of the clever people, Meadows. You think a doctor is of no good unless he gives you pills and draughts. But don't be alarmed, Jack, boy. I am not going to give you either."

"What then?"

"Nothing, I tell you. Yes, I am; fresh air—fresh water."

"Yes; and then?"

"More fresh air, and more fresh water. Look here, Meadows; food is the best medicine for his case—good, wholesome food, and plenty of it as soon as he can digest. I want to hear him say, 'What's for dinner to-day?' That's a fine sign of a boy being in good health."

"Well, Jack, what do you say to all this?" said Sir John.

"I don't know what to say, father," replied the lad. "I did not know I was unwell."

"I suppose not," interposed the doctor. "But you are, and the worst of it is that you will get worse."

"Then give your instructions," said Sir John, "and we will try and follow them out—eh, Jack?"

"I will do anything you wish, father," said the boy, with a sigh.

"Yes, of course you will, my boy. Well, doctor, we are waiting. Let's take the stitch in time."

"Ah! but we can't now," said Doctor Instow. "We shall have to take nine, or eighty-one, or some other number in what our young philosopher calls geometrical progression—that's right, isn't it, Jack, eh?"

"Yes, I suppose so," said the lad, smiling. "Well, then, thread the needle for us, Instow," said Sir John merrily; "and we will begin to stitch, and be careful not to neglect our health for the future. Now then, we're both ready."

"Yes; but I'm not," said the doctor thoughtfully. "This is a ticklish case, and wants ticklish treatment. You see I know my patient. He is so accustomed to one particular routine, that it will be hard to keep him from longing for his customary work and habits. Suppose I prescribe outdoor work, riding, walking, cricket or football, according to the season; I shall be giving him repellent tasks to do. I can't make him a little fellow eager and longing to begin these things which he sees his bigger school-fellows enjoying. He would be disgusted with games directly, because others would laugh at him and call him a muff."

"Yes," said Sir John with a sigh, "the rent has grown very large, and I don't see how we are to sew it up."

"Neither do I," said the doctor; "it's past mending. We must have a new coat, Jack."

"You mean a new boy, Doctor Instow," said the lad, smiling sadly. "Had you not better let me be?"

"No," cried Sir John, bringing his fist down heavily upon he table. "That won't do, Jack. We've done wrong, taken the wrong turning, and we must go back and start afresh—eh, Instow?"

"Of course," said the doctor testily, "and give me time. I've got plenty of ideas, but I want to select the right one. Ah! I have it."

"Yes," cried Sir John eagerly, and his son looked at him in dismay.

"That's the very thing. Right away from books and the ordinary routine of life—fresh air of the best, fresh people, fresh scenes, constant change; everything fresh but the water, and that salt."

"Some country place at the seaside," said Sir John eagerly.

"No, no; bore the boy to death; make him miserable. Seaside! No, sir, the whole sea, and get away from the side as soon as possible."

"A sea voyage!" cried Sir John; and his son's face contracted with horror.

"That's the thing, sir. You have always been grumbling about the narrowness of your sphere, and envying men abroad who send and bring such fine collections home. Be off together, and make a big collection for yourselves of everything you come across worth saving."

"Yes; but where?"

"Anywhere—North Pole; South Pole; tropics. Start free from all trammels, open new ground away from the regular beaten tracks. You don't want to go by line steamers to regular ports. Get a big ocean-going yacht, and sail round the world. Here, what are you grinning at, patient?"

"At your idea, sir. It is so wild."

"Wild to you, sir, because you are so tame. It may have seemed a little wild for Captain Cook and Bougainville and the old Dutch navigators, with their poor appliances and ignorance of what there was beyond the seas. Wild too for Columbus; but wild now! Bah! I'm ashamed of you."

"You must recollect that Jack is no sailor," said Sir John, interposing. "He was very ill when we crossed to Calais."

"Iii! A bit sea-sick. That's nothing."

"I am not sailor enough to manage a yacht."

"What of that? Charter a good vessel, and get a clever captain and mate, and the best crew that can be picked. You can afford it, and to do it well, and relieve yourself of all anxieties, so as to be free both of you to enjoy your cruise."

"Enjoy!" said Jack piteously.

"But the responsibility?" said Sir John thoughtfully. "I should like it vastly. But to take a sick lad to sea? Suppose he were taken worse?"

"Couldn't be."

"Don't exaggerate, doctor. Fancy us away from all civilised help, and Jack growing far weaker—no medical advice."

"I tell you he would grow stronger every day. Well, take a few boxes of pills with you; fish for cod, and make your own cod-liver oil, and make him drink it—oil to trim the lamp of his waning life and make it burn. He won't want anything of the kind—rest for his brain and change are his medicines."

"I dare not risk it," said Sir John sadly, and Jack's face began to light up.

"Well then, if you must do something foolish, take a doctor with you."

"Ah, but how to get the right man?"

"Pooh! Hundreds would jump at the chance."

Jack sighed, and looked from one to the other, while Sir John gazed hard at the doctor, who said merrily—

"There, don't sit trying to bring up difficulties where there is nothing that cannot be surmounted. What have you got hold of now?"

"I have not got hold of him. I am only trying to do so."

"What do you mean?"

"The doctor. Will you go with us, Instow?"

"I?" cried Doctor Instow, staring. "Only too glad of the chance. I'm sick of spending all my days in the sordid practice of trying to make money, when the world teems with wonders one would like to try and investigate. If I did not know that I was doing some little good amongst my fellow-creatures, my life would be unbearable, and I would have thrown it all up long ago."

"Then if I decide to follow out your advice, you will come with us?"

"No," said the doctor firmly; "it would not do."

Jack brightened up again.

"Why would it not do?" said Sir John anxiously. "The plan is excellent, and I am most grateful to you for the suggestion. Come with us, Instow, for I certainly will go."

Jack groaned.

"Look at him," cried the doctor. "There's spirit. The sooner you get to sea the better."

"Yes, I have decided upon it, if you will come."

"No, no; impossible."

"Because of leaving your practice?"

"Oh no; I could arrange that by having a *locum tenens*—'local demon' as the servant-girl in *Punch* called him."

"Then what objection is there?"

"Why, it's just as if I had been planning a pleasure-trip for myself at your expense."

"That's absurd, Instow, and an insult to an old friend. Look here, if you will come I shall look upon it as conferring a great favour upon us. We shall both be under a greater obligation to you than ever."

"I say, don't tempt me, Meadows. I'm not a bad doctor, but I'm a very weak man."

"But I will tempt you," cried Sir John eagerly. "Come, you can't let your old friend go without a companion, and stop here at home, knowing that there will be times when you could help Jack there on his way to health and strength."

"No, I can't—can I?" said the doctor, hesitating. "But no, no, it wouldn't do."

"Here, Jack, come and help me press him to go with us."

"I can't, father; oh, I can't," cried the boy despairingly.

"Oh, that settles it!" said Doctor Instow, jumping up. "You've done it now, Jack. You're worse than I thought."

"Then you will come?" cried Sir John, holding out his hand.

"I will," cried the doctor, "wherever you like to go;" and he brought down his hand with a sounding slap into his friend's. "Here, Jack," he cried directly after, "shake hands too. Come, be a man. In less than six months those dull filmy eyes of yours will be flashing with health, and you'll be wondering that you could ever have sat gazing at me in this miserable woe-begone fashion. There, pluck up, my lad. You don't know what is before you in the strange lands we shall visit. Why, when your father and I were boys of your age, we should have gone wild with delight at the very anticipation of such a cruise, and rushed off to our bedrooms to begin packing up at once, and crammed our boxes with all kinds of impossible unnecessaries—eh, Meadows?"

"Yes; our skates, cricket-bats—" cried Sir John.

"And fishing-rods, and sticks. I say, though, we must take a good supply of sea and fresh-water tackle. Fancy trying some river or lake in the tropics that has never been fished before."

"Yes, and a walk at the jungle edge, butterfly-catching," cried Sir John eagerly.

"Yes, and a tramp after rare birds, and always in expectation of bringing down one never yet seen by science," said the doctor.

"And the flowers and plants," said Sir John, "We must take plenty of cases and preserving paste."

"And entomological boxes and tins."

"Plenty of spirits, of course, too," cried the doctor. "I say, my little cooking apparatus I designed—it will be invaluable; and I shall treat myself to a new double gun, and a rifle."

"No need, my dear boy; I have plenty. But we must have a thoroughly good supply of fishing-tackle of all kinds."

"And cartridges," said the doctor. "What do you say to clothes for the rough work?"

"We must have plenty, and flannels and pyjamas," said Sir John. "A couple of small portable tents, too."

"And boots for the jungle—high boots. A deal depends on boots."

"No, not high," said Sir John, "they're a nuisance—good lace-up ankle boots, with knickerbockers and leggings."

"Yes, I believe you are right. My word, old fellow, we've got our work cut out to prepare."

"Yes; how soon would you go?"

"As soon as ever we can get away."

"That's the style. Nothing like striking while the iron is hot."

And, full of enthusiasm, the two friends sat throwing suggestions at one another, nearly forgetting the presence of Jack, who did not catch a spark of their excitement, but sat gazing at them with lack-lustre eyes, and a weary, woe-begone expression of countenance, for it seemed to him that all was over, that he was to be dragged away from his studious pursuits to a dreary end. His father and their old friend the doctor meant well, no doubt; but he knew that they were mistaken, and when the doctor left at last, it was for Sir John to wake up to the fact that he had never seen his son look so despondent before.

"Why, Jack, lad, what a face!" cried Sir John merrily.

The boy looked in his eyes, but said nothing. "Come, come, the doctor's right. Put away the books, and help me to prepare for our cruise."

"Then you really mean for us to go, father?" said the lad.

"Yes; I have quite made up my mind." Jack sighed like a girl.

"But you will let me take a few boxes of books, father?"

"A few natural history works of reference, nothing more. Bah! don't be so narrow-minded, boy. We shall be where Nature's own grand library is always open before us to read. We shall want no books. Come, pluck up, my lad; all this means ill health. Instow is perfectly right, and the sooner we begin our preparations the better."

"Father!" cried the boy passionately, "it will kill me."

"No," said Sir John, taking the boy's hand, and laying his own right affectionately upon his shoulder; "if I thought it would hurt you I would not stir a step; but I feel that it is to bring you back to a healthy life."

Jack sighed again, and shook his head.

"Ah," he argued to himself, "life and all that is worth living for—all passing away."

Chapter Three
In doleful dump

"Beg pardon, sir."

Jack raised his head wearily from where it was resting upon his hand by the fireside, and looked dreamingly at the footman who had entered the warm library next morning.

"Head ache, sir?" said the man respectfully; and the well-built, fair, freckled-faced, but good-looking fellow gazed commiseratingly at his young master.

"My head ache, Edward? Yes, sadly, sadly."

"Begging your pardon, sir; it's because you sit over the fire too much."

"What!" cried Jack angrily; "have you got that silly idea in your head too? How dare you!"

"Beg pardon, sir. Very sorry, sir. Don't be angry with me, sir. You see I don't know any better."

"Then it's time you did."

"So it is, Master Jack, so it is; and I want to know better, if you'll help me."

"How can I help you?" said Jack, staring at the man.

"Well, you see, sir, it's like this: I don't get no chance to improve my mind. Up at six o'clock— No," cried the man emphatically, "I will speak the honest truth if I die for it! It ain't much before seven when I begin work, sir, for you see I have such a stiff beard, and it does grow so, I'm obliged to shave reg'lar. Well, say quarter to seven I begin, and it's boots and shoes. When they're done it's hard work to get my knives done before breakfast. Then there's the breakfast cloth to lay, and the toast to make, and after breakfast master's and your dress-clothes to brush; and them done, my plate to clean. That brings me up to laying the cloth for lunch, and—"

"Look here, Edward," cried Jack impatiently, "do you suppose I want to learn all you do in a day?"

"No, sir, of course not. I only wanted you to understand why it is I've no time to improve my mind."

"So much the better for you, Ned," cried Jack. "I've improved mine, and Sir John and the doctor say that I've been doing wrong."

"Do they, sir, really? Well, they ought to know; but all the same I feel as if I want to improve mine."

"Let it alone, Ned," said the boy drearily.

"No, sir, I can't do that, when there's such a chance in one's way."

"Chance! What for?" said Jack, whose interest was awakened by the man's earnestness.

"That's what I'm telling you, sir, a chance to improve myself."

"How?"

"Well, you see, sir, I've got ears on my head."

"Of course you have."

"And can't help hearing, sir, a little of what's said."

"Look here, Ned," cried Jack, "I'm unwell; my head aches, and I'm very much worried. Tell me what it is that you want as briefly as you can."

"Well, sir, begging your pardon, sir, I couldn't help hearing that Sir John and you and the doctor's going abroad."

"Yes, Ned," said Jack moodily; "we're going abroad."

"Well, sir, I'd thank you kindly if you'd speak a word to master for me."

"What, about a character? There is no need, Ned; you will stay here till we come back—if ever we do," he added bitterly.

"Oh, you'll come back right enough, sir. But don't you see that's just what I don't want, unless I can come back too."

"What do you mean, Ned? Can't you see that you are worrying me dreadfully?"

"I am sorry, sir, for if there's a thing I can't abear, it's being talked to when I've got one o' them stinging 'eadaches. But I keep on explaining to you, sir. Don't you see? I want you to speak a word to Sir John about taking me with you."

"You!" cried Jack. "You want to go with us round the world?"

"Now, Master Jack," cried the man reproachfully, "would you like to spend all your days cleaning knives and boots and shoes, when it wasn't plate and waiting at table?"

"No, of course not; but you must be mad to want to do such a thing as go upon this dreadful journey."

"Dreadful journey! My word of honour, Master Jack, you talking like that!" cried the man. "You talking like that!" he repeated. "A young gent like you! Well, I'm about stunned. Do you know it would be about the greatest treat a body could have?"

"No, I don't," said Jack shortly. "It means nothing but misery and discomfort. A rough life amongst rough people; no chance to read and study. Oh, it would be dreadful."

"Well!" exclaimed the man; and again, "Well! You do cap me, sir, that you do. Can't you see it means change?"

"I don't want change," cried Jack petulantly.

"Oh, don't you say that, sir," cried Edward reproachfully; "because, begging your pardon, it ain't true."

"What! Are you going to begin on that silly notion too? I tell you I am not ill."

"No, sir, you're not ill certainly, because you don't have to take to your bed, and swaller physic, and be fed with a spoon, but every bit of you keeps on shouting that you ain't well."

"How? Why? Come now," cried the boy with more animation, as he snatched at the opportunity for gaining an independent opinion of his state. "But stop: has my father or Doctor Instow been saying anything to you?"

"To me, sir? Not likely."

"Then tell me what you mean."

"Well, sir; you're just like my magpie."

"What!" cried Jack angrily.

"I don't mean no harm, sir; you asked me."

"Well, there, go on," cried Jack pettishly.

"I only meant you were like him in some ways. You know, sir, I give one of the boys threppuns for him two years ago, when there was the nest at the top of the big ellum."

"Oh yes, I've seen the bird."

"I wasn't sure, sir, for you never did take much notice of that sort of thing. Why, some young gents is never happy unless they're keeping all kinds of pets—pigeons and rabbits and hedgehogs and such."

"I wish you wouldn't talk quite so much," cried Jack sharply.

"There, sir, that's what it is. You want stirring up. I like that. You haven't spoke to me so sharp since I don't know when."

"What, do you like me to scold you?"

"I'd like you to bully me, and chuck things at me too, sooner than see you sit moping all day as you do, sir. That's what made me say you put me in mind of my magpie. He sits on his perch all day long with his feathers, set up, and his tail all broken and dirty, and not a bit o' spirit in him. He takes the raw meat I cut up for him, but he doesn't eat half of it, only goes and pokes the bits into holes and corners, and looks as miserable and moulty as can be. It's because he's always shut up in a cage, doing just the same things every day, hopping from perch to perch that often—and back again over and over again, till he hasn't got a bit of spirit in him. I'm just the same—it's boots and knives and plate and coal-scuttles and answer the bells, till I get tired of a night and lie abed asking myself whether a strong chap like me was meant to go on all his life cleaning boots and knives; and if I was, what's the good of it all? I'm sick of it, Master Jack, and there's been times when I've been ready to go and 'list for a soldier, only I don't believe that would be much better. The toggery's right enough, and you have a sword or a gun, but it's mostly standing in a row and being shouted at by sergeants. But now there's a chance of going about and seeing what the world's like, and its works, and how it goes round, and you say you don't want to go. Why, it caps me, it do, sir, really."

"Yes," cried Jack angrily; "and it 'caps me,' as you call it, to hear a good servant like you talk about giving up a comfortable place and want to go on a long and dangerous voyage. Are you not well fed and clothed and paid, and have you not a good bed?"

"Yes, sir; yes sir; yes, sir," cried Edward; "but a man don't want to be always comfortable, and well fed, and to sleep on a feather bed. He's a poor sort of a chap who does. I don't think much of him. It's like being a blind horse in a clay mill, going round and round and round all his life. Why, he never gets so much change as to be able to go the other way round, because if he did the mill wouldn't grind."

"Pooh!" cried Jack sharply. "It is not true: you can have plenty of change. Clean knives first one day, and boots first the next, and then begin with the plate."

"Ha—ha! haw—haw! he—he!" cried the man, boisterously, laughing, and in his enjoyment lifting up one leg and putting it down with a stamp over and over again.

"Don't stand there laughing like an idiot!" cried Jack angrily. "How dare you!"

"Can't help it, sir, really, sir; can't help it. You made me. But go on, sir. Do. Chuck some books at me for being so impudent."

"I will," cried Jack fiercely, "if you don't leave the room."

"That's right, sir; do, sir; it's stirred you up. Why, you have got the stuff in you, Master Jack. I do believe you could fight after all if you was put to it. You, sir, actually, sir, making a joke about the knives and boots. Well, I wouldn't have believed it of you."

"Leave the room, sir!"

"Yes, sir, directly, sir; but do please ask the governor to take me, sir."

"Leave the room, sir!" cried Jack, starting to his feet.

"Certainly, sir, but if you would—"

Whish!—Bang!—Jingle!

In a fit of petulant anger Jack had followed the man's suggestion, caught up a heavy Greek lexicon, and thrown it with all his might, or rather with all his weakness, at the servant's head. Edward ducked down, and the book went through the glass of one of the cases; and at the same moment Sir John Meadows entered the library.

Chapter Four
A ready-made man

"What's the meaning of this?" cried Sir John angrily, as he stood staring in astonishment at his son's anger-distorted, flushed face, then at the footman, and back at his son.

"I—I—this fellow—this man—Edward was insolent, and—and—I—father—I—ordered him—to leave the room—and—and he would not go."

"Oh, I beg pardon, Master Jack, sir," said Edward reproachfully. "I said I'd go, and I was going."

"Silence, sir!" cried Sir John, frowning. "Now, Jack, he would not go?"

"I was angry, father—and—and—"

"And you threw this book at him, and broke the pane of glass?"

"Yes, father," said the boy, who was now scarlet, as he stood trembling with excitement and mortification.

"Humph!" ejaculated Sir John, crossing to raise the very short skirt of his brown velveteen Norfolk jacket, and stand with his hands behind him in front of the fire. "Pick up that book, Edward."

"Yes, Sir John."

"And tell one of the housemaids to come and sweep up the pieces."

"Yes, Sir John," said the man, moving toward the door.

"Stop! What does that signal to Mr Jack mean?"

"Well, Sir John, I—"

"Wait a minute. Now, Jack, in what way was Edward insolent to you?"

"Only laughed, Sir John."

"Be silent, sir! Now, Jack!"

"He irritated me, father," said the lad hastily. "He came to worry me with an absurd request, and—and when I ridiculed it, he burst out laughing in a rude, insolent way."

"Beg pardon, Sir John," said the man respectfully.—"Not insolent, Master Jack."

"Say Mr Jack."

"Certn'y, Sir John. *Mister* Jack actually made a joke,—it wasn't a good one, Sir John, but it seemed so rum for him to make a joke, and then get in a passion, that I bust out larfin, Sir John, and I couldn't help it really."

Sir John looked wonderingly at his son for an explanation.

"It was only a bit of petulant nonsense, father," stammered the lad. "I'm very sorry."

"And pray what was the request Edward made?"

"Well, father, it was about this dreadful business."

"What dreadful business?"

Jack was silent for a few moments, but his father's stern eyes were fixed upon him, and he stammered out—

"This going abroad."

"Oh!—Well?"

"He came to beg me to ask you to take him with you."

"With *us*," said Sir John.

"Ye–es, father, if we went."

"There is no *if* about it, Jack," said Sir John quietly; "we are going. Humph! and you wanted to go, Edward?"

"Yes, sir, please, Sir John," cried the man earnestly. "I'd give anything to go."

Sir John looked at the man searchingly.

"Humph!" he said at last. "Well, I suppose it would sound attractive to a young man of your age."

"Attractive ain't the word for it, Sir John," cried the man.

Sir John smiled.

"Some people differ in their opinions, my lad," he said, with a meaning glance at his son.

"Yes, Sir John, meaning Master—Mister Jack; but he don't half understand what it means yet."

"You are quite right, Edward. In his delicate state he does not quite grasp what it means."

"Oh, father," cried the lad reproachfully; "don't speak like that. Once more, indeed I am not ill."

"Humph!" said Sir John, smiling, "not ill? What do you think, Edward?"

"No, Sir John, not ill, cert'nly," said the man.

"There, father!" cried Jack excitedly, and with a grateful look at their servant, but it faded out directly.

"He ain't no more ill than I am, Sir John, if I may make so bold. It's only that he wants stirring up. He reads and reads over the fire till he can't hardly see for the headache, and it's what I told him just now, he's all mopey like for want of change."

"Humph! You told him that?" said Sir John sharply.

"Yes, Sir John," faltered the man. "I know it was not my place, and I beg pardon. It slipped out quite promiskus like. I know now I oughtn't. It made Master—Mister Jack angry, and he chucked the book at me. Not as I minded the act, for I was glad to see he'd got so much spirit in him."

"And so you would like to go with us?"

"Oh yes, Sir John," cried the man, flushing with excitement. "But you wouldn't want me to go in livery, of course?"

"No," said Sir John quietly. "I should not want you to go in livery. I cannot consent to take you at all."

"Oh, sir!" cried the man appealingly.

"I am not sorry to hear you make the application, for it shows me that you are satisfied with your position as my servant. But the man I should select to take with us must be a strong active fellow."

"That's me, Sir John. I haven't been neither sick nor sorry all the five years I've been with you, 'cept that time when I cut my hand with the broken decanter."

"An outdoor servant," continued Sir John, rather sternly, passing over his man's interruption—"a man with something of the gamekeeper about him—a man who can tramp through woods, carry rifles and guns, and clean them; use a fishing-net or line; row, chop wood and make a fire; set up a tent or a hut of boughs; cook, and very likely skin birds and beasts. In short, make himself generally useful."

"And valet you and Mr Jack, Sir John," interposed the man.

"Certainly not, Edward; we shall leave all those civilised luxuries behind. You see I want a thorough outdoor servant, not such a man as you."

"Beg pardon, Sir John," cried the man promptly; "but it's me you do want, I'm just the sort you said."

"You?" said Sir John, smiling rather contemptuously.

"Yes, Sir John. I was meant for an outdoor man, only one can't get to be what one likes, and so I had to take to indoor."

Sir John shook his head.

"You are a very excellent servant, Edward," he said, "and I shall have great pleasure in giving you a very strong recommendation for cleanliness and thorough attention to your duties. I cannot recall ever having to find fault with you."

"Never did, Sir John, I will say that; and do you think I'm going to leave such a master as you and Mr Jack here, though he does chuck big books at me!" he said with a grin. "Not me."

"I thank you for all this, Edward, but—"

"Don't, don't say no, Sir John—in a hurry," cried the man imploringly. "You only know what I can do from what you've seen; and you know that having a willing heart and 'and 's half-way to doing anything."

"Yes," said his master with a smile; "I know too that you're a very handy person."

"Hope so, Sir John; but I'm obliged to stick up for myself, as there's no one here to do it for me. There ain't nothing you want done that I can't do. Father was a gamekeeper and bailiff and woodman, and when I was a boy I used to help him, cutting hop-poles with a bill-hook, felling trees with an axe, and I've helped him to make faggots, hurdles, and stacks, and tents, and thatched. I've helped him many a time use the drag and the cast-net, fishing. I can set night lines, and I had a gun to use for shooting rabbits and varmint, and I learned to skin and stuff 'em. We've got cases and cases at home. I used to wash out the master's guns, and dry and oil them; and as for lighting fires and cooking, why, I beg your pardon for laughing, Sir John, but my mother was ill for years before she died, and I always did all the cooking. Then I've had a turn at gardening and stable work; and as for the water, I can row, punt, or sail any small boat. I don't say as I could tackle a ship, but if there was no one else to do it, I'd have a try; and—beg pardon, Sir John, there's the front-door bell."

"Go and answer it," said Sir John quietly.

"And if you would think it over, Sir John—"

"Go and answer the bell."

The man darted out, and Sir John turned to his son to gaze at him for a time.

"You're a pretty good scholar for your age, Jack," he said; "but I wish you possessed some of Edward's accomplishments."

"Oh, father!" cried the boy hastily.

"But you have more strength in your arm than I thought for. That is plate glass."

"Doctor Instow," said Edward; and the doctor entered like a breeze.

"Morning!" he cried boisterously.

"Don't go, Edward," said Sir John; and the man stayed by the door, looking white with excitement.

"I was obliged to run in," said the doctor. "Well, Jack. Why, hulloa! You've got a bit more colour in your cheeks this morning, and your eyes are brighter. Come, that's good. You're beginning to take then to the idea?"

"No," said Jack firmly.

"Stop a moment, doctor," cried Sir John. "Here is some one of a different opinion. This foolish fellow has been laying before us his petition."

"Who? Edward?"

"Yes; he wants to go."

"Well," said the doctor; "we shall want a good smart handy man."

Edward's cheeks began to colour again.

"Yes; but what do you think? We want a strong fellow, not a fireside servant."

"Quite right, but— Here, take off your coat, my man."

Edward's livery coat seemed to fly off, and displayed his white arms with the shirt-sleeves rolled right above the elbows, spotted a little with rouge from plate-cleaning.

"Hum! ha!" said the doctor, taking one arm and doubling it up so that the biceps rose in a big lump. "Hard.—Stand still."

He laid one hand upon the man's chest and thumped it in different places; laid his ear to it and pressed it close.

"Now breathe.—Again.—Now harder.—Hold your breath."

Then he rose and twisted the man round, and listened at his back between the shoulder-blades before making him open his mouth, and ended by looking into his eyes, while the father and son watched him.

"Ha! that will do," said the doctor dryly. "Sleep well, I suppose?"

"Oh yes, sir."

"And you can eat and drink well?"

The man's face expanded in a broad smile.

"Goes without saying. There, put on your coat."

Edward began to put it on.

"Sound as a bell," said the doctor. "Strong as a horse."

"Yes, but we want something besides a healthy man."

"Of course: a good handy, willing fellow, who would not want to come home as soon as he had to rough it and do everything."

"There ain't anything I wouldn't do, gentlemen," cried Edward. "If you take me, Sir John, I'll serve you faithful, and you shan't repent it. May I tell the doctor, Sir John, what I can do?"

"There is no need. He boasts, Instow."

"Beg pardon, Sir John, it ain't boasting, it's honest truth."

"Yes, Edward, I believe you feel that it is. Well, Instow, he says he has been accustomed to outdoor life with his father from boyhood. His father was a gamekeeper and woodman. That he can shoot, fish, clean guns, manage nets, ride, sail boats, punt and row. Do everything, including building huts and cooking."

"Don't want any cooking. I shall do that myself."

"In addition, he can skin birds and beasts."

"Ha!" ejaculated the doctor. "Well, if we engage a stranger, we don't know how he'll turn out, and it would be very awkward to have a man who would turn tail at the first bit of discomfort. Look here, sir, it will be a rough life."

"If you only knew, doctor, how hungry I am for a bit of rough outdoor time, you'd put in a word for me," cried the man excitedly.

"And suppose we get in a hot corner, and have to fight for our lives against black fellows?"

There was a grim look in the man's face at once—a regular British bull-dog aspect, as he tightened his lips, and made wrinkles at the corners, as if putting his mouth in a parenthesis, and then he began to tuck up his cuffs and double his fists.

"That will do, Edward," said the doctor quietly. "We know him, Meadows, for a steady, straightforward fellow, sound in wind and limb, who has never given me a job since he tried to cut his hand off with a bit of glass. What he don't know he'd soon learn; and I should say that we are not likely to get a more suitable fellow if we tried for six months."

Edward's face was a study, as he glanced at Jack, and then turned to gaze imploringly at his master as if he were a judge about to utter words upon which his life depended.

"That will do, Edward, you may leave the room."

A look of despair came across the man's face, as in true servant fashion he turned to obey orders, and went straight to the door.

"Stop," said Sir John. "That way of obeying orders has quite convinced me that you will be our man. You shall see about your outfit at once."

"And go, Sir John?" faltered the man, as if he could not believe his luck.

"Yes."

"Hoo—"

He was going to add "ray!" but he recollected himself, and went quickly and promptly out of the room.

"The very fellow, Meadows," said the doctor.

"Yes," said Sir John. "He'll do."

"Then one knot is solved," cried the doctor. "I had come in to consult you upon that very point."

"A man?"

"Yes; and here he is ready-made and proved."

"Not yet."

"Oh," said the doctor, "I'll answer for that."

Chapter Five
The "Silver Star"

A busy fortnight followed, during which Jack Meadows accompanied his father and the doctor up to town pretty well every day, to visit tailors, hatters, hosiers, gunsmiths, fishing-tackle-makers, naturalists, provision dealers, and help to spend money at a liberal rate upon the many necessaries for a long voyage. To do the lad justice, he tried hard to hide his distaste for all that was being done, and assumed an interest in the various purchases, making Sir John appear pleased, while Doctor Instow patted his shoulder, and told him that he looked brighter already. But when alone at night his depression came back, and there were moments when, tired out, he told himself that he could not bear it all, and that he must tell his father the next morning that it was impossible—he could not go.

But when the morning; came he said nothing, for on rising the matter did not look so black and gloomy by daylight, after a night's rest; and he felt that it would be too cowardly to make such a declaration, when his father was doing everything and going to so great an expense entirely for his sake.

"Because he thinks me weak and ill," he said to himself; "and nothing will persuade him that I am not."

That very morning, after a good sound night's rest, the boy woke with the sun shining brightly into his bedroom, and he got up thinking he had over-slept himself, but on looking round he found that his hot-water can had not been brought in, nor his freshly-brushed boots and clothes, so he rang impatiently.

"Disgraceful!" he said peevishly. "Ned thinks of nothing now but the voyage, and everything is neglected."

But all the same his bell was not neglected, for in a very short time there was a sharp tap at the door, and as the lad stood by his bedside in his dressing-gown, the white top of a pith helmet appeared slowly, followed by the lower part of a grinning face, a dark-brownish coarse canvas jacket, or rather a number of pockets stuck one above another, and attached to a pair of canvas sleeves; and next, a pair of leather breeches, ditto leggings, and to support all a very stout pair of lace-up boots.

As soon as all were inside the door, a familiar voice said—

"Morning sir. You are early."

"Early!" cried Jack angrily; "what do you mean by early?"

"Ten past six, sir."

"Nonsense! it must be nearly eight."

"Then all the clocks are wrong, sir, including my larum-scarum, for I set it for half-past five, so as to be up early and try 'em on."

"And what do you mean by coming here dressed up in that Guy Fawkes fashion?"

"Guy Fawkes! Oh, I say, Master Jack, don't be hard on a fellow."

"You look ridiculous."

"I say, sir! Why, they fit lovely, all but this pith helmet, as is two sizes too large, and reg'larly puts one out. These came home late last night. Just the thing, ain't they?"

"Go down and take them off, and bring me my hot water, and clothes and boots."

"Why, they ain't cleaned yet, sir, and the kitchen fire ain't alight. There's no hot water neither. You don't mean to get up now?"

Jack looked undecided, and ended by getting back into bed.

"I thought it was late," he said, in a somewhat apologetic tone.

"Not it, sir—extra early, sir. I say, Master Jack, this is a topper, isn't it?" said the man, taking off the helmet. "A'most do for an umbrella in a big shower."

"Preposterous!"

"Think so, sir. Oh, I don't know what sort o' thing people wear in hot climates. But I have got a rig-out, sir, and a waterproof bag, a bullock trunk, and I dunno what all—most as many things as you have."

"Don't bother me about your things: go down, if it's so early, and come back and call me at the proper time."

"Yes, sir; cert'nly, sir," said the man, stealing a glance at himself in the looking-glass, and then standing examining his pith helmet as he held it upon his outstretched hand.

"Well, then, why don't you go?" cried Jack. "I was a-thinking, sir. I say, as you are awake, and there's plenty of time, why don't you try on some of your noo things?"

"Bah! because I don't want to make myself ridiculous," said the lad peevishly.

"You wouldn't look ridiculous, sir. You try 'em, and if I was you I'd go down to breakfast in 'em. Sir John would be as pleased as Punch to see you begin to take a little more interest in going."

"Look here!" cried Jack, springing from his pillow to sit upright in bed, "when I want any of your advice, sir, I will ask for it. Such impertinence!"

"Oh, I beg your pardon, sir, but I only thought you might like to do what Sir John would wish to see. I put 'em all straight last night, and laid a suit of tweeds, with knickerbockers, brown plaid worsted stockings, and high-laced brown shooting-boots, all ready for you."

"Then it was like your insolence, sir."

"Yes, sir, and the boots are lovely, sir; just the thing! Stout strong water-tights as lace on right to the knee. Leather's as soft as velvet. They'll be grand for you when you're going through the jungle where there's leeches and poisonous snakes."

"Ugh!" ejaculated the boy with a shudder.

"Oh, you needn't mind them, sir; I've been reading all about 'em in the Natural History Sir John's lent me. They always run away from you when they can."

"And when they cannot they bite venomously," cried Jack.

"That's it, sir," said Edward, "if they can."

"And they can," said Jack.

"If you don't kill 'em first," said the man, laughing, "and that's the proper thing to do. Kill everything that wants to kill you. Don't want me then yet, sir?"

"Only to go," said Jack, throwing himself down again and drawing up the coverings close to his ear.

"Yes, sir; I'll be back again at half-past seven."

Jack made no reply, and the man went off laughing to himself.

"He's getting stirred up," he said. "I never saw him take so much notice before."

Jack lay perfectly still for another hour, apparently asleep, but really thinking very deeply of his position, and of how hard it seemed to be that he should be obliged to give up his calm quiet life among his books to go upon a journey which, the more he thought of it, seemed to grow darker and more repellent.

He was still thinking and wishing that he could find some way to escape when Edward came into the room again, bearing clothes, boots, and hot-water can.

"Half-past seven, sir," he said.

"Thank you."

"Very fine morning, sir," continued the man, arranging the things for his young master's toilet, but there was no response.

"Looks as if it was going to be settled weather, sir."

Still no response.

"Just been to Sir John, sir, and he says that he forgot to tell me Doctor Instow would be over to breakfast."

Jack did not move, and Edward went close to the bedside.

"Beg pardon, sir," he said loudly; "it's more than half-past seven."

"Will you go away, and not pester me," cried Jack, turning upon him fiercely.

"Yes, sir; certainly, sir; beg pardon, sir, but you said I was never to leave you till you were regularly woke up."

Jack said something inarticulate, and Edward went out once more grinning.

"My word!" he muttered; "he is coming round."

"I don't get a bit of peace," cried the boy peevishly, and he sprang out of bed, washed in hot water, shivered as he dried himself, and then turned to begin dressing, and paused.

Which way should he go?

On two chairs a yard apart lay his clothes: on the left his things he had worn the previous day; on his right, a suit specially made for the life ashore that they were to live abroad; and after a little hesitation he began to dress in that, finding everything feel strange, but certainly very comfortable, and at last he stood there in garments very much like those in which the man had come in, and he looked at himself in the glass.

Nothing could have been more comfortable and suitable, as he was fain to confess; but all the same the inclination was strong to take them off. He resisted, however, and in due time went down, feeling strange and half ashamed of being seen.

Sir John was in the breakfast-room, and he looked up from his newspaper rather severely, but as soon as he caught sight of his son's altered appearance, the paper dropped from his hands and he rose quickly.

"Thank you, Jack," he said warmly. "You did this to please me, and I am more than pleased. It shows me that you are trying to make the brave fight I expect of you, as my son should. Hah! you will see the truth of it all before long."

He would have said more, but the doctor was heard in the hall, and directly after he entered in his bluff fashion.

"Morning, morning," he cried; "splendid day for our trip. Why, bravo, Jack! The very thing. Your get-up is splendid, my lad, and it makes me impatient to be off. You are going with us of course?"

"I suppose so," said Jack with a sigh.

"I don't mean on our trip, but to see the vessel."

That sounded to the boy like a temporary reprieve, and he looked inquiringly at the doctor.

"I had not said anything about it to him," said Sir John. "We have had particulars from my agent of a large ocean-going steam yacht, my boy, which sounds well. It is really a sailing vessel, but fitted with a screw for occasional use in calm or storm. She is lying at Dartmouth, and we are going down to see her to-day. Will you come?"

"Do you wish me to come, father?" said Jack.

"Of course I do, but what I do wish is to see you take an interest in all our preparations."

"I am trying to, father."

"Yes, and succeeding," said the doctor, "or you would not have come out like you are this morning."

"How soon do you start?" said Jack hurriedly, to escape the doctor's allusions to his dress.

"In half-an-hour. We have to get up to town, and then go across to Paddington."

"I'll hurry through my breakfast then, and go and change my things."

"What for?" cried the doctor. "You couldn't be better."

"But I should look so absurd, sir, dressed like this."

"Absurd?"

"The absurdity is only in your imagination, my boy," said Sir John. "Go as you are."

Jack looked troubled, but he said nothing, for he was making a brave fight to master his antipathy to his father's projects, and without another word he went on with his breakfast, receiving the next time he caught his father's eye a nod of approval which meant a good deal.

But the pith helmet was a severe trial just before the carriage came to the door, and he stood in the hall with the round-topped head-piece standing on the table, for it would recall Edward's extinguisher, and his own remark that morning concerning the Guido-Fawkes-like aspect of their man.

"Don't seem to like your topper, Jack, lad," said the doctor, smiling.

"Well, who could?" cried the boy sharply. "It looks so absurd."

"Because you are not used to it, and will probably not see any one else wearing one. Now for my part, I think it the very reverse of absurd, and a thoroughly sensible head-piece, light, well ventilated, and cool, a good protection from the sun, and thoroughly comfortable."

"What, that thing?"

"Yes, that thing. It is a hot sunny day, and we shall be out of doors a good deal when we get into Devonshire, so it is most suitable. Now between ourselves, what would you have worn if left to yourself?"

"My black frock-coat and bat," said Jack quickly.

"Nice costume for a railway journey. Orchid in your button-hole of course, and a pair of straw-coloured kid gloves, I suppose? I have observed that those are your favourite colour."

Jack nodded.

"Bah! Try and be a little more manly, my lad," said the doctor kindly. "A healthy young fellow does not want to be so self-conscious, and to dress himself up so as to look pretty and be admired — or laughed at."

"I'm more likely to be laughed at dressed like this, and with a thing like half an egg-shell on my head."

"Fools will laugh at anything," said the doctor dryly; "but no one whose opinion is worth notice would laugh at a sensible costume. You would have gone down in a tall glossy hat, ironed and brushed up till it shines again. Hard, hot, uncomfortable, roughened at a touch, and perfectly absurd in a shower of rain. But it is the fashion, and you think it's right. Ladies study fashion, lad; look at them after they have been caught in a shower. Now in that rig-out you could go through anything."

"Ready?" said Sir John, taking a soft wide-awake from the hat-stand.

"Yes, and waiting," said the doctor; and they entered the carriage, which was driven off, Jack's last glance on leaving being at Edward on the doorsteps, as he patted his head, evidently in allusion to his young master's pith helmet.

"Oh, if I had only been behind him!" thought the lad indignantly; which, being analysed, meant that a most decided change was taking place, for a month earlier Jack Meadows could not by any possibility have harboured the thought of kicking any one for a mocking gesture.

In good time the terminus was reached, and soon after the fast train was whirling along, leaving the busy town behind, and off and away through the open country with gathering speed. Father and friend chatted away to the lad, but he was listless and dull, refusing to be interested in anything pointed out; and at last a meaning look passed between his companions, the doctor's eyes saying plainly enough—"Let him be: he'll come round by and by."

But this did not seem likely to be the case, Jack not even being attracted by the first glimpse of the beautiful estuary of the Dart when it was reached in the evening, and they looked down from the heights as the train glided along, at the town nestling up the slopes upon the other side of the water.

He did turn sharply once when the doctor said suddenly: "There are the two training ships for the naval cadets," and pointed at the old men-of-war with their tiers of ports, moored in midstream; and was feeling a strange sense of pity for the lads "cooped up," as he mentally called it, in the narrow limits of a ship, when the doctor suddenly exclaimed, "Look, look! both of you. I'll be bound to say that's our yacht."

Jack glanced sharply at what seemed in comparison with the huge men-of-war, and seen at a distance, a little three-masted, white-looking vessel with a dwarfed funnel, lying at anchor, but he turned pale and listless again, utterly wearied out with his journey, nor did he revive over the comfortable dinner of which he partook without appetite.

Sir John looked uneasy, but the doctor gave him a meaning nod.

"You won't care about going to look over the yacht this evening, Jack?" he said.

"I!" said the lad, almost imploringly. "No, not to-night."

"No; we're all tired," said the doctor. "I did not say anything to you, Meadows; but I thought we had done enough, so I sent off word to the captain to say that we had come down, and I shouldn't be surprised if he comes over to the hotel by and by."

It fell out just as the doctor had said, for about half-an-hour later the waiter came into the room to say that Captain Bradleigh would be glad to see Sir John Meadows; and Jack looked up curiously as a ruddy, tan-faced, rather fierce-looking man, with very crisp hair, beard sprinkled with grey, and keen, piercing grey eyes, shaded by rather shaggy brows, entered, glanced quickly round as he took off his gold-braided yachting cap, and at once addressed Sir John, as if quite sure that he was the principal.

"Sir John Meadows?" he said courteously, but with a ring of authority in his words.

"Yes; will you sit down. This is my friend, Doctor Instow; my son."

The captain shook hands with the two elders, giving them a firm, manly grip, short and sharp, as if he meant business; but his pressure of Jack's thin, white hand was gentle, and he retained it in his strong, firm palm as he said—

"Ah! father—doctor—you have been ill, young gentleman?"

"I? No," said Jack, with a look of resentment.

"Unwell, not bad," said the captain kindly. "Only want a sea-trip to do you good;" and he smiled pleasantly, looking like an Englishman full of firmness and decision, such a one as people would like to trust in a case of emergency.

"I got your message, gentlemen," he said, as he took a chair, "and I came on at once."

"Thank you," said Sir John.

"The agent wrote me a long letter, saying you might come down; but I did not think much of it, for I have had so many from him that have come to nothing."

"People don't like the yacht then?" said Sir John, rather anxiously.

"Oh yes, sir, they like the yacht," said the captain, with a little laugh. "No one could help liking her. They don't like the price."

"Ah, the price," said Sir John quietly; and the captain gave him a searching look.

"Yes, sir, the price; and it is a pretty good round sum; but I give you my word it is just one-third of what it cost Mr Ensler."

"Oh! you know what it cost?" said Sir John.

"Well, I ought to, sir," said the captain, smiling, a peculiarly frank, pleasant smile. "When he came over from New York five years ago, I was recommended to him, and he trusted me fully. She was built under my eyes, up in the Clyde, and I watched everything, as she was fitted up of the very best material, regardless of expense. The cheques all passed through my hands, so I think I ought to know."

"Yes, of course. The agent told me the yacht was built expressly for an American gentleman."

"That's right, sir. He's one of these millionaires who don't know how rich they are, for the money comes on rolling in. Restless, nervous sort of men who must be doing something, and then they want to do something else, and get tired of the idea before they've begun. He had an idea that it would be a fine thing to imitate Brassey, but do it better, and sail round the world. So the *Silver Star* was built, rigged and finished in style. I selected as good a crew of fifteen picked, sea-going fellows as were procurable, and just a year ago we started."

Jack began to grow interested.

"But you see, gentlemen, he was disappointed in her from the first."

"Hah!" said the doctor sharply; "now frankly, captain, what was her failing?"

"Failing, sir?" said the captain, turning in his chair, and fixing the doctor with his clear eyes. "I tell you as a man, I can't find a failing in her, except perhaps there's a little too much French polish about the saloon cabin, more in the stuffed cushion line than I quite care for. You see, for an ocean-going boat I think you want to study strength and sound workmanship more than show; but that's a matter of fancy."

"Of course," said Sir John, who was watching the captain very narrowly.

"Well, sir, I did my very best, what he called level best, and when she was done I was as proud of her as—as—well, as your young son here might have been of a new plaything."

Jack winced, and looked indignant.

"But Mr Ensler didn't like her: said she was a miserable little cock-boat, and not fit for a long voyage."

"And frankly, between man and man, isn't she?" said the doctor sharply.

"Well, gentlemen," said the captain, showing his regular white teeth in a smile, "that's a matter of opinion. I'm not interested in the matter. I'm in command with a good crew on board, and we have our pay regular as clockwork. She may be sold, or she may not; but I can only say what I think. I did all that a man who has been at sea pretty well everywhere for thirty years could do, and I say this: if you gentlemen like to buy her and engage me—mind, with a good picked crew—I'll sail her wherever you like. If, on the other hand, you like to pick your own man, I can tell him as a brother sailor that he can't get a better found boat in either of the yacht squadrons or in Her Majesty's navy."

"But Mr Ensler was dissatisfied with her."

"He? Yes," said the captain contemptuously. "He has been coming and going for years in the Cunard and the American liners, and his ideas were built on one of those floating palaces. As I told him, it was absurd. He wanted an ocean-going gentleman's yacht, and there she lies. I'd trust my life in her anywhere a deal sooner than I would in one of those coal-swallowing monsters. She's as light as a cork, easy to manage from her fore and aft rig, with a small picked crew, and has a magnificent engine with the best kind of boilers, which get up steam quickly, ready for any emergency; for of course as a yacht she's a boat in which you would depend most upon your sailing."

"Exactly," said Sir John, "that is what I meant."

"Then she'd suit you to a tittle, sir."

"Has she made any long voyages?" said the doctor.

"No, sir, but she has been in some rough weather. I brought her round from Glasgow in the dirtiest weather I was ever in on our coast; and from here we sailed to Gib, and right away through the Mediterranean, meaning to go through the Canal and on to Ceylon; but long before we'd got to Alexandria he was sick of it, and pitched it all. I must say that we did have rather a nasty time, but, as I told him, it only showed what a beautiful boat she was. It was wonderful how we danced over the waves with close-reefed canvas. But he'd had enough, gave me my orders to bring her here to Dartmouth, and he went back to Marseilles by one of the Messageries Maritimes, and across home. When we got back, first thing I saw was the advertisement that she was for sale."

"You have a good crew on board then?" said Sir John thoughtfully.

"As good a crew as I could pick, sir, and they are well up to their work. For I'm rather a hard man, young gentleman," continued the captain, turning to look sharply at Jack, "as stern about discipline as they are in the Royal Navy; but work done, I like to see my men play, and somehow I think they get on very well with me. But of course, gentlemen, if you bought the yacht, you are not bound to take the captain and crew."

"Oh no, of course not," said Sir John quietly.

"There, gentlemen, I've been doing all the talking: Perhaps now you would like to ask me a few questions."

"I think we might defer most of them till we have seen the yacht, eh, Meadows?" said Doctor Instow.

"Yes, certainly, unless anything occurs in our conversation with Captain Bradleigh."

"Anything you like, gentlemen, though there is very little that I could say more than I have said. She's a splendid craft in every respect. There is only one fault in her from a buyer's point of view."

"What is that?" said the doctor sharply.

"Price, sir."

"But to a man of means, who would give his cheque down, Mr Ensler would take considerably less?"

The captain shook his head.

"No, sir, I don't believe he would. He don't want money, and I have always lived in the hope that he would take a fresh sea-going trip; but it does not come off. He has had several offers for the boat, but sent a sharp answer back that he had fixed his price."

Sir John sat tapping the table with his finger-tips, watching his son, who seemed to be brightening up, evidently in the hope that the transaction would fall through.

"So you are going to have a few cruises, young gentleman," said the captain, turning to Jack, for the doctor too was looking very thoughtful, and was nibbling at his nails as he glanced at Sir John. "I suppose so," said the lad coldly. "Do you good," said the captain. "Fine thing the pure sea-air. Why a trip round the coast for a few weeks, and you'd be quite a new man. Like the sea?"

"I? Like the sea?" said Jack with a shiver. "My son thinks he will not like it at all," said Sir John, smiling.

"Thinks, sir," said the captain, laughing. "Ah, he don't know. Not like the sea! My word, what a weary world this would be if there were no sea. Storm or calm it's grand or beautiful. There's nothing like the sea. Oh, he don't know yet. You mean a short cruise or two, sir, or a trip round the island from port to port. She's a little too big for that."

"No," said Sir John, rousing himself from a reverie. "I intended to go from here through to Ceylon, then on to Singapore, and along the islands, touching here and there, till we reached some place at which we would like to stay."

"Perhaps round by the Horn, touching at Monte Video, Rio, and the West Indies?" cried the captain excitedly.

"Perhaps," said Sir John, smiling. "It depends."

"That means a couple of years to do it well, sir."

"I am not tied for time," said Sir John.

"That's a lot of money for a yacht," said the doctor thoughtfully.

"Yes, sir, a pretty good sum, but she's worth it, and whether you buy the *Silver Star* or no, I say, as an old seaman, don't you undertake such a trip without a good boat under you, a man who knows his business for sailing her, and a good crew. If you mind that, weather permitting, you'll have a pleasant voyage worth a man's doing. With a clumsy craft, a bad captain, and a scraped together mutinous crew, it will be a misery to you from the day you start to the day you come back—if you ever do."

"That is quite right," said Sir John, rising, for the captain had risen and picked up his cap. "What time shall we come on board to-morrow?"

"Come now if you like, sir."

"No, no; my son is tired. Will ten o'clock suit you?"

"Any hour you like to name, sir."

"Ten then," said Sir John. "Of course we can easily find a boatman to take us off?"

"At ten o'clock, sir, a boat will be waiting for you at the pier end," said the captain in a sharp businesslike tone. "Good-evening, gentlemen. Weather seems to be settling down for fine. My glass is very steady."

"Hah!" said the doctor, "I rather like that man."

"I don't," said Jack sharply. "He is insufferable. He treated me as if I were a child."

Sir John raised his brows a little in surprise to hear his son speak so sharply.

"Don't judge rashly, Jack," he said. "You don't know the man yet; neither do I; but he impressed me as being a very frank, straightforward fellow, one of Nature's rough gentlemen."

"Would you mind my going to bed, father?" said Jack hastily. "I am very tired."

"Go then, and have a good long night's rest."

"Yes," said the doctor; "and I say, Jack, leave your window open. Sea-air is a splendid tonic."

"Good-night," said Jack shortly; and, shaking hands quickly, he hurried out of the room, and went to bed, after carefully seeing that the window was closely shut.

"That's a pile of money for a yacht, Meadows," said the doctor, as they sat together to watch the moon rise over the hills in front of the hotel away across the estuary.

"Yes, it is a heavy sum, Instow, but if it answers the captain's description the yacht must be worth the money."

"Yes, if it does. Seems to be an honest sort of fellow, and he's right about having a good ship and crew for such a voyage."

"Of course."

"But it's a deal to pay down."

"I'd pay ten times as much down to-morrow to see my poor boy hale and hearty—a frank, natural lad with an English boy's firmness and strength."

"Instead of a weak, irritable, sickly, overstrained, nervous fellow, who would give me the horrors if I did not know that I can put him right."

"You do feel this, Instow?"

"Of course I do. Why look at him to-night. He is tired, and speaks sharply, and almost spitefully; but already he is showing twice as much spirit, though it is in the way of opposition."

"Yes; the feeling that he is to exert himself is beginning to show itself," said Sir John musingly. "He'll come round if he is given something to call out his energy."

They sat very silent till bed-time, and on saying good-night, Sir John turned quickly upon his old friend.

"This is a chance, Instow," he said, "and if the vessel comes up to his description I shall close at once."

Chapter Six
Jack begins to wake

The waters of the Dart were dancing merrily in the bright sunshine next morning, when, nervous and so anxious that his breakfast had been spoiled, Jack walked between his father and the doctor toward the pier, wondering what sort of a vessel the *Silver Star*, which had been finished too finely for the captain's taste, would prove.

"There she is," said the doctor suddenly. "That must be the yacht, for there is nothing else in sight at all answering her description."

"Yes, that is she, the one we saw as we came in yesterday. Why she must be quite half-a-mile away."

"Are we to go off to the yacht in a small boat?" asked Jack nervously.

"Yes, my boy," said Sir John. "You heard that the captain, said one would be waiting for us at ten, and it is now nearly that time. Look, there's a man-o'-war gig coming towards the pier. How well the men look in their white duck shirts and straw hats, and with the naval officer in the stern sheets. Those men row splendidly."

They stopped to look at the beautiful little boat glistening and brown in its varnish, with its three little fenders hanging on either side to protect it from chafing against boat-side or pier, and its rowlocks of highly polished gun-metal, and then lost sight of it behind the pier.

"Bringing the officer to land, I suppose," said Sir John. "I dare say she comes from the *Britannia*."

"No," said the doctor suddenly. "Why that's our captain and our boat."

"Oh no," said Sir John quickly. "That was a regular man-o'-war craft."

"I don't care; it was ours," said the doctor. "You'll see."

He proved to be right, for as they went on to the pier, they saw Captain Bradleigh climb up from a boat lying out of sight close in, and he came to meet them.

"Morning, gentlemen," he said. "You are punctuality itself. It's striking ten. This way. We'll go off at once, while the tide is with us, and save the lads' arms."

He led them to the end of the pier, where the so-called man-o'-war boat lay just beneath them, one of the sailors holding on by a boat-hook, while the other three smart-looking fellows sat quietly waiting on the thwarts. The gig was in the trimmest of conditions, and looked perfectly new, while it was set off by a gay scarlet cushion in the stern sheets, contrasting well with the brown varnished grating ready for the sitters' feet.

"But we are never going to the yacht in that crazy little boat?" whispered Jack nervously.

"The sailors came to shore in it," said Sir John quietly, "so why should we mind?"

"But it seems so slight and thin," faltered the boy to his father.

"Are you afraid, Jack?" asked Sir John gravely. "If so you had better stay on the pier while we go."

The lad was silent. That he was afraid was plainly written in his face—plainly, that is, to those who knew him. To a stranger it would have seemed to be the pallor of his complexion.

Sir John said no more, but made way for Doctor Instow to step down into the boat, and at a sign he descended and held out his hand to Jack.

"I can manage, thank you," said the lad, and he jumped down on to one of the thwarts, and then, without assistance, took his place in the stern sheets; his father and the captain followed, the latter gave a short, sharp order, the boat was vigorously thrust away into the stream, and the next minute the four men were sending her along with a regular stroke which seemed to make the slightly-built boat throb and quiver.

For a few minutes the utterly foreign sensation was absolutely painful to the boy; and as the land appeared to glide away from them, a sensation of giddiness attacked him as he sat hearing conversation going on, but understanding nothing, till, as he turned his eyes in the captain's direction, he saw that this gentleman was watching him curiously.

A pang shot through him, and the blood began to rise to his white cheeks, as he made a tremendous effort to master the miserable sensation of abject fear which troubled him, and succeeded so far that in a minute or two he was able to give himself the appearance of looking about him, as if examining the boats they passed.

"There, young gentleman," said the captain suddenly, "there's the *Silver Star*. What do you say to her? Doesn't she sit the water like a sea-bird?"

Jack looked at the graceful curve and taper spars of the vessel, and began to wonder at the way in which she seemed to grow as they drew nearer; or was it that the boat in which he was gliding onward was shrinking?

He had not much more time for examination of the delicate lines traced upon the sky by the yards and cordage, for the boat was cleverly run close up, the oars tossed on high, and as the bowman hooked on to a ring-bolt the boat was drawn beneath a side ladder.

Jack felt the tremor returning as he thought of the danger of such an ascent, when his father said in a low voice —

"You did that very bravely, my boy; now make another effort."

Jack was on his feet in an instant. He stepped forward, seized the lines on either side of the ladder, and climbed up very clumsily, but managed to reach the deck without accepting the assistance of the mate and one of the men, who stood in the gangway and made room for him to step for the first time in his life upon the deck of a ship.

Sir John and the doctor followed, and the captain remained silent, while his visitors stood gazing about the clean white deck, where everything was in the most perfect order, ropes coiled down so that at a distance they looked like pieces of engine turning, the hand-rails of polished brass and the ship's bell glistening in the sunshine, and the pair of small guns seeming to vie with them. The sails furled in the most perfect manner, and covered with yellowish tarpaulins, yards squared, and every rope tight and in its correct place and looking perfectly new, while the spare spars and yards were lashed on either side by the low bulwarks, smooth and polished till they were like ornaments.

"Well," said the doctor at last, "I am not a sailor, Captain Bradleigh, but everything here appears to be in the most perfect condition."

"I hope so, sir. My men are proud of our vessel, and we do our best."

Sir John glanced at the men, who were all at their stations, and felt a thrill of satisfaction as he noticed that they well deserved the term of "picked," being the smart, athletic, frank, manly-looking fellows we are accustomed to see in the Royal Naval Reserve.

The captain then led the way to the cabins, which were thoroughly in keeping with what had been seen on deck, elegantly decorated and furnished, and with every inch so contrived that the greatest of convenience was given in the smallest space. Berths, steward's room, cook's galley, all were inspected in turn, and then the captain opened a door with a smile.

"I don't know whether you gentlemen care for sport, but Mr Ensler had this little magazine fitted up, and it is well furnished."

The contents seemed nothing to Jack; but the doctor and Sir John exchanged glances of surprise, as they saw on each side the sliding glass doors in which, in the most perfect order, were ranged double and single fowling-pieces, rifles from the lightest express to the heaviest elephant guns, as well as a couple of large bore for wild-fowl shooting and one with its fittings for discharging shells or harpoons. Lances, lines, nets, dredges, sounding-lines, patent logs, everything that a scientific sportsman or naturalist could desire.

"There's a good magazine forward, gentlemen," said the captain, "which I will show you by and by, with, I should say, an ample supply of cartridges of all kinds—the best. Cartridge and ball for the big guns, and many chests of empty brass cases, canisters of powder, and bags of all-sized shot, and the like, so that I may say the yacht is well found in that respect."

"But these are Mr Ensler's," said Sir John, who appeared thoroughly interested, while his son looked on and listened in a careless way.

"Well, yes, sir, his, of course; but they go with the boat."

"At a valuation?" said the doctor.

"Oh no," replied the captain, smiling. "Everything in the yacht—stores, provisions, extra tackle, spare anchors, cables and sails—and I'll show you directly, gentlemen, the stores are well worth looking at—go with the yacht at the price named. I wouldn't be answerable for the state of some of the tinned provisions, of course, for they've been on board some time, but they were of the best, and I have had them gone over, and only found a few cases to condemn."

Sir John said nothing, and the captain led them on, showing them the store-rooms, the place devoted to provisions, and then the magazine, which he pointed out as being solidly constructed at the bottom and sides, but exceedingly light overhead.

"So you see, gentlemen," said Captain Bradleigh, "the powder and cartridges are so divided, that if there were an explosion it would be a small one, though of course it would be followed by others; but with the light construction overhead the force would fly upwards, and there would be no fear of our going to the bottom."

There was no farther progress to be made forward, a strong iron bulkhead lined with woodwork dividing the yacht here in two; and after the magazine had been carefully closed, the captain opened a couple of arm-chests, in which were rifles, bayonets, and cutlasses, the belts and cartouche boxes hanging in a row from pegs.

"Men are all well-drilled, sir," continued the captain, "and have regular small-arm practice, for Mr Ensler said there was no knowing where we might find ourselves; and there's no mistake about it, gentlemen, there's plenty of piracy out in the East still, specially in the Malay and Chinese waters."

Jack was interested now, and he gave the captain so sharp a look of inquiry that he smiled and nodded.

"Oh yes, young gentleman, there are plenty of cut-throat scoundrels out there, as I know well, who would be a deal better out of the world. Now we'll go back on deck, please."

They followed him up, and he went forward, taking them to see the engine and stoke-hole, then down into the cable-tiers and another store-room, where the extra tackle and various appliances were kept. Then into the carpenter's and smith's workshops, and lastly into the forecastle, and the men's cook's galley, the former being well-fitted, ventilated, and supplied with a case of books. Finally, after quite three hours' inspection, Captain Bradleigh led the way back to the saloon, where quite an elegant lunch had been spread, and the steward and his mate were in attendance.

"Oh, there was no need for this," said Sir John hastily.

"I am only obeying instructions, sir," said the captain, smiling. "Mr Ensler said that if any gentlemen took the trouble to come all the way to Dartmouth to see the yacht, the least we could do was to give them some refreshments. I think I've shown you everything, gentlemen, as far as I could, but of course if you thought anything of the yacht you would have her thoroughly gone over by a trustworthy marine surveyor."

Sir John and the doctor exchanged glances again.

"Oh, there's one thing I did not show you, gentlemen," cried the captain. "It may interest our young friend here. We have no figure-head."

"Is the man mad?" said Jack to himself, giving him a look full of contempt. "What interest could I possibly have in a ship's figure-head?"

"It was a whim, a fad of Mr Ensler's. He went to a lot of expense over it. I don't suppose you noticed it, but just out over the cut-water close to the bowsprit, there's a great cut-glass silver star, fitted inside with a set of the most wonderful silver reflectors, parabolic they call them, and when the big lamp inside is lit it sends rays out in all directions, so that when you are a way off, it looks just like the evening star shining out over the water. Going back to-night, gentlemen?"

"No," said Sir John quietly; "I shall not return to-night."

Jack winced and looked troubled.

"Then as soon as it's dusk, young gentleman, I'll have the star lit up. It's of no particular use except as a bow-light, but it looks mighty pretty, as good as the fireworks you've let off on fifth o' Novembers many a time, I'll be bound."

"Ha! ha! ha!" roared the doctor, turning to Jack merrily.

"I!" cried the lad, impatiently, and giving the captain a scornful look; "I never let off a firework in my life."

"I have," said the captain dryly, "many a one, and made them too. But boys—some of 'em—are a bit different to what they were when I was young."

"Oh, they're the same as ever, captain," said Sir John, smiling thoughtfully, as if in recollection of the past. "As a rule, a boy is a boy, but no rule is without an exception, you know."

"That's right, sir."

"And my son has been delicate, and has always led a studious, indoor life."

"Ah, I see, sir, and now you are going to let him rough it a bit, and make a man of him."

"Yes, a healthy man," said the doctor.

"Ah, doctor," said the captain merrily, "there's a beautifully fitted medicine-chest in that cupboard, with plenty of physic and books of instructions for that, and a bit of surgery; and I've had to dabble in it a little myself. We captains often have to do that out away abroad. Why, sir," he continued, with a queer humorous look at Jack, "I'd back myself to give a pill to any man against all the doctors in Christendom."

Jack looked disgusted.

"But," said the captain, "I was going to say, if our young friend here goes off with his father on a voyage, he won't want you or any other doctor, sir."

"And a good job too, captain," cried Doctor Instow, "for I like a bit of travel and rest as well as any man. But you are quite right. It is what I prescribed. Two or three years' voyage and travel."

"Well, gentlemen," said the captain, as they rose from the lunch-table; "Mr Ensler wished everything to be straightforward and above-board; is there anything else I can show you?"

"Well, yes," said Sir John, after exchanging glances once more with the doctor; "I have come down on purpose to inspect this yacht, and I should feel obliged if you would show me over it again."

"Certainly, sir," said the captain bluffly; "I have nothing else to do, I'm sorry to say. Here I am at your service."

"And in the evening," continued Sir John, "I hope you will give me the pleasure of your company to dinner at the hotel."

"Well, sir," said the captain, in rather a hesitating way, "I'm not much of a dining-out sort of man, and besides, I should like you to go about the town a bit, and make a few inquiries about me and my principal and the yacht. Seaside people are pretty knowing, and you'll soon hear a boat's character if you begin to ask questions."

"Oh yes, of course," said Sir John; "but we should like to know a little more of you personally, Captain Bradleigh."

"Well, that's very kind of you, sir," said the captain bluffly. "Thank you then, I'll come. But perhaps you gentlemen would like to go over the yacht alone? I want to write a letter or two. You go about and talk to my boys. They're not primed, gentlemen."

"Well, I think we will," said the doctor quickly, "Eh, Meadows?"

"Yes, Captain Bradleigh," said Sir John; "one does not decide upon a thing like this in a minute."

"Certainly not, sir. You go and have a good rummage, she'll bear it, and you jot down in your log-book anything you see that you'd like to draw attention to. Call any of the men to move or overhaul anything you wish."

For the next three hours, to Jack's great dismay, his father and Doctor Instow roamed and hunted over the yacht. Nothing seemed too small for the doctor to pounce upon, though he devoted most attention to the magazine-room, amongst the sporting implements; but one way and another they thoroughly overhauled the yacht from stem to stern, even to examining the cable-tier and the well, and having several long talks with the men, before, to Jack's great satisfaction, as he sat against the aft bulwarks, his father came to him and said—

"Tired, my boy?"

"Wearied out, father," was the reply.

"Well, we have done now. What do you think of the yacht?"

"Nothing, father;" and then hastily, as he saw the look of trouble in Sir John's eyes, "I don't understand anything."

"Humph! No. Of course not. Well, come down into the saloon."

The captain looked up from where he was writing, having carefully abstained from joining them since lunch.

"Well, gentlemen," he said, smiling, and a quiet triumphant look beaming on his face, "done?"

"Yes," said the doctor, wiping his forehead; "I haven't worked so hard for months."

"Like the look of her, sir?"

"Very much indeed," said Sir John quietly; and a pang of misery shot through the boy.

"Ah, you don't know her yet, sir; but I'm glad you think well of her."

Sir John took a seat and was silent for a few moments, Doctor Instow watching him with an inquiring look, while Jack was in agony.

"Look here, Captain Bradleigh," said Sir John at last, "I do not profess to be a judge of such matters, but everything here seems to me to speak for itself, and I can fairly say that I never saw a vessel in such perfect trim before."

"That's a high compliment to pay me, sir," replied the captain, "and I thank you for it. Well, I'm glad to have met you, sir, and it is a break in rather a monotonous life. Don't apologise, sir, I know it is a very heavy price for the craft, and of course it is on account of her having fittings that not one gentleman in ten would think of putting in a yacht. You were quite welcome to see her, and as for anything I have done—"

"I do not quite understand you," said Sir John.

"No, sir? Well, I take it that what you say is to smooth down that the craft will not quite suit you."

"You are entirely wrong," said Sir John; "I think she would suit me admirably, and save me a great deal of labour in preparation."

"Oh!" cried the captain; "then I was on the wrong tack."

"Decidedly. Now, Captain Bradleigh, about yourself. I judge you to be a perfectly straightforward, honourable man."

"Thank you, sir," said the captain, smiling. "I hope for my own sake that you are a good judge."

"I hope so too. Now, Captain Bradleigh, between man and man, will you give me your word of honour that this yacht is thoroughly sound, and one that you would advise a man you esteemed to buy?"

"That I will, sir, straight," cried the captain, holding out his hand, and giving Sir John's a tremendous grip. "She's as perfect as the best builders and fitters can make her, out of the best stuff. But you, if you think of buying her, get down a couple of the best men you can to overhaul her, and if they give a straightforward report, buy her you will."

"I don't see any need for so doing," said Sir John quietly. "I would rather have your opinion than any man's."

"But you don't know me, sir."

"I think that any observant man would know you, Captain Bradleigh, in half-an-hour."

The captain reddened.

"Well, sir," he said, "I didn't know I had my character written on my face."

"Perhaps not," said Sir John quietly; "but now about yourself. I don't wish to spend more money than I can help, and I am not an American millionaire, only a quiet country gentleman rather devoted to natural history and a love of collecting."

"That's better than being a millionaire, sir. Money isn't everything, though it's very useful."

"Exactly. Well, if I buy the yacht, will you go with me wherever I wish to sail?"

"That I will, sir, with all my heart, and do my duty by you as a man."

"Thank you," said Sir John; "and now about the crew. It is rather a large one."

"Twice too big in fair weather, sir, but not a man too many in foul."

"You think them all necessary?"

"I do, sir, unless you like to depend on steam; then you might knock off half-a-dozen, but you'd save nothing; coals at the depôts abroad are very dear. Better trust to your sails and keep the men."

"Yes; I think you are right," said Sir John. "What do you say, Instow?"

"Quite," said the doctor.

"Very well then. Now about the crew; would they be willing: to engage to sail with me wherever I please, to bind themselves not to break their engagement without my leave till we return, even if it is for three years?"

"I could say yes, sir, for they'd follow me wherever I went, but I'll ask them."

"Do," said Sir John.

The captain touched a table gong, and the steward appeared promptly.

"Go and ask Mr Bartlett to pipe all hands aft," said the captain.

The man ascended, and the next minute the clear note of a whistle rang out, to be followed by the trampling of feet, and the captain rose, evidently satisfied at the promptitude with which his order was obeyed.

"They're waiting sir," he said.

Upon the party going on deck, there were the crew drawn up, quite as smart as men-o'-war's men, and all looking as eager as schoolboys to learn the meaning of their summons.

"'Tention!" said the captain; and, to use the old saying, the dropping of a pin could have been heard. "This gentleman, Sir John Meadows, Bart., is going to buy the *Silver Star*."

"Hurrah!" shouted a man.

"Steady there!" cried the captain sternly. "He means to sail right away east, through the Canal, and along the islands, to stop here and there where he likes—two or three years' cruise—and he wants to know if you will sign articles to go with him, and do your duty like men."

There was a dead silence, and as the men began directly after to whisper together, Jack, who but a minute before had felt in his misery and despair that he would give anything to hear the men refuse, now, by a strange perversity of feeling, grew indignant with them for seeming to hesitate about doing their duty to his father.

"Well, my lads, what is it?" said the captain sternly. "What are you whispering about? Can't you give a straightforward yes or no?"

There was another whispering, and the words "You speak," "No, you," came plainly to Jack's ears, followed by one man shouting—

"We want to know, sir, who's to be in command?"

"Why, I am, my lads, of course."

"Hooray!" came in a roar; and then—"All of us—yes, sir, we'll go," and another cheer.

"There's your answer, sir," said the captain; and then turning to the men—"Thankye, my lads, thankye."

"Yes, that's my answer," said Sir John, "and an endorsement of my feeling that I am doing right."

"And thank you, sir," said the captain warmly. "We'll do our duty by you, never fear. Perhaps you'll say a word to Mr Bartlett, sir," he whispered. "Good man and true, and a thorough sailor."

"You will, I hope, keep your post, Mr Bartlett," said Sir John, turning to him.

"Oh yes, Sir John," said the mate; "I'm obliged to. Captain Bradleigh's kind enough to say I am his right hand."

"And I can't go without that, can I, young gentleman?"

Jack, who was feeling unduly thrilled and excited by the novel scene, was chilled again, and he only muttered something ungraciously.

"Mr Bartlett will join us at dinner, I hope," said Sir John; and this being promised, the men were ordered forward, the boat was manned, and, as the whole crew was watching every movement on the part of the visitors, Jack shook hands with captain and mate, and stepped down a little more courageously into the gig, but turned dizzy as he dropped into his seat.

The next minute it was pushed off, and the thrill of excitement ran through the lad again, as the crew suddenly sprang to the shrouds of the three masts, to stand there, holding on by one hand, waving their straw hats and cheering with all their might.

"Jump up, Jack, and give them a cheer back," cried the doctor.

There is something wonderful about a sharp order suddenly given.

In an instant Jack was on his feet, waving his white pith helmet in the air, and giving, truth to tell, a miserably feeble cheer, but the crew of the boat took it up and joined in.

Then, as it was answered from the yacht, Jack sank down in his seat again, looking flushed and abashed, and he glanced from one to the other to see if they were laughing at him; but nobody even smiled. Still the lad could not get rid of the false shame, and the feeling that there was something to be ashamed of after all.

Chapter Seven
First sniffs of the briny

"He's beginning, Meadows," said the doctor, as they sat together in their room at the hotel, waiting for the guests of the evening.

"Think so?" said Sir John sadly.

"Of course I do," cried the doctor.

"But it's very pitiful to see a lad of his years shrinking like a timid girl, and changing colour whenever he is spoken to. He seems to have no spirit at all."

"He has though, and plenty, only it's crusted over, and can't get out; I noticed a dozen good signs to-day."

"A dozen?" said Sir John.

"Well, more or less. Don't ask me to be mathematical. You'll want to know the aliquot parts next," said the doctor snappishly.

"I see you want your dinner," said Sir John, with a smile.

"I do—horribly. This sea-air makes me feel ravenous. But, as I was going to say, there were abundant signs of the change beginning. He's ashamed of his—his—"

"Well, say it—cowardice," said Sir John sadly. "Yes, poor fellow! he is ashamed of it, as I well know."

"But he can't help it, weak and unstrung as he is. It will come all right, only let's get him out of his misery, as we used to call it. Get him to make his first plunge, and he'll soon begin to swim. Did you see what a brave fight he made of it over and over again to-day? There, I'm sure we're right; and, my word, what a chance over this yacht."

"Yes, it would have been folly to hesitate."

"But it's going to cost you a pretty penny, my friend."

"I do not grudge it, Instow, if we can bring him back well. We'll be off as soon as I can get the preliminaries settled."

"These things don't take long when a man has the money."

"Hush!" said Sir John; "here he is. Don't say anything to upset him."

Jack came in, looking sad and dispirited.

"Ah, Jack, my boy, ready for dinner?"

"No, father."

"Hah! chance for the doctor," cried that gentleman merrily. "Let me administer an appetiser."

"No, no, Doctor Instow; I'm sure it would do no good."

"Wait till you hear what it is, O man of wisdom, and be more modest. You don't know everything yet. Now then: prescription—take a walk as far as the kitchen door, wait till it is opened, and then take four sniffs quickly, and come back. That will give you an appetite, my boy, if you want one; but I don't believe you do, for you have a lean and hungry look, as Shakespeare calls it. It's the sea-air, Jack; I'm savage."

"Some one coming," said Sir John, and a minute later the waiter showed in the two guests.

Jack did not notice it himself, but others did: he ate about twice as much as he was accustomed to, and all the while, after looking upon the dinner and the visitors as being an infliction, he found himself listening attentively to Captain Bradleigh, who was set going by a few questions from the doctor, and proved to be full of observation.

"Oh no," he said, "I'm no naturalist, but I can't help noticing different things when I am at sea, and ashore, and if they're fresh to me, I don't forget them. Let me say now, though, Sir John Meadows, how glad I am that you will buy the yacht and go on this cruise. The lads are half wild with excitement, for we've all been, as the Irishmen call it, spoiling for something to do. It has seemed to be clean and polish for no purpose, but I told them they ought to feel very glad to have had the yacht in such a state. I trust, Sir John, that you will never have cause to regret this day's work."

"I have no fear," said that gentleman. "I shall be glad, though, as soon as you receive notice of the transfer to me, if you will do everything possible toward getting ready for sea."

"Getting ready for sea, sir? She is ready for sea. Fresh water on board, coal-bunkers full. Nothing wanted but the provisions—salt, preserved, and fresh—to be seen to, and that would take very little time. As soon as you have done your business with the owner, send me my orders, and there'll be no time lost, I promise you."

Jack bent over his plate, and was very silent, but he revived and became attentive when the doctor changed the subject, and began to question the captain about some of his experiences, many of which he related in a simple, modest way which spoke for its truth.

"I suppose," said Sir John merrily, after glancing at his son, "you have never come across the sea serpent?"

The captain looked at him sharply, then at the mate, and ended by raising his eyebrows and frowning at his plate.

"That's a sore point for a ship captain, sir," he said at last, "one which makes him a bit put out, for no man likes to be laughed at. You see, we've all been so bantered about that sea serpent, that when a mariner says he has seen it, people set him down for a regular Baron Munchausen, so now-a-days we people have got into the habit of holding our tongues."

"Why, you don't mean to say that you have ever seen it, captain?" cried the doctor.

"Well, sir, I've seen something more than once that answered its description pretty closely."

"I always thought it was a fable," said Sir John.

"No, sir, I don't think it is," said the captain quickly. "As I tell you, I've seen a great reptile sort of creature going along through the sea just after the fashion of those water-fowl that are shot in some of the South American rivers."

"The darters," said Sir John; "*Plotius.*"

"Those are the fellows, sir; they swim with nearly the whole of their body under the surface, and look so much like little serpents that people call them snake birds. Well, sir, twice over I've seen such a creature—not a bird but a reptile."

"And they are wonderfully alike in some cases," said the doctor quietly.

"So I've heard, sir, from people who studied such things. Mine was going along six or seven knots an hour, with its snake-like head and neck carried swan-fashion, and raised fifteen or twenty feet out of the water as near as I could judge, for it was quite half-a-mile away. It was flat-headed, and as I brought my spy-glass to bear upon it, I could see that it had very large eyes. I kept it in sight for a good ten minutes, and could not help thinking how swan-like it was in its movements. Then it stretched out its neck, laid it down upon the water, and went out of sight."

"And you think it was a sea serpent?"

"Something of that kind, gentlemen. Bartlett saw it too, and he was sure it was a great snake."

"Yes, I feel sure it was," said the mate quietly.

"Very strange," said Sir John, who noted how Jack was drinking it all in.

"Strange, sir, because we don't often see such things. That was in my last long voyage, a year before I was introduced to Mr Ensler, but I don't look upon it as particularly strange. Why, I hope that before very long we shall be sailing through bright clear waters where I can show you snakes single, in pairs, and in knots of a dozen together basking at the surface in the sunshine."

"What, huge serpents?" said Jack shortly.

"No," replied the captain, turning upon him with a pleasant smile, while the doctor kicked at Sir John's leg under the table, but could not reach him. "They are mostly quite small—four, five, or six feet. The biggest I ever saw was seven feet long, but I've heard of them being seen eight feet."

"Yes, I saw one once seven feet nine. It was shot by a passenger on his way to Rangoon, and they got it on board," said the mate quietly.

"Oh, but that's nothing of a size," said Jack.

"No, Mr Meadows," replied the captain; "but we know it as a fact that there are plenty of sea serpents of that size, just as we know that there are adders and rattlesnakes on land."

"Yes, poisonous serpents," said Jack.

"So are these, sir, very dangerously poisonous. I have known of more than one death through the bite of a sea snake. But, as I was going to say, we know of adders and rattlesnakes, and we know too that there are boas and pythons and anacondas running up to eight-and-twenty and thirty feet long on land. There's a deal more room in the sea for such creatures to hide, so why should there not be big ones as well as small there?"

"That's a good argument," said Sir John, "and quite reasonable."

"And you think then," said the doctor, "that yours which you saw were great serpents swimming on the surface?"

"No, sir, I thought they were something else."

"What?" said Jack, with a certain amount of eagerness.

"They struck me as being those great lizard things which they find turned into fossils out Swanage and Portland way. I dare say you've seen specimens of them in the British Museum."

"No," said Jack, colouring a little, "I have never taken any interest in such things."

"No?" said the captain wonderingly. "Ah, well, perhaps you will. Now it struck me that these things were—were— Do either of you gentlemen remember the name of them?"

"Plesiosaurus. Lizard-like," said Sir John.

"That's it, sir," cried the captain, glancing at the speaker, and then looking again at Jack. "And I tell you how it struck me, and how I accounted for their being so seldom seen."

"Yes!" said Jack, who had laid down his knife and fork, and was leaning forward listening attentively. "How did you judge that?"

"From its large eyes."

"What had that to do with it?"

"It meant that it was a deep-sea living creature. You'll find, if you look into such matters, sir, that things which live in very deep water generally have very large eyes to collect all the light they can."

"But yours were living on the top of the water," said Jack.

"To be sure," cried the doctor, giving Sir John a sharp glance. "Come, captain, that's a poser for you."

"Well, no, sir," replied the captain modestly, and with a quiet smile; "I think I can get over that. Perhaps you know that fish which live in very deep water, where the pressure is very great, cannot live if by any chance they are brought to the surface. The air-vessels in them swell out so that they cannot sink again, and they get suffocated and die."

"But if it was their natural habit to live in deep water," said Jack, "they would not come to the surface."

"If they could help it, sir," said the captain; "but when a creature of that kind is ill it may float toward the surface, and turn up as you see fishes sometimes. I fancy that my great lizard things are still existing in some places in the mud or bottom of the sea, that they are never seen unless they are in an unnatural state, and then they soon die, and get eaten up by the millions of things always on the look-out for food, and their bones sink."

"I should like to see one," said Jack thoughtfully.

"And I should like to show you one, sir," said the captain. "There's no knowing what we may see if we cruise about. Well, I'll promise you sea-snakes and whales and sharks. I can take you too where there are plenty of crocodiles for you to practise at with a rifle. Good practice too to rid the world of some of its dangerous beasts."

Jack shuddered, and wanted to say that he did not care to see anything of the kind, but he did not speak, and just then the captain rose from the table, drew up the blind, and looked out.

"There you are, sir," he said. "Come and look. The lads were ready enough when I told them to light up to-night. Looks nice, don't she?"

Jack followed to the window, to see that it was a glorious night, with the sky and sea spangled with gold, while out where he knew the yacht lay, there shone forth with dazzling brilliancy what seemed to be a silver star, and dotted about it, evidently in the rigging of the yacht, were about thirty lanterns of various colours, but only seeming to be like the modest beams of moons in attendance upon the pure white dazzling silver star.

The boy gazed in silence, impressed by the beauty of the scene, as the captain now quietly opened the window to admit the soft warm air from off the sea, while faintly heard came the sound of music from some passing boat.

"How beautiful!" said Sir John, who had come unheard behind them.

"Yes, sir," said the captain quietly, "with the simple beauty of home; but you will have to see the grand sunrises and sunsets of tropic lands to fully understand the full beauty of God's ever-changing ocean. But even now, Mr Meadows, I think you can hardly say you don't like the sea."

Jack made no reply, but drew a deep breath which sounded like a sigh.

"Well, Jack," said Sir John, when they were about to retire that night, "what do you think of Captain Bradleigh?"

"I liked him better this evening, father," said the boy thoughtfully. "He did not treat me as if I were a child, and he left off calling me 'young gentleman.'"

"Good-night, Meadows," said the doctor, a short time after; "I wish you weren't going to spend so much money, but Jack has had his first dose of medicine."

"Yes," said Sir John; "and it has begun to act."

Chapter Eight
Ned feels the motion of the vessel

All aboard after the preliminaries had been arranged in the most satisfactory way, Sir John's arrangements made, and Jack, like a dejected prisoner, taken down to Dartmouth one day, following Edward, who had gone on in advance with the last of the luggage.

He was waiting in the station when the train came in, looking as eager and excited as a boy, and as full of delight as his young master was depressed. Captain Bradleigh was there too, and one of the yacht's cutters hanging on at the pier, ready for rowing the party on board the *Silver Star*.

"The luggage, Edward?" said Sir John.

"All aboard, Sir John, and things ready in the cabins," said the man.

"Then see that our portmanteaus are placed in the boat."

"All in, Sir John. I set the porters to get 'em from the van."

"Come along then, Jack, let's take our plunge."

Jack gave a wild look round, his eyes full of despair, but he said nothing, only felt that he was bidding good-bye to home, land, ease, and comfort for ever, and followed his father to the boat.

Two hours after they were standing out to sea, with Jack, Sir John, and the doctor watching the receding shore, the two latter feeling some slight degree of compunction at the last; but Edward was below inspecting the cabins once more, and as soon as he had done this, in spite of the yacht beginning to heel over so that the cabin floor was a good deal higher on one side than the other, he folded his arms, frowned, set his teeth, and began the first steps of a hornpipe, but before he had gone far a lurch sent him head-first toward the port bulkhead. Here he saved himself by thrusting out his hands, turned, and began again.

"Very well, uphill if you like," he cried, and he danced from port toward starboard. But this time his legs seemed to have turned wild, and he staggered to right.

"Wo-ho! heave-ho! you lubbers!" he cried, and giving a lurch to right, but with desperate energy he saved himself from a fall, and tried to begin again.

"Now then," he cried, "from the beginning! Wo-ho! No, I mean yo-ho!" he muttered. "Why, it's like trying to dance on horseback. Here goes again. Tiddly-um-tum-tum! Tiddle-liddle-iddle iddle-liddle iddle-rum-tum!"— "*Bang.*"

Edward crashed against one of the little state-room doors, cannoned off, and came down sitting on the cabin floor.

"Oh, that's it, is it?" cried the man. "Well, if you're going to dance it, I'll wait till you've done."

"Anything the matter?" said a voice, and the steward came in.

"Nothing particular," said Sir John's man, "unless it's the yacht gone mad."

"Oh, this is nothing," said the steward. "A bit lively after being at anchor so long."

"Oh, that's it, is it?" said Edward, rising. "You'll soon get used to it. Not much of a sailor I suppose?"

"Not a bit of one, but mean to be. I say, who are you?"

"Steward, and I suppose you are to be my mate?"

"Oh, am I?" said Edward; "very well, anything for a change."

The steward turned and left the cabin, for there were steps, and directly after Jack appeared at the door, tried to walk steadily to a seat, but a sudden careening over sent him to port, and he would have fallen heavily if the man had not made an effort to save him, when they went down together, the man undermost.

"Quite welcome, sir," said Edward, struggling up and helping Jack to a seat. "Sorry I ain't a bit fatter, sir; only if I was you I'd hold on till I get used to it, in case I'm not always there to be buffer."

"Oh!" groaned Jack, whose face was ghastly.

"Why, Mr Jack, sir, don't look like that. You fight it down. Feel a bit queer?"

"Horrible, Ned. Help me to get to my berth."

"Oh, I wouldn't cave in, sir. It'll soon go off."

"Will it?" groaned Jack. "I was afraid to come down for fear they should see and laugh at me. Oh, how bad I am! Why did we come?"

"I dunno, sir. It was the guv'nor's doing. But you try and keep up."

"It is impossible. You don't know how bad I feel."

"No, sir, but I know how bad I feel."

"You!" said Jack dismally. "Surely you are not going to be ill?"

"Why not, sir? I feel just as if my works had gone all wrong, but I haven't got time to be ill. Come on deck, sir."

"No. Help me to my berth."

"Right, sir," said the man; and waiting till the vessel seemed steadier, he took tightly hold of his young master's arm, helped him to his legs, and tried to guide him across the cabin to his little state-room; but at the first step Jack made a dive, and they went down together.

"Please, sir, this ain't swimming lessons."

"Let me crawl," groaned Jack.

"No, sir, don't do that. Here, give me your hand again. Up you gets. That's the way. This time does it. Told you so. Here we are."

"Don't, please don't talk to me," said Jack in a low voice. "Help me into the berth.—Yes, thank you. Now go away and leave me."

"Won't roll out, will you, sir?"

"Don't—don't talk to me. Please go."

"Poor chap!" muttered Edward. "I do wish he'd got just a little bit o' pluck in him. But it do make you feel a bit queer. S'pose I go and shake it off on deck."

He went up, saw that the gentlemen were right aft, and he walked forward to where the crew were busy here and there, and nodded first to one and then another in the most friendly way, as if he had known them all his life. Then he thrust his hands in his pockets, trying to look perfectly unconcerned, and balanced himself so as to try and give and take with the vessel.

But it was no good; he fought against the inevitable as long as he could, and finally staggered to the cabin hatch and descended to where Jack was lying. "Here's a go, sir," he cried. "I thought it only wanted a bit of pluck, and it would be all right."

"Oh, go away," groaned Jack. "Don't bother me. I'm dying."

"I'm worse than that, sir," said the man piteously. "What's to be done, sir?"

"Oh, go to your hammock or berth. I can't bear to be bothered now."

"But it will be dinner-time soon, sir, and I shall have to help wait at table. I couldn't carry the soup or fish, sir. I couldn't carry myself. What will the guv'nor say?"

"Ned, will you please to go!" said Jack with a groan.

"Certainly, sir; directly, sir; but I can't move."

"Nonsense!"

"Yes, sir, that's what I thought about you, and that you'd only got to make a try; but it isn't to be done."

"Go away," groaned Jack.

"Wish I could, sir. I oughtn't to have come. It's all through being so jolly cock-sure that I could do anything, and I can't. Wish I was at home cleaning the plate. Oh, Master Jack, can you feel how the boat's a-going on?"

"Yes, it's dreadful," sighed Jack.

"Is it going to be like this always, sir?"

"Don't! pray don't bother me. Can't you see how ill I am?"

"No, sir, not now. I can only see how bad poor miserable me is. Oh dear! did you feel that, sir? she give a regular jump, just as if she went over something.—Master Jack!"

There was no reply.

"Master Jack!" groaned the man. "Oh, please, sir, don't say you're dead."

"Will you go away and leave off bothering me!" cried the boy angrily.

"Wish I could, sir; I'd be glad to."

There was a pause, during which the yacht bounded along before a fine fresh breeze. Soon Edward began again.

"Mr Jack!"

No answer.

"Mr Jack, sir!"

"Ned! will you go!"

"I can't, sir. 'Strue as goodness, sir, I can't."

"Where are you?" moaned the boy, who was lying on his back staring with lack-lustre eyes up at the ceiling just above his head.

"I dunno, sir; I think I'm lying on the carpet, sir, close to the shelf I put you on."

"Then go away somewhere; you make me feel as if I could kill you."

"Wish you would, sir," groaned the man. "I'd take it kindly of you."

"Oh, don't talk such nonsense," sighed Jack. "Oh, my head, my head!"

"Oh, mine, sir, and it ain't nonsense at all. It's real earnest. Why was I such a fool as to come, and why did I grin at you, and say as you was a poor-plucked 'un? It's like a judgment on me. But I always was so conceited."

"Call some one to help you to your berth."

"I dursn't, sir. If I did, those sailor chaps would see as it was all over with me and pitch me overboard."

"Ned, you are torturing me," said Jack; and he turned himself a little to look down at the miserable being on the floor.

"Very sorry, sir, but something's torturing me. Do you think we've got as far as France yet?"

"Oh, I don't know."

"Do you think, if I give master warning, he'd have me set ashore at once?"

"No," said Jack, with a touch of exultation in his words; "I'm sure he wouldn't. You'll have to go with us now."

"I couldn't, sir, I couldn't really. Why, I couldn't go round this room—cabin, or whatever you call it. Oh dear! oh dear! to think of me turning all of a sudden like this! It's awful."

"Here, Jack! Jack, lad! Aren't you coming on deck?" cried a voice down through the cabin skylight.

"Oh, there's the doctor," groaned Edward. "Why don't he come down?"

"Jack! are you there? It's splendid. Come up."

"Come down, sir, please," groaned the man.

"Hullo!" said the doctor to himself. "Why surely they're not— Oh! they can't be so soon."

He hurried down the cabin steps, and came breezily into the cabin, to see at a glance the state of affairs.

"Why, Jack, my lad, this is cowardly," he cried.

"Don't, sir, don't," groaned Edward. "I said something like that. Don't you, sir, or you may be took bad too."

"Why you ought to be able to stand a little sea-going, my man," said the doctor; "this is a break down. Here, make an effort and go to your berth."

"Make an effort, sir? I couldn't do it even if the ship was a-sinking."

"Nonsense!"

"It's true. I'm afraid it's all over, and Sir John will want another man."

"There, jump up and go to your berth. You share the same cabin as the cook and steward, don't you?"

"I was to, sir, and it was a very small place, but there'll be more room for them now."

"Nonsense, I tell you; jump up."

"Jump, sir!" groaned the man; "did you say jump?"

"Well then, crawl. Here, steward!" cried the doctor, "come and help this man to his cabin."

"Can't you give me something to put me out of my misery, sir?" groaned the man.

"Absurd! There, try and get on your legs. I'll help you." For the steward had come in promptly, smiling at the state of affairs, and poor Edward was set upon his legs.

"Come, stand up," said the steward, for Edward's knees gave way like the joints of a weak two-foot rule.

"Yes, stand up," cried the doctor; "don't be so weak, man."

"'Tain't me, sir, it's my legs," said the man faintly. "Don't seem to have no bones now."

"Why, Edward, I thought you were a smart manly fellow," cried the doctor.

"That's just what I always thought of myself, sir, but it wasn't a bit true. Would you mind asking Sir John, sir, to have the yacht stopped and me put ashore?"

"Of course I would. It's absurd."

"But I shan't be a bit of use, sir; I shan't indeed. I'm ashamed of myself, but I can't help it."

"There, I know," said the doctor kindly; "get to your berth and lie still for a few hours. You'll be ready to laugh at your weakness before long."

"Laugh, sir? laugh? No, I don't think I shall ever laugh again."

The door swung to after the man's exit, and the doctor returned to Jack's cabin.

"Well," he said, "feel very queer?"

"Can't you see, doctor?" said the boy, giving him a piteous look.

"Yes, of course I can, my lad; but lie still, and you'll soon get over it. Some people do get troubled this way. Haven't you read that Lord Nelson used to have a fit whenever he went to sea?"

Jack made no reply, for he was in that condition which makes a sufferer perfectly indifferent about everything and everybody, and when it is no satisfaction to know that the greatest people in the world suffered in a similar way. All they can think of then is self.

Sir John came down soon after, and sat with his son for awhile, trying to encourage him, but poor Jack hardly answered him, and at last he began to be anxious, and went to join the doctor, who was on deck chatting with the captain.

"I wish you'd go down and see to the boy," he said; "he looks so white, I feel anxious."

The doctor shrugged his shoulders and went below, to come back at the end of five minutes.

"Well?" said Sir John anxiously.

"Usual thing; nothing to fidget about. Your man's worse."

"What, Edward?" cried Sir John, staring. "I saw him forward there chatting with the sailors not long ago."

"Yes, and now he's in his berth talking to himself about what a donkey he was to come. Who knows! perhaps it will be our turn next."

But it was not, although it began to blow hard from the west, and the sea crew rougher as the yacht dashed on.

But the next evening Edward was about again, looking rather pale, but very proud and self-satisfied, as he went to Jack's berth.

"Don't you feel any better yet, sir?" he said.

"No; can't you see how ill I am?" replied Jack faintly.

"Ah, that's because you don't try to master it. Hasn't Doctor Instow told you that you ought to try and get the better of it?"

"Yes; but what is the use of telling me that?" groaned Jack, with his eyes shut; but he opened them directly and gazed discontentedly at the man, as if feeling that it was hard and unfair of fate to let the servant recover while the master was so ill. "Are you quite well again?"

"Me, sir? Oh yes, sir," said Edward carelessly.

"And I—I feel as if I shall never live to go far."

"Ah, that's the way of it, sir, I felt just like that; but you'll come all right again before you know where you are. Like me to get you a bit of anything, sir? The kitchen place is splendid, and the cook would knock you up something nice in no time. What do you say to an omelet, sir?"

Jack ground his teeth at the man, and then closed his eyes and feebly turned his back.

"Poor chap, he has got it bad," muttered the convalescent, as he went out of the cabin on tip-toe. "But I don't think he's quite so bad as I was, after all."

Chapter Nine
"When the raging seas do roar."

Jack Meadows started up in his berth with a great fear upon him, and he started down again with the great fear turned for the moment into a great pain, caused by his having struck his forehead sharply, for about the tenth time, against the top of his berth.

"Am I never going to recollect what a miserable, narrow, boxed-up place it is," he said to himself angrily.

Then the fear came back, and he rolled out feeling confused and horrified.

He had turned in over-night without undressing, further than taking off jacket, waistcoat, and boots, so that he was almost dressed, for he had lain down in terror to rest himself so as to be quite ready if an alarm was given that the yacht was sinking; and he knew now that he must have been asleep, for it was early morning by the pale grey light which stole in through the glass. The weather seemed to be worse, the yacht pitching and tossing, and there was a dull, creaking, horrible sound which kept on, but was smothered out at intervals by a tremendous bump, which was always followed by a sound as if the vessel had sailed up the rapids of Niagara river and then beneath the falls.

The confusion increased with the noise, and, holding on with one hand, Jack pressed the other to his forehead as he stared straight before him at a big tin box which appeared to his sleep-muddled brain to be walking about the saloon table, when he opened the tiny state-room door.

Yes, there was no mistake about it; that box was alive, just as frightened as he was by the fearful storm, and was trying to escape, for all of a sudden, after edging its way to the end of the table, it made a bound, leaped to the floor, and began to creep and jump toward the door at the foot of the cabin stairs.

"What did it all mean?" thought Jack, and he tried hard to collect himself. Yes, they came on board three or four days before, he was not sure which. He remembered that. He had been frightfully ill, and oh, so sick. He remembered that too. Then he recalled about preparing for the worst last night, when the storm increased, and thinking as he lay down in his berth, weak as a baby, that it was very grand to be able to act as his father and Doctor Instow did, for they were perfectly resigned, and he had seen them sitting down playing a game of chess with a board full of holes into which the chess-men stuck like pegs.

Then in full force his brain seemed to assert itself. The worst had come, and it was his duty to awaken his father and Doctor Instow, so that they might all save themselves by taking to one of the boats or a raft.

Boomp! Splash. U–r–r–r–r!

A wave striking the yacht's bows—the water deluging the deck.

A spasm of fear shot through him, and he made a dash to catch up his yachting cap and pea-jacket with gilt anchor buttons which he had had on the previous night; but as soon as he quitted his hold, he was literally at sea, and the floor of his little state-room rising up, he seemed to be pitched head-first into his berth as if diving, but he managed to save himself from injury, and dropped on to the floor, crawled to his jacket, slipped it on, and then out into the saloon, to see that the tin box—one which the doctor had had brought on board full of necessaries for their fishing and collecting trips—had reached the saloon door, but could get no further.

But what was a box to a man? Jack crept to his father's door, beat upon it, and then dragged it open to find the berth empty.

"Gone and left me," groaned the lad in his misery and despair. "How horrible! No; he is making a raft, and will come and fetch me soon.—Oh!"

He clutched at the door to save himself, for the yacht suddenly made a dive, and he felt that they were going down into the vast depths of the sea; but he did not save himself, for the door played him false and helped to shoot him right across the saloon, and he was brought up by the door of the doctor's tiny room.

Recovering himself he desperately clutched at the handle, dragged the door open, and as the yacht prepared for another dive, he shot in against the berth, punching its occupant heavily in the ribs, and snatching at the clothes as he held on.

The doctor uttered a deep grunt, but did not stir. "Doctor! doctor!" panted Jack. "Wake up! Quick! We're sinking."

"Eh? All right!" came in a deep muffled voice. "Oh, wake up, wake up!" cried Jack. "I can't leave him to drown. Doctor! doctor!"

"All right!" came fiercely, as Jack seized the sleeper by the shoulders. "Tell 'em—only jus' come abed."

"Doctor! doctor!"

"Tell 'em—give—warm bath—mustard."

"But we're sinking," cried Jack wildly. "Eh? Whose baby is it? What's matter—Jack? Taken ill?"

"No, no. Quick! Come on deck."

"Just won't," growled the doctor; and he turned his back and uttered a deep snore.

Jack stared in horror, and then dropped on all fours to crawl to the foot of the cabin stairs, and fetch help to drag the drowning man on deck, being fully imbued with the idea that Doctor Instow had taken some drug in his despair, so that he might be unconscious when the yacht went down.

In passing he saw that the captain's and the mate's berths were both empty, and, how he knew not, he crawled up the cabin stairs, looked on deck, and saw that his father was standing by the weather bulwark, and the captain close by.

There was the man at the wheel, and a couple more forward in shiny yellow tarpaulins; and as he gazed at them wildly, there was a thud and a beautiful curve over of a wave which deluged the deck and splashed the two men, but they did not stir.

He saw no more then, for the yacht careened over from the pressure on the three great sails, and it seemed to the lad that the next moment they would be lying flat upon the water, so he clung to the hatchway fittings for dear life. But the next moment the *Silver Star* rose from the wave in front, and literally rushed on, quivering from stem to stern like a live creature, the waves parting and hissing to form an ever-widening path of foam astern.

Jack caught the full fresh breeze in his teeth as he struggled on deck, and breathlessly staggered to the side, looking as if he were going to leap overboard; then clinging to the rail, he crept hand-over-hand to where his father now stood with the captain.

"That you, Jack?" cried Sir John. "Good-morning. Well done! Come, this is brave."

"Splendid!" cried Captain Bradleigh. "Why you have soon come round."

Jack woke fully to the fact now that it was a false alarm, and strove hard to get rid of the scared look with which he had come on deck for help to drag Doctor Instow up. But still he was not quite assured, for he started suddenly as, *plosh!* there came another rush of water over the bows. "What's that?" he cried.

"Sea having a game with the yacht," said the captain merrily. "Splashing her nose. Look how she rises and glides over that wave. Regular racer, isn't she?"

"Yes, going so fast," panted Jack breathlessly. "But—but is there no danger—of her sinking?"

"Just about as much as there would be of a well-corked-up bottle, my lad. The more you pushed her under, the more she'd bob up again. Oh no, she won't sink."

"I'm glad you came up," said Sir John. "This breeze is glorious, and I never saw the sea more beautiful; look how the waves glisten where the moon falls upon them on one side, and how they catch the soft pearly light from the east on the other. It is a lovely effect."

"Yes, father, very beautiful," said the boy sadly. "Are we far from land, Captain Bradleigh?"

"Yes, and getting farther every minute. Don't want any steam with this breeze. If it holds, we shall regularly race across the bay."

"Bay?" said Jack, feeling that he must say something to keep them from seeing how nervous he was. "Mount's Bay?"

"Mount's Bay?" said the captain, smiling, "No; the Bay of Biscay. We passed Mount's Bay three days ago, while you were lying so poorly in your berth. Oh, that's nothing to mind," he added quickly. "I was horribly bad for a week in smoother water than you've had; you've done wonders to get over it so soon."

"Yes, you've done well, Jack," said Sir John, who looked gratified by the way in which his son was behaving. "Mind! keep tight hold of the rail."

For just then the yacht made a dive, rose, shook herself, and then, after seeming to hang poised on the summit of a green hillock, she started again with a leap.

"Yes; better hold tight till you feel more at home. One easily gets a heavy fall and bruises at first. But you'll soon find your sea-legs, and give and swing with the vessel just as if you belonged to her."

"Why didn't you bring the doctor up?" said Sir John; "he is losing a glorious sight."

"I tried hard to wake him," replied the lad, "but he was too sleepy."

"Yes; he likes his morning sleep," said Sir John.

The captain walked forward to speak to the two men of the watch, and an intense longing came over the boy to undeceive his father, who had not grasped the true reason of his appearance on the deck. But try hard as he would, shame kept him silent, and he began to give way again to the nervousness which oppressed him.

"Don't you think," he began; but his father checked him.

"Look—look—Jack!" he said; and he pointed to something about a quarter of a mile away.

For a few moments, as it appeared and disappeared, the lad could not catch sight of it; but at last he did.

"A serpent—a huge serpent," he cried. "Is it coming this way?"

"It, or rather they are not coming in this direction, but going on the same chase, my boy. No, it is not a serpent; serpents do not travel up and down in that fashion, though some people think they do, but undulate their bodies right and left."

"But look, father," cried Jack, forgetting his nervousness in the interest of what he saw. "It must be a great snake, you can make out its folds as it goes along."

"No, you look—take a good long look, and don't come on deck again without your binocular. That is a little shoal of seven or eight porpoises. They follow one another like that, and keep on with that rising and falling manner, coming up to breathe, and curling over as they dive down again. They do strangely resemble a great snake."

"But breathe, father?" said Jack; "fish breathe?"

"Those are not classed as fish, my lad. They cannot exist without coming up to get air. A fish finds enough in the water which passes over its gills."

"Yes, I've read that," said Jack; "but I had forgotten."

"Well, gentlemen, looking at the porpoises?" said the captain, coming up behind them. "Nice little school of them. They always go along like that. I used to think when I first saw them that they were like a troop of boys running along and leaping posts. They're after a shoal of fish; mackerel perhaps. Well, Sir John, how do you think the yacht runs with this breeze?"

"Splendidly," said Sir John.

"Breeze! Splendidly!" said Jack to himself, as he tried to restrain a shudder, for the breeze had seemed to him a storm.

"Well, sir, she's good on every tack. I can do anything with her; I never felt a boat answer the helm as she does. But I like to hear you talk about it; I feel a sort of vanity about her, seeing she is like a child of mine, and I want to be quite convinced that you are satisfied with your hasty bargain."

"Once for all then, Captain Bradleigh, be satisfied on that point; for I feel myself most fortunate," said Sir John.

"Thank you, sir, thank you!" cried the captain warmly. "That will do then; I will not refer to it again. By the way, Mr Jack, now you are getting your sea-legs, you will have to begin your education."

"My education?" said the lad, staring. "Yes, sir; you must not go on a two or three years' cruise without making a thorough sailor of yourself, so as soon as you feel yourself fit, I'm ready to teach you to box the compass, and a little navigation."

"Oh, thank you," said Jack coldly, and the tips of his horns, that, snail-like, were beginning to show signs of coming out, disappeared.

The captain gave Sir John a meaning look, and went on.

"You gentlemen will find Bartlett a capital fellow, and very useful. He's quite at home over all kinds of sea-fishing, and you had better begin to give him a hint, Mr Jack, that you'll want a good deal of his help. Capital knowledge of sea-fish; not book knowledge, but practical. It's of no use now with the yacht going at this rate, but when we get into calmer waters."

"Shall we soon get into calmer water?" said Jack anxiously.

"Oh yes. We're going due south now, and shan't be long first. I dare say by the time we have passed Cape Finisterre, and are running down the Spanish coast, you will find it smooth enough. Like an early cup of tea, gentlemen?"

"I? No," said Sir John, "I'll wait for breakfast. What do you say, Jack?"

Jack said nothing, but looked disgusted.

"Don't like the idea of taking anything of course, sir," said the captain; "but wait a little, I'm quite a doctor over these troubles, and I'll give you some good news."

"I'm sure he will be grateful for it," said Sir John, for Jack was silent.

"Here it is then," said the captain bluffly; "and you may believe it, for I know. You've had a sharp little spell since we left port; but it's over now, and, as we say, you're quite well, thank you."

"I quite well?" cried the lad indignantly; "I feel wretchedly bad."

"And think me very unfeeling for talking to you like this," said the captain, smiling; "but I'm nothing of the kind. Of course you feel wretchedly ill. Faint and weak, and as if you could never touch food again. That's why I wanted you to let the steward bring you a cup of tea. Human nature can't go without food for three or four days without feeling bad."

"Of course not," said Sir John.

"But now look here, Mr Jack, I talked about good news, and told you that you were well now. Here's the proof. There's a nice stiff breeze on, the water's very lively, and the yacht's dancing about so that we shall have to mind how we handle our breakfast-cups; and look at you! You are holding on because you haven't learned to give and take with the springs in your legs, but you are taking it all quite calmly. Why, the other day as soon as we began to career over a bit, the doctor had to take you below. Now do you see the difference?"

"No," said Jack. "You cannot tell how ill I feel."

"My dear lad, I know exactly," said the captain. "Come, pluck up your courage; we're going to have a glorious day, and the wind will drop before noon. Take my advice: go below to have a good tubbing, and dress yourself again, and by breakfast-time you'll be beginning to wonder that you should have felt so queer; and mind this, sea-sickness isn't a disease: it's a—well, it's a— Ah, here's the doctor. Morning, Doctor Instow, you're just in time. What is sea-sickness?"

"A precious nuisance for those who are troubled with it," said the doctor heartily. "Morning. Morning, Meadows. Why, Jack, lad, this is grand. You've quite stolen a march on me. I say, you mean you're over your bit of misery then. My word, what a jolly morning. Hullo! going below?"

"Yes," said Jack quietly, as he began to move toward the cabin hatch.

"Take my arm, Mr Jack," said the captain kindly.

"No, thank you," said the lad. "I want to get to be able to balance."

Sir John said nothing, but stood with the others watching the lad's unsteady steps till he disappeared.

"He'll do now, sir," said the captain.

"Do?" cried the doctor; "I should think he will. Why, Meadows, he has got all the right stuff in him: it only wants bringing out. Nothing like the sea for a lad, is there, captain?"

"Nothing, sir," said that gentleman. "It makes a boy manly and self-reliant. He may turn out a bit rough, but it's rough diamond. Sir John, pray don't you think from what I say that I'm one of those carneying, flattering sort of chaps who ought to be kicked all round the world for the sneaks they are. What I say is quite honest. That's a fine lad of yours: he's as nervous now as a girl, and no wonder, seeing how weak and delicate he is, but I watched him this morning, and he's fighting it all down like a fellow with true grit in him, at a time too when he's feeling downright bad. You won't hardly know him in a month."

Sir John nodded and walked away, to go and stand by himself looking out to sea.

"Whew!" whistled the captain, turning to the doctor. "I hope I haven't offended our chief."

"Offended him? no," said the doctor, taking his arm and walking him off in the other direction. "It's all right, captain. You spoke out the truth, and he'll tell you before the day's out that he is obliged. Poor fellow! he is very tender-hearted about his boy. Lost the lad's mother, you see, and he worships him. But you're quite right, my plan's good, and I shall bring him back a healthy man."

"You shall, doctor, for we'll all try and help you; there!"

Chapter Ten
Jack begins to come round

"Oh dear, I do feel so ashamed of myself," said the doctor at breakfast that morning. "Edward, bring me another egg, and some more of that ham."

"Well, sir, if you do," said the captain, smiling, "I ought to be, but I'm not. More coffee, Sir John?"

"Thanks, no, I'm taking tea. Jack, my boy, will you try another cup?"

The lad hesitated for a moment, and then drew aside for Edward to refill his cup, with which he had been eating sparingly of some well-made toast.

"Find that rather stale, Mr Jack?" said the captain.

"No; it is very nice," said the lad. "Ah, the toasting takes it off. Four days out. That's as long as we go with the same bread. Begin making our own to-morrow."

Just then Edward handed Doctor Instow a goodly rasher of broiled ham, upon which was a perfectly poached egg; and directly after the man came round behind Jack, and quietly placed before him, with a whisper of warning that the plate was very hot, another rasher of ham, and at the first sight of it the lad began to shrink, but at the second glance, consequent upon a brave desire not to show his repugnance, he saw that it was a different kind of rasher to the doctor's, and that there was no egg. It was small and crisp and thin, of a most beautiful brown, with scarcely any fat, and showing not a drop in the hot plate. There was a peculiar aroma, too, rising from it, grateful and appetising, and after sipping at his fresh hot cup of tea—the second—twice, Jack broke off another fragment of his crisp toast and ate it slowly.

A minute passed away, his four companions eating in sea-going fashion, which is rather costly to the person that caters, and they were talking aloud meantime, but every one present made a point of not taking the slightest notice of the sensitive lad.

That hot tea at the first mouthful of the first cup was nauseating, and Jack glanced toward the door and waited before venturing upon a second.

But that second mouthful was not so bad, and it seemed to him that the captain certainly had good tea provided. Then Jack had broken off a scrap of the brown toast and eaten it, feeling at the end of a minute or two that he had never before known what well-made toast was like.

And so he had gone on very slowly, but certainly surely, till that piece of broiled ham—just such a piece as might tempt an invalid—was placed before him by Edward, who winked afterwards at the steward.

Jack would have resisted with scorn the suggestion that he was an invalid, and he was in utter ignorance of the doctor having entered into a conspiracy with the steward and cook just before they sat down; but that triumvirate had conspired all the same, and the result was that dry toast and that thin shaving of brown ham, which from the moment it was placed under his nose began to tempt him.

What wonder! Three days lying in a berth aboard ship, three days of hardly touching food; and now at last sitting at a pleasant breakfast-table in an exasperating appetite-sharpening atmosphere, which came in through the open window along with the bright sunshine, while four people were cheerily chatting and eating away like men who knew how good breakfast can be.

Then, too, there was that insidious preparation—that sending in of skirmishers of dry toast to attack the enemy before a bold advance was made with the ham.

Was it strange then that after another glance round, and telling himself that it was really to keep the others from thinking him too squeamish, Jack daintily cut off a tiny brown corner of the fragrant, saline, well-flavoured ham, and placed it in his mouth?

No: it did not disgust him in the least, and he ate it, and then glanced half-guiltily at the doctor, who was bending over his plate and gilding one of his own ham fragments with yolk of egg; but the doctor had very heavy eyebrows, and from behind them he had been watching the lad's acts, and as he saw him begin to cut another piece a little browner than the last, he winked to himself twice, and then burst out with—

"I say, captain; I suppose when we get into smoother water we might get a bit of fresh fish for the table?"

"Oh, yes, something of the mackerel kind; eh, Bartlett?"

The mate entered into the conversation directly, and in a quiet, modest way chatted about the possibilities of success, but advised waiting until the yacht was gliding steadily before a light breeze.

Still nobody turned to say a word to Jack, who sat and listened, growing by degrees a little interested over some remarks that were made about "the grains," which gradually began to take shape before him as a kind of javelin made on the model of Neptune's trident, and which it seemed had a long thin line attached to its shaft, and was thus used to dart at large fish when they were seen playing about under the vessel's counter, though what a vessel's counter was, and whether it bore any resemblance to that used in a shop, the lad did not know.

It was somewhere about the time of the last remarks being made by the mate, in which "the grains" were somehow connected with the bobstay, that Jack proceeded to cut another fragment of that crisp juicy ham; but he did not cut it, for the simple reason that there was none left to utilise the knife and fork, which he laid together in his plate with a sigh.

And somehow just the most filmy or shadowy idea of the possibility that the steward might ask him if he would take a little more crossed his mind, along with a kind of wondering thought that if the man did, what he would say in reply.

But the man did not ask, and Jack glanced at the toast-rack, which was, like his tea-cup, empty.

There was a pause now in the conversation, the captain looked inquiringly round, and then tapped the table lightly and said grace.

"Like to see how we take observations by and by, Mr Jack?" he said.

"With a telescope?" said Jack quickly, feeling relieved that no one asked him how he felt now.

"Well, yes, we do use a little glass in the business attached to the sextant. But you thought I meant observations of the land?"

"Yes."

"No, we are far away from land now. We take our observations from the sun at twelve o'clock, and then I can give you the exact spot where we are upon the chart."

"That's curious," said Jack.

"Yes, sir; curious, but quite commonplace now. It's worth noticing though how cleverly scientific men have worked it out for us, and what with our instruments, the chronometer, and the nautical almanac, we only want a bit of sunshine to be able to find out our bearings and never feel afraid of being lost."

"I'll come and see how it's done."

"Do, sir, at noon; and you'll like to see the heaving of the log as well."

The captain was right; the wind dropped—and quite suddenly—a good hour before noon, and Jack found himself beginning to feel a little hungry and hollow inside just about the time when the sextant was brought out, but he felt interested in what was being done, and found himself beginning to think that perhaps after all there might be something during the voyage to compensate for the deprivations he was to suffer with respect to his regular studies and his books.

It was curious, too, how little he began to think of the rising and falling of the vessel, as she glided over the waves, which were rough enough, and sparkled brilliantly in the sunshine; but the fore-part of the deck was dry now and warm, while the yacht looked picturesque and cheery, with the crew busy over various matters connected with the navigation.

But nobody made the slightest allusion now to his having been ill, or asked how he felt, and the colour came into the lad's cheeks once as he caught his father's eyes, which somehow seemed to wear a more contented and satisfied look, but he only said quietly—

"I say, Jack, lad, do you think we could sit down in a chair now without being shot out?"

Jack felt obliged to reply, so he said—

"Let's try."

Chapter Eleven

Jack's eyes begin to open.

"No," said Sir John, in reply to a question addressed to him by the captain, one beautiful moonlight evening, as they were running down within sight of the coast of Portugal; "unless it is necessary, or my son wishes to see the towns, I should prefer going steadily on eastward. For my part I want to get away from civilisation, and see Nature unspoiled or unimproved, whichever it is."

"And that depends upon individual taste, eh, Jack?" said the doctor.

"I suppose so," said the lad.

"Bah! he's going back again," said the doctor to himself.

"Would you like to stop at Gibraltar and see the Rock and its fortifications, Jack?"

"No, father, thank you," said the lad.

Sir John looked disappointed, but he said quietly—

"Then we'll go right on, captain, according to your plans. Let's see, what were they?"

"If you wish to get right away to the East, then I propose that we just touch at Gib, and stay long enough to fill up our water-tanks and take in fresh provisions and vegetables, run straight on to Naples, do the same there again, and then make for the Canal, unless you would care to see Vesuvius. Naples and its surroundings are very fine."

"Yes, very," said Sir John.

"Oh yes," growled the doctor; "but the place swarms with visitors. I want to get where we can land on some beautiful coast with our guns and collecting tackle, where we shouldn't see a soul, unless it's a naked savage."

"So do I," said Sir John. "What do you say, Jack?"

"Wherever you like, father," said the boy resignedly; and he rose and walked right forward to where a couple of the men were on the look-out, and Mr Bartlett was walking slowly up and down with a glass under his arm.

Sir John sighed, and there was perfect silence for a few minutes.

"It is very disappointing," he said at last.

"What is?" cried the doctor sharply. "Rome wasn't built in a day."

"But he seems to take it all as a duty, and as if he was compelled to obey me."

"And a good thing too," cried the doctor sharply. "What's better than for a son to feel that he is bound to obey his father? If I had been a married man instead of a surly bachelor, and I had had a son, I should have expected him to obey me and do what I thought was for his good; eh, captain?"

"Yes, sir, of course; and on your part, tried to be reasonable."

"Of course. Well, we—I mean Sir John—is reasonable. No, he isn't now. He wants Rome built in a day with the fresh paint on as well, and a grand procession of big drums and trumpets and soldiers with flags to march through the principal streets."

"Come, not quite so bad as that, Instow. Don't be cross."

"Then don't make me so. Now, I appeal to the captain here. Has not the boy been wandering about the deck all day with Bartlett, asking him questions about the sails, and talking to the men, and using his glass whenever there was a good bit of the land to see?"

"Well, yes."

"Well yes, indeed! What more do you want? We can only go on two legs, we men; we can't fly."

"Captain Bradleigh seems of a different opinion with this yacht. He makes us swim and pretty well fly."

"Yes, but what was Jack a month ago? Going about the house like a boy in a nightmare, or else with his hands supporting his heavy head, while he was A plus B-ing, squaring nothing, and extracting roots, or building up calculations with logs. He isn't like the boy he was when he came on board."

"That's true," said the captain quietly. "His interest is being awakened, and something else too—his appetite."

"Yes; he certainly eats twice as much, and is not so particular as to what it is."

"There!" cried the doctor triumphantly. "And what does that mean?"

"That the sea-air makes him hungry."

"Bah! that isn't all. It means that Nature keeps on asking for more bricks and mortar to go on building up the works that were begun years ago and not finished—muscle and bone and nerve, sir, so as to get him a sound body; and mind you, a sound body generally means a sound brain. Everything in a proper state of balance."

"I suppose you are right," said Sir John.

"Right? of course I am. Only give him time."

"Where is he now?"

"Along with Bartlett," said the captain.

"Yes, I can see him. They're examining something over the bows. Found something fresh. Isn't that a healthy sign? He was only a bit tired and bored just now. Look here, Meadows, you and I must not be too anxious, and keep on letting him see that we are watching him. Why, look at the other morning when he was just up from his sea-sickness. Do you think if I had begged him to eat that rasher of ham he would have touched it? Not he. Let him alone, and he'll soon be coming to us."

"Certainly that will be the best course. I should like to see though what he is doing now?"

"Better leave him alone. Sensitive chap like that, with a body like a little boy and a head like an old man, don't want to feel that he is being led about by a nurse. But there, I must humour you, I suppose. Come away."

The doctor set the example by rising, and they walked slowly forward, hearing Jack talking in an animated way as they drew nearer, and, as if in obedience to an order, one of the sailors trotted by them.

As they reached the port bows Jack turned round where he was leaning over the starboard side, as if to look for the man who had gone on some errand, and he caught sight of his father.

"Come and look here, father," he cried. "Something so curious."

"Eh? What is it?" said Sir John coolly, and, followed by the doctor, he crossed to where his son stood with the mate.

"Look over here, straight down into the black water," said Jack.

"Hah! Yes, very beautiful, looks as if we were sailing through a sea of liquid pale gold."

"And it's all black where it is not disturbed. As soon as the yacht's prow rushes through, everything is flashing out with phosphorescent light, and you can see myriads of tiny stars gliding away."

"Yes, beautiful," said Sir John. "Grand," cried the doctor.

"And Mr Bartlett here says it is nothing compared to what he has seen off Java and the other islands. Look now! it's just as if the sea as deep down as we can pierce was full of tiny stars. Oh, here's the pail."

The sailor had returned, and way was made for him to drop the bucket at the end of a rope down into one of the brightest parts, and bring it up full of the phosphorescent water.

Just then the doctor gave Sir John a dig in the ribs with his elbow, as much as to say, "Now, who's right?" While mentally agreeing that his friend was, Sir John moved out of the way, so as not to receive another poke.

Then followed rather a learned discourse from the doctor on the peculiarities of the wonderful little creatures which swarmed in the bucket, whose contents in the light seemed to be so much clear sea-water, but which in the darkness flamed with light as soon as it was disturbed by a hand being passed quickly through.

"Why, it makes my hand tingle and smart just slightly," said Jack.

"Oh yes," said the mate. "If you bathe in a sea like this you can feel quite an irritation of the skin, while the large jelly-fish sting like a nettle."

"Then are these jelly-fish?"

"Yes, almost invisible ones," replied the doctor.

"But it seems so strange. Why is it?" said Jack.

"Well, we know that fish prey upon these things wholesale, and my theory is that the tiny things have the stinging power as a defence by day, and the ability to light up to make the fish think they will burn their mouths at night and leave them alone. Sounds absurd, eh? But I believe that's it."

Jack spent an hour having bucketfuls of water drawn up from the spots where the luminous cold fire seemed to burn most fiercely, the mate and Edward, called in to assist, entering into the business with the greatest of enthusiasm, and helping, after Sir John and the doctor had gone, in another way, fetching tumblers and a glass globe from the steward, Edward having to carry these well-filled into the cabin, where, chuckling to himself, the doctor brought out his small microscope, and using a tiny water-trough designed for the purpose, proceeded to examine these little wonders of the world.

Gibraltar was reached a couple of days later, and a very brief stay made, Jack contenting himself with watching the huge mass of rock with his binocular. Then away over the rather rough sea, with a favourable wind, they ran for Naples, where it grew calmer, and at night the slow from the summit of the burning mountain was seen reflected on the clouds, while by day these clouds could be seen to be of smoke.

On again for the Canal, and the doctor confided to Sir John his belief that he was a little anxious now.

"It will be so tremendously hot down the Red Sea, that I'm afraid it will upset the lad; so as you are getting up steam for the run through the Canal, if the wind is light or contrary, I should use the screw till we get to Aden."

"And make up our coal-bunkers there," said the captain. "Yes; good advice, sir, for that is about the hottest place I know; but it's not often we get a contrary wind for the *Silver Star*. She'll sail closer to the wind's eye than anything I ever saw."

"But I feel disposed to say, steam through to Aden," said Sir John anxiously, "for if the wind is north-west, we shall have it like a furnace from the African desert."

"Yes, sir," said the captain, smiling, "but, according to my experience, it isn't much better from the Arabian side. There's no getting over it: the Red Sea might almost be called the Red-hot sea."

The business going on in the engine-room seemed to be a break in what so far had been rather a monotonous voyage, and, to the father's great satisfaction the following morning, he came suddenly upon Jack ascending to the deck, wiping his face, and followed by the mate, just as they were slowly steaming into the Canal.

Sir John said nothing, but noted that the lad went with the mate right aft, where they stood leaning over and gazing down at where the screw was churning up the water, the mate explaining its fish-tail-like action and enormous power in propelling the yacht.

"Have an eye upon him, Instow," said Sir John; "the heat is getting intense, and it can't be good for him to go down into that engine-room."

"Just as if I ever had my eyes off him," replied the doctor. "You let me be."

"But he seemed to be dripping with perspiration."

"Best thing for him. Open his pores, which have been shut up all his life. Grand thing for him. He couldn't be going on better. I was afraid that the heat would depress him, and lay him on his back: don't you see that so long as he keeps active he will not feel it so much?"

"I am not a doctor," said Sir John simply. "I suppose you are right."

"Well, give me a fair chance, old fellow. You've had your turn with the bow, and made an old man of him."

"Not I—his masters."

"Well, let me now try if I can't make a boy of the old man. Look at him. Can you believe it?"

Jack walked by them, in his white duck suit and pith hat, just then, with the mate.

"Find it too hot, father? Shall I fetch your white umbrella?"

"No, no, thank you, my boy; I'm going to sit under the awning and watch the shipping. But—er—don't expose yourself to the heat too much; the sun has great power."

"Yes, it is hot," said Jack quietly, "but I like it."

"Yes, Mr Jack, sir," said Edward, who had overheard his master's remarks, "and so do I like it; but it's a sort of country where you feel as if you would like to have a great deal of nothing to do, and lie about on the sand like the niggers. I've just been watching 'em, and it seems to me that they don't eat much, nor drink much. You see 'em nibbling a few dates, or swallowing lumps of great green pumpkins."

"Melons, Ned," said Jack, correcting him.

"Melons, sir? Yes, I know they call 'em melons, but they're not a bit better than an old pumpkin at home, or an old vegetable marrow gone to seed. I know what a melon is, same as Mackay grows at home, red-fleshed and green-fleshed, and netted. They're something like; but as for these— have you tried one, sir?"

"No."

"Then you take my advice, sir. Just you don't try 'em, for they're about the poorest, moshiest-poshiest things you ever tasted."

"But the people here seem to like them."

"Oh yes, they like 'em, sir. They seem as if they'd eat anything, and I suppose that's why their skins are so black. But, as I was saying, they don't seem to want beef, or mutton, or pickled pork, and yet they get fat. It's the sunshine, I believe. They go on swallowing that all day long. I mean to try how it acts as soon as I get a good chance."

"You're quite lazy enough without doing that," said Jack, laughing.

"Now I do call that 'ard, Mr Jack, sir—reg'lar out an' out hard. I'm sure I never neglects anything. You don't want, nor Sir John neither, anything like so much valeting as you do at home. There's no boots to brush, nor clothes neither. I'm sure, sir, I never neglected you, only just for that little bit when I seemed to be standing on my head because my legs wouldn't hold me up—now, have I, sir?"

"Oh no. You've always been very attentive, Ned."

"Then that's why I call it 'ard, sir. Ever since you've been growing sharp and quick, and wanting to do something else besides read, you've been getting 'arder to me, sir, and I don't like it."

"Oh, nonsense. I've only laughed at you sometimes."

"Well, sir, look at that. You never used to laugh at me at home, nor you usen't to order me about, nor you usen't to—well, you never used to do nothing, sir, but read."

Jack frowned, and reddened a little.

"I put out your clothes and boots for you, and you put 'em on—just what I liked to put for you. You used to get up when I called you, and you'd have eat anything that was put before you, and said nothing. While now you're getting particular about your food even, and you order me about—and I won't say bully me, because it ain't quite true; but you've said lots o' sharp things to me, and I feel 'mazed like sometimes to hear you, for it don't sound like you at all. It's just as if you'd got yourself changed, sir."

"Perhaps I have, Ned, for I feel changed," said the boy.

"Yes, sir, you are changed a lot, and I hope it's right."

"I hope so, Ned," said Jack, and he walked away.

"Don't even use his legs like he did a month ago. I can't quite understand it, but it ain't my business. Couldn't have been right for him to be always sitting over a book, and when he got up, looking as if he was still all among the Romans and Greek 'uns. But it seems so sudden like, and as if he might go back again. But I s'pose we shall see."

Chapter Twelve
A finny prize

The run through the Canal did not seem monotonous to Sir John, for a new feeling of satisfaction was growing within him, and everything looked bright. The crew appeared contented, and the work went on with an ease and regularity that was pleasant to see. The various objects of interest were pointed out, but Jack paid very little attention to them, his attention being principally taken up by the working of the yacht, and he was, in spite of the heat, up and down several times, the engine, with its bright machinery and soft gliding movements, so full of condensed power, having a strange fascination for him.

Then they were out in the Red Sea, with its sandy and sun-baked mountains, and the water flashing like molten silver.

Here it was perfectly calm, and Jack watched when the speed was increased; and as the captain wished to show Sir John what the yacht could do under pressure, the order for full speed ahead was given by the touch of an index, and they cut through the dazzling water, sending up an arrow-shaped wave of displacement, and for the next two miles going at a tremendous rate.

Then all at once the captain began to give orders, and the neatly-furled canvas was cast loose and hoisted, for puffs of air came from the northeast like as if from a furnace mouth, and away they glided once more. The fires were drawn, the steam blown off, and their rate decreased, though it was not far behind that of one of the great steamers which passed them on its way to China.

Once well on their way, lines were brought out from the little magazine and furnished with sinkers of lead selected by the mate to suit the speed at which glittering silvered artificial baits were thrown out to drag forty or fifty yards behind; but though every kind of lure on board was tried, hours and hours went by without a touch. But long before this Jack had turned to the mate, who was leaning over the stern on the opposite side.

"Isn't this very stupid?" he said.

"Oh no," said Mr Bartlett merrily. "It's a capital practice for patience."

"I don't know that I want to practise patience," said the lad thoughtfully. "But I say, I felt it when we started. Surely the fish will not be stupid enough to bite at these baits."

"It does not seem like it," said the mate, smiling.

"They will sometimes when the water's a bit rougher and we're going fast, but they are too clever for us to-day."

"Then we can give up," said Jack with a sigh of relief.

"Give up? No, that will never do. If we could only catch one fish, we could use it to cut up for bait."

"Ugh! the cannibals," cried Jack.

"Yes, plenty of fish are; but as we haven't one, and don't seem as if we can catch one, I'll go below and see if the cook can help me to a bit of pork skin to cut into a bait or two."

He made his line fast and went forward, while, standing now in the shadow cast by the great sail behind him, Jack held the line in a quiet listless way, gazing at the distant mountains and wondering at the beauty of the colour with which they glowed in the pure air. He felt calm and restful, and the soft sensuous warmth of the wind was pleasant. It was restful too this gliding over the sea, with the yacht gently rising and falling and careening over to the breeze. The trouble of the days to come seemed farther off, and for a few moments the germs of a kind of wonderment that he should have looked upon this voyage as a trouble began to grow in his mind.

Then he was roused from his pleasant musings as if by an electric shock attended by pain. The line he had coiled round his hand suddenly tightened with a jerk which wrenched at his shoulder and cut into his fingers, and he uttered a shout for help which made the man at the wheel turn to look. A big black-haired fellow, who was busy with a marline-spike and a piece of rope, dropped both and ran to the lad's help, but not before he had brought his left hand up to help his right, taking hold of the fishing-line and holding on with the feeling that the next minute he would be dragged overboard, but too proud to loose his hold all the same.

"Got him, sir?" said the sailor. "I've got something," panted Jack. "It's horribly strong."

"They are in here. Let him go."

"What!" cried Jack indignantly; "certainly not."

"I don't mean altogether, sir. Let him run, or the hook will break out."

"But how?"

"You've plenty of line on the winch, sir; let him have some loose to play about and tire himself."

"Oh yes, I see; but it's jerking dreadfully." The man picked up the big wooden winch upon which the line was wound and held it fast.

"Now, sir, hold on tight with your left hand, while you untwist the line from your right. That's the way. Now catch hold tight and let the wheel run slowly. There's a hundred yards more here. It will let him tire himself. That's it, he won't go very far; then you can wind in again—giving and taking till he leaves off fighting."

"Hallo! here, Mr Meadows," cried the mate; "this is hardly fair. Why you're the best fisherman after all. That's it, let him go every time he makes a dart like this: now he's slacking again. Wind up, sir, wind up."

Jack obeyed very clumsily, for it wanted practice to hold the big wooden winch steady with one hand while he wound with the other, and before he had recovered ten yards the fish made a fresh dart, not astern, but away nearly at right angles with the course of the ship, tiring itself by having to drag the now curved line through the water.

"Now again," cried the mate; "wind—wind."

Jack's inclination said, "Give the line over to the man who understands it," but pride said "No"; and he wound away till the wheel was nearly jerked from his hands by a fresh dart made by the captive.

And so it went on for some minutes, till the fish began to show symptoms of becoming exhausted; so did Jack, upon whose face the perspiration was standing in beads.

"Here, Lenny," cried the mate, "go and get the big gaff-hook. We shall have this fellow."

The man ran forward, and Jack, with eyes fixed, began to play his fish with a little more *nous*, but it was terribly hard work.

"Tell me when you're tired," said the mate.

"Now."

"Shall I play him for you?"

"No, no! Don't touch it," cried Jack, who was unaware for some moments that he had an audience to look on.

"Oh no, I won't touch till you tell me," said the mate.

"Bravo!" cried the doctor; "capital. Well done, Jack, that's the way. I ought to have been here. Why you've got hold of a thumper."

So it proved, for the fish showed no sign of giving in for another quarter of an hour, and various were the comments made as to the probability of its being got on deck; but at last the darts grew shorter and shorter, and far astern they saw a gleam from time to time of something silvery and creamy as there was a wallowing and rolling on the surface, and now the mate took hold of the keen hook attached to a light ten-foot ash pole.

"Perhaps you'd like to gaff him, Doctor Instow," said the mate.

"No, no," replied the doctor. "Fair play. You two were fishing. Land him yourself."

"What shall I do now?" said Jack, who was panting with his exertions.

"Let the winch go down on the deck, and haul the fish in hand over hand till you get him close in."

Jack followed his instructions, and the captive, completely exhausted, now came in fast enough, proving to be far larger than any of those present had expected to see, but about a tenth of what Jack had imagined from the strength the creature had displayed. In fact there had been moments when the lad had again been calculating whether at one of the fiercest rushes he would not have to let go and so escape being dragged over the rail.

But now, half drowned by being drawn through the water, the fish came in slowly and quietly, the lad having all the hauling to himself, till, leaning over, the mate made a dart and a snatch with the great gaff-hook, the weight on Jack's arms suddenly ceased, and, helped by the big dark sailor, Mr Bartlett hauled the prisoner quickly in over the rail, for it to lie beating the white boards with sounding slaps of its crescent-moon-shaped tail.

"Well done!" cried Sir John. "What brilliant colours!"

"Hah! yes," cried the doctor. "This is something like fishing. What is it, captain?"

"Oh, one of the great mackerel tribe fellows they have in the Mediterranean. It isn't a bonito, for it's too big, but just as bright in its colours. Can't be a small tunny come down through the Canal, can it?"

"I'm puzzled," said the mate, bending over the beautiful prize. "It may be; but whatever it is, Mr Meadows here has had a fine stroke of luck, and we shall have fish for dinner."

Jack flushed with the excitement of the capture, and stood looking on at the beauty of the creature's colours in the bright sunshine, while the mate placed the end of the gaff-pole between its jaws before attempting to extract the great triple hook which hung by a swivel beneath the silvered shining bait.

"I should say it is one of the bonitos," said the doctor thoughtfully. "It has that slimness just before the tail fin spreads out, and there are plenty of flying fish here, of course."

"Plenty, sir," said the captain. "I dare say if you go forward you'll see them beginning to skip out of the water, startled by the yacht. Seen any yet, Mr Jack?"

"Not yet," was the reply.

"Yes," said the doctor, "I think that's what it is. They chase the flying fish, and this fellow must have taken your long spoon-bait for one of them. Don't you think so, Bartlett?"

"Yes, sir, you are right; but without exaggeration I never saw so fine a one as this. Why," he continued, clasping his hands round the thin part near the tail and raising the fish for a few moments before letting it fall back on the white boards, "it is very little short of forty pounds."

"It must be quite that," cried the doctor. "Well, it's always the way, the new beginner catches the biggest fish. I should have liked to hook that fellow. Did he pull much, Jack?"

"Dreadfully. My arms feel strained by the jerks it gave."

"I congratulate you, my boy," said Sir John. "It is a beauty."

Then the captain spoke:

"When you've done admiring it, gentlemen, there is some one else would like to have a word. I mean the cook. This fellow is fresh now, but they go off at a tremendous rate, and it will be worthless in a few hours. Pass the word there for the cook."

The word was passed, and the worthy in question came up smiling.

"What do you say to him?" said the captain. "Too big and coarse?"

"Oh no, sir," cried the man. "I'll answer for it I can send some cutlets off it that will be excellent, and make plenty for the crew as well."

It seemed a pity to Jack for the beautifully coloured prize to be handed over, but already some of the bright tints were fading, and as soon as it was borne off the mate made a sign to Lenny, who brought a swab and a bucket to remove the wet and slime.

"What do you say to another turn, Mr Meadows?" said the mate, smiling.

Jack smiled and began to rub his shoulder, so the tackle was hung in loops to dry, and the lad went forward to watch the flying fish spin out of the water and glide along upon their transparent wing-like fins; and he returned to watch the beautiful little creatures again and again as, evidently taking the hull of the yacht for some huge pursuing fish, they darted up from under her counter to drop back far away after their forced journey, and swim on till they gathered force and with swallow-like skim took another flight.

"Isn't it near dinner-time?" he said at last to the doctor, who was by his side watching the flights.

"Must be, I should say," was the reply, as that gentleman glanced at his watch. "Yes: close upon it. Glad of it, for I begin to feel a bit peckish in spite of this heat. I wonder what your fish will be like."

He soon learned, for the cook was right, and all pronounced it excellent; but there was something more than ordinary flavour about the fish from the Red Sea, and the doctor gave Sir John a meaning look, one to which Jack's father responded by a short nod.

Edward had had his opinions too, about his young master—opinions which sometimes made him look pleased, at others shake his head.

"Young governor's going it," he muttered, as he stood near watching the fishing. "Fancy him getting excited over hooking a fish, and holding on by the line. Beats anything I ever knew of before. There, you never know what's in a boy till you begin to get it out of him. Why that line must have cut his hands awful, but he never reg'larly 'owled about it, only rubbed the places a bit when he got a chance. Wonder whether the doctor's giving him some kind of physic as makes him come out like this. If he is, I should like to have a dose or two to bring me up to the mark. It's wonderful what a change he's made."

Edward ceased for a few moments.

"Wonder how he gives it him, and what he takes it in. He don't know he's taking it, that's for certain. It must be on the sly, or I should have seen it, and the glass and spoon. That's it. He puts it in his coffee; I'll be bound to say that's it—in his coffee. I'll be on the watch."

"Dunno why I should though," said the man, after a few moments' musing. "'Tain't my place to know anything about it, and if it does him good, where's the harm? And it is doing him good, that's for certain; but I should like to know what it is, and when he gives it."

Chapter Thirteen
Beginning to grow backward

"Regular volcanic cinder heap, Jack," was Sir John's not new opinion of sun-scorched Aden, where, while the coal-bunkers were filled up again, the lad had amused himself by inspecting the place with his glass as he sat contentedly under the awning, preferring to submit to the infliction of the flying coal-dust to a hot walk through the arid place. Then he leaned over the side and half-contemptuously threw threepenny-bits and sixpences into the clear water in response to the clamouring young rascals who wanted to scramble for them far below and show their swimming and diving powers.

"Come on board," cried the doctor, blowing his nose hard and coughing to get rid of the black dust. "Sacks counted, iron stopper put back in the pavement, and the wagon's gone, Jack."

The lad looked up at him as if wondering whether he had gone out of his senses.

"What are you staring at, sober-sides?" cried the doctor. "I know it's poor joking, but I'd have done better if I could. Hallo! what's the matter?" he continued, as, in what seemed to be a motiveless way, the boy threw sixpence over the side. "Got too much money?"

"No: look!" said Jack.

The doctor glanced over the rail to where the bright piece of silver was sinking fast and flashing as it turned over, while two merry little young scamps were diving down after it, racing to see which would get first to the coin. This soon disappeared in the disturbed water, while the figures of the boys grew more and more shadowy and distorted by the varying refraction.

"My word!" cried the doctor, "how the little niggers can dive! Look: here they come again."

It was curious to see them rising with the water growing more still as their frantic struggles ceased, and their forms grew plain as they rose quickly, one dark head suddenly shooting up like a cork on a pike line after the fish had rejected the bait, and its owner showing a brilliantly white set of teeth as he shouted, "Nurrer! nurrer!"

The next moment a second head shot into the brilliant sunshine, the boy's lips opening into a wide grin of delight as he showed his white clenched teeth with the captured sixpence held between them.

"Tell him to put it in his pocket, Jack," cried the doctor. "Puzzle him, eh? Hold your noise, you chattering young ruffians," he shouted. "Come, a dozen of you. Here, Jack, I'm going to waste a shilling, for it won't do the young vagabonds any good. It's only encouraging them to run risks of asphyxiating themselves or getting caught some day by the sharks."

He held up a shilling as he spoke, and quite a dozen boys of all sizes splashed in out of canoes, and left the pieces of wood and one old boat to which they clung. They came swimming about near where the doctor and Jack looked over, shouting, splashing each other, and generally clamouring for the piece of money to be thrown in.

"Ah! we must have a race for this," said the doctor, and he drew himself up and made a feint of throwing the shilling.

There was a rush like a pack of black water spaniels going after a thrown stick, but the boys had been tricked too often by passengers stopping at Aden in the regular steamers, and they did not go far, but turned round, treading water and shouting.

"Come back then," cried the doctor. "Here, close to the yacht."

In all probability the boys did not comprehend a word, but the gestures made with the hand containing the shilling brought them all back, and they ranged themselves in a line close in, and shouted and splashed away till the doctor, whose left hand had been in his pocket, threw the shilling shining and twinkling through the sunny air as far as he could.

Away went the boys with a tremendous rush, making the water foam, and naturally the biggest and strongest took the lead, leaving three little fellows well behind.

The doctor had anticipated this, and drew their attention with a shout, at the same time holding up another shilling, and as they turned to swim back, he suddenly dropped the coin about six feet away from the yacht's side, where the water was still.

Plop! down went one little fellow, who rose up, turned over, sent his heels gleaming in the sunshine, and disappeared, as *plop! plop!* down went the two others.

"Just like a lot of dabchicks," cried the doctor; "now we shall see them race for it. See the shilling, Jack?"

"Yes; here it goes."

"Yes, and here they come. Look at them. Why, they go down faster than the coin. It's wonderful."

Wonderful it was, for the dark little figures glided through the crystal water like seals, and every motion could be followed till the coin was reached and ceased to twinkle as it sank. Then once more the dark figures grew plainer and rose and rose, but somehow more and more astern, and Jack looked startled.

"Why, there must be a tremendous current here," he cried. "They're being swept away. A boat! a boat!"

The doctor looked as much startled as his companion, but a very gentle vibration enlightened them the next moment, for the engine was once more in motion, the screw revolving slowly, and the *Silver Star's* prow was gradually coming round in answer to the helm, till she pointed straight for the open sea, where the throbbing and quivering of the vessel increased as she went easily ahead, and then faster still over the perfectly calm water, for there was not a breath of air.

Then away and away through the burning sunshine the yacht glided, with the sea glistening like damascened steel frosted with silver, till the mountains above the coaling port grew distant; and away over the burning Afric sands there was a wondrous orange glow which deepened into fire, vermilion, crimson, purple, and gold of the most refulgent hues, and soon after it was night. It seemed to Jack as he stood gazing forward that they were gliding on between two vast purply black basins studded with stars, which were larger and brighter than any he had seen before, while deeper and deeper in the wondrous depths there were more and more, till the farthest off seemed like clusters and patches of frosted gold.

There was not a breath of air when they went on deck after dinner, and with the exception of the throbbing and humming of the engine and propeller, and soft whish of the sea as it was divided and swept along the sides, all was wonderfully still. But the silence was soon after broken by a sharp call from somewhere forward, a clear musical voice rang out, and then, sounding very sweet and melodious on the soft air, the men began glee-singing, showing that they had good voices among them and no little knowledge of singing in parts. They were simple old glees and madrigals, and no doubt the surroundings helped, but Jack sat listening and thinking he had never heard music so sweet and beautiful before.

"Why, captain," said Sir John, "this is a surprise."

"Is it, sir? Hope you don't mind."

"Mind?" echoed Sir John and the doctor in a breath.

"Bartlett's fond of a bit of music, and he has a good voice too, but he is so precious modest you can't get him to sing alone; he's singing with the men though now. He trains them a bit when we're not busy, and they like it. Nothing pleases men like them more than singing in chorus; you see, they're most of them Cornish and Devon lads, and they take naturally to it. Many's the time I've heard the fishermen going out on calm evenings to their fishing-ground singing away in parts, so that you'd think that they had been well taught, and perhaps not one of them knowing a note of music."

The glee-singing went on for about an hour, and ceased as suddenly as it had begun. Then the watch was set, and after standing leaning over the bows gazing at the glittering stars reflected in the deep water, and seeing the phosphorescent creatures add to the lustre as they were disturbed by the yacht's prow, or some large fish darting away, Jack heaved a deep sigh and turned to go aft to the cabin.

"Unhappy, my boy?" said a voice at his elbow, which made the lad start and remain silent for a few moments, utterly unable to give expression to his feelings, before he said softly—

"No, father, not unhappy, but low-spirited and sad."

"Sad, my boy?" said Sir John.

"No, it isn't sad, because somehow, father, it makes me feel happy, and—and I can't explain it, but I never felt that I cared to stand and look at the sea and sky like this before. It seems so grand and beautiful, and as if—as if—"

"The great book of Nature was being opened to you for the first time, my boy. Yes; this wonderful soft air, this glorious star-lit heaven, and the silence of the ocean through which we are gliding, impress me too in a way I cannot explain. But tell me now, my boy, are you sorry we came?"

"Sorry!" cried Jack excitedly, as he caught at his father's arm. "No; glad."

That night the melody of one of the old West-country ditties the men had sung in parts seemed to lull Jack Meadows to rest, and he slept one of those deep healthy slumbers which give us the feeling when we awake on a bright sunny morning, that a strange vigour is running through our veins, and that it is a good thing to live.

Chapter Fourteen
Doctor Instow paints a picture— with his tongue

A quick run with a favourable wind across to Colombo, a very brief stay, and then on again. There were baffling winds and a sharp storm, during which it was found necessary to get up steam, but the yacht was as good in foul weather as in fair, and to Jack's great satisfaction he found that, in spite of the pitching and tossing of the vessel, he was not ill, but found a strange pleasure in being on deck in mackintosh and leggings, watching the yacht career over and race through the foam. Every now and then a wave would appear gliding along like some huge bank of water, ready to roll over them and sweep the deck, but the well-trained hands at the wheel sent her racing up the watery slope, to hang poised for a few moments and then rush down again.

"Isn't it glorious, Jack, my lad?" said the doctor, wiping the spray out of his eyes and off his beard, just in the height of the storm. "I don't know how you find it, but it excites me."

"I like it," said Jack quietly; "it seems so grand, and as if the yacht was laughing at the waves and tossing them off to right and left. I wonder whether Captain Bradleigh would let me steer."

"I hope not," said the doctor, with a droll look of puzzledom in his face. "Why, what's come to you, you reckless young scamp? No, thank you. If you're going to be indulged in any luxuries of that kind, I'm going to land at Penang or Singapore, and make my way home by the next boat that touches."

Jack laughed.

"Don't believe it," he said. "But doesn't it seem as if it would be nice to have full command of the yacht like that, and send her here and there just as one liked?"

"Can't say that my desires run in that groove, Jack, my lad; I'm quite content to play the part of looker-on. But this storm is grand, and it's splendid to see how the little vessel shakes the water off her and rushes through it all. But I did want some calmer weather; we haven't done a bit of fishing since we left the Red Sea, and I meant to try every day. Well, captain, how long is this going to last?"

"Another twelve hours, I should say," replied the captain, "and then we shall have calm weather all the way to Singapore, and with the exception of a few thunderstorms, light winds among the islands."

It turned out exactly as the captain had said. The weather calmed rapidly, and their run down to the equator, between the Malay peninsula and Sumatra, was in brilliant hot weather all through the morning; while early in the afternoon, with wonderful regularity, there came on a tremendous thunderstorm, with peals heavier and lightning more vivid than anything Jack had ever encountered, and then at the end of a couple of hours all was clear again, and the evening was comparatively cool and beautifully fine.

Singapore was so fresh and attractive that of necessity a few days were spent there, before a fresh start was made for a cruise through the islands in the region which was now exciting Jack's expectations. Soon after they were passing great heavy-looking junks with their Celestial crews, or light Malay prahus with their swarthy, coffee-coloured sailors in tartan skirts, in whose folds at the waist the formidable wavy dagger known as a kris was worn, the handle, like the butt of a pistol in form, carefully covered by the silk or cotton sarong to indicate peace.

"If you see one of them with the handle bare," said the mate to Jack, "one has to look out, for it means war."

Malay prahus were so thoroughly connected in the lad's reading with piracy, that he looked curiously at the first they encountered, and eagerly scanned the calm, rather scornful faces of the men who apathetically stood about the bamboo deck, and watched the passing of the swift, white-sailed yacht, while they distorted their cheeks by slowly chewing something within.

"What's that fellow doing?" said Jack, handing his double glass to the mate, who gave a quick glance through and handed it back. "Look for yourself."

Jack resumed his inspection of the prahu's deck, for it was not above forty yards away.

"Doing something with a bit of—I don't know what, which he has taken out of a little bag."

"Betel-nut from one of the palms which grow in these parts," said the mate.

"Now he has slowly taken a leaf out of the same bag."

"Sirih leaf; a kind of creeping pepper plant which runs up trees," said the mate.

"And now he is opening a little brass box, which has something that looks like a white paint."

"Lime," said the mate, "lime of a very fine kind, made by burning shells."

"And he is spreading some of it with one finger upon the leaf."

"Yes! See what he does next."

"Rolled the piece of nut in it and put it in his mouth."

"Yes," said the mate; "all the Malays do this betel-chewing."

"What for?"

"It is a habit like our sailors chewing tobacco. The Malays think it is good for them, and keeps off all choleraic attacks."

"Does it?" asked Jack.

"Ah, that I can't say. You must take the doctor's opinion."

But Jack was too much interested in watching the prahu, which, in spite of only having matting sails, sped along over the calm water at a rapid rate, and he went on questioning his companion.

"They seem fierce-looking fellows, and as if they could do a deal of mischief. Are they such terribly bloodthirsty people?"

"Certainly not," said the mate. "I have always found the better-class Malays simple, gentlemanly, and courteous if they are properly treated; but if injured, I believe they can be treacherous and relentless."

"But I remember once reading how bloodthirsty the Malay pirates are."

"I don't think the English, Spanish, or French pirates were much better," said the mate, laughing. "Pirates are generally the scum of the ports they sail from; reckless, murderous ruffians. But I should say that of all pirates out in the East, the gentle, placid, mild-looking Chinaman makes the worst; for he thinks nothing of human life, his own or any one else's."

"But there are no pirates now, of course," said Jack quietly.

The mate turned and looked him in the eyes.

"Do you want me to tell you some murderous narrative?"

"Oh no; I don't care for such things. I know, of course, that there used to be plenty."

"So there are now," said the mate. "They have hard work to carry on their piracies; but every now and then we have a bad case. They mostly come from the Chinese coast; but they are made up of ruffians of all kinds."

Jack was silent for a few moments.

"I heard Captain Bradleigh say that the men were all trained to use the small-arms," he said at last quietly. "Would they fight if we were attacked?"

The mate hummed over a bit of a once popular song, beginning, "We don't want to fight, but by Jingo if we do."

"That pretty well expresses the nature of English sailors, sir," he said quietly. "They don't want to fight, and never would if they were left alone. But if they do fight—well, Mr Jack, if they do they hit very hard."

Jack laughed merrily, to the great satisfaction of two gentlemen across the deck, who turned their heads so as not to seem as if they noticed anything.

"I dare say," continued the mate, "you remember how it was at school; you never wanted to fight, but when you had to I suppose you hit hard?"

Jack was silent again, and at last said quietly—

"I never did have a fight at school."

During the next few days they sailed slowly on at a short distance from the coast of the long island of Java, and except that the weather was very hot, and that they could see in the distance mountain after mountain rising up like a huge, blunt cone, several of them showing a cloud of smoke drifting slowly away before the wind, sailing here seemed in nowise different from by the coast of Spain or Portugal. But Jack was to see the difference before long.

One evening over dinner their plans were discussed, the captain saying—

"Then I understand, Sir John, that you quite leave the choice to me?"

"Certainly. We have not sailed these thousands of miles for the sake of visiting towns and show places. Take us to some one of the islands such as you described to me; uninhabited if you can. If you could cast anchor by one never yet trodden by the foot of man, so much the better."

"Ah, that I can't promise you, sir," replied the captain, "for the people out this way are nearly all venturesome sailors, and for any number of years have put to sea in the most crazy of bamboo craft, and set sail to land where they could, some of them even going in mere canoes. So you see we may come upon people in the most unexpected places. But I have several islands in my mind's eye, between here and the east end of New Guinea, where you gentlemen may collect to your hearts' content."

"Birds?" cried the doctor.

"Birds, sir? Yes; some of the most beautifully coloured to be found on the face of the earth. Parrots, cockatoos, birds of paradise, sun-birds, something like the little humming-birds of the West Indies and South America. Oh yes; you'll find as many birds as you want."

"Butterflies?" asked Jack.

"Yes, and moths, some of them bigger than a cheese-plate."

"Flies, of course?" said Sir John.

"Oh yes, sir, and beetles too, some of the ugliest you can imagine, and some of them looking as if made of burnished metal. Then of course you'll have plenty of fireflies and mosquitoes too."

"Of course we shall get them," said Sir John. "But what about serpents?"

"Plenty, sir, sea and land; curious lizards too."

"There will be no animals to shoot," said the doctor rather regretfully.

"Tigers, elephants, or leopards? No, not unless we make for the mainland. But there is a great deal of unexplored country on the coast of New Guinea and Borneo, and there's no knowing what we might come across. There are elephants in Borneo, and our old friend the orang-outang."

"Let's try one of the smaller islands first," said Sir John. "I'm getting eager to begin doing something."

"I can't exist much longer doing nothing but parade up and down this deck. My joints are growing up. How do you feel, Jack?" said the doctor.

"Lazy. I feel as if I could go on doing nothing for any length of time."

"Here, this won't do," cried the doctor in mock horror. "'Bout ship, captain, and let's get back home, or else to one of these wonderful islands that make my mouth water. Let me see, something of this kind: a beach of coral with the waves always rolling over and breaking in foam, so that just within there is a beautiful blue lagoon of water, calm as a lake. Across the lake stretched right and left golden sands, at the back of which are cocoa-nut groves, with their great fern-like leaves rustling in the sea-breeze, crabs and fish scuttling about beneath them; and farther on where the land commences to rise the glorious tropic forest begins, trailed with orchids and wonderful creepers. Great palms rise like columns, and huge trees of the fig persuasion spread and drop down at several spots to form green bowers, and capital places to make huts. Monkeys climbing about. Birds swarming—nesting or swinging by the rotan canes. Farther on the land rising and rising, and all forest till it begins to be seamed with valleys, or rather deep gorges which run up to the central mountain, from which they radiate all round down toward the sea, and all of them forming glorious collecting grounds for naturalists. Then higher up the air growing cooler, save for a peculiar hot puff now and then with a taste in it of sulphurous steam. Then the trees growing thinner and not so majestic, but the flowers more abundant and the valleys more moist, where the streams trickle down; and here and there are little waterfalls, over which in the spray enormous fronds spread their green lace-work and sparkle with the fine pearly dew which is formed by the spray from the falling water. Here an icy spring of crystal purity gushes from amongst the mossy stones, and oddly enough a little farther on we come upon another spring, from which steam rises, but the water itself is of wonderful clearness, so hot that you cannot bear your hand in it, and the basin is composed of delicate pinky-white as beautiful as the inside of some of the shells which lie in the glorious marine garden at the bottom of the lagoon which spreads all round the island. We push on and at last leave the trees behind, to find the vegetation curiously dwarfed, masses and tufts of wiry grass, and we have to tramp over sandy, cindery stuff which gives way under our feet, and sets some of the big stones in motion. For we have come upon a slope which grows steeper and steeper, and runs up and up, till, quite breathless, we stop short among the great grey masses of pumice-stone and glassy obsidian which cut our boots. We look about and see from where we are over one side of the island, in whose centre we nearly stand. The forest is glorious, the lagoon looks like turquoise, and the coral reef which forms a breakwater round the place seems from our great height to be one mass of creamy foam, while beyond it stretching far and wide is the glorious sapphire sea. We are terribly hot with our climb, but the air here is splendidly invigorating, and we turn to finish our last hit of a few hundred feet over loose lava, pumice, and scoria. It is hard work, but we give one another a hand, and at last we stand at the edge of a tremendous depression like a vast cup in the top of the mountain, whose other side, similar to that on which we stand, is a mile away, while below its the cup is brimming with the verdure which runs up from a lovely blue lake a thousand feet below. All is beautiful, so beautiful, that it seems to take away our breath, for flowers are all about, the gorgeous butterflies are on the wing, noisy paroquets are climbing head up or head down, and there is nothing to show that we are on the edge of the crater of some tremendous volcano, but we catch sight of a thin thread of steam rising to form a cloud over a bare rock-strewn patch on one side. That tells us the fierce gases below are not quite extinct, but are smouldering ready to burst out at any time, sending forth the fiery rain to destroy the verdure, torrents of molten stone to run in streams down to the sea, or a flood of boiling mud to turn the lovely island into a wilderness. All is so beautiful that we can hardly turn away to begin our descent to where the yacht is lying in the lagoon, which forms a perfectly safe port into which it has been towed by the crew. But go down we must, for we are choking with thirst—at least I am, through talking; so long, and I'll trouble you, steward, for another glass of water."

"Oh," cried Jack, who had been drinking in every word, his face flushed and eyes bright with excitement as he pictured mentally the glorious place the doctor had described, "what a cruel mockery to raise one's expectations like that. It's like waking one suddenly from a beautiful dream."

"Don't quarrel with him, my boy. I say, Jack! I did not know the doctor could be so florid."

"I didn't either," said the doctor, laughing, "not till I tried."

"Capital!" cried the mate, clapping his hands softly.

"Yes, excellent," said the captain, smiling, with a peculiar twinkling about the eyes. "But it seems to me, Sir John, that you do not need any guide."

"Why not?"

"Because I see the doctor has been there."

"I never was farther from home than Switzerland in my life."

"That's strange," said the captain, "for that's the very island I am making for now."

"Oh! won't do," said the doctor. "Mine was all exaggeration, built up out of old books of travels."

"The description was perfect, sir," said the captain quietly. "Eh, Bartlett?"

"Photographic," said the mate.

"Come, come, gentlemen, that won't do," said the doctor merrily. "I gave rein to my fancy. I knew that the coral islands are very lovely, and the volcanic islands very grand, and so I said to myself, I'll paint a regular tip-top one, such as ought to please friend Jack here, and I joined the volcanic on to the coral and astonished myself."

"And me too," said Sir John, laughing.

"And disappointed me horribly," said Jack; "I really thought there was such a place."

"So there is, Mr Jack, and we're sailing for it now," said the captain quietly.

"Aha! Which?" cried the doctor merrily, as he felt that he was trapping the captain fast,—"coral or volcanic?"

"Both, sir," said the latter, and he looked at Jack as he spoke. "There are plenty of islands where a volcano has risen from the sea, and the coral insects in the course of ages have built a rampart of limestone to act as a breakwater, and thus prevented the lava and pumice from being washed away. The island I am making for is one of these."

"But not so beautiful," cried Jack.

"Well," said the captain, "our friend here the doctor did lay the paint on very thick in the picture he drew, and used all the brightest colours he had in his knowledge-box; but after all Nature's colours are purer and lovelier than any we can mix, and well as he painted he did not quite come up to the mark; and I think, sir, that when we've climbed up to the top of the mountain you will say the same."

"Oh!" cried Jack rapturously, and he turned to his father.

"*If*!" said the captain, very emphatically.

"If? If what?" said Jack.

"There has not been an eruption, and the whole island blown away."

Jack felt as if some one had suddenly poured cold water all down his back.

Chapter Fifteen
Jack is wide-awake

"Land ho!"

It was Lenny, the black-bearded sailor, who raised the cry at sunrise one morning, and made Edward spring out of his berth and run up, closely followed by Jack, who appeared on deck half-dressed, and with his face lit up by a strange look of animation, but he gazed round over the golden waters in vain.

But it was not only a golden sea that met his eyes, for the sky was golden too, and the *Silver Star* from deck to truck, with every yard and rope, appeared to be transmuted into the glittering metal. "Morning," cried the captain, coming up to him. "Did you hear the hail?"

"Hear it? yes," said Jack, "and it's a mistake, unless the land's hidden by the sun. I can see nothing."

"No?" said the captain, smiling. "Well, it would take long-trained eyes to make it out on a morning like this, when everything is dazzling. But let's try."

As he spoke the captain took his glass from under his arm, laid it on one of the ratlines of the mizzen shrouds to steady it, and took a long and patient look through.

"Ah!" he said, raising himself and keeping the glass in position. "Now take a peep through my spy-glass. One moment: do you see that little patch of cloud like fire, just a little north of the sun?"

"Is that north? Yes. I think I see the patch you mean."

"Then fix your glass on the horizon just on the line where the sea melts into sky, under the middle one of those three patches. Quick, before they change."

Jack took the glass and looked through.

"See it?"

"No," he said.

"Haven't got the glass straight perhaps," said the captain. "Take a shot with it first as if it were a gun—look along the top and fix it upon the horizon line, and then sweep it right and left till you make the land."

"I've got it," cried Jack.

"The land?"

"No, the line of the horizon. I wasn't looking through the eye-piece. That's it; now I can see the edge of the sea quite plainly."

"Then you are clever," said the captain, laughing. "I never did. Well, sweep it about to right and left. See the land?"

"No," said Jack after a good long try. "Isn't it a mistake?"

"Let me try again," said the captain, taking the glass. "Yes, there it is plainly enough, just under the little golden cloud to the right; they are floating northward. Try again."

Jack took the glass, brought it to bear, and was silent.

"See it?"

"No. I can make out that beautiful golden cloud."

"Well, now look under it."

"Yes, I've been looking right under it, but there's nothing there but a little hazy patch."

"Then you do see it," said the captain.

"That?"

"Yes; what did you expect to see?"

"Why, the island you talked about."

"Well, I don't say that is it, because I want to make an observation first, but I feel pretty sure that it is the place."

"But that looks so little."

"It's a little island."

"Yes, but that looks so very small."

"So would you seem small if you were thirty or forty miles away," said the captain, taking the glass and having another good long look. "The air is very clear this morning, and the island looms up. But we shall see better by and by."

They had been steadily sailing east for some days, and land had been sighted several times since. Jack had stood gazing longingly over the starboard rail at the tops of the Java volcanoes, which had followed one another in succession, some with the clouds hanging round their sides and their peaks clear, but two with what looked in the distance like tiny threads of smoke rising from their summits, and spreading out into a top like a mushroom.

This long island had tempted him strongly, and he had suggested to his father that they should make a halt there, but Sir John and the doctor both shook their heads.

"No," said the latter, "I vote against it. I believe Java to be a very interesting country, but for our purpose it is spoiled."

"Yes," said Sir John; "we don't want to get to a place full of plantations and farms; we want an out-of-the-way spot where the naturalist and traveller have not run riot over the land; where Nature is wild and untamed."

"And where we can find something new," said the doctor. "That place the captain talked about is the very spot."

"But we may not find it," said Jack.

"Let's chance it, my boy," said his father; "and even if we do not hit upon that, there are plenty of places far more interesting to us than Java is likely to be."

And now at last they were in sight of the very place, and a wild excitement began to fill the boy's breast as he went over the doctor's imaginary description, one which the captain declared to be perfectly accurate, for so many islands existed formed upon that very plan.

It did not occur to Jack that a great change had come over him, nor that people on board were noticing him when he hurried down to finish dressing that morning, and back on deck with his powerful binocular glass, to stand gazing away toward the east.

"This is clearer and better than the captain's glass," he thought to himself, "and easier to use," as he made out the misty little undefined patch, but was disappointed to find how slightly it had changed in the time he had been below.

He ate his breakfast hurriedly, and came on deck again with his excitement growing, and Sir John and the doctor exchanged glances, but nothing was said, as they leisurely finished their meal and then followed him.

"When shall we make the land, captain?" said Sir John.

"Perhaps not till to-morrow morning," was the reply, "under sail: the wind's falling."

"Why, where is Jack?" said the doctor suddenly. "He came on deck."

The captain gave him a queer look, and jerked his head backward, as he stood facing the wheel.

"Forward in the bows?" said the doctor.

"No: look up."

Sir John and the doctor looked up in astonishment to find that Jack had mounted the mainmast shrouds, and was now perched in the little apology for a top, with his arms about the foot of the topmast, against which he held his glass, gazing east.

Sir John drew a deep breath, and looked at his friend.

"Don't take the slightest notice," said the latter; "treat it as quite a matter of course. He has taken his spring and is out of his misery. He won't want any corks to swim with now, nor for us to hold him up."

"That's right, gentlemen," said the captain. "His spirit's rising, and that will carry him along. I wouldn't notice anything."

"Hi! father!" cried the lad, as he lowered his glass and caught sight of them. "I can't make much out even here. I say, Captain Bradleigh, are you sure this is the island?"

"Well, I'm sure it's land," replied the captain.

"But we don't seem to get a bit nearer."

"Sun's getting higher and makes it fainter. But the wind is falling, and we'll clap on a little more sail."

As the morning went on sail after sail was added, the men springing aloft and shaking out the squaresails, while long triangular pieces of canvas were run up the stays till the yacht was crowded, and she glided along with a delightfully easy motion.

But it was all in vain; the wind sank and sank, till at mid-day the sails hung motionless in the glowing sunshine, while, save for a slow soft heaving, the glassy transparent sea was absolutely without motion.

"Oh, this is vexatious!" cried Jack impatiently.

"Yes, you'll have to whistle for the wind, Jack," said the doctor, stretching himself under the awning and lighting his cigar.

"Whistle for nonsense!" said the lad irritably. "So tiresome, just too as we have come in sight of the place."

"Practice for your patience, my boy," said Sir John merrily. "Oughtn't he to come under the awning out of the scorching sun?" he continued to the doctor, as Jack went forward to where Captain Bradleigh was giving orders about lowering some of the studding-sails.

"Won't hurt him so long as he does not exert himself," replied the doctor. "The sun, sir, is the real fount of life. Nature incites all animals to bask in it, even the fish. There's a shoal swimming yonder. We'll have a try for some presently. Do him good."

"Then why don't you go and lie in it?" said Sir John, smiling.

"Because I don't want doing good. Too idle. I'm drinking all this in. I never felt so well in my life."

"Nor I," said Sir John, watching his son's movements, "but I begin to feel as if I should like to be doing something active. What's Jack about?"

The answer came in the boy's voice, heard distinctly enough in the clear air,—

"I say, don't take the sails down, Captain Bradleigh," he said; "the wind may come again soon."

"Not before sundown," replied the captain, "and then we shan't want stuns'ls."

"But it might!"

"Yes, and it might come with a sudden touch of hurricane, my lad. We're getting where dangers lie pretty quickly, and we old sea-going folk don't like to be taken unawares."

"What would it do then if a touch of hurricane did come?"

"Perhaps take our masts short off by the board before we could let everything go. Not nice to have half our canvas stripped away. You haven't been at sea so long as I have, squire."

"No, of course not," said Jack impatiently. "But I say, why don't you get up steam?"

"Because we want to keep our coal for an emergency, or when we want to get on."

"Well, we want to get on now."

The captain smiled.

"Go and ask your father what he thinks."

"Yes; come with me."

The captain humoured him, and they walked aft to where the awning cast its grateful shade.

"Here, father, hadn't we better have the steam up and get on?"

"I hardly think so, Jack. What do you say, captain; will the calm last?"

"Only till sundown, sir; then I think we shall have a nice soft breeze again."

"Then I say no, Jack," said Sir John. "We're quite hot enough, and it does not seem fair to the men to send them down making roaring fires when there is so little need."

"You'd be getting brown on both sides at once, Jack," said the doctor. "Look yonder; fish rising. What do you say to having a try?"

"Yes," said Jack eagerly, "let's get up the lines. Hi, Mr Bartlett, come on."

The mate had taken the captain's place, and was superintending the lowering of the studding-sails.

"Yes, all right, Bartlett," cried the captain, "I'll see to that;" and giving the lad a friendly nod, he went forward, the mate coming aft.

"Look! Fish!" cried Jack. "What had we better do, Mr Bartlett?"

"Yes; send out some light lines floating in the current," said the doctor.

"No, I don't think we should do much that way. More likely to get something from close in under the bows with the grains," replied the mate thoughtfully. "But what I should do would be to lower a boat and gently scull her toward one of those shoals; we might do something then."

"That's the way," cried Jack. "Here, hi! Lenny, we want you."

The big black-bearded fellow looked inquiringly at the captain, who nodded, and the man came aft, while Jack and the doctor went below, the former in a hurry, the latter with a good deal of deliberation. The mate and the man then proceeded to lower the light gig and cast off the falls, leaving her hanging by the painter.

"Strong tackle and bright artificial baits, Jack, my lad. The water's wonderfully clear."

These were selected from the ample store, and carried up to the boat, into which a basket, a bucket, and a big stone bottle covered with a felt jacket, and full of fresh water, were lowered.

"Won't you come, father?" said Jack suddenly.

"Well—er—no," said Sir John; "there is hardly room for another in that boat."

"Then we'll have a larger," cried Jack in a decisive tone, speaking as his father had never heard him speak before.

"No, no," cried Sir John; "don't alter your plans. But look out there."

He pointed away from the side of the yacht, and Jack shaded his eyes, for the sun flashed from the surface.

"Fish of some kind," said the lad eagerly. "Look, Mr Bartlett; what are they—eels?"

"Snakes—sea-snakes," said the mate quietly; and they stood gazing at a little cluster of eight or ten beautiful mottled creatures lying close to the surface, almost motionless, except that one now and then changed the S-like figure into which it lay by bending and waving its long sinuous body into some other graceful curve, progressing by a slight wavy motion of its tail.

"Proof positive, Jack, that there are sea-snakes," said Sir John.

"We shall have to look out," said the doctor, laughing. "Perhaps these are the babies, and papa and mamma not far off."

"Hallo! what have you got there?" said the captain, coming up. "Snakes, eh? Plenty of them to be found."

"And big ones?" asked Jack eagerly.

"I don't say that, my lad," replied the captain. "There's a pretty good big one there though."

"What, that?" cried Jack. "Three or four feet long."

"Nearer eight when he is out of the water."

"Would they take a bait?"

"Doubtful. But I would not try. Those things can bite, and, as I said, I've known cases out in the Indian Ocean where men have died from their bites. They're best dealt with from a distance. Why don't you shoot one for a curiosity? You could keep it in spirits."

"Ah, why not?" said the doctor; and he ran below, to return directly with a double gun and some cartridges, a couple of which he inserted at the breech.

Sir John looked at his friend inquiringly.

"There you are," said the doctor, handing the gun to Jack. "I'd rest the barrels on the rails as we're rolling a little. Then take a good aim as we're rising, not as we're going down, and fire as if you wanted the shot to go under its head."

Jack hesitated, and shrank a little, but mastering his feeling of trepidation, he took the gun, and rested the barrels on the rail.

"Why am I to fire under if I want to hit the snake?" he said.

"Because you will be in motion, and if you do not, your charge of shot will be carried above the reptile for one thing; another is to allow for the refraction, which makes the snake seem higher in the water than it is."

"But that one has its back right out."

"Yes: quick! a quick aim, and then draw the trigger."

Jack had never fired a gun in his life, and he shrank from doing so now, but every one was watching him; and as the barrels still lay on the rail, he glanced along between them as he had along the captain's telescope that morning, and pulled the trigger, but no explosion followed.

"Quick!" cried the doctor. "Do you call that quick?"

"It won't go off," said Jack, with a touch of irritation in his voice.

"Of course it won't," cried the doctor. "Why, you had not cocked it."

Jack had had no experience of guns, but he knew what ought to be done, and quickly drawing back the hammers, he took aim just beneath the largest of the snakes, and fired.

He had not placed the stock close to his shoulder, so he received a sharp blow, and the report sounded deafening, the smoke was blinding, and it was some moments before he was able to see what luck had attended his shot.

Better than he expected. The large snake was writhing and twining about in the water, and splashing it with blows from its tail, but the others had disappeared, and the mate had dropped down into the boat, and taken up the long-handled gaff-hook.

"Mind what you're about, Bartlett," cried the captain. "Don't lift it into the boat while it's so lively."

"I'll take care," was the reply, and after giving the gig a thrust which sent it near enough, the mate watched his opportunity, and lowering the hook made a snatch with it, catching the snake somewhere about the middle.

The touch seemed to fill the reptile full of animation, and quick as thought it twined itself in a knot about the hook, bit at it, and began lashing at the strong ash pole with its tail.

"Don't be rash, Bartlett," cried the captain. "We mustn't have any accidents. There, keep the end down in the water while Mr Meadows here gives it the other barrel."

"Fire at it again?" said Jack, who was full of excitement.

"Yes; give it him and finish him off," cried the doctor.

Jack raised the piece again, and it was none too soon, for the serpent was beginning to make its way along the pole toward the mate's hands, while it held on by tightening the folds of the lower part of its body.

The lad took aim at the knot twined round the hook, and then shivered as he saw the head of the dangerous beast gliding, or more correctly thrust along the ash handle, and changing the direction of the muzzle of the piece a little to the left, he once more fired, when the snake's head fell with a splash into the sea, the tight knot about the hook relaxed, the tail fell limply, and writhing with a feeble motion, the two ends hanging down together, prevented from falling by one twist round the gaff.

"Bravo! well done, Jack!" cried the doctor. "I say, my lad, if you begin by shooting like that you'll turn out a good shot. Now, Bartlett, let's have the beast on board and see what it's like."

The mate placed the gaff across the bows of the gig and thrust an oar over the stern, sculling the boat alongside, with the snake trailing in the water. Then taking hold of the gaff handle, climbed on board, and the prize was drawn on the deck, to lie writhing feebly and quite beyond the power of doing mischief, but it was scarcely disfigured, the small shot having done their work without much injuring the skin.

"Well, this is something to begin with," said Sir John, examining the beautifully mottled creature, as it lay in the sun, the dark, almost black ground of the skin showing up the ochre yellow markings, while in certain lights the black glistened with iridescent hues.

"A good eight feet long," said the captain; "but you'd better be careful. Cut his head off: he won't revive and show fight then."

"What, and spoil that beautiful skin!" cried the doctor. "No!"

"Get a length of stout fishing-line, Lenny," said the captain quietly; and the man trotted forward, his companions of the crew making way for him to pass, and then closing round again to examine the capture, which kept on raising its head a little and letting it fall back on the deck, after which a wave ran along the body right to the tail, which, instead of being round and tapering off, showed the creature's adaptability for an aqueous life by being flattened so that the end was something like the blade of a sword.

"We had better start a spirit tub at once," said the doctor; and he bent down over the head. "What sharp eyes!" he continued. "Malignant looking little beast."

"That's right," said the captain, as Lenny came up with the stout line. "Now make a noose in it. No, no, not at the end: a couple of fathoms in. That's the way. Take hold, one of you others. Now together draw the loop over the thing's head."

"What are you going to do?" cried Jack excitedly.

"Take care that he doesn't do any mischief, my lad," cried the captain; and standing about a dozen feet apart, the two sailors carefully drew the noose along the deck, till the bottom touched the snake's head, but it would not pass under.

"Bring your gaff, Bartlett," cried the captain, "and raise the head a little."

Hardly had he uttered the words, when the snake lifted it of itself a few inches from the white deck, and its whole body was in motion.

"Look out," cried Jack; and several of the men started back, but the sailors who held the line stood fast, and drew the noose over the reptile's head, and with a quick snatch tightened the strong cord about its neck.

The effect seemed magical, and the shot to have done nothing more than stun the creature for a time. It was now apparently as strong as ever, twining itself into knots and then writhing free again, to beat the white deck with its tail.

But this did not last many minutes, and as the men kept the line tight across the deck the reptile gradually stretched itself out, till it hung perfectly limp and almost motionless by the neck. Then a small cask was brought on deck, a stone jar of prepared spirit poured in, and the snake drawn over the mouth and allowed to sink in. Then the head of the cask was held ready and the tightened fishing-line cut short off. There was a hollow splash, and the cask was covered and secured.

"That's specimen the first," said the doctor, with a smile of satisfaction. "We shall have to fill that pickle-tub up before we go back, Jack. There, go and put away the gun and let's have our fish."

"I'll take the gun, Mr Jack, sir," said Edward, who had been watching all the proceedings with the greatest interest. "I must clean it before it's put away."

Jack handed him the piece, and the man whispered quickly—

"Mr Jack, sir; do please tell me to come."

"What, with us? Impossible," said Jack hastily. "You heard my father say that there was not room for another."

"Yes, sir, of course, not room for another like him, but I'm nobody. I don't want any room; I can sit down in the bottom, or kneel down. And I should be so useful, sir. I could cut up bait, or put on hooks, or take 'em off, or anything."

"What, do you understand fishing?"

"Me, sir? yes: I used to go up our river when I was a boy. I've caught roach and chub many a time, not that they were very big. Do take me, sir."

Jack hesitated.

"Say you will, sir," cried the man eagerly. "I can clean the gun after we come back."

"I don't like to refuse you, Ned," said Jack.

"That's right, sir: keep on don't liking, and say I may come. You don't know how useful I'll be."

"Very well: come then."

"Hurray!" whispered the man, "who'd be without a good master? I'll be back directly, sir."

He ran below with the gun, laid it in his berth ready for cleaning, and was up again just as the mate and Doctor Instow approached the side.

"Hallo, sir, you coming?" cried the latter.

"Yes, sir."

"But we don't want you."

Edward's face became puckered with disappointment, and his eyes were full of misery, as he turned them piteously upon his young master.

"Yes, I want him," said Jack, in response to the appealing look, and the man's hopes rose.

"What for?" said the doctor, and Edward's aspirations went down to zero.

"I don't know," said Jack coolly; "to unhook the fish. I'm not going to soil my hands."

"Oh, very well," said the doctor; "I don't mind, but we had better catch the fish before you take them off the hook. Now then, in with you."

Lenny and the mate stepped down into the boat, Jack and the doctor followed, and then, looking flushed and excited as a boy, Edward jumped in, giving, his young master a grateful look as soon as the doctor was not looking.

Chapter Sixteen
An awkward customer

There was no need to go far afield in search of sport, for before Lenny and the mate had rowed them a couple of hundred yards, with Jack and the doctor preparing their lines, they were passing close by a large shoal of fish, another being some distance astern.

These were leaping and playing about on the surface, making the water ripple and sparkle, and every now and then there was a flash as of a bar of silver darting into the sunny air, and falling back with a loud splash.

"This looks promising," said the doctor; "but my word, how hot the boat is. I touched that copper rowlock, and it quite burned my band."

"I could hardly bear mine on the side," said Jack; "but let's begin."

"Yes, we must have a few of these fellows, Jack. I wish we had rods, we could throw so much better."

"I don't think you will need them," said the mate, as he finished attaching a spoon-bait to Jack's line; "the current will carry the bait right through the shoal."

"Yes, but fair play, Jack. I'm not ready, let's start together."

But he was too late. Jack dropped his bait over the side as the doctor spoke, and away it glided, sinking slowly and turning and twinkling in the sunlit water, while when, in obedience to the mate's instructions, Jack checked the line as it ran over the side, and drew it a few feet back, the resemblance to a fish was strangely apparent.

"There you are," cried the doctor, as, after laying a quantity of line in rings beside him, he threw his own bait so cleverly that it fell with a light splash nearly on a level with his companion's.

"Now then; a race for the first fish!" he cried, and they let out a good fifty yards of line, with the result that, while, by Lenny giving a gentle stroke or two with the oars, the boat was kept pretty well in its place, the artificial baits were carried by the current right into the middle of the shoal of fish playing about on the surface.

"Now for it," said the doctor, who looked as excited as the boy. "We must have one directly."

"If they will take the artificial bait," said the mate. "Keep jerking your line, Mr Jack."

"That way?"

"Yes; capital. Fish like to take a bait that seems to be trying to escape from them."

"Then why don't they do it?" said the doctor impatiently.

"Give them time," said the mate, smiling.

"Time and line too, but they don't seem to notice the bait."

"They notice mine," said Jack. "Look here."

He gave a snatch with his line, Edward sitting ready to unhook the fish, and as he drew the bait along toward him, there was a rush made while it passed, but whether in pursuit or to escape from the novel object the occupants of the boat could not make out for some time. At last, though, the mate came to the conclusion that the spoon-bait scared the shoal.

"That shows what a set of ignorant savages they are, Jack," cried the doctor; "never saw a spoon-bait before in their lives, and don't know it's meant to catch them. But never mind, we shall have one directly, and then the others will know better."

"And go right away," said Jack dryly, as he kept on taking advantage of the mate's instructions, and making his bait play about in the bright water in a way which ought to have tempted a run, but without effect.

"Let's try another kind," said the mate, and the line being drawn in, an artificial sand-eel was fastened by the stout twisted wire hook to the swivel on the line.

"I'll wait and see what luck you have, Jack, before I change mine," said the doctor.

"I don't think I shall have any," replied the lad.

"The fish may be stupid and ignorant, but I don't think they will be so stupid as to try and bite at the absurd thing I have on now."

"There's no accounting for what fish will do," said the mate, smiling. "That's right; let it go. I've caught mackerel often enough on the Cornish coast with a hook at the end of a piece of gut run through a broken scrap of clay tobacco-pipe."

"Yes, mackerel are splendid fellows to bite. I've caught them myself with a soft white goose feather tied on to a hook, and thrown as if it were a fly, and—"

"Oh!" cried Jack, with a cry of excitement, "I've got one," and Edward half rose in his excitement from his seat.

For as he let the line run gently through his fingers from where it lay in rings at the bottom of the boat, it was suddenly snatched away and began to run rapidly.

"Stop it! Catch hold quickly," cried the mate; and Jack seized the line again and held on.

"I've got it!" he cried, as he felt thrill after thrill run up his arms in the fish's struggles to escape.

"Haul him in, Jack," said the doctor. "Bravo! first one to you. We shall begin to take some now."

"It won't come," cried Jack, as he held on by the line, with the fish evidently diving down into deep water in its frantic efforts to escape.

"Pull, lad!"

"But it's a monster, and the line cuts my hand. No, no, not you," he cried to his man.

"Let me try," said the mate.

"No, no, I mean to catch it myself," said Jack excitedly. "Ah, don't touch it."

"Only to see what it's like," said the mate, reaching over so as to take hold of the line.

"Not a very large one," he said, "two or three pounds perhaps. There, I think you can haul that in; I'll lift it into the boat with the gaff."

"Oh, don't touch it with that," cried Jack quickly; "it's all snaky, and we shall want to eat the fish."

"I'll give it a good wash in the water," said the mate, smiling.

"No; let me lift it in when I get it to the side," said Jack excitedly. "Yes, it's coming now."

"But if you try to lift it in, the hook will drag out of the fish's jaws," said the mate.

"Yes; let him lift it in, Jack," said the doctor. "Don't let it get away, or it will go and tell all the other fish not to bite."

"Of course," said Jack dryly, "and give a full description of me and my line."

"I shall have to try a fresh bait," said the doctor, beginning to draw in.

"I caught a glimpse of him," said Jack, as he hauled slowly on his line. "How strong a fish is in the water!—Ah!—Oh, I say, Mr Bartlett, how can you say it is not a big one!" cried the lad, as there was a tremendous jerk given at the line, and then a series of sharp tugs, followed by a steady drag which made the line begin to run through the fisher's hands again.

"It cuts! it hurts! I can't hold it!" cried Jack excitedly, and he was about to let go, when Edward caught hold, and then the mate's firm strong hands reached over and took hold of the line beyond his and began to haul.

But at the first drag he made at the line, the fish gave a peculiar wallow, which felt as if it had spun itself round in the water, and began in spite of the mate's efforts to move off, the line gliding through his fingers, till by a sudden action he twisted the slack round his hand and held on.

"Now isn't it a big one?" cried Jack. "Look here, doctor."

"I'm looking. Why, Jack, you've got hold of that snake's grandfather. Mind what you're doing, or you'll have the sea serpent aboard."

"What!" cried the lad, looking aghast.

"Hurrah! I've got one too," cried the doctor. "Humph! only a little one;" and he began to haul in. "Hurrah! something else has taken it," he shouted. "Here, Bartlett, I've got hold of a whale."

"We've got a shark," said the mate. "Look at the boat."

"Let go—let go quick!" cried Jack excitedly; "the fish is running away with us."

"And no mistake," said the doctor. "Mine's helping. Why, Jack, this is something like sport."

"How can you laugh!" cried the boy; "it must be horribly dangerous. Cut the line;" and Edward's knife was hastily opened.

"Oh no," said the mate, "we don't want to lose that, it will break directly close to the hook."

"Think we could get them both alongside?" said the doctor.

"Not with tackle like this," replied the mate; "we should want fine rope and a bit of chain. Mine must be six feet long. Look what a rate we're going at."

"Why, it's like being fast to a whale," cried the doctor.

"Not quite so bad as that," said the mate, laughing. "There he goes," he added, as the line suddenly hung loose in his hands.

"Gone?" cried Jack with a sigh of relief.

"Yes, and it's a good proof of the quality of the lines. They are wonderfully strong to hold out so long. Cut into my hands pretty well."

"Come and give me a hand, Jack," cried the doctor.

The boy moved unwillingly, but he reached over and took hold, half expecting to see a head come out of the water, a pair of menacing jaws open close to his hands, and a pair of fierce eyes give him a questioning look as to what he was doing to a peaceable inhabitant of the deep. But he had hardly felt the throbbing drag at the end of a hundred yards of line when the shark dived, and he and the doctor sank back in the boat, whose steady progress through the water was checked.

"How do you like fishing?" said the doctor merrily.

"But I don't quite understand," said Jack. "Oh, it's easy enough, boy," cried the doctor, smiling; "we threw out little fish or imitations. Bigger ones took them. Then a pair of monsters seized the bigger ones and began to tow the boat; and if we had held on much longer we should have had a pair as big as the yacht take our monsters, and end by swallowing us, boat and all."

"But you don't think they were sea serpents?" said Jack, whose face looked a little sallow.

"Oh no," said the mate. "Sharks without doubt. Look here, the twisted wire is regularly cut through, as if by a pair of shears," he continued, as he held up the end of the line he had drawn in. "How is yours?"

"Haven't got the end yet," said the doctor, who was hauling away. "Here we are," he cried; "mine's broken where the snood joins on. What's to be done now?"

"Put on fresh baits," said Jack sharply; and Edward reached for the basket.

The mate and the doctor exchanged glances. "Very well," said the latter; "but I expect it only means another fight like the last. Eh, Bartlett?"

"I'm afraid so. The sharks are evidently following this great shoal to pick up a helpless one now and then."

"But it's so disappointing," said Jack. "I wanted to see what we had caught, and take them aboard for dinner."

"Yes, it's disappointing," said the doctor. "What do you think they were that we had hold of—there in the shoal?"

"They look to me like some kind of sea perch," said the mate, "something like the bass one gets down in Cornwall."

"Seem like it from their playing about," said the doctor, and drawing the basket toward him, he proceeded to fit on another artificial bait. "I'll try and stir them up again with the spoon," he said, with a droll look at Jack.

"I shall keep to the imitation fish," said Jack, who was deeply interested. "I think we ought to pull them in more quickly, before the sharks have time."

"Couldn't pull in more quickly than I did," said the doctor. "Well, we will have this try, and if we don't succeed we had better give it up. We don't want to be towed right away from the yacht."

"What?" said Jack, looking up sharply. "I say it would be rather awkward to be towed out of sight of the yacht."

Jack gave an anxious glance in the direction of their sea-going home, and then laughed.

"No fear of that," he said; and as soon as Lenny had placed the boat once more quietly at a little distance from the shoal, the boy threw in his bait, seeing the fish rush in all directions; but directly after there was a jerk, and a thrill, and he felt that he was fast to a big fish.

This time he began to haul at once, as quickly as he could, hand over hand, while after a few frantic dashes the fish gave in, and was half-way to the boat, then three-parts of the way, showing its silvery sides, and apparently about two feet long, and all before the doctor had thrown out.

"Get your hook, Mr Bartlett," cried Jack eagerly.

"All ready."

"Washed?"

"Yes, thoroughly."

"Now then, here he is! Oh!"

"Murder! Look out!" shouted Edward, ducking down.

There was a tremendous splash, the water being thrown in their faces as Jack and the mate stood up, the one drawing in the fish, the other ready to make a snatch with the gaff-hook, when a great dark object suddenly rose within six feet of the boat, taking the fish in its jaws, curved over, and dived down, waving a great grey and black tail high in the air, and sending the water flying over them as it disappeared with the line running rapidly out.

"Let me come, Mr Jack," cried the mate; "it's of no use to let it burn or cut your hands. I'll show you."

As he spoke he stooped, took hold of the line a few rings below those which were rapidly gliding over the side, and passed it round the copper rowlock, letting it still run, but at a slower rate, and gradually adding weight, till the boat began to move, when he checked the line entirely by giving it another turn round and holding on.

"Now take hold. You can let him run or make him tow us, whichever you like," he said to Jack, who seized the line, and stood there feeling as if he were driving in a marine chariot drawn by sea monsters that were quite under his control.

"The line cannot bear such a strain long," said the mate. "If we had heavy tackle we might haul the brutes alongside, and kill them with a lance or a shot."

"Let's try next time," cried Jack excitedly. "How it is pulling us along."

"Yes; we are going pretty well," said the doctor dryly. "I *hope* the brute won't turn round and attack us."

"Not likely, is it?" said Jack with an anxious look. Then quickly, "Well, let it come. You take hold of the boat-hook, Mr Bartlett; you would spear it with that."

"But I say, Jack, don't you feel frightened?" said the doctor.

"Him frightened! likely!" muttered Edward.

"No; I don't think I do," said the lad frankly. "I feel a curious fluttering kind of sensation, as if my heart was beating very fast, but I don't think I'm frightened—I'm sure I'm not," he added gravely, and with a simple sincerity far removed from boastfulness.

"How can you be sure?" said the doctor, giving him a searching look.

"Because if I really were frightened I should cut the line."

"Of course you would," said the doctor. "Stands to reason. But I didn't come out prepared for shark-fishing, so I'm beginning to think we may as well cut or break the line, and go back. We don't want to have far to row on such a day as this."

"Oh, don't do that," cried Jack. "It's so exciting and strange to be dragged along like this."

"What do you say to trying to get the fellow up to the surface, so as to have another look at him?"

"But suppose it attacks us?"

"I don't think there is any fear," said the mate, smiling.

"Try and get it up then," said Jack eagerly. "Come and lend a hand, Edward," said the mate; and they began to take a slow, steady pull on the line, drawing in the strong hemp fathom by fathom, till the number of rings in the bottom of the boat showed that they must be near their captive, but there was no sign of it till another dozen yards were hauled in, and then, as Jack leaned over the bows, he could dimly see deep down a shadowy form going right onward, slightly agitating the water as it passed through.

Then as the pair in the boat hauled, the dark shadow began to show more and more clearly, proving that the buoyancy of the boat was beginning to tell upon it, and draw it nearer to the surface.

"Can't stand this much longer, Jack," said the doctor; "the line must break."

"I wonder it has not parted before now," cried the mate. "It is of wonderfully good quality, and stretches like india-rubber. Hah! he's coming up now. Will you take the boat-hook and give him a prod, doctor, if he is disposed to show fight?"

"Well, yes, unless you would like to, Jack."

"Yes, I should like to," said the lad, with a couple of red spots appearing in his cheeks; and he bent down, picked up the light boat-hook, and stood with one foot upon the thwart, holding the implement as if it were a lance.

"Bravo! Mr Jack," whispered Edward. "See him plainly?" said the mate. "Yes, very clearly now. It is not above six feet down, a great long black creature. Would it be a shark?"

"Oh yes, that's a shark, sure enough," said the mate. "I saw him plainly enough when he took your fish. But you had better watch him, for at any moment the line may give way."

Another pull or two resulted in the great fish being brought so close to the surface that its back fin showed from time to time.

"Aren't we quite near enough?" said the doctor in a low tone to the mate; "it's a big, dangerous-looking creature."

"The line will go at the first struggle it makes," replied the mate, "and there is no danger. A splashing is the worst thing that can happen. Let him do as he likes."

"What's the matter? What are you whispering about?"

"I was just thinking of cutting loose," said the doctor, taking out a knife.

"No, no; let it be," cried Jack. "Look here; we are nearly over it, and you can see how it tows us along by just gently waving its tail. Pull, Mr Bartlett; both of you pull."

Bang!

At the fresh tightening of the line, which drew the bows of the boat partly over the fish, there was a tremendous blow delivered on the side, accompanied by a shower of spray, a violent ebullition which rocked them to and fro. Then the line hung slack, and the last fathom was drawn on board by the sailor, while the mate went down on his knees and examined the slight planking of the boat to make sure that it was not stove in.

"Oh!" groaned Edward; "look at that!"

"Any damage, Bartlett?" said the doctor hastily.

"No; but I was a little startled. What enormous power these creatures have in their tails!"

Jack laid down the boat-hook, looking rather serious.

"What would have happened," he said, "if the shark had made a hole in the boat?"

"All depends on the size," said the mate, laughing. "If it had been very small we might have plugged it with our jackets till we managed to row back, or the skipper, seeing we were in distress, sent another boat after us. If it had been a very large hole we should have had to hold on to the gunwale outside all round, for she wouldn't have sunk, and then again the captain would have sent a boat to pick us up, if he sent in time."

"What do you mean by in time?" asked the lad rather huskily.

"Before the sharks had pulled us all under, and there was no one left to pick up."

Edward turned sallow, and looked at the speaker in dismay.

"Are you saying that to frighten me?" asked Jack.

"No, I don't make jokes about such things as that, sir," said the mate quietly. "I ought to have known better than to run such a risk, but I did not imagine that a shark could strike such a tremendous blow."

"It was my fault," said Jack quickly. "I wanted to see how far it would drag us before the line broke."

"And the sharks would have picked us all off," said the doctor thoughtfully. "Humph! Not a very pleasant look-out. There's a deal of trouble and disappointment in the world; eh, Jack? Especially in fishing."

"Yes, I suppose so," replied the lad, looking at the speaker curiously.

"But take it altogether, it's a very grand and glorious place, and full of wonders for those who like to use their eyes. I don't think I should have liked for our voyage to have been brought to a sudden end like that, eh?"

"No; it is too horrible to think of," said the lad with a shudder, and he cast a wistful look around him at the silver-looking sea, and the white yacht standing up apparently at the top of a slope.

"Won't try any more fishing to-day, will you?"

"No. Let's row back now, and come another time with one of the big boats, stronger lines, and a lance."

"Oh, then you haven't had enough of it?" said the doctor.

"Enough? No. I want to catch some of those fish, and have a try if we cannot kill one of these sharks. My father would like the adventure too, I'm sure."

"Well, yes, I'm thinking he would," said the doctor, looking quietly at his young companion as if he were studying him. "What do you say to another try to-morrow? I think I should like to have another turn."

"I hope we shall be at the island to-morrow," replied Jack, as the doctor followed the mate back to the stern sheets. "But the first time there is an opportunity."

He seated himself on the fore thwart as he spoke, and held out his hands.

"Let me have one oar, Lenny," he said. "I want to try and learn to row."

"Rather too hot for you, won't it be, sir?" said the man, smiling.

"It is hot; but I can leave off if I'm tired," replied Jack.

"Here you are then, sir," said the man; "I'm stroke, and you bow, so you take your time from me, and hittings in the back don't count fair."

The next minute they were rowing slowly back toward the yacht, with the doctor looking on very silent and thoughtful, as he furtively watched the young oarsman.

"Boat ahoy!" came at last from the yacht's deck. "What sport? Caught anything?"

Jack answered in the familiar old way in which fishermen do reply to that question.

"*No!*"

"Tired, Jack?" said his father, as the boat grazed the yacht's side.

"A little—not much," replied the lad; and he sprang on deck actively enough, and ready for the dinner which was to follow in due course.

"Brayvo! Mr Jack, sir!" said Edward, who had followed him to his cabin. "I never see anything like the way you're going on now. It's grand, that it is."

"Look here, Ned," cried the boy, flushing; "do you want to offend me?"

"Offend you, sir? Why, of course not. I said it to please you."

"Well, it doesn't please me a bit," cried Jack. "I don't like flattery, so don't do it again."

"Why, that ain't flattery, sir," cried the man indignantly; "that's plain honest truth, sir, and it was because I felt so proud of you."

"Why?" said Jack sharply.

"Because of what you used to be a bit ago, sir. Why, a couple of months back I wouldn't have believed it, for you were just like a great—"

The man's tongue had run away with him, and he now pulled up short.

"Well, like a great what?" said Jack.

The man set his teeth hard and compressed his lips now it was too late.

"Why don't you speak, sir?"

"Beg pardon, Mr Jack, sir," stammered the man.

"I know what you were going to say," cried Jack angrily. "You were going to say that I was like a great girl. Now then—the truth. You were going to say that, were you not?"

"Well, sir?"

"Speak out, or I'll never believe in you again, Ned."

"Don't say that, Mr Jack, sir. I didn't mean to make you cross. I only spoke because I was so proud to see you picking up so, and getting to be such a man."

"A man now!" cried Jack sharply. "You were going to say a great girl a little while ago."

Edward was silent.

"Once more, will you speak out frankly?" cried Jack.

"Yes, sir, that was it, sir," said Edward hastily. "Wish I'd held my tongue, but it would come."

"Like a great girl, eh?"

"Well, sir, I can't help it, sir. You did seem more like a young lady in those times. But you're as different as can be now, sir. You really aren't like the same."

"That will do," said Jack. "You can go now."

"Yes, sir," said the man with alacrity; "but you won't leave me behind another time, sir, for speaking out so free?"

"Wait and see," said Jack shortly; and the man was obliged to content himself with that reply, and left the cabin.

"My word, he is getting a Tartar," said Edward to himself as he went to his own quarters. "Fancy him dropping on to me like that! Well, it's a change; and after all he's better so than being such a molly as he was."

"Like a great girl—like a great girl," muttered Jack as soon as he was alone. "To say that to me! How it shows what people must have thought. It was quite time there was a change. But I wonder what they all think of me now."

A burning sensation made him turn to the glass, to see that his face was growing brown, while in each of his cheeks there was a bright spot.

Chapter Seventeen
Jack sees a volcano light up

"Is there going to be any wind to-night, captain?" said Sir John as they went on deck. For answer the captain pointed away to the west, and Jack saw here and there dark patches of rippled water, but the sails that were left still hung motionless from the yards.

"In half-an-hour we shall be bowling along, Mr Jack," said the mate; "and if the wind holds, before morning we shall be lying off the land."

"Then I think I shall sit up," said the lad eagerly, for his brain was buzzing with expectation, and as full of exaggerated imaginations as it could possibly be.

But with the nightfall, in spite of the inspiriting, cooling breeze which sent them, as the mate had it, "bowling along," there was the familiar sensation of fatigue, and at the usual time, after a long look out into the darkness, Jack went to his cot, to dream that the island was getting farther and farther off, and woke up at last with the sensation that he had only just lain down.

For a few minutes he was too sleepy and confused to think, but all at once the recollection of what he expected to see came to him, and he leaped out of his berth and ran to the cabin window, but from thence he could only see the long level plain of water.

Hurriedly dressing himself, he ran on deck, to see that the dawn was only just appearing in the east, and as they lay to, rocking gently, with the sails flapping, there rose up before him, dim and dark, one vast pyramid which ran up into the heavy clouds, and filled him with a strange sensation of awe, the greater that there was a heavy booming sound as of thunder right and left and close at hand.

He grasped the fact directly after that it was not the low muttering of thunder which he heard, but the booming of the heavy billows which curved over about a couple of miles away and broke upon a reef which extended to right and left as far as the dim light would let him see.

Then came a sense of disappointment which was almost painful. Had they sailed by without stopping at any of the lovely islands they had encountered, to come to this awfully gloomy-looking spot in the ocean? The captain must be half mad to speak so highly in its favour, and for a few moments the boy felt disposed to return to his berth and try to forget his disappointment in sleep.

He took a few steps, and suddenly came across Edward.

"That you, Mr Jack, sir?" said the man.

"Can't you see it is?" replied the lad shortly.

"Yes, sir, and sorry for you I am."

"What do you mean?"

"Why, sir, about the island. They've been a-cracking it up to us, and making believe as it was the loveliest place as ever was, and now we've got to it, why it's all gammon."

"Then you've seen it, Ned?"

"Seen it, sir? I wish I hadn't. It's a trick they've played on us because we're what they call longshore folk. Makes me long for the shore, I can tell you. A jolly shame, sir."

"It does look dreary, Ned."

"Dreary aren't the word for it, but you can't gammon me. I know what it is; I've read about 'em. It's one of them out-of-the-way stony places where they used to send convicks to. 'Rubbish may be shot here' spots. And a lot of the rubbish used to be shot there if they tried to escape. Oh, it is a dismal horror place. Give me the miserables as soon as I saw it, after spoiling my night's rest for fear I shouldn't wake up at daylight to see what it was like. I've seen it though, and I don't want any more, thankye. Don't want me, I suppose, sir?"

"No, Ned. I'm going back to bed."

"Are you, sir? Well, that's a good idea, and I don't see why I shouldn't do the same."

"Let's have another look at the place first."

"No thankye, sir. If it's all the same to you, I'd rather not. Once was quite enough. Of course, if you say I am to look, sir, there I am."

"Oh no, I don't want you. Go back to bed. It's a miserable place, Ned, but I dare say there will be some good fishing."

"Take a lot of good fishing, sir, and they'd have to be very fresh, to make it worth staying for. Good-night, sir."

"Good-morning, Ned," said Jack with a faint smile, and the man went below, while, feeling chilly and depressed, and as if it would be wiser to follow the fellow's example, he walked moodily forward, gazing over the side in the direction of the island, and noticing now that there was a low line of thick mist lying just over where the billows broke in foam and produced the deep thunderous roar.

Cold, chilling, and repellent as it was, Jack could not repress a shiver, and the feeling of dislike to the voyage, which had been rapidly dying out in the new interests he felt, came back with renewed force.

"Why did we come?" he muttered.

As his eyes grew more accustomed to the gloom, he saw that the low clouds seemed to be in bands above each other, increasing the strangely forbidding aspect.

Just then there was a light step on the deck, and the mate came up.

"Morning," he said. "Here we are, you see."

"See? Yes; but what a place!"

"Eh?" cried the mate in surprise; "what, don't you like the look of it?"

"No; it is horrible. Just a black and grey mountain rising out of the sea. Are we at anchor?"

"No; only lying-to, waiting for the full light, so as to find the opening through the reef. There is no anchorage out here; I dare say the lead would go down a mile."

"What, so close to the shore?"

"Oh yes. These volcanic mountains rise up suddenly—steeply, I mean, from very great depths, and then the coral insects begin building upon them, and form regular breakwaters of solid stone all round, and these coral reefs rise just to the surface, and keep the waves from washing the sides of the volcano away."

"What a pity!" said Jack mockingly. "I don't see any good in preserving a great black-looking heap like that."

"Don't you?" said the mate, smiling, and looking back up at the gloomy eminence.

"No, I don't," replied Jack, with a touch of early morning ill-humour in his tones. "But isn't that nonsense? The sea could not wash away an island like that."

"What! Why, give it time and it will wash away a continent. But an island like this would be nothing to it without the coral insects stopped it. Some volcanoes rise in these seas and never get much above the surface—the waves wash them away as fast as they form. You see they are only made up of loose cinders and ashes which fall over outside as they are thrown up. Others are more solid if liquid lava boils over the edge of the crater and runs down. This gradually hardens into massive rock, and resists the beating of the sea till the coral insects have done their work, building up to the surface of the sea, and then going on at the sides."

"I suppose you are right," said Jack with a yawn, "but the sooner we get away from this ugly place the better."

"Think so? Well, wait and see it by daylight first. Look!"

He pointed to where, nearly a mile above them, a bright golden spot had appeared.

"Why, the volcano's burning," cried Jack excitedly. "Look! It's red-hot, and gradually increasing. There's going to be an eruption. How grand! But shall we be safe here?"

"Quite," said the mate, smiling, and he stood watching his companion's face, and its changes in the glowing light of the magnificent spectacle, as the golden red-hot aspect of the mountain top rapidly increased, displaying every seam, ravine, and buttress, that seemed to be of burning metal, fiery spot after fiery spot, that the minute before was of a deep violet black. And this went on, with the fire appearing to sink gradually down till the whole of the mountain top was one grand blaze of glory, which went on apparently sinking behind a belt of clouds, till from being of dark and gloomy grey they began to glow and become of a wonderful translucency.

"Oh!" panted the lad, "I never saw anything so grand as that. Look how the awful fire is reflected in the sky all round there."

"Yes, it's brightening it well up," said the mate, smiling; and then the boy looked in his face, and the truth came to him like a flash from the great orb to enlighten his understanding.

"Why, you're laughing at me," he cried. "How stupid! I thought the mountain was burning. You should have told me. How was I to— Yes, I ought to have known that mountain tops first caught the light. Oh, I wish I were not so ignorant."

"You are not the first who has been deceived," said the mate quietly. "Well, the mountain does not look so gloomy now, does it?"

"Glorious! Up there it is grand. I wish we were on the top."

"All in good time. But you know how quickly the full day comes here near the equator. Keep looking."

Jack wanted no telling, and for the next few minutes, with a curious sense of awe, wonder, and delight, he stood watching the line of light descending and making the beauties of the volcanic island start out of the gloom. The bands of cloud which hung round the sharp slope became roseate, golden, orange, and purple, and soon after the lad was gazing below the barren, glowing rocks at patches of golden green, then at the beginning of billows and deep valleys running down, the former of wonderful shades of green, the latter of deep dark velvety purple, across which silvery films of vapour were floating.

And still the light came down, casting wonderful shadows, setting towering pyramidical trees blazing as it were; and then all at once the boy could have believed that he was gazing where there was a gash of liquid fire pouring down into a dark valley, flashing and coruscating till it disappeared.

And still lower and lower, with wonderful rapidity now, as the great glowing disk was seen to rise above the edge of the sea, till the whole island was ablaze in the morning sunshine, and the gloomy, forbidding mass was one glorious picture of tropic beauty. Forests grouped themselves about the lower mountain slopes, lovely park-like stretches could be seen lower still, and beneath lower groves of palm-like trees a band of golden sand. Nearer still, thin lines of cocoa palms edging what appeared to be a lake of the purest blue, edged in turn with a sparkling line of foam, where the billows seemed to be eternally fretting to get over the surrounding reef and plunge themselves into the placid, perfectly calm lagoon.

Lastly there was the dark sea, now lit up into a gleaming plain of gently heaving waves; all being shot as it were with purple, where again patches of rippled damascened silver flashed in the opening of a new day.

"It is too beautiful," muttered the boy to himself. "It seems almost as if it hurt and made one sad. Oh," he said aloud, "and I never called him up to see."

"Eh, what's that?" said Sir John. "Think we were sleeping through all this? Oh no! What a glorious sunrise, my boy."

"Glorious," cried the doctor, grasping the boy's arm. "I didn't think Nature could be so grand. Here, I don't feel as if I could wait for breakfast. Oh, Jack, my lad, what times we're going to have out there."

"Well, gentlemen," said the captain, coming up with his face shining in the morning light, "will this do for you? What do you say to my island now?"

"Thank you," said Sir John, offering his hand. "I don't think we shall want to go any farther, Bradleigh. There will be enough here to last us for life."

"Right," cried the doctor, rubbing his hands. "Only to think of our pottering away our existence at home when there were places like this to see. I say, you know, Nature isn't fair. The idea of such grand, clever chaps as we are—or think we are—having to put up with our gloomy, foggy island, and a set of naked savages having such a home as that. I say it's quite unnatural."

"I don't suppose they appreciate the beauties of the place," said Sir John.

"Will it do?" cried the doctor. "I'm philosopher enough to say that this is just the sort of place where a man can be happy. You don't get me away from here, I can tell you. I mean to stay."

"For the present, at all events," said Sir John. "I question though whether Captain Bradleigh here will want to stop very long."

"Just as long as you like, gentlemen," said the captain. "I can make myself contented anywhere. That is," he added with a laugh, "if I can find good safe anchorage for the vessel I command. Well then, if you think this place will do for a stay, the first thing to be done is to find the way through the reef into the lagoon. There's an opening somewhere near here."

Just about that time Jack cast his eyes aft and saw that Edward was standing by the cabin hatch with one of Sir John's serge jackets in his left and a clothes-brush in his right hand, for though the clothes on ship-board seemed as if they could not by any possibility gather dust—they did get some flue in the corners of the pockets—Edward gave them all a thorough-going turn every morning before he rubbed over the shoes with paste, the blacking bottle remaining unopened and the brushes unused.

Jack went quickly up to him, and Edward began rubbing his head with the back of the clothes-brush; but before the lad could speak the man began.

"Beg pardon, sir," he said, "but you didn't happen to see me on deck in the middle of the night, did you?"

"No, Ned," said Jack, staring.

"Of course you didn't, sir," said the man, speaking as if relieved. "Made me feel as if my head was getting a bit soft."

"No wonder, if you keep on tapping it with the clothes-brush."

"Oh, that won't hurt it, sir, my head's hard as wood. I'm a bit late this morning—over-slept myself. Had the rummiest dream I ever knowed of."

"What did you dream?"

"Dreamt as I come up in the middle of the night, just when it was thinking about getting to morning, and we'd sailed to about the horridest place as ever was, and then I looked round and saw you like a black shadow going about the deck without making a sound."

"I had no shoes on," said Jack.

"Then it wasn't a dream, and it was only that the place looked so dismal drear in the dusk."

"Of course it was, Ned."

The man gave his head a rap with the clothes-brush. "Then that's a lesson for a man never to be in too much of a hurry. 'Pon my word, Mr Jack, sir, when I came just now and had a look, I felt as if I must have been dreaming, for as soon as I went below I lay down for a snooze, and went off like a top."

"The light has made a wonderful change, Ned," said Jack. "Well, what do you think of it now?"

"It's beyond thinking, sir, it's wonderful. We've seen some tidy places as we come along, but this beats everything I ever saw. Seems to me that we'd better stop here altogether. They say 'there's no place like home,' but I say there's no place like this."

"It really is beautiful, Ned. You should have stopped on deck and seen the wonderful transformation as the sun rose."

"Couldn't have been anything like coming upon it sudden, sir, after going below feeling that you'd been cheated. How I should like to send for my poor old mother to see it. But I dunno: she wouldn't come. She's got an idee that Walworth is about the loveliest place in the world. But it ain't, Mr Jack, you may believe me, it really ain't, not even when the sun shines; while when it don't, and it happens to be a bit muddy, or it rains, or there's a fog, it's—well, I don't think there's anything short of a photo to show what it really is like, and one of them wouldn't do it credit. But this isn't Walworth, sir, and the next thing I want to do is to go ashore and see what the place is like."

"All in good time, Ned. I suppose we shall soon begin collecting now."

"Any time you like, Mr Jack, sir, and please remember that your obedient servant to command, Edward Sims, is aboard, and whether it's sticking pins through flies and beetles like Sir John does, or shooting and skinning birds and beasts like the doctor, I want to be in it. My word, there ought to be some fine things here."

"There's no doubt about it."

"Then if you'll remember me, sir, as the song says, there isn't anything I won't do, even to being your donkey for you to ride when you're tired, and," added the man with a smile full of triumph, as if defying any one to surpass his offer, "you can't say fairer than that."

"I'll try for you to come, Ned," he replied.

"Do, sir, if it's only to carry the vittles. Thankye, sir, all the same."

Chapter Eighteen
Finding the way in

Meanwhile the captain went forward. The men were piped on deck, and in a short time they were under easy sail in search of the opening, the captain keeping about a mile from the lovely shore, which Jack scanned eagerly with a glass as they glided on, but he saw no sign of inhabitants either in the open or among the palms.

Then he searched the open spots which could be seen here and there among the trees where the ground began to rise, but there was nothing in the shape of hut or shelter of any kind.

"Well, can you make anything out?" said Sir John, coming up to where Jack was resting his elbows on the rail and sweeping the island in a peculiarly effortless way, which only necessitated his keeping the glass steadily to his eye and holding himself rigid, the result being that the object glass had three separate motions given to it by the yacht, namely, its gliding straight on, its fore and aft rise and fall as it passed over the gently heaving swell, and thirdly the careening movement as the *Silver Star* yielded to the pressure of the wind. Hence every part along the shore was being thoroughly searched.

"No, father, nothing. I thought I should see some canoes drawn up on the shore of the lagoon, but there is no sign of any one being there. Oh, I do hope it is an uninhabited island."

"So do I, my boy; but we may come at any time upon a village. The place is quite big enough to hold towns even on the other side, hidden from us by the mountain."

"But Captain Bradleigh thinks that if we do find any one there it will only be a wandering party who have sailed from some other island. He says that they are famous people in this direction for taking long journeys in their canoes, sailing from island to island, for the sea is dotted with them in every direction for hundreds and hundreds of miles."

"So I suppose," said Sir John thoughtfully; "but I do not see any signs of an opening in the reef to let us through into the smooth water. All depends upon that, for if we do not get into a sheltered part we can only make a few short visits."

The wind began to fall so light when they had sailed a few miles, that it was evident that before long they would have a similar calm to that which they had experienced on the previous day.

"My brain's a little foggy about where the opening in the reef is," said the captain soon after breakfast; "and I am rather anxious to get inside before the wind drops, for one never knows what weather one is going to have in these latitudes at this time of year, especially after a calm."

"Are you sure there is an opening in the reef?" asked the doctor anxiously.

"Oh yes, I'm sure of that," said the captain, "for I rowed through it and landed; but it's some years ago, and one can't recollect everything. Suppose you go aloft, Bartlett, with the glass, and see what you can make out."

"May I come with you, Mr Bartlett, and bring mine?" said Jack eagerly.

"Glad of your company," replied the mate. "You take one side and I'll take the other."

"Ay, that will be best," said the captain; "for our main-top is not like that of a man-o'-war."

Sir John looked a little anxious, but he said nothing, and stood watching as Jack went to the starboard main shrouds and began to ascend rather awkwardly but with a quiet determination which soon landed him in the little top, where he and the mate levelled their glasses, and began to trace the edge of the reef where the great rollers were foaming, but nothing was visible, till all at once Jack said—

"What will the opening be like?"

"A spot where there is no foam—no breakers curling over."

"I've found it then," said Jack quickly, "but it seems to be a very long way off."

"I'm afraid you are mistaken," said the mate, who repeated the process of sweeping the reef with his glass. "My eyes are pretty good ones, but I can make out nothing but breakers. Try again, and see if you see the place now."

Jack had not taken his double glass—a very good one presented to him by his father—from his eyes, and a minute had not elapsed before he said—

"Yes, there it is: a dark bit in the white rollers. It's a long way off, but I can see it quite plainly."

"Make anything out?" cried the captain anxiously, as he watched them from the deck.

"I can't, sir," replied the mate, "but Mr Jack here says he can see it quite plainly."

"Well done, young mariner," cried the captain. "Good for the first voyage. Have another look, Bartlett, and see how far it is off."

The mate looked again through his long glass, and Jack with his short one.

"Yes, there's the dark spot," said the latter. "Can't you see it now?"

"No. Your eyes are better than mine, my lad."

"Perhaps it's my glass that is better than yours," said the lad. "Try."

The mate lowered his own telescope and took the little binocular handed to him, had a look, focussed it a little better for his own sight, and then cried sharply—

"Yes, sir, there's the gap in the reef."

"How far away?"

"About a couple of miles, sir."

"Tut—tut—tut—tut!" ejaculated the captain; "and we shan't make it till the wind rises at night."

"What! be rocking out here all day again?" said the doctor.

"Yes, sir, I'm afraid so."

"But we could land here in the boat."

"What, through that surf, Sir John? Impossible. It looks very trifling from here, but it would be a certain capsize if it was attempted, and the boat smashed to pieces. But we must do better than that;" and giving the orders sharply, the firemen and engine-driver turned to below, and five minutes later the great wreaths of black smoke were pouring out of the funnel and rising high, forming a huge feather that was very slowly left behind.

Before there was steam enough to use they were once more in a dead calm, but the swell consequent on the check given to the current by the obstacle formed by the reef was far heavier than on the previous day, and the captain frowned as the yacht rocked from side to side, her masts describing arcs against the sky.

"I don't like that," he said. "Bad place to be in if we had a bit of a hurricane, with that reef just under our quarter."

"But there seems to be no likelihood of such a misfortune, for the glass promised fine weather."

"All the same, though, sir," said Captain Bradleigh, "I am always anxious when I find myself in a place which might prove dangerous, and I am not so situated that I could get out of it."

At last there was a welcome hissing sound from the valve, the order was given, and once more the yacht began to throb, as if it had its heart pulsating rapidly, and the distance which separated them from the opening in the reef was soon passed, the panorama being lovely in the extreme. Once there the engine was slowed, stopped, and the captain gave orders for one of the boats to be lowered.

"Why not steam in at once?" asked Jack.

The captain smiled.

"It is some years since I was here, my lad. Then we rowed in, with the lead being heaved all the time, and there was plenty of water for a ship to sail in; but since then the coral insects may have been busy building up walls or mushroom-shaped rocks, or a bit of a mountain top ready to make a hole in our bottom, so we must feel our way. Going with them?"

For answer Jack sprang into the boat, and they pushed off, riding easily over the swell caused by the breakers stretching away in a long line to right and left; and as they rowed on, a man in the bows kept on heaving the lead, and sounding to find deep water everywhere.

"Make a pretty loud din, don't they?" said the mate quietly, as, with a feeling of awe beginning to increase as they neared the opening, Jack sat watching the great rollers which came gliding in with the tide, and then, as if enraged at the barrier to their progress, rose up foaming and curved over to fall with a boom like thunder.

This increased as they drew nearer, the opening proving to be about a hundred yards in width, and the water, which had seemed to be so smooth and calm at a distance, being just outside one wild turmoil of eddy and cross currents consequent upon the action of the breakers on either side.

The boat danced about so at last, as they rowed slowly on to enable the man in the bows to sound more frequently in this the entrance part, that Jack was unable to keep back the question he felt ashamed to put.

Out it came.

"Is it safe for such a small boat as this to go through there, Mr Bartlett?"

"If it were not I should row back," said the mate with a quiet smile. "Oh, yes, we could go through far worse places than this. But look there to the right; you see now why the captain said no boat could cross the reef."

Jack could not forbear a shudder.

"The oars are nearly useless in that broken water, nearly all foam. The men can get no grip. But here we could run in twice as fast if we liked. Seems to be deep water. Capital channel. Not a suggestion of a rock."

Then after contenting himself with letting the lead go down a few fathoms in the deep water, the man began to keep to one level length of ten fathoms, and this always went down without finding bottom till they were well in the jaws of the reef, when all at once he cried the depth—"By the mark nine," and repeated the announcement again and again. Then it was eight, then seven, and as they glided out of the turmoil into perfectly smooth water the depth shallowed to six fathoms, and kept at that, no less, wherever they rowed.

"Plenty of good anchorage in shelter," said the mate, slewing the boat round head to the opening once more, and they rowed out, sounding again as they went back, after proving that there was a perfectly clear channel for the yacht to pass in.

Once well outside the mate bade the men lie on their oars, and he hoisted the boat-hook with a handkerchief on the end for the signal agreed upon with the captain.

Then the *Silver Star* began to move, and glided slowly in, picking up the boat as she passed.

Half-an-hour later the anchors were dropped, and the yacht lay moored in perfectly still water, through which Jack gazed down at a wonderful submarine garden, and then at the line of cocoa-nut trees in the sandy beach to their right. Then his eyes went wandering over the forest, and up and up to the perfectly formed volcano which shot skyward.

And so on till his eyes grew misty, and the back of his neck ached with the way in which it had been bent, and he was still gazing through his glass when the announcement came that the meal was ready.

All too soon, for the boy did not know he was hungry, there had been too much mental food to devour.

But he found that he could eat and pay attention to the conversation too, which was upon the glorious, to him, subject of going ashore that afternoon in the boat for the sake of a little exploring before the night closed in, and ended what was to Jack a most exciting day.

Chapter Nineteen
The first run ashore

Jack dropped down into the boat with a feeling of pity for the men who had to stay on board with the mate. Sir John, the doctor, and Captain Bradleigh were of the party, all well-armed, and, to Jack's excitement and satisfaction, he found that the crew of the boat all wore cutlasses, with the peculiar hilt which enables the wearers to fix them bayonet-fashion to the muzzles of their rifles.

"Just as well to be prepared, Mr Jack," said the captain, smiling, as he saw the interest the boy took in the men's appearance. "I don't think we shall find a soul in the island. If there had been, they must have caught sight of us, and would have shown themselves, even if they had gone off into the woods when they saw us coming ashore. Well, what do you say to this for a treat? Think it's as good as Doctor Instow described?"

"Better, ever so much," said Jack excitedly; "but please don't talk to me now. There is so much to see, I want to look about me. It is all so fresh and beautiful. But are there cocoa-nut trees?"

"Yes, of all sizes, from little ones a year old, to old ones in full bearing. There they are."

"But I thought cocoanuts grew on a sort of palm-tree which went up from the ground as straight as an arrow."

"No: never. The cocoa-nut sapling springs up with a beautiful curve like you see yonder, all alike, and no matter how the wind blows they keep to it, bending down and springing up again as if they were made of whalebone. They get it badly though when there is a hurricane; scarcely anything can stand that. But look down."

"Look down?"

"Yes, into the sea. You must not pass that over."

The boy glanced over the side of the boat, as the men rowed gently across the lagoon, to find that they had gradually come into a shallow part, whose waters, save for the disturbance made by the boat's passing, were perfectly calm and of crystal clearness. As they neared the sandy shore, the bottom, by the refraction, seemed to come nearer and nearer to the surface, through which he sat gazing into one of Nature's loveliest aquaria, strewn with the most wondrous corals and madrepores, not dry, harsh, and stony, but glowing in colours imparted by the many creatures which covered them. The seaweeds were exquisite, and the flowers of this submarine garden were sea anemones of wondrous tints, some closed like buds, others open wide, aster-like, and as bright in tint, but with a slow, creeping movement of their petal-like arms, as some unfortunate water creature touched them and was drawn into the central mouth.

Shell-fish too of wondrous forms lay or crept about in the grottoes of coral rock. Some were anchored oyster-like, and of gigantic size, lying as traps with shells apart, like the mouth of some terrible monster lying hidden among the weeds; others with strange, striped shells crawled snail-like over the bottom, amidst many so small that they were mere specks. And all the while, as the boat glided on over the surface, there were flashes of gold, silver, ruby, topaz, sapphire, and amethyst, for shoals of fish, startled by their coming, darted through the sunlit water, to hide in the waving groves of sea-weed, or nestle down among the coral stones.

"Stop rowing, please," said Sir John suddenly; and Jack turned to see that his father and the doctor had been gazing down into the water from the other side of the boat. "Only for a few minutes, captain: we must not pass over this too quickly."

"You have only to give your orders, sir," said the captain, smiling with satisfaction; and as the men sat with their oars balanced, the boat glided slowly on, hardly disturbing the surface; but her shadow was sufficient as it darkened the water to still startle the fish from their homes.

"Here's work, Meadows—here's collecting. Jack, boy, what do you think of it?"

"Oh!" ejaculated the lad, without raising his eyes from the wondrous scene he was watching once more.

There does not seem much in that simple little interjection; but the meaning put into it by the tone and the face of the lad who uttered it spoke volumes.

"Ah, it is oh!" cried the doctor. "Here, Jack, it's all nonsense, I can't be thirty-six; I feel only sixteen, and I want to begin wading in here."

"I'd advise you to wear very thick boats then," said the captain. "Some of these things are knife-edged, some sharp as thorns. You'll have to take care."

"Oh, we will; eh, Jack?"

"Yes; but we must get a lot of these as specimens. Here, look—look!"

"Ah, one of those snakes," said Sir John. "One? Look—look! there are dozens of them gliding about."

"Then I shan't wade," said the doctor decisively. "I don't want any patients this trip, and there wouldn't be much fun in laying myself up with a bad leg, and having myself to attend. I shall do my wading in a boat."

"Yes; and we must fish for and catch some of these little fellows. Do, father, look at that one gliding along by that clump of branched stuff, plant or coral, or whatever it calls itself. Why it's like a gold-fish with a great, broad bar of glittering blue across it."

"Lovely!" cried the doctor.

A discordant burst of shrill, whistling screams came from the cocoa-nut grove ashore, and Jack looked up sharply.

"Paroquets," said the captain. "There they are, quite a flock of them."

Jack's hand stole behind him toward the guns and just then there was a fluttering of wings, and a little cloud of green, shot with orange yellow and blue, glided out of the grove and flew inland.

"Let's land," said Sir John. "There is so much to see, that we had better content ourselves with a preliminary look round."

"Yes," said the doctor, "and devote separate days after to some particular branch. Pull away, my lads."

"Yes; but very gently," cried Jack; and they glided on, the men guessing the wishes of those on board by swinging together with a slow, steady motion, and just lightly dipping their oars without a splash, so that, as they glided on toward a patch of sand some four hundred yards away, where the grove of palms was the highest, and the shade from the glowing sun the deepest, a glorious view of the submarine treasures was enjoyed. Jack sighed as the boat's prow touched the sands, the men sprang out on either side in the shallow water, and ran her right up on the shore, close to a great cocoa-nut tree, ready for the painter to be attached in case the tide should rise as high.

Two men were left as keepers, and the party, shouldering their arms, prepared to start inland.

"It will be best, gentlemen," said the captain, "to make our way along the open ground between the lagoon and the forest to-day, and to keep well together. I don't think there is a soul but ourselves on the island, but it is as well to take every step as if we were in face of enemies. For no doubt once upon a time the people who live among these tropical islands were fairly amiable when not provoked; but I'm sorry to say that they have been so ill-used by the sailors and traders of all nations, that whatever they may have been, they are often now ready to behave in a very treacherous manner to white people."

"Quite right," said Sir John; "and it is hard to make them understand that we are perfectly peaceable. I quite agree with Doctor Instow that our pleasant voyage ought not to be made arduous to him and painful to us all by any sad accident. We do not want any patients suffering from spear-thrust, or poisoned arrow sent from blow-pipe or bow, and I beg that every one will understand that I should look upon it as a calamity if, in defence of our lives, we were forced to fire upon a set of ignorant savages. Captain Bradleigh, we trust to your guidance on board, we will continue to do so, please, on shore."

"Thank you, Sir John," said the gentleman addressed; "you have uttered my sentiments exactly, and I am glad to say that I can trust my lads thoroughly. So now, then, we'll go west slowly and easily, so that you can take a look at anything which takes your fancy, and we will just skirt the woodland patches while we go as far as seems reasonable in this direction, our main object being to find out whether we have the island to ourselves."

"But we shall only be examining the narrow band by the water side. What about inland?" said the doctor.

"If we go partly to-day and partly to-morrow round the island, I fancy we shall learn all we want," replied the captain. "If there are any of the black fuzzy-headed Papuans here, or the browner South Sea Islands type of men, more like the Maoris, or lastly the Malay flat-nosed fellows, we are sure to find traces of them by the shore or up the little rivers. They don't care for the inland parts of an island like this, where there is a volcano still more or less active. They generally give these mountains a wide berth, unless there happens to be a tribe of the original people who have been driven inland by the more warlike folk, who go filibustering about searching for new lands in their great outrigger war canoes."

"Hang their war canoes!" said the doctor gruffly, "we don't want them here."

"You, my lads," said the captain to the two men by the boat, "will not leave your posts, and you will keep the cutter just afloat, so that you can leap aboard and keep her off at the first sign of danger. If there is anything you will fire two shots sharply, as a warning to Mr Bartlett, though probably he will see it first and send help to you. Then keep on firing a shot every minute till you get an answer from us, followed by one shot, and then two more, which mean that we have heard you and are coming back. Now I don't expect anything of the kind, but we must be on the look-out till we have examined the place. You understand?"

"Yes, sir."

"That's right. Don't leave your rifles, and don't go to sleep."

"Right, sir."

"Then now, gentlemen, we'll advance in a line. No straggling, mind. When one halts, all will stand fast. Forward!"

Jack shouldered his perfectly new double gun and stepped out, not feeling the weight of either that or the satchel and cartridge pouch slung by cross-belts, while from that at his waist hung a leather holster containing a revolver and a strong, handy sheath knife, suitable for a weapon, for skinning a specimen, or for hacking a way through tangled scrub. A feeling of subdued excitement set his heart beating steadily, and a thrill of returning health made his muscles feel tense, while his eyes flashed with eagerness, and there was an elasticity in his step that sent a feeling of satisfaction home to his father.

He was between Sir John and the doctor as they stepped off in a line over the soft sand, and the latter turned for a moment, looking serious.

"One word to you two," he said,—"medical adviser's word. This is a new country, and you are new to it. Just mind this: with quiet steady going you can do a great deal; but there must be no over-exertion so as to get too much heated. Chills are easily taken in these tropic lands, and they mean fever and weakness, so let there be no false delicacy or shame, and fighting to keep up with men better fit for the work than we are. If either of you feels tired, stop at once and rest."

"That's all meant for me," said Jack, smiling.

"No, it isn't," cried the doctor sharply. "It's meant as much for your father, who has a deal more weight to carry than you have, and if I am not much mistaken, Jack Meadows, Esquire, he is a good deal older. Now you understand. No over-exertion, no drinking cold water while you're hot. As I told you before, I don't want patients till I get back home. I've come out to enjoy my trip, so have a little mercy, if you please."

They tramped on under the blazing sunshine, and where they could under the shade of trees, starting crabs running in all directions, fish which had been basking on the wet sand by the water's edge wriggling and flopping back into the lagoon, and birds of brilliant colours from the trees they passed; all of which excited a desire in Jack to begin trying his skill with his double gun; but it was an understood thing that shooting was not to commence that day, but every hour be devoted to exploring.

Everything looked superlatively beautiful. Metallic-armoured lizards darted over the dry sand to hide amongst the scattered blocks of sun-baked coral, lovely butterflies and other insects flitted amongst low growth, in company with tiny sun-birds which seemed clothed in brilliant burnished mail, and at every few steps larger birds, perfectly new to the visitors, took flight or hurried thrush-like to take refuge beneath the bushes.

On their left the wondrously blue lagoon glittered through the tall stems of the cocoa-nut trees which fringed the shore; on their right they had the open park-like stretches of land, dotted with bush and stately tree; and every here and there, through an opening, they had glimpses of the forest, which rose upward covering the flanks of the mountain.

At the end of an hour, long after—through the curving of the shore—the yacht had disappeared from view, they made their first halt. They stopped at a valley-like opening which ran in a sinuous manner up and up till they had a glimpse of the central mountain nearly to its highest part.

The captain, in his caution, set a man on the highest part to act as sentry and guard against a surprise, and he himself took another and walked a quarter of a mile farther in search of traces on the sands of canoes.

Jack threw himself down beneath a group of cocoa-nut trees, with the soft sand for his couch, and was delighted and puzzled at the pleasant, restful sensations he enjoyed. Sir John and the doctor sat down a little apart, and the sailors chose another group of cocoa-nut trees to indulge in a quiet chat.

Jack had just half-closed his eyes, to lie gazing through the lashes at dazzling light and rainbow-like effects seen in the mist caused by the breakers on the reef, when a rustling sound behind him made him start and find that it was their man.

"Only me, Mr Jack, sir. Hope I haven't woke you out of a nap."

"Oh no. I was not asleep, Ned."

"Tired, sir?"

"No, not a bit."

"Feet hurt you?"

"No. Why should they?"

"With the walking, sir. You see, you're not used to it."

"No, I'm not used to it, Ned; but I soon shall be."

"That's right, sir. If they had been hurting you and your boots felt tight, I was going to say, come down to the water's edge and paddle your feet a bit."

"But they're all right."

"Glad of it, sir. Mine ain't. At least they're better now. That's what I went and did, and it's lovely. Thirsty, sir?"

"Well, yes, I am thirsty."

"Then I'll get you a drink, sir, same as the men's had. Two of 'em's been up one of those trees—these trees like we're under, sir. They calls 'em cocoa-nut, but that's all nonsense. They're not nuts."

"Oh yes, these are real cocoa-nut trees, Ned."

"Well, sir, I don't like to contradick you; it wouldn't be my place. But if these are real cocoanuts, them we buys—I mean I buys—at home are sham ones."

"Oh, they're all the same, Ned."

"Well, sir, 'tain't for me to contradick. I dessay you're quite right and they are all the same, but they're quite different. Them at home's hard shells with rough shaggy hairs on 'em, and inside they're white solid nut."

"So are these, Ned."

"Beg pardon, sir, have you tasted one? You must have seen 'em hanging here in the trees."

"Of course I've seen them."

"Yes, sir, and they're twice as large as ours, with a cover to 'em like a piece of solid door-mat."

"That's the outer husk, Ned."

"Oh, is it, sir? I thought it was something. But you ain't tasted one?"

"No."

"Well, sir, it's hard work to cut them at home with a knife, they're that hard; as for these here they're too soft to cut with a spoon. Have one, sir?"

"Oh no, I'm not disposed to eat nuts," said Jack, laughing.

"But you don't eat 'em here, sir; it's more drinking of 'em. Let me get you one, sir."

"Very well: I do feel as if I could drink something."

"Then these are the very thing, sir," said the man, and he hurried off, Jack lying back watching him till he reached the knot of sailors enjoying the shade.

Then as Jack watched quite out of hearing, a kind of pantomime began, in which the sailors seemed to be laughing, and Ned gesticulating, and holding his hand first to one and then another, slapping his knee afterward, and seeming to go on in the most absurd manner; but the next minute Jack began to grasp dimly what it all meant, and that the sailors were daring their man to do something, and telling him it could not be done.

There it all was: directly after Ned slipped off his straps and belt, pulled off his jacket, and then rapidly got rid of his boots.

Jack did not hear him say, "Now, my lads, I'll show you," but he seemed to say it, after shading his eyes and staring upward for a few moments before spitting in his hands, taking a run and a jump, and beginning to hug and climb one of the cocoa-nut trees, while the sailors all sprang up to stand clapping their hands, and evidently bantering him or urging him on.

This brought Jack into a sitting position, and the next minute he had out his glass, and was watching with the actor apparently close at hand, drawing himself up a few inches at a time, as one would mount a scaffold-pole, and his wrinkled forehead, compressed lips, and determined eyes so plain that Jack could have fancied that he heard him breathe.

"I wonder whether he'll do it," said the lad softly. "He is just one of those obstinate fellows who, if they make up their minds to do a thing, manage it somehow."

And feeling as deeply interested as the man himself, Jack felt ready to run across to the cocoa-nut grove and shout encouragement.

"Look so precious undignified if I did. But how strange it seems! There was he only the other day in his quiet livery and white tie valeting us, and waiting at table, and now he's climbing that tree like a boy."

"Or a monkey, Jack," said the doctor, who had come up behind, and Sir John with him. "I didn't hear you," said Jack, starting. "Not likely when you were talking aloud with your ears glued to that lorgnette. Well, eyes then. But it's the air, my lad; I feel ready to do any stupid thing of that kind. I'd challenge you to climb the two next trees if we were alone."

"*I* hope the foolish fellow will not meet with an accident," said Sir John.

"Pooh! not he," said the doctor. "The lads have been challenging him, I suppose."

"I think that's it, but he has gone to get a cocoa-nut for me."

"You did not send him to do it, Jack?"

"No, father: he came and proposed it."

"Tree's getting gradually thinner," said the doctor. "Easier to climb."

"I hope he will be successful," said Sir John. "The men will banter him so if he fails."

"How the tree begins to bend!" said Jack anxiously. "Why don't you shake it?" he cried, without considering that his words could not be heard. But, oddly enough, just at that moment the idea seemed to have occurred to Ned, who held on with his legs and shook the tree violently.

"You will not do it like that, my fine fellow," said the captain, coming up; "and lucky for you that you can't. A crack from one of those nuts would be no joke."

"Yes, they must be pretty heavy," said Sir John.

"Heavy enough to kill any one if they fell upon his bare head."

"Oh, look how the tree's bending over!" cried Jack.

"Yes, he had no business to choose such a slight one," said the captain, as the tree swayed beneath the man's weight.

"Had I better stop him?" said Sir John.

"I think perhaps you had better not startle him and make him nervous, father. We don't want any accidents."

"Indeed we don't," said the doctor; "better let him be. Why, if he goes on like this the tree will bend over like a fishing-rod, and he can drop from the top to the ground."

Then silence fell upon the group, and the sailors ceased to cheer, as, with the elastic rod-like tree bending more and more over, and swaying up and down, Ned climbed on, till the last part of his progress was after the fashion of a sloth, hanging back downward, and at every movement coming nearer, till the great crown of leaves and nuts, which had stood forty feet in the air, was not more than twenty.

"Another two or three feet will do it," said the doctor; "but I'm afraid he will not be able to get the nuts off."

"Oh yes; he can screw them off," said the captain.

"What I'm afraid of is—"

Crack!

A sharp loud snap, and the top of the tree came down, the big leafage hiding Ned; but he was standing up close to the broken-off tree, which was now like a thick pole, and rubbing himself hard, with the sailors about him, when the lookers-on reached the spot.

"Oh, Ned!" cried Jack, who was first up.

"Yes, sir, it is 'Oh, Ned!'" replied the man angrily.

"Hurt?" cried the others in a breath.

"Don't know yet, Sir John," said the man, "I think my right leg's broke, though."

"Here, let me see," cried the doctor eagerly.

"No, it ain't, sir," said Ned, giving a kick. "It's the left one."

"Bah!" roared the doctor; "how could you stand upon it and kick out like that if it were broken?"

"Right you are, sir; of course I couldn't. But something's broke, for I heard it go. Maybe it's my arms."

"Maybe it's your head," said the doctor sarcastically, "for you are talking in a very crack-brained fashion. Let me buckle your belt round it tightly to hold it together."

The man stared wonderingly at the doctor, feeling his head all over the while, and his eyes having a puzzled look in them, as if he couldn't quite make out whether the doctor was speaking seriously. But the next moment he took it as a piece of chaff and grinned.

"It's all right, sir, but it did come an awful whack against one of these nuts."

"Better see if you've damaged the nut," said the doctor sarcastically. "No, never mind. Head's too soft."

Ned grinned again, and gave himself a rub as he looked down at the crown of the tree and then at the broken stump, snapped off a good five-and-twenty feet from the ground.

"Here," he said, turning to the group of sailors, "you were precious full of your brag about climbing, and saying I couldn't. But I did, and now let's see one of you do that."

There was a roar of laughter, and Sir John turned away, but the captain spoke rather seriously.

"I wouldn't advise you to do this sort of thing again, young fellow. Now then, how do you feel? Can you go on with us, or will you wait here till we come back?"

"Me wait here, sir?" cried Ned. "What, all alone? No, thank you, I'm all right, sir. Walk as well as any of them."

"Then whoever wants a cocoa-nut had better have it, for we go on in five minutes."

"Will you give me your knife, sir?" said Ned, turning to his young master. "Thankye, sir; I know how it's done;" and chopping off the husk and the top of the soft shell of one of the great nuts, he handed it to Jack, the sailors quickly getting the rest of the others and serving them the same, to hand to Sir John, the doctor, and captain, who all partook of the deliriously cool, sub-acid pulp. Then the word was given and the march commenced once more.

Whether Ned suffered or not he kept to himself, for he resumed his jacket, boots, and belts, clapped on his pith hat, and stalked off with the rest, the way seeming to grow more and more beautiful, and the natural history specimens more attractive at every hundred yards they left behind.

But there was no shooting, the object of the exploration being rigorously kept in mind, and they were just rounding what seemed to be the end of a great artificial dike that ran down from the slope on their right, when one of the men cried—"Look out! They must be close here." Every one stopped short, and guns and rifles were brought to the ready.

"What is it?" said the captain in a low voice. "What did you see?"

"Didn't see nothing, sir," replied the man. "I smelt 'em."

"What do you mean?"

"Must be some huts or cottages close here, where the people keeps pigs."

"Yes, look, sir," cried another man, pointing; "they've been down here to the sea."

He pointed to where, about a dozen yards away, there were abundant traces of a drove of pigs, and as the captain advanced, the odour which the sailor had noticed now became plain to all.

Sir John looked inquiringly at the captain. "A good find," said the latter, smiling. "We shall be able to shoot some fresh young porkers. Wild pig is not bad."

"Wild?" cried the doctor.

"Yes, there is evidently a herd of wild pigs in the island, if not several. They have been down here lately."

"But surely there would not be wild boars and sows in an island like this?" said Sir John.

"No," said the captain, "but pigs that have run wild. You see, the old voyagers left two or three pairs in a good many places, and they have increased largely. This must have been one of the favoured islands."

Further proof was given a short distance farther on, for they had a glimpse of a herd which seemed to be fifty or sixty strong, whose leaders stood grunting and staring at the new-comers for a moment or two before whisking round and dashing off among the trees, to be hidden directly by the low growth, a head or a tail being seen at intervals; and then every sign was gone.

"Well," said the doctor to Jack, "that's another discovery to the good: fresh pork and poultry."

"You can't eat parrots," said Jack, laughing.

"Why?" said the doctor.

"Oh, those highly-coloured birds can't be good."

"Wait a bit, my young philosopher. I never knew that gaily-coloured barn-door cockerels were 'bad', and I know that a young peacock is as good as a pheasant; so where is your theory now?"

"Yes, Jack, you are beaten," said Sir John merrily.

"Oh, but I meant parrots and cockatoos and birds of paradise," said the lad hurriedly.

"Parrots and cockatoos live on fruit," said the doctor; "fruit is good, ergo parrots and cockatoos are good, and I'll have a curry made of the first I skin."

"You are right about the birds of paradise though, my boy," said Sir John. "I should not like to try one of those, because they are so nearly related to the crow."

"A bird of paradise related to a crow—a black crow?"

"Oh yes, you'll find some of the most gaily painted birds out here in the tropics very nearly related to some of our more common friends at home."

"Yes; look, there goes one, Jack. I could bring him down easily."

The lad had already caught sight of a lovely bird upon the ground, which stood looking at them for a few moments before hopping away beneath the bushes and undergrowth, appearing again farther on, and then spreading its wings for a short flight, and displaying the lovely colours with which it was dyed, the most prominent being shades of blue relieved by delicate fawn and pale warm drab.

"What's that?" cried Jack eagerly.

"That's a thrush," said the doctor.

"A thrush!"

"Yes; not one of our olive-green, speckled-breasted fellows, but a thrush all the same, and saving its colouring, wonderfully like one of ours."

There was plenty to say about bird and insect as they went on, keeping just where the sand gave place to firm ground, for the birds were excessively tame, and gave evident proof that they were not much disturbed; while every now and then amid the lovely insects which thronged wherever there were flowers, appeared some magnificent butterfly, several inches across its wings, tempting Sir John to cease exploring for the sake of making captures.

But everything was given up to the main object, and mile after mile was tramped, every step seeming to reveal some new beauty—peeps through the groves at the broad blue sea, or wonderful landscapes up ravines, with the mountain towering up behind.

The natural history objects they encountered were plentiful enough. In fact very few steps were taken without something attracting attention. Lizards which seemed as they basked on pieces of the heated rock to have been cut out of glittering metal, till, at the jar of a footstep, or the shadow of any one cast across them, they darted away. In one place the doctor pointed out sinuous markings on the sandy ground which looked as if freshly made.

"Yes, a snake," said Sir John, "and a good-sized one too."

"How large?" said Jack with suppressed excitement.

"Seven or eight feet long, I should say," replied his father.

Jack looked with an expression of mingled dread and longing at the patch of dense growth into which the track led, and directly after Edward exchanged glances with him, the man's look seeming to say—

"I've marked down that spot, sir."

Glen after glen was passed, every one full of beauty and interest, and at last they were brought up short by what looked like some huge pier running right across their way, down over the sands, and ending suddenly about a hundred feet out in the beautiful blue lake. At the first sight it seemed like some great landing-place or wharf, but there was no sign of handiwork about it, and the lad gazed at it in awe, as the doctor explained that it was the end where it had cooled and solidified in the lake of a huge lava-stream which had flowed down from the mountain, high up on their right.

"But that means it must have run like so much liquid fire for miles."

"Yes, that's exactly what it does mean, Jack," said Sir John; "six or seven or eight. We shall know some day, when we have explored the place."

"And that will be like a high-road to the top," said the doctor, "only I'm afraid it would be a rather rough one."

"We'll try it some day," said Sir John.

"Rather hard for your boots, sir," said the captain. "Look at it: like glass, and as sharp in places."

"Why, it must be quite fresh," said Jack.

The captain smiled and shook his head.

"But some of these pieces look quite bright," said Jack.

"Yes; and these trees look quite green, and many of them may be a hundred or two hundred years old."

"What has that got to do with it?" said Jack. "Oh yes, I see now: they would have been burned up. Of course."

"Yes," said Sir John, as he stood looking at the huge solidified stream; "everything about here must have been burned to ashes, and it would, even with the rapid tropic rate, have taken fully a hundred years for these trees to grow."

"How wide is the stream?" said the doctor; and he led the way to climb up, startling something, which went off with a tremendous rush inland.

"What's that?" said Sir John.

"Couldn't catch a glimpse of it; but it wasn't a man. Four-legged creature of some kind. There, that's its cry."

A peculiarly weird howl rang out, and was answered from a distance off; but though the party waited in the hope of seeing what it was that had been started, they were disappointed.

"Never mind," said the doctor; "we have proof that there are animals about. Now then, how wide do you make the lava-stream to be?"

"About four hundred paces," said Sir John.

"Quite that," said the captain. "Well, gentlemen, what do you say to making a halt just beyond the lava there—under one of those trees, say, beside that stream?"

"Couldn't be a better place," cried Jack. "I am getting hungry."

"I think we all are," said the doctor, smiling, "for we have been tramping quite two hours since Edward had his adventure on the cocoa-nut tree."

"If I might suggest, Sir John, I'd make this the farthest limit of our tramp to-day. We shall be about four hours going back; and to-morrow we might go in the other direction—sail round the island, if you like."

"I think we would prefer to explore it on foot, captain," replied Sir John.

They crossed the remainder of the solidified stream of stone, ascended to the beautiful grove of trees on the other side, where a swift stream of the purest water ran gurgling along to the sea, and here enjoyed, in the cool shade, a delicious *al fresco* meal, to which every one did ample justice. After which a start was made for the yacht; but the heat proved to be so intense, there not being a breath of air, save a succession of hot puffs which seemed to be wafted down from the mountain, that the men began to flag and show signs of being overcome. Consequently, first one and then another halt had to be called, and when they were still a good three miles from where they had left the boat, the sun went down, and the night came on with startling suddenness, so that at the end of a quarter of an hour it was dark as pitch beneath the trees, and the order was given to bear off to the right, so as to follow the sand.

"Can't go wrong," said the captain, "if we keep within touch of the sea."

"Hark! hark! What's that?" cried Jack.

There was no need for him to speak, for every one had stopped short, and was listening intently to the echoes which ran reverberating along a valley, after what seemed to have been the firing of a heavy gun.

Chapter Twenty
Floating blacks

"Is that Mr Bartlett firing one of the yacht's guns for a recall?" said Sir John.

"No, sir; they could not make a noise like that."

"It could not be thunder," said Jack.

"Oh yes, it could," said the captain. "I've heard short sharp cracks like that often out here, but I don't think that was thunder."

"Must have been," cried the doctor. "Why, I saw the flash. There! Look!"

A bright light suddenly appeared from somewhere inland, followed at a few seconds' interval by a heavy detonation, exactly like the firing of a great gun.

"Now what do you say, Captain Bradleigh?" cried Sir John.

"That it is what I thought at first, sir. The mountain yonder is firing a shot or two. If we had been out at sea, I dare say we should have seen a great red-hot stone flying up and falling back."

"Then there is going to be an eruption," cried Jack in excited tones.

"That does not follow at all. Some of these volcanoes do no more perhaps than make a rumbling, and send up a few red-hot stones now and then. Forward now, gentlemen. Close up, my lads, and follow two and two."

The mountain, if the captain was right, made no farther sign, and now began the most interesting part of the journey. With the exception of having to be careful not to stumble over the blocks of coral limestone which lay here and there in their road, it was easy walking in spite of the darkness, while this latter was modified by the brilliant stars overhead, the dazzling scintillations of the fireflies, which flittered out whenever any of the bushes which fringed the sands were approached—and the soft, luminous, oil-like appearance at the edge of the lake.

But the sand was soft, and it seemed to Jack as if they would never reach the boat.

In the darkness Edward edged up close to his young master, and whispered—

"Tired, Mr Jack?"

"Dreadfully."

"Makes one's legs feel as if they were made of cast lead."

"Or stones," said Jack.

"Well, p'r'aps you're right, sir. Stone is more like it. Let me carry your gun, sir. Seems to get heavier every step, don't it?"

"Yes; and the cartridges too. Thank you, Ned. I should be glad to get rid of them. No, you've got your own to carry, and—I say, how do you feel now? I mean, after your fall."

"Oh, bit stiff, sir. There's nothing broken; but I don't go quite so well as usual. Shan't be sorry to get back to the yacht. Better give me your gun, sir."

"Better give me yours to carry, Ned."

"What, sir? Well, 'pon my word, Mr Jack, you do talk. I do wonder at you."

Just then Jack started, for a hand was laid on his gun.

"Who's that?" he cried.

"Only me, sir—Lenny," said a dark figure behind him. "Let me carry your gun, and pouch too. I heerd what you said. Take hold of t'other's weapon, mate," continued the man to the sailor by him, and Jack and his man tramped the rest of the way relieved of their loads, heartily glad to hear at last a hail from somewhere away in the darkness.

It came from the boat; and directly after a bright light flashed out over the calm lagoon, like a star just rising to shine across the sea, and the men gave a cheer.

"Is that the *Silver Star*, Captain Bradleigh?" said Jack eagerly.

"Yes, my lad. That's better than a figure-head, eh?"

It was extremely beautiful just then, and looked very attractive and suggestive of rest and a good meal, beside being a guide to them along the lagoon, the men as they bent to their oars having the straight path of light to follow right up to the yacht's bows, and soon after the efforts of the cook and the cheery aspect of everything made Jack forget his weariness.

"Well, gentlemen," said the captain after their late dinner, "I think that there ought to be another exploration to the east to-morrow."

"Certainly," said Sir John; "I want to feel that we can go about in safety."

"I suppose you'll be too tired to go, Jack?" said the doctor.

"Too tired? Didn't I keep up well to-day?" said the lad quickly.

"Capitally; but you look done up."

"I shall be ready in the morning," said Jack shortly.

"Don't attempt too much at first, Jack," said his father.

"Oh no, I will not do that. But I can't be left behind."

There was no need for any question about the matter, for the captain now joined in the conversation again.

"I propose, Sir John," he said, "that we should have the first cutter and the gig to-morrow morning, and let the men row gently along the lagoon, close in shore. It will be a change; we can get along faster, and land as often as you wish. I could have the awning rigged up."

"Yes, capital!" cried the doctor. "If you decide on that, Sir John, I should advise a start at daybreak, and a halt for breakfast when the sun begins to get hot. But, of course, we should have some coffee and biscuit before we start."

The captain's plan was agreed upon, and in what seemed to be the middle of the night, Jack was awakened from a dream of watching a cup-headed mountain playing at throwing up and catching a huge red-hot ball, by a voice at his berth-side saying—

"Coffee's about ready, Mr Jack—t'other gents has begun to dress."

For some moments Jack stared at him stupidly. "What time is it?" he stammered at last. "Some bells or another, sir—I dunno; but the men have got the boats out, and the things in for breakfast and lunch. They were at it before I woke."

"I won't be long," said Jack, yawning, and wishing the expedition at the bottom of the sea, for he felt dreadfully sleepy, and as if he would have given anything for another hour or two's rest. It seemed absurd to be getting up in the dark when there was all the day before them, and altogether he was in that disposition of mind which people say is caused by getting out of bed the wrong way first.

The doctor noticed it as the lad left his cabin to find a comfortable meal spread by the light of the cabin lamp, and the odour of coffee coming fragrantly from a steaming urn.

"Here, look at him," cried the doctor. "Mind, or he'll bite."

"Why, Jack, my boy," cried Sir John merrily; "don't look so fierce as that."

"I didn't know I looked fierce," said the lad in an ill-used tone. "I can't help feeling tired and sleepy."

"Of course he can't," said Doctor Instow. "He had a very hard day yesterday. Here, I'll set him right. You go back to bed, Jack, and lie there till we come back. You'll be as fresh as can be then."

"What, let you go without me?" cried the boy, with a sudden display of animation. "Of course. It is too much for you."

"Give me some coffee, Ned," said the boy irritably. "Is there no new bread?"

"No, sir. Too soon. Dry toast, sir?"

"Bother the dry toast! you know I don't like dry toast."

"Yes, and it isn't well-made, Jack. You go to bed."

The lad gave the doctor an angry glance, spread some marmalade upon the dry toast, and began to eat and sip from his coffee as fast as the heat thereof would allow.

"Well, are you going to take my advice?" said the doctor, who was pretty busy over his own early breakfast.

Jack made no reply, but went on sipping his coffee, and feeling much better.

Sir John looked up, and raised his eyebrows a little.

"Doctor Instow spoke to you, my boy," he said gently, and, to the speaker's surprise, his son said coolly—

"Yes, father, I heard him."

"Then why do you not answer?"

"Because he doesn't expect me, father. He knows what I should say."

"Knows?"

"Yes, father; he's only making fun of me. He only said that to make me speak out."

"Then why do you not speak out? If you are so tired, it is excellent advice for you to go and take a good long rest."

"And be fidgeting in that hot berth, thinking about the adventures you are having? It would do me harm instead of good. Bring, me some more toast, Edward."

The doctor threw himself back in his revolving seat at the table, and clapped his hands on his knees.

"Well done, Jack!" he cried. "Bravo, lad! You've got the stuff in you that good strong men are made of, after all. You're quite right. I did want to stir you up and make you speak. Stop in bed all day! Not you."

The captain came in.

"How are you getting on, gentlemen?" he said in his bluff way.

"Nearly ready," said Sir John. "Then you will not go with us to-day?"

"No, sir. Let Bartlett have a turn, and I'll take care of the yacht. One word though. I don't for a moment think you will come across savages, but if you do I should like you to take the lead. You don't want to fight, only to get back safely to the yacht, so make the best retreat you can."

"Of course," said Sir John, and Jack looked from one to the other in an excited way, "I expect the doctor here would like a fight," said the captain with a grim smile.

"I! Why?" cried Doctor Instow, with a surprised look.

"So as to be getting a specimen or two to take home. I know what you naturalists are."

"Oh, pooh! nonsense! absurd!" cried the doctor, taking a good deep draught of the coffee Sir John's man knew so well how to provide. "Doctors want to save life, not to destroy it—clever doctors do; and I'm not such a very bad one, am I, Jack?"

"I can't talk properly with my mouth full," was the reply.

"But this is not breakfast, my boy," said Sir John, smiling.

"He's quite right, sir," said the captain. "Always make your hay while the sun shines, especially when you're travelling."

There was no sign of any light when they went on deck, to find the men in the boats, and the mate waiting with Edward who had slipped up by his side.

"Hullo!" cried the doctor. "You're not going, Ned?"

"Yes, he is, doctor," said Jack quickly. "I want him."

Sir John said nothing, but stepped down into the large boat.

"I'll go in the other," said the doctor.

"You'll come with us?" said the mate to Jack.

"No; I'll go in the little boat," replied the lad; and he followed the doctor, Edward, whose face by the gleam of one of the lanterns was puckered up by a broad smile of satisfaction, entering the gig after him.

"You'll be able to go a bit farther to-day, sir," said the captain at parting. "I'd halt at the best place you can find at mid-day, and have a good meal, rest for a couple of hours, and then make the best of your way back."

Sir John nodded.

"Save the men all you can, Bartlett. You have the sails."

"Yes, sir," cried the mate. Then the oars dropped into the dark water and they rowed away, the lesser boat about a length behind.

They seemed to Jack to have started too early, for it was very dark, and the lanterns they carried in the bows shed a strange light across the smooth water. There was the black forest on their left, and the ghostly-looking reef with its billows on their right, with the dull thunderous roar sounding strangely awe-inspiring, and the boy could not help feeling a sensation of nervousness as he thought of what the consequences would be if they rowed on in the dark to a part of the lagoon where the protecting coral bank came to an end.

"You're very quiet," said the doctor suddenly, from his seat in the stern sheets. "What are you thinking about?"

The boy told him.

"Shouldn't have much chance then, my lad," said the doctor. "But no fear, we should have ample warning long before we came to such a spot. The water of the lagoon would not be like this. Perhaps, though, there is not another opening, for though the waves are always breaking on the outside, the little coral insects are always building on the in. But only think; we must be passing over the most wonderful specimens here, and we can't see a thing. How long is it going to be before the light comes?"

"It's coming now," said Jack, pointing up to his left at a bright golden speck that seemed almost over their heads, and once more they witnessed all the glories of a tropic sunrise, the change from darkness to light being wonderfully quick, and soon after their eyes were aching with the beauties of coast and lagoon.

"Oh, this is tiresome," cried the doctor; "fancy wasting our time hunting for danger when there are such chances for collecting. Look at those birds flying into that grove."

"Yes, and this glorious garden under us. It's so clear that the bottom seems close enough to touch with the hand."

"Look at those fish too. Did you ever see such colours in the sunshine?" cried the doctor.

"There goes a snake," said Jack, "quite a big one; and what's that long shadowy-looking creature?"

"Small shark," said the doctor. "Take notice. Water's tempting for bathing, but it won't do here. There's a shell! Why, Jack, that great oyster must weigh a couple of hundred-weight!"

"What's that?" cried Jack. "Father's pointing to the shore. I see: a lizard. No, it's too big; it must be a crocodile."

"Couldn't be in a bit of an island like this. It is, though. Ah, I see, there's a little river runs up into the land. Look, it's one of the valleys. I wonder the water's so clear. Comes over rocks, I suppose."

"There he goes," cried Jack, for just then the great heavy saurian, which had crawled out at daybreak to have a nap in the warm sun, divined danger, shut its jaws with a loud snap, and rushed clumsily into the water, giving its tail a flourish as it disappeared in a heavy swirl.

"I should have liked his head," said the doctor, "but he may keep it for the present. We'll remember this place and come and look him up another time."

"Is it true that their horny skulls can't be penetrated by a bullet?" asked Jack.

"I should be sorry to trust to it if a man was taking aim at me with a rifle, Jack. Oh no: I dare say if you shot at one and it hit the beast at a very sharp angle it might glance off, but a fair straight shot would go right through one of them. Look at that butterfly—or moth."

"There's something drinking—two somethings—four or five. What are they?"

"Legs and loins of pork, all alive oh!" said the doctor merrily. "Dear me! and we must not fire at them. What a pity! Look at that little fellow. He's just the size for the larder."

"You mustn't speak so loud, doctor," cried Jack, laughing; "the pigs hear what you are plotting against them."

"Seems like it. My word, how they can run!"

"And swim," cried Jack. "I did not see that fellow in the water."

For one had suddenly appeared from behind a rock about a dozen yards from the sandy shore. It was swimming as easily as a dog, in spite of what old proverbs say about pigs and the water, and it was evidently making eager efforts to reach the sands and rush after its companions, which had probably been making a breakfast off shell-fish, and were now disappearing among the trees.

"Ah! look at that," cried the doctor.

For suddenly the pig threw up its head, screaming dismally, and pawing at the air.

"Stupid thing! it could have reached the sands in another half-minute."

"It won't now," said the doctor, reaching back to pick up his double gun.

"Let's row and try and save it from drowning," cried Jack eagerly.

"It isn't drowning," said the doctor quietly. "Look! there it goes."

Still squealing horribly, the unfortunate little animal suddenly seemed to make a dart backward several yards farther from the shore, but with its head getting lower, till the water rose above its ears, and as it still glided farther, less and less was visible, till only its wail-producing snout was above the surface.

"Poor wretch! it must be in a terrible current," cried Jack. "Row, row, row."

The men pulled hard, but the doctor shook his head and laid down his gun, for the pig's snout disappeared with a horrible last gurgling wail.

"Yes, it's in a terrible current," said the doctor, "going down something's throat."

"What!" cried Jack, upon whom the truth now flashed.

"Yes, crocodile or shark has got him, my lad. Another warning not to try and bathe."

"Yes, and to try and kill all the crocodiles and sharks we can."

"Which comes natural to all men," said the doctor.

"See that, Jack?" came from the other boat.

"Yes, father. Horrible."

A soft wind began to fan them as they rounded a well-wooded point, and the men stepped small masts and ran up a couple of lug-sails which carried the boats swiftly gliding along over the hardly rippled water. But the lovely garden below was now blurred and almost invisible, so the attention of all was taken up by the shore along which they coasted, and for hours now they went on past cocoa-nut groves, park-like flat, lovely ravines running upward, and down which tiny rills of water came cascading; past three huge black buttresses of lava, the ends that had cooled in the water of as many streams of fluent stone; and above all, grey, strange, dotted with masses of rock, seamed, scored, and wrinkled, rose from out of the dense forest, which rail up its flanks, the great truncated cone, above whose summit floated a faint grey cloud of smoke or steam—which they could not tell.

But when mid-day arrived they had seen neither hut nor canoe, and in accordance with the captain's instructions they rowed into the mouth of a little river and landed in a lovely shady ravine, whose waters at a couple of hundred yards from the lagoon were completely shaded by the boughs of ancient trees.

Their halting-place was a pool, at whose head the advance of such salt tide as ran up was checked by a huge wall of volcanic rock, down which trickled the bright clear waters of one stream, while another took a clear plunge only a few yards away right into the pool.

"What a place for a lunch!" said Sir John, as the occupants of the two boats now met on shore, and Mr Bartlett placed one of the two keepers from each boat in good places for observation of sea and land, so as to guard against surprise.

Edward was now in his element, and while men went with buckets to get water from the springs by climbing up the side of the huge lava wall, he spread a cloth for the gentlemen's lunch and emptied a flat basket.

The sailors soon selected their spot a dozen yards away, and their preparations were very simple.

"Hold hard a minute," cried Edward to the men as they returned with the buckets filled. "I want one of those. Let's see which is the coldest. Here, Mr Jack, sir, just you come and try this," he cried the next minute, and on the boy approaching eager enough, the man plunged a glass into the first bucket and dipped it full of the most brilliantly clear water possible, and handed it very seriously to his young master.

"Oh, this won't do, Ned," cried the boy; "it isn't cold—why it's hot."

"Hot it is, sir, but just you taste it. I did."

Jack took a pretty good sip and ejected it directly.

"Ugh!" he cried with a wry face. "It's horrible; hot, salt, bitter, filthy, like rotten eggs; and yet it's as clear as crystal."

"Yes, sir, it's about the worst swindle I ever had."

"Here, father—Doctor Instow," cried the boy; and they came up and tried the water in turn, and looked at each other.

"Regular volcanic water," said the doctor. "Why that would be a fortune in England; people would take it and bathe in it, and believe it would cure them of every ill under the sun, from a broken leg up to bilious fever. There's no doubt where that comes from. Look how full it is of gas."

He pointed to a stream of tiny bubbles rising from the bottom of the glass.

"Sea-water ain't it, sir?" said Edward respectfully; "but how did it get up there?"

"Sea-water? no, my man. Beautifully clear, but strongly charged with sulphur, magnesia, soda, and iron. Which spring did it come from?"

"That one which shoots out into the pool, sir," said one of the men.

"And is the other the same?" cried Jack.

"No, sir; cold as ice and quite fresh."

Jack and the doctor climbed up to see the sources of the two springs, finding the hot not many yards from the edge of the rocky wall, where it was bubbling up from a little basin fringed with soft pinky-white stone, while the bottom of the pellucid source, which was too hot for the hand to be plunged in, was ornamented with beautiful crystals of the purest sulphur.

The source of the cold stream of fresh water they did not find, for it came dancing down the dark ravine, which was choked with tree-ferns, creepers, and interlacing boughs laden with the loveliest orchids, and their progress was completely stopped when they had advanced some hundred yards or so.

"The beginning of the curious features of the place," said Sir John as they sat down to their pleasant meal, gazing through an arch of greenery at the sapphire lagoon and the silver foam of the billows on the creamy reef half-a-mile away.

Never did lunch taste more delicious to the rapidly invigorating boy, never was water fresher, sweeter, and cooler than that of which he partook. Then a good long hour's rest was taken as they all lay about listening to the hum of insects, the whistle, twitter, and shrieking of birds; and beneath it all, as it seemed, came the softened bass from the reef.

"What do you say to a start back, Mr Bartlett?" said Sir John at last, as he glanced at his son, who had just risen and gone knife in hand to dislodge a cluster of lovely waxen, creamy orchids from a tree overhanging the pool.

"I think we ought to be going soon, sir," said the mate.

"Here, Jack, my lad, what's the matter?" cried the doctor, springing up, as he saw the lad holding the flowers he had cut at arm's length. "Ah! stand still! Don't move whatever you do."

"Help, help!" shouted Edward. "Snakes! snakes!"

"Down flat, my lads, quick!" cried the mate; and as the men obeyed he pointed out across the lagoon to where a great matting sail came gliding into sight, looking misty and strange as seen through the veil of foam hanging iridescent about the reef, and twice over rising up sufficiently for the long low hull of a great sea-going canoe crowded with men to come into sight.

Chapter Twenty One
An adventure

Jack did not see the canoe, for his attention was taken up by the little serpent which had suddenly flung itself upon his hand, as he disturbed the cluster of flowers, and struck at his arm sharply—twice.

Sharply does not express the way in which the reptile attacked him, for the whole business from its springing, coiling, and striking seemed instantaneous. The effect upon the lad was peculiar. He had man's natural horror of all creatures of the serpent kind, and as he broke off the sweetly-scented bunch of flowers a pang shot through him—a sensation of pain which made him turn cold and wet, while his senses felt exalted, so that sight, smell, hearing, and feeling were magnified or exaggerated in the strangest way, but his muscular power seemed to have failed. His man's cries for help sounded deafening; the fragrant odour of the orchids made him feel faint; the little serpent appeared enormous, and its eyes dazzling, while the cold touch of its scaly body against his bare hand was of some great weight, and when it rapidly compressed his fingers with its folds, to give itself power to strike, and struck twice, the concussion of the lithe neck and jaws felt like two tremendous blows which paralysed him, so that he stood there as if turned to stone, with his arm outstretched staring down at the—as it seemed to him—gigantic head, which glided about over his enormously swollen arm, the sparkling malicious eyes seeming to search into his, and then about his arm for a fresh place at which to venom.

It was in its way beautiful, in its golden-brown and greenish tints, while the back appeared to be shot with violet and steel, as the light which flashed from the glittering sea was thrown up beneath the trees. Jack was so utterly fascinated for the time being that his eyes took in every detail, and he noted how the reptile's tightly-closed mouth resembled a smile of triumph, and thought that the tiny forked tongue which kept on flickering in and out of the orifice in the front part of the jaws mocked at him as the creature laughed silently at his helplessness.

"It has killed me," was the predominant thought in the boy's mind, as he stood there for what seemed to be a long space of time, with Edward shouting for help and calling upon him to act, the words thundering in his ears.

"Throw it off, Mr Jack, sir. Chuck it away. D'ye hear me? Oh, I say, do something, or you'll be stung."

But the lad did not stir, merely remained in the same attitude with his arm outstretched. He was, however, fully conscious of what was going on, and he watched with a feeble kind of interest the action of the man, wondering what he would do.

For Ned, as he grasped his young master's peril, did the most natural thing in the world to begin with, he called loudly for help; but fully grasping the fact that as he was nearest the first help ought to come from him, he dashed to Jack's side.

"Ugh!" he cried angrily, "I can't abear snakes and toads. If I touch him he'll sting me too. Tied himself up in a knot too. Don't try to chuck it off, Mr Jack, the beggar will only be more savage and begin stinging again. If I could only grab him by the neck I could finish him, but he'd be too quick for me. Here, I know. That's right! Stand still, sir."

This last was perfectly unnecessary, for the lad could not have stood more motionless and rigid if he had been carved in marble.

"What a fool I am!" muttered Ned. "Thinking about cutting sticks when there's something ready here to be cut. I don't want a stick."

He whipped his long hunting-knife out of the sheath fitted to his belt, and the light flashed upon the keen-edged new blade which had never yet been used.

"Now then," he said softly, "if I can only get one cut at you, my gentleman, you shan't know where you are to-morrow."

The plan was good, but not easy of performance, for he could not cut straight down at the reptile's neck without injuring Jack's arm, and for a few moments he stood watching and waiting for an opportunity, but none seemed likely to occur, and the serpent still held on by the boy's wrist, and the front of its long, lithe, undulating body kept on gliding about over the brightly-ironed white duck sleeve, the head playing about the hollow of the elbow-joint, turning under the arm, and returning to the top again and again.

"I can't get a cut at him—I can't get a cut at him," muttered Ned; and then a happy thought came: he stretched out the point of the glistening blade toward the serpent's head, till it was a few inches from it.

"I don't like doing it," he muttered fretfully; "it's running risks, and setting a dose myself, but I must—I must;" and he made the blade glitter and flash by agitating his hand.

It had the desired effect, for the head was raised sharply from the lad's arm till it was six or seven inches above it, and the reptile seemed to be attracted for a moment by the bright light flashing from the steel.

Then the head was drawn back sharply, and darted forward as Ned expected, and with a slight jerk from the wrist he flicked the blade from left to right.

"Hah!" he cried joyfully, as the head dropped at his feet, and the long thin body writhed free from the lad's hand and wrist; "a razor couldn't have took it off cleaner. Hurray, Mr Jack! He half killed himself. But don't—don't stand like that. You're not hurt bad, are you?"

"Here, let me look," cried the doctor, who had now climbed up to where they stood, closely followed by Sir John. "Snake, was it?"

"Yes, sir; there's his body tying itself up in knots, and here's his head."

As he spoke, the man stooped down quickly, made a dig with the point of his knife, and transfixed the cut-off portion through the neck just at the back of the skull, and the jaws gaped widely as he held it up in triumph.

"Here, let me see," cried Sir John excitedly. "Yes, look, Instow, the swollen glands at the back of the jaw, and here they are like bits of glass—the poison fangs. Jack, lad, where did it strike you?"

"Strike me?" said the lad feebly, and shuddering slightly, as he stood with his eyes half-closed, and dropped the cluster of orchids.

"Yes; speak out, quick!" cried the doctor, grasping the lad by the arm. "Where are you hurt?"

"Twined round my hand, and bit at my arm twice—just there."

He stood pointing dreamily at the thickest part of his forearm, just where the jacket-sleeve went into wrinkles through the bending of the joint.

"Yes, I see," cried the doctor. "Here, Ned, man, jump down there and get my flask. You'll find it in my coat. A plated one full of ammonia."

Ned leaped in a break-neck way down the lava wall, and the doctor forced his patient into a sitting position and stripped off his jacket. Then he snapped off the wrist button and turned up the shirt-sleeve, to begin examining the white skin for the tiny punctures made by the two bites, while Sir John knelt by him, supporting his son, who looked very white and strange, and as if he were trying to master the sense of horror from which he now suffered.

"See the places?" said Sir John hoarsely.

"No," replied the doctor, shifting his position and raising the arm a little. "The fangs are like needle-points, and make so small a wound. Can't see anything. Whereabouts was it, Jack?"

"Just there," said the lad, speaking more decisively; and he laid his left finger on his arm. "Two sharp blows."

"And a keen pricking sensation each time?" said the doctor, looking curiously at his patient.

"No; I did not feel anything but the blows."

"Here's the silver bottle, sir," panted Ned.

"Hold it," said the doctor. Then to Jack, "Did the snake strike at you anywhere else?"

"No."

"Pray, pray give him something," cried Sir John impatiently; "the poison runs through the veins so quickly."

"Yes," said the doctor quietly, as he wrinkled up his forehead, and, dropping the boy's arm, he caught the jacket from where it lay.

"Nothing here," he muttered. "Pish! Wrong sleeve."

He hastily took the other, and turned the sleeve up to the light.

"Hah!" he cried; "here we are. Look, Meadows!"

"Never mind the jacket, man," cried Sir John passionately.

"Why not?" said the doctor coolly. "Nothing the matter with the lad. Touch of nerves. Horribly startling for him. See this?"

He held up the sleeve, and there upon the puckered part were two almost imperceptible yellowish stains, in each case upon the raised folds.

(Half a page of text missing here.)

"I couldn't help it," said Jack.

"Of course you couldn't," said the doctor.

"But father thinks that I was a dreadful coward."

"Then he ought to know better," said the doctor quickly. "Nothing to be ashamed of, my lad. Imagination's a queer thing. I once fainted because I thought I had cut myself, while I was skinning a dog which had been poisoned. I was a student then, and knew the dangers of wounds from a poisoned knife; and, by the way, we must take care of the wounds from poisoned arrows. Well, when I washed my hand there wasn't a scratch. You couldn't help it, Jack. Any man might be seized like that after seeing Death make two darts at him and feeling him strike."

(Half a page of text missing here.)

"Is any one hurt?" said a voice then; and Mr Bartlett's head appeared above the edge of the lava wall.

"No; all right. Only an alarm, and a narrow escape. How about the savages?"

"They're gone in the direction of the yacht, gentlemen, and we must get back as quickly as we can."

"Ah, look! look!" cried Ned excitedly, as he pointed out to sea; "there's a canoe—two canoes—three."

They followed the direction of his pointing finger, and saw plainly enough three long, low vessels full of men gliding by, with their matting sails glistening in the sun, and not two miles out from where they stood.

"Worse and worse," said the mate. "We must get back to the yacht, gentlemen."

"Of course," said Sir John, drawing a deep breath. "Why, there must be a hundred men in those canoes."

"Quite that, sir, I'm afraid," replied the mate. "Quick, please. It will be terrible if they attack the captain while he is so short-handed."

"But he has the big guns, and the men are well-trained," said the doctor, as they hurried down to the boats.

"What is the use of them, sir, when a crowd of reckless savages are swarming over the sides? He is lying at anchor too, and the yacht is made helpless."

The men were soon in their places, pulling a long, steady stroke, and thinking nothing of the hot sunshine.

"It is of no use to try and hide ourselves," said the mate, "for it is a race between us who shall get there first."

"But they can't know the yacht is there," said Sir John.

"Perhaps not, sir; but they will soon sight us, and then run for the opening in the reef, if they were not already going there."

"Well, there's one advantage on our side," said the doctor; "they can't attack us till they get through the reef, so we're safe till then."

"Yes, sir," said the mate bitterly; "but I was thinking of the captain, and his anxiety, alone there."

"Yes, of course," said Sir John; and he looked at the mate when he could do so unobserved; and it seemed to Jack that he thought more highly of Mr Bartlett than ever.

They had been rowing abreast, with the waters of the lagoon perfectly smooth; but as they began to round one of the huge buttresses of lava which had run down into the lake, they saw that the water all beyond was disturbed by a breeze.

The mate started up and began to give his orders directly. The mast in the bigger boat was stepped, the sail hoisted, and he shouted to one of the men to throw a line from the bows of Jack's boat, to make fast to their stern.

"We can take you in tow, doctor," he said, with the men still rowing and the sail flapping; then a little spar was set up from the stern, and a triangular sail hoisted from the bows to the mast in front.

"Four men in here," cried the mate; "unless you two gentlemen would like to come."

"No; we'll stay here," said the doctor. "Eh, Jack?"

"Yes; we'll stay."

"You'll manage better with men who can work, we shall be in the way."

"I want them for ballast to steady us with all this sail up," said the mate, smiling; and without any pause the second boat was drawn close up astern, four men crept into the leader, and the rope was allowed to run out again.

"Think we're going to have a fight, Mr Jack?" whispered Ned, as the doctor sat forward trying to make out the canoes through the sparkling cloud of spray here about a mile away; "It seems like it, Ned; but I hope not."

"You hope not, sir?"

"Of course."

"Oh, well then, I needn't mind saying I hope not too. I never was anything in that line, sir, even when I was a boy."

"What difference does that make?"

"Difference, sir? Oh, all the difference. Men can fight, of course; but if I was a king, and wanted to have a good army, I'd make it of boys."

Jack stared at him, and in spite of the peril of their position, felt disposed to smile.

"Why?" he said at last.

"Because they can fight so. They're not so big and strong; but then they're not so easily frightened. They're always ready for a set-to, and 'cepting where there's snakes in the way, they never think of danger, or being hurt. And when they are hurt, the more they feel it, the more they go, just like horses or donkeys."

"Excepting in the case of snakes," said Jack bitterly.

"Oh, don't you mind about that, sir. I was as scared as you were, I can tell you. I remember when I was a boy I wasn't good at fighting, and I used to get what we used to call the coward's blow, and that was the rum part of it."

Jack stared.

"Ah, you don't understand that, sir. But it was rum. You see it was like this; t'other chap as was crowing over me because I wouldn't fight, would give me an out-and-out good whack for the coward's blow, and then he wished he hadn't."

"Why?" asked Jack, after a glance at the doctor, who was still in the bows.

"Because it hurt me, and made me wild. And then I used to go at him and give him a good licking. That's what I was when a boy, sir, and I am just the same now; I don't feel at all like fighting, and, coward or no coward, I won't fight if I can help it; but if any one hurts me, or begins to shoot at us, I think I shall get trying what I can do. But you see it won't be fist-fists."

"No," said Jack thoughtfully; "it will not be fists."

"Hi! look out!" shouted Ned. "You'll be over."

For a sudden puff of wind had caught the boat in front, and she heeled over so much with the large spread of sail that the water began to creep in over the leeward side. But at a word from the mate half-a-dozen men shifted their positions to windward, and there were two or three inches clear once more, as the boat with her three sails well-filled began to rush through the water.

"And now they're goin' to take us under," said Ned, nervously seizing the side with one hand. "My word, we are beginning to go."

"Yes; this is different to rowing," cried the doctor, as their boat danced about and ran swiftly through the disturbed water left by their companion. "But, unfortunately, the wind will help the canoes as much as it helps us."

"But if it does not help them more, we shall be up to the yacht first."

"There's another side to that, Jack," said the doctor; "suppose they sail faster than we do. What then?"

This was unanswerable, and they sat back in the boat, running through the water with a little wave ever-widening on either side.

"I hope the painter won't give way," said the doctor at last, "and that they will not leave us behind."

"They'd miss us directly," said Jack. "Their boat would go so much faster."

"Couldn't go faster than she is. Why, Jack, it must be a clever canoe that can beat us."

"Goes too fast to please me," whispered the man at the first opportunity. "Strikes me, Mr Jack, that one of these times when they swing over to the left so they'll drag us under, so that our boat will fill and go down; and if we do, what about that there pig?"

"What pig?" said Jack wonderingly.

"Why, you know, sir, close in there as we came along. If there's things in this water that can pull down pigs, won't they be likely to pull down us?"

"There's plenty of real trouble to think about," said Jack quietly, "without our trying to make out imaginary ones. The boat will not fill."

"Eh? what's that?" said the doctor; "this boat fill? Oh no; she rides over the water like a cork. Can't see anything of the enemy, Jack; the spray along the reef makes a regular curtain, and shuts off everything. I hope it hides us well from our black friends, for I don't want to get into a row of that kind. Well, Ned, if it comes to the worst, do you think you can manage a gun?"

"Cleaned Sir John's guns often enough, sir."

"Yes, but can you shoot?"

"That means holding the gun straight, sir, and pulling the trigger. Oh yes, sir; I can do that."

"That isn't shooting: you have to hit."

"So I suppose, sir; but some of the governor's friends, who come down in September and October, go shooting in his preserves and over the farms, but they don't always hit anything."

"But you will try if we want you, eh?"

"Yes, sir, if the governor orders me. And what about a cutlass? Can you handle that, do you think?"

"Don't see why not, sir. I'm pretty handy with a carving-knife, both with meat and on the knifeboard."

"Well," said the doctor gravely, "I hope we shall not have to come to anything of that kind, for all our sakes."

"How long will it take us to get back?" said Jack, after a silence, during which the thoughts of the danger seemed to be chased away by the beauty of the shore along which they glided.

"Hours yet," said the doctor. "This wind will not last. If it would, we might be there before the canoes."

Very few greetings passed between the two boats, for every one engaged in the race seemed in deadly earnest. There was the possibility of the people proving to be friendly, but as in all probability these great sea-going canoes belonged to a fighting fleet upon some raiding expedition, the hope in the direction of peace was not great.

About half of the way had been accomplished, when, as Jack sat watching the foaming waves break upon the reef, he caught sight of something misty and weird-looking apparently just on the other side, but it was too undefined for its nature to be made out.

He pointed it out to the doctor, who gave his opinion directly.

"One of the canoes," he said. "That's good, Jack. It shows that they have not distanced us."

A hail from the mate told them that they too had sighted the canoe from the boat in front; but though they gazed long and watchfully, they saw no more.

Not long after the wind dropped suddenly, came again, and then fell altogether, the appearances being so marked that the mate had the sails lowered, and stowed after the oars had been going for some time, and now they made out from the boat astern that Mr Bartlett had divided his crew into two watches, one rowing hard while the other rested.

It was all plain enough to those astern that everything was admirably arranged, so that the well-drilled men shifted their places without any confusion or difference in the speed of the boat, the men changing one at a time.

And so the afternoon wore on.

"We shall be no sooner," said Jack at last. "In an hour it will be dark."

"Yes," said the doctor with a sigh. "It would not matter if the blacks are not there first, but the worst of it is, as soon as it's dusk the captain will be lighting up that firework business for a beacon, and that will show the canoes where to steer."

It proved just as he said. The darkness came on with awful rapidity as soon as the sun disappeared beneath the waves, all searching the edge of the reef most anxiously during the last rays which flooded the sea; but in vain; and then for a full hour they rowed steadily on, guided by the gleaming of the fireflies against the black darkness ashore, but all at once a bright star shone out.

"There she is!" cried Jack excitedly. "Look how Mr Bartlett has turned the boat's head straight for the light."

"Yes; we shall follow the bright path straight away now," said the doctor.

"How are you getting on there?" came from the boat in front. "Hungry, or will you wait till we get on board?"

"We'll wait, father," shouted Jack.

"Yes. Only half-an-hour now. Mr Bartlett thinks we've distanced the canoes."

They were soon to learn for certain, as they followed the bright path of light which minute by minute grew clearer, till they could see as it were right up to the anchored yacht.

"Shall we hail the captain?" said Jack.

He had hardly spoken when he felt a jar run through the boat, and found that the towing-line had been hauled upon till the prow of the second boat touched the stern of the first.

"Hist there!" said the mate. "Perfect silence, please. We must creep alongside so as to give warning. There must be no hailing. This is the most dangerous time."

"How far are we away?" said the doctor in a whisper.

"About five hundred yards."

"How is it the oars go so quietly now?" whispered Jack.

"Muffled, and the men are just dipping them, so as to keep a fair way on."

The next two or three minutes were passed in silence, Jack's boat having once more dropped astern to the full length of the rope.

The lad had risen to stand up and watch the line of light extending from them right up to the source of the rays ahead, and from his position he could look right over the foremost boat.

"How deceptive it is!" he thought. "One can hardly tell how near we are, and—ah!—"

"What is it, boy?" whispered the doctor.

For answer Jack pointed right ahead to where something dark could be seen crossing the line of sight.

"One of the canoes," said the doctor quickly. "We shall be right aboard her."

He crept forward, but Jack forestalled him, and was hauling in the line till they wore close up.

"Mr Bartlett—father!"

"Yes; what is it?"

"You are rowing right into one of the canoes."

Chapter Twenty Two
A sharp lesson

The men ceased rowing, and Jack sat with his heart beating painfully, his mind full of memories of accounts he had read concerning encounters with savages, and wounds inflicted by poisoned arrows and spears.

As he sat in the intense darkness, watching the brilliant star-like lamp, it all seemed to be dreamlike and impossible that he should be there—he who so short a time before was leading that quiet student life in the study or library at home.

But there was the black canoe gliding by the light, and like so many silhouettes the dark, clearly-defined figures of the savages busy paddling.

No, it could not be the canoe he had seen first, it must be another, and the next minute he had proof thereof, in this canoe passing across the disk of radiant light, leaving it for a few moments clear, and then another appeared, and he watched the little black silhouettes steadily moving as they paddled, till the long boat had gone by, when another appeared and passed.

"Give way!" came in a whisper; then the oars dipped silently, and they began to move onward.

"We must make a dash for it, or they will surprise the yacht," whispered the mate. Then he leaned over backward, and the exciting words came— "Astern there. Guns ready and load."

A faint whisper or two from the mate's boat told that the men not rowing had received a similar command, and Jack, as he thrust a couple of cartridges into the breech of his gun, felt that the canoes would be paddling round the yacht, and have reached the other side by the time they were alongside.

"Are we not going to shout and alarm Captain Bradleigh?" whispered Jack to the doctor.

"No; sit still," said that gentleman sternly. "He and your father are the leaders. We have only to obey. Don't fire till you receive orders."

A low deep sigh came from Ned, but it was accompanied by a faint "click—click; click—click."

"Both barrels at full cock," thought the lad. "But how horrible to have to fire at any one, even if he is black."

But all the same, horrible or no, the lad cocked both locks of his own piece, and felt the flap of his cartridge satchel to try whether everything was handy if he had to reload; and just then, as they glided silently along in the full glare of the great artificial star, a feeling of angry resentment ran through him, and he said half aloud—

"Serve them right. Why can't they leave us alone?"

"And so say all of us, Mr Jack," whispered Ned, startling him he addressed, for he was not aware that his words were heard.

The only sounds to be heard now were the regular heavy boom of the breakers on the reef—a sound so deep and constant that it had already begun to count as nothing, and curiously enough did not seem to interfere with their hearing anything else, acting as it did like the deep bass in an orchestra or great organ, and making the lighter, higher-pitched notes more clear—and the light soft dip of the boat's oars as the men silently pulled home.

Then, all at once, as Jack strained his ears to catch the paddling of the canoes, the deep voice of Captain Bradleigh rang out as if from the other side of the yacht.

"Ahoy! What boat's that?"

Then in the midst of a dead silence there was a quick flash, and Jack held his breath, expecting to hear the report of a gun, but his eyes conveyed the meaning of the flash, not his ears.

The darkness was profound, for the light from the great star had been shut off in their direction, and directly after the shape of the graceful yacht stood out clearly, every spar and rope defined against a softly diffused halo as the star was made to perform the duties of a search-light, sweeping the lagoon beyond and showing plainly the long low shapes of four great canoes, each with its row of men, and about a quarter of a mile away.

Then all was black as pitch.

"Now for it, my lads," whispered the mate. "Pull with all your might."

The men made the water hiss as they drew hard at the long tough ash blades, and above this sound they could hear the hurry and rattle of something going on aboard the yacht. Quick short orders were issued; then Captain Bradleigh's voice was heard again.

"Ahoy there! Sir John!"

"Right. Here we are."

What the captain said in reply was confined to the word "Thank—" The rest was smothered by a sharp crash, and a check which took the small boat in which Jack sat sharply up against the other's stern.

The crash was followed by a savage yelling and splashing; and as they went on again directly, the men pulling with all their might. Jack was conscious of struggling and blows, and he grasped the fact that they had rowed at full speed against the stern or bows of another canoe which had been invisible in the darkness, and that some of her occupants had seized the men's oars on the port side. The blows, he found, were delivered by their men to shake off their adversaries, some of whom he dimly saw struggling in the water as the boat passed on; and, unable to control himself, Jack leaned over and caught at a hand just within his reach, the fingers closing upon his in a fierce grasp and nearly jerking him out of the boat, a fate from which he was saved by Ned, who seized him round the middle and dragged him back.

"Got him?" cried the doctor excitedly.

"You should have said 'Got it,' sir," grumbled the man, with a drawing-in of his breath as if in pain. "But he's all right. I wish I was."

"What's the manner, man?"

"Him a-holding his gun like that. Oh, my crikey! What a whack I got on the cheek!"

"What an escape, Jack!" cried the doctor.

"But the poor wretch was drowning. Hark! their canoe must be sinking—men struggling in the water."

"Never mind: let them," said the doctor. "They can swim like seals, and their canoe will float like a log."

"But the sharks!" panted Jack.

"We can't stop to think of them," said the doctor.—"Are you all right there?"

"Yes, and alongside," cried the mate, and there was the rattle of the oars being laid in.

"Thank heaven!" cried the captain from the deck, as both boats ground against the yacht's side. "Quick, all aboard! Now then, hook on those falls and up with the boats."

The boats were run up to the davits in regular man-o'-war fashion, the gangway was closed, and the men who were busy went on rigging up a stout net about six feet wide along from stanchion to stanchion, and shroud to shroud, while, after a word or two of congratulation upon their safe return, the captain went on giving his orders.

"Nearly surprised us, Sir John," he said; "and it would have been awkward with us so weak-handed. All go to your stations; they may try to board at any time. Here, Mr Jack, you'd better go below."

"What for?" said Jack quietly.

"To be out of danger, sir," said the captain angrily. "Quick, sir, I have no time to be polite."

"Are you going below, father?" said the lad.

"I? No, my boy. I shall stay."

"So shall I," said Jack; and a voice whispered at his ear—

"That's it, Mr Jack. You stop; we don't want to be out of the fun."

Sir John was silent, and stood behind the captain, who looked out ahead at the canoes, shown up clearly by the search-light as four lay in a cluster together, their occupants watching the light as if puzzled.

The next moment the light was sent sweeping round to the other side; and there, plainly seen, was the fifth canoe, its gunwale level with the surface, and only its high stem and prow standing well above the water. And there clinging to her on either side were her crew, paddling away by striking the water, and sending the injured vessel slowly along, so as to cross the yacht's stem, and take her to where the rest lay waiting, as if their leaders were uncertain what to do.

"There, you see, Jack," said the doctor. "But what a crash! our speed saved us from being stove in, just as the tallow candle is said to pass through a deal board when fired from a gun."

"Do you think they are all there?" said Jack.

"Oh yes, they would help one another; but I don't think we should have been all here if they had had their way with us."

They stood watching the damaged canoe till it had passed the yacht, and then the light was suddenly turned so that it lit up the four canoes, in which there might have been close upon a couple of hundred men; and to Jack's horror he saw that they had altered their position, and were prow toward them in regular battle array, and only about forty or fifty feet apart.

"Does that mean coming on?" said Jack, and he thought of their own weakness.

"I expect so," replied the doctor; "but I dare say a few volleys of small shot will give them such a sickening of the white man's magic that they will turn tail. Why look at that."

The light was now turned on to its full power, and the man who managed it kept on changing its position so that it blazed right upon each canoe in turn, with a singular result, each doing the same. For, as if startled by the light, the occupants began to paddle backward in a hurried way, till the beam was shifted, when they ceased.

"Why they're regularly scared at the lamp, captain," cried Doctor Instow.

"Yes, that's so, sir," replied the captain; "and it looks as if they knew that their deeds were evil, shunning the light in this fashion; but it can't last. They'll soon get used to it; and if they can only be scared until I get the steam up I don't mind."

"Are you getting the steam up, captain?" asked Jack eagerly.

"Yes; can't you hear the fires going?"

Jack had been too much excited to notice any one special thing in the preparations to resist an attack, but he was now conscious of a dull humming sound which he knew was the softened roar of the furnaces.

"The yacht's like a useless log lying here becalmed," continued the captain; "but once I have a good head of steam on she becomes a living creature, and I can do anything with her—and with them if they don't behave themselves. I don't want to run down and drown any of the poor wretches; but if they attack us they must take the consequences."

"Poor ignorant creatures!" said Sir John. "I suppose they don't know our power."

"That's it," replied Captain Bradleigh. "The more savage a man is, according to my experience, the more vain and conceited he seems. He believes in himself thoroughly, for he is generally vigorous and active as a wild beast, and looks down on an ordinary white man with a kind of scorn. You would be surprised, Mr Jack, what a number of lessons have to be given him before he will believe in our machinery and weapons of war, unless you can appeal to his brain by making him believe that they are what the Scotchman calls uncanny. If you once find him thinking that steam, or the gun which kills a man a couple of hundred yards away, is the result of fetish or the bunyip, or a diabolical spirit, he's the greatest coward under the sun. Give them another brush over with the light, my lad."

The man in charge of the great star sent the rays sweeping over the sea, once more making the dazzling beam play here and there at his will, upon first one and then another of the blacks in the canoes, with the result that they were all thrown into a state of confusion, each as the light dazzled his eyes ducking down right into the bottom of his vessel, or trying to bend behind his neighbour and to escape from the terrible blazing eye, which seemed to go through him.

"That's right," said Sir John.

"Now if we can only keep them off for an hour longer I don't care. Give me that time and I'll chase them all out to sea before they know where they are, or send them to the bottom if they don't mind."

The suppressed excitement on board the yacht was tremendous, but the men worked without a word. The thick net was strongly fixed so as to act as a barrier to the enemy who might try to climb on board. The yacht's guns were cast loose, well shotted with small grape, and cartridges were ready for use. The men whose duty it was to repel attempts at boarding stood ready with their sword-bayonets at the ends of their rifles, and the engineer and firemen were below doing their best to get up steam, the humming noise going merrily on the while.

The captain paced the deck very calmly and quietly, night-glass in hand, with which he watched the movements of the savages, and handed it more than once to Jack to take a look through at the enemy, making remarks the while about their bows and arrows, spears and war-clubs, while the doctor and Sir John stood aft, well-armed and ready for any emergency, Sir John's servant being close at hand.

"Don't seem quite the thing, Jack," said the doctor, as the lad came along the dark deck to where they stood.

"What doesn't seem quite the right thing?" said the boy, glad to have an opportunity to talk and have some cessation of the terrible strain which kept his excited nerves at the highest pitch of tension.

"Why, the standing here with a double gun loaded with slugs, ready to pepper the niggers. I'm a curer, not a killer."

"We must defend ourselves," said Jack.

"You must. I ought to be below turning the cabin or the steward's place into an operating room, getting my instruments, tourniquets, silk, and bandages ready."

"Oh, don't talk like that!" cried the lad with a shudder.

"Why not? Doctors must prepare for the worst."

"Hope we shall have no worst, Doctor Instow," said the captain, coming up. "If I could only get the signal that steam was ready! We are just swinging by the head to the buoyed cable, so that I can slip at any moment. Halloo! What's going on now?" He ran forward, gave a word to the man in charge, and the beam of light swept round the yacht and back; but there was no fresh danger coming up, and the shouting and yelling which had taken the captain forward evidently proceeded from the two central canoes.

"Why, where's the sunken one?" said Jack, as he shaded his eyes and peered forward.

"They've floated her right astern of them," replied the captain, "half-an-hour ago, and the crew are distributed amongst the four. But I don't quite make out what they were shouting about. Why— Steady there, my lads. You at the guns, be ready. The canoes are coming on. Oh!" he added to himself, "if there were only a capful of wind!"

But there was not a breath of air, as a loud yell from one voice was heard, and followed by a burst from the whole party. Then the paddles were plunged into the water on both sides, making it foam and sparkle in the bright light of the star, the canoes began to move very slowly, and Captain Bradleigh turned to the yacht's owner—

"They mean mischief, sir. I'm afraid we must fire."

"Only as a last resource," said Sir John.

"If we wait for a last resource, sir," said the captain sternly, "it may be too late. My lads could sink one of the canoes now, and that might check the advance. The guns are useless if we let them come to close quarters."

"But I am dreadfully averse to what may prove wholesale slaughter," said Sir John.

"So am I, sir," said the captain dryly. "It is for you to decide."

Jack stood quivering with excitement, and wondered what Sir John would say. But he said nothing, for all at once, as the canoes were coming on faster and faster in the bright light shed by the star, and the little crews of the two bright guns laid them ready for the shots they expected to hear ordered from moment to moment, the strange silence on board was broken by the clear loud *ting* of a hammer upon a gong close to where the principals stood.

"At last!" cried the captain; and before Jack could utter the question upon his lips as to what that stroke meant, order after order was delivered in quick succession.

At the first the cable was slipped. At the second, the star, which was vividly lighting up the approaching canoes, suddenly went out, leaving everything in darkness, for there was not another light visible on board. And at the third, a peculiar vibration made the slight yacht quiver from stem to stern, for the engine was in motion under a good head of steam, and the propeller revolved slowly in reverse, so that the yacht moved astern as fast as the canoes approached.

This went on for a few minutes, with captain and mate standing by the wheel, and the former suddenly turned to Sir John.

"I can't keep this up in the dark, sir," he said. "Perhaps we had better give them a shot or two."

"Why not keep on retreating?"

"Because at any moment we may retreat on to a sharp coral rock, and be at their mercy."

"Try everything first."

"I will, sir," said the captain; and suddenly changing his tactics, the order was given, the light flashed out again, and the canoes were made out four times the distance away, the men paddling with all their might, but stopping instantly in utter astonishment, for they were in perfect ignorance of the distance having been put between them, all being invisible in the darkness which followed the shutting off of the light.

There was another yell now, and plunging their paddles in again, the water once more flashed and foamed in the brilliant light.

Then there was a stroke on the engine-room gong down below, and the propeller began to revolve; two more strokes, directly after, another three, and the yacht gathered more and more way till she was rushing on full speed ahead, her light, like a brilliant star, hiding everything behind her, and apparently just above the surface of the water, bearing rapidly down for the centre of the little fleet of canoes.

On she went, and as she neared the rate at which the paddles were used increased in speed too, but it was to get out of the way, for the steersmen turned off to starboard and port, and though the slightest turn of the wheel would have sent the *Silver Star* crashing through either of the canoes the captain had chosen to select, she was steered straight through the little fleet till she was three or four hundred yards astern, and the canoes were invisible in the darkness. Then by a clever manoeuvre she was swung round in very little more than her own length, the light which had been shut off as soon as they passed being opened upon the enemy again, and the occupants of the deck saw the two pairs of canoes now lying waiting as if undecided.

Once more the order to go on full speed rang out, and the yacht was steered for the nearest canoe.

No movement was made at first, but the moment the enemy made out that the light was rushing silently at them again, they uttered a wild shout of horror and dismay and began to paddle as hard as they could for the opening in the reef, to escape from the fiery star that had dropped from the heavens and was now chasing them to burn them up.

Ignorance and fear went hand in hand, for there was the dazzling star but nothing more to be seen. There might have been no yacht in existence for all they could tell. It was enough that the fiery light like a great eye was fixed upon them in full pursuit, and away they went, faster probably than canoes ever travelled before, till the dark portion was reached where there were no breakers, and the leading canoe rushed out, followed by the others, and away to sea, horror-stricken at the great mystery they had seen, and in no wise lightened by the fact that the star suddenly disappeared as the last canoe dashed out from the lagoon.

"I think that has startled them," said the captain, as he had the light shut off and gave the order for the yacht to go slowly astern, as he made, as well as the darkness would allow, for their old quarters, but did not reach them, it being more prudent to drop another anchor at once.

No lights were shown and the strictest watch was kept, when the gentlemen went below to their late dinner, and discussed over it the probabilities of a return of the enemy.

"No, you won't receive another visit from them in the dark, gentlemen," said Captain Bradleigh merrily. "The star they saw will be talked about among them for years. That big light must have been a scare; but I expect we shall have them again by daylight, for this yacht would be a prize worth having. But we shall see."

"Well," said the doctor, "I should think that the maker of that light would be surprised if he knew to what purpose it was put."

"Yes," said the captain, "I should say it is the first time an illuminated figure-head was used to scare a war-party of blacks."

"What about to-night, Captain Bradleigh?" said Jack anxiously.

"Well, if I were you, sir, I should go to bed and have a good long sleep."

"Oh, impossible," cried the lad; "I could not close my eyes for feeling that the blacks were come back."

"Try, sir," said the captain; and when the others went to lie down, on the captain's assurance that steam would be still on and the strictest watch would be kept, Jack lay down to try.

But he did not try, he had no time. Wearied out with the dangers of the day, he laid his head on his pillow, after placing a double gun and loaded revolver close to the bed's head, and just closed his eyes.

They did not open again till Ned stood there and announced that it was "some bells," and that it was time to rise.

"How many, Ned?" said Jack sleepily.

"Oh, I dunno, sir, only that it answers to seven o'clock."

"And the savages?" cried Jack excitedly.

"Nowhere in sight, sir; but they've left the broken canoe as a present for you. It's floating close in to the sands where we made our start the day before yesterday. Lovely morning, sir, but I wish the neighbours hadn't been quite so friendly and wanted to come and see how we were getting on."

Chapter Twenty Three
The use of the lance

Edward was right. There, a few hundred yards from the yacht, and close in shore, lay the great canoe; but not floating, for she was aground, with the water lapping over her, and only the prow and raised stern standing above the surface.

Jack had a good look at the vessel through his glass, and then turned to watch the proceedings going on, just as Captain Bradleigh came up to him.

"Well, squire!" he cried, "that was a bit of a scare for us."

"Yes; it was horrible. But are they quite gone?"

"We can't make out any signs of them from the mast-head; but as they know we're here, they may set over their fright and come back."

"Why, we're steaming," said Jack in surprise.

"We are, my lad. This is just the time when steam is useful; it helps me to run back gently to our old moorings; and as soon as Sir John comes up, I'm going to propose that we take a run right round the island from outside the reef, so as to make sure that the blacks have no village here."

Directly after that the yacht hooked up the tub which buoyed the cable, and they swung in their old moorings.

"Now then," said the captain, "I'm going to have a look at that canoe; will you come with me?"

"Of course," cried Jack.

"Get your gun and cartridges then. It will not do to go unarmed anywhere now we have found that there is an enemy."

Jack fetched his double gun, wondering whether he would ever have occasion to use it, and on returning to the deck he found the captain examining the stem of the cutter, now hanging from the davits.

"Look here, Squire Meadows," he said, "this is a specimen of the value of good things. Now if this had been a common, cheaply-made boat her planks would have been started, and a lot of carpenter's work wanted before she would have been any use. As it is, she will want a bit of varnish there, and a few taps of the hammer where the copper covers the front of the keel. You came a pretty good crash into that canoe, I suppose?"

"I was not in the boat; but they seemed to."

"I suppose so. Well, come and jump in."

He led the way to where Lenny was seated in the dinghy, and they stepped down, and were rowed by the man toward the submerged canoe.

"Keep a sharp look-out along the edge of the trees," said the captain quietly. "I don't think any one can have landed; but there is no harm in being safe."

Jack began sweeping the green edge just beyond the golden sands, but his attention was taken off by the captain as they approached the canoe.

"Look at the brutes," he said, pointing. "Half-a-dozen of them under her."

Jack looked at him in horror.

"There, you can see their dusky bodies against the sand."

"I thought they all escaped by swimming and hanging on to her," he said a little huskily.

"Escaped by swimming?" replied the captain wonderingly. "What are you talking about?"

"The savages."

"Oh!" cried the captain, bursting into a hearty laugh, to the boy's great disgust, "I see. Well, I meant the savages too, but a different sort. Look down there."

"I don't care to!" cried Jack hoarsely. "Perhaps it is cowardly; but I don't want to satisfy a morbid curiosity by gazing down at the dead bodies of my fellow-creatures."

"Rather fine language, young gentleman," said the captain, patting him on the shoulder; "but I like the sentiment all the same, and I should not have drawn your attention to them if it had been what you thought. The bodies I mean are those of half-a-dozen sharks. There they are."

"Oh, I beg your pardon, Captain Bradleigh!" cried Jack. "How stupid of me!"

"Nothing to ask pardon for, sir," said the captain, smiling. "See them?— Hold hard, Lenny."

"Yes; quite plainly now. Six. How shadowy they look! Not very big though, are they?"

"Plenty big enough to tear a man to pieces. Why, that one's a good nine feet long, and there isn't one under six, I should say. But isn't it strange how they seem to smell out danger? You know how they'll follow a ship? Well, these brutes must have been following the canoes, expecting to get something, and this one being wrecked, they're waiting by it as if they were ready for a grab at some poor wretch."

"How horrible!"

"Ay, my lad, it is. I'm as bad as any of the sailors. Of course it's the brutes' nature; but I feel a thorough satisfaction when one is caught and killed; and if it was not that I don't want to have any firing just now, I'd go back and make some kind of a dummy with a ship's fender and some old clothes, and we'd pitch it overboard. It would tempt them to come at it, and we'd put in ball-cartridge and try a bit of shooting, and finish off this lot."

"I wish you would," cried Jack eagerly.

"Well, we'll see after breakfast."

Jack took up his gun and cocked it as he gazed down at the long, lithe creatures lying perfectly motionless beneath the injured canoe.

"No, no; don't fire!"

"Not unless I'm obliged," said Jack, who looked excited. "This boat is so small and slight, I thought that perhaps they might attack us."

"Oh no; they will not do that. Scull round her bows, Lenny; I want to see where the cutter struck her."

The man obeyed, and there about twenty feet from the prow, seen perfectly through the clear water, was a large gap where the cutter had acted up to her name, and gone right through the side, completely disabling the barbarian craft.

"Ah, shows the strength of our boats," said the captain. "Fine canoe, too. Perhaps they'll come after her, and tow her away to mend her. Takes them too long to make such a canoe as that to give her up easily. Humph! a good sixty feet long. That must have been a fine tree before it was cut down."

"Was that made out of one tree?"

"Yes; all the bottom part. They cut one down, and hollow it out by burning and chopping, and then they raise the sides, and bows, and stern by pegging and lashing on planks. There, you can see the rattan cane they lash the planks on with. Look how the holes are plugged and filled up with gum. It's rough, but good, strong work; and it's wonderful what voyages they make from island to island in a canoe like that."

"Look!" said Jack excitedly, "there's one of the sharks rising."

"Yes," said the captain coolly. "Give me the little boat-hook, my lad."

Lenny smiled grimly as he passed the little pole from where it lay.

"Like to have a prod at him?" said the captain.

Jack hesitated a moment, and then said, "Yes."

The captain nodded approval, but did not hand the boat-hook.

"Better let me," he said. "You shall have a turn with a lance, first chance. Look, here he comes. Wonderful how these things can move through the water. You can't see him moving a fin, but he is rising slowly, and when he likes he can dart through like an arrow. One lash with the powerful tail sends the brutes a long way. I believe he is rising now from some management of the air-bladder. Swells himself out and makes himself lighter."

Jack made no reply, for he was half fascinated, as he gazed down into the water, by the way in which, after passing under the canoe, the shark gradually and almost imperceptibly rose, with its head toward them, the sharply-rounded snout projecting over and completely hiding the savagely-armed jaws.

"Sit fast and don't move," said the captain, poising the little boat-hook; "he is sure to lash out, but it will be behind, and can't touch the boat."

Only a few moments passed, but expectation made them seem minutes, during which the shark's head came nearer and nearer, and its shadow cast by the sun was perfectly plain on the sands a few feet below.

Then with all his force the captain drove the pole down; the aim was good, for the next instant there was a tremendous swirl in the water, the long, heterocercal tail, through which the creature's spine was continued to the end of the upper lobe, rose above the surface, and was brought down with a tremendous blow which raised a shower, and at the same time Captain Bradleigh's arms were dragged lower and lower, till he loosened his hold, and the pole of the boat-hook disappeared.

"I didn't mean that, Mr Jack!" he cried, laughing, as the boat danced up and down, and the lad sat waiting to fire if the need arose. "My word, what a tug! Enough to jerk a man's arms out of the sockets."

"Will it attack us?" said Jack.

"Not he. Gone to get rid of that thing sticking in his head. No; got rid of it directly. Lucky for him. I dare say if it had stopped there his beloved brothers and sisters would have been at him for a cannibal feast."

For about twenty yards away the handle of the boat-hook suddenly shot above the surface, and floated, bobbing gently up and down like a huge quill float, the metal on the end weighting it sufficiently to keep it nearly upright.

A touch or two with the oars sent the dinghy within reach, and the boat-hook was recovered, but with its gun-metal head a good deal bent.

"Got a good strong skull," said the captain, holding the end for Jack to see. "Look under the canoe now."

Jack glanced over the side, and there was not a shark to be seen as the agitated water grew calm again; but even as he looked, first one and then another shadowy object reappeared, until five had resumed their places, waiting for the dead that might float out of the canoe, but in this case waiting in vain.

"The horrible wretches!" said Jack.

"It's their nature, sir. They are the scavengers of the sea in their way, just as the crocodiles are of the great rivers.—Row back, Lenny.—There is your father on the deck."

"And Doctor Instow too," said Jack.

"Here, I say," cried the doctor, "play fair. Don't have all the adventures to yourselves. Been harpooning fish? Ugh!" he continued. "Sharks. I should like a turn at them."

Over the breakfast the position was discussed.

"Well, you saw, Sir John, we would be obliged to camp out for one, perhaps two nights, if we tried to row inside the reef, and it would be dangerous with the enemy about."

"And the steam is up, and we could run round outside the reef, and be back here in the evening."

"Why not try inside?" said the doctor.

"I was thinking of it," replied the captain. "There is the risk of coming upon shallow water; but if Sir John likes we'll try. I can have a couple of men sounding."

"It would be much more interesting than going out to sea," put in Jack. "It's so much better than having to be always looking through a glass."

"Try inside, Bradleigh," said Sir John.

"It means coals, sir."

"Never mind that," said Sir John, who had just drawn a deep breath full of satisfaction to see the intense interest his son was taking in everything now.

"And what about our friends the blacks?" said the doctor.

"Well, sir, we should find out whether they are neighbours or visitors from some other island. I expect the latter," said the captain, "but I want to know."

"Wouldn't there be time to try for the sharks first?" said Jack.

"Oh yes, we could give an hour to that," said the captain; "for perhaps while we are rounding the island our friends of last night will come and fetch their boat. They are welcome to it, I suppose, Sir John. You don't want to take it back to England as a specimen?"

"No," said Sir John, smiling, "let them have it; and I hope we shall see no more of them while we are here."

There was a little excitement among the men as the cutter was lowered down, and a couple of small harpoons, two lances, and a little tub containing a hundred yards of fine strong line carefully coiled in rings were handed down, along with three rifles.

Jack was looking on deeply interested after going with the doctor and Edward to fetch these and the necessary ammunition from the little museum-like place set apart for them and the magazine. He was so much occupied with the preparations and his eagerness to get back that he did not notice a peculiar cough which was uttered behind him twice.

But when it was delivered again with peculiar emphasis close by, and followed by a touch on the arm, he turned sharply round to find Edward looking at him with a most agonised expression of countenance—so bad did the man seem that Jack was startled.

"Why, Ned," he cried, "what's the matter? Here, doctor! doctor!"

"Hush! don't, sir, pray," whispered the man. "He couldn't do me no good. Don't call him, pray."

"But you look horrible," cried Jack.

"So would you look horrible, sir, if you was like me."

"Then why don't you speak out and tell me? Are you in pain?"

"Well, yes, sir, it is pain, and yet it ain't, if you can understand that."

"Well, Ned, I can't. Let me fetch Doctor Instow."

"No, no, sir, please don't; he'd only laugh at me."

"He would not be so unfeeling, I'm sure."

"But he couldn't do me no good, sir. Please don't. Nobody but you could do me any good."

"What nonsense, Ned! Just because I gave you a seidlitz powder once."

"I don't mean powders, sir."

"Then what is the matter?"

"Oh, sir, you'd be just the same if you was like me. Can't you see?"

"No; only that you look rather yellow."

"Oh, don't laugh at a fellow, sir. It does seem so hard. Sharks! and me left behind."

"That's it, is it?" cried Jack, laughing.

"Yes, sir; ain't it bad enough? But I say, sir, it does do a fellow good to see you laugh like that."

"Absurd! But I meant you to go, Ned."

"Did you, sir?" cried the man joyfully.

"Of course. My father said the other night that I was to take you with me everywhere I liked, and have you as my regular attendant."

"Did he, sir?" cried the man joyfully. "Think of that now. Well, I was going to ask him to raise my wages, and now I won't. I say, Mr Jack, sir, ain't it a lovely morning?"

"I thought it looked rather cloudy just now, Ned," said Jack dryly.

"Now, my boy, are you ready?" said Sir John, coming up.

"Yes, father, but you're not."

"No, I'm not coming this morning. There'll be plenty in the boat without me."

"Oh!" ejaculated the lad, "you go, and I'll stay behind."

"Certainly not. You'll have the doctor with you."

"And Mr Bartlett," said the captain, strolling up.

"But you're coming," cried Jack. "No; Bartlett's a better hand at this sort of work than I am. He and Lenny will show you plenty of sport, and help to rid the seas of some of these dangerous brutes. Now then, over with you."

Ned did not need the order, for he had already stepped over the side with the oarsmen.

"Make anything out, Bartlett?" shouted the captain.

"No," came from the mast-head. "I've swept well round, and there's nothing in sight."

"Come down then, and I'll send up one of the watch."

The mate came down and joined the party in the boat, which pushed off in the direction of the sunken canoe.

"Stop," cried Jack before they had gone fifty yards.

"What is it?" cried the doctor. "Captain Bradleigh said that he would have a kind of bait made to attract the sharks."

"Here it is, Mr Jack, sir," cried Ned from the bows. "I'm sitting on it."

Curious to see what it was like, Jack went forward, the men laughingly making way for him to pass as they tugged against rather a swift current, for the tide was setting toward the opening in the reef; and the next minute he was examining a nondescript affair made of two ship's fenders—the great balls of hempen network used to prevent injury to a vessel's sides when lying in dock or going up to a wharf or pier. These were placed, one inside an old pea-jacket, the other in a pair of oilskin trousers, and all well lashed together so as to have some semblance to the body of a man.

"But a shark will never be stupid enough to bite at that," said Jack contemptuously.

"Oh yes, he will, sir," said the black-bearded sailor, grinning. "The cook's put a bit of salt pork, beef, and old grease inside. They'll smell that soon enough."

It was soon put to the proof, for the boat was steered by the mate well beyond the sunken canoe. The men kept near there by clipping their oars, and then Jack and the doctor were each furnished with a lance, and the mate took the harpoon and attached it to the line in the tub.

"Would either of you gentlemen like to have first try?"

"No, no, I want to learn," said the doctor. "What do you say, Jack?"

"No, thank you," said the lad merrily; "I should be harpooning one of the men."

"Not unlikely," said the mate, smiling. "Don't lift your lances till they are wanted, and then handle them carefully. I don't say though that I shall strike a fish," he continued, as he rose in his place and stood ready, with one foot on the side. "Now then, Lenny, overboard with the dummy, and make a good splash. Give it plenty of line, and let it sail by the canoe; then bring it back toward me; and you, my lads, try and give me a chance by backing water gently. Ready?"

"Ay, ay, sir."

"Over she goes then."

Splash! went the awkward-looking bundle the next moment, and began to float toward the stern of the canoe, beneath which the sharks had lain that morning, but were too far off now to be visible.

"I say, this is exciting, Jack," cried the doctor, rubbing his hands. "I hope they'll bite. Pike-fishing's nothing to it."

But there was no sign of anything stirring, as the unwieldy bait was allowed to float on between the stern and bow of the canoe; and though Jack watched, holding his breath at times in his excitement, there was not a ripple, and the dummy was dragged back alongside.

"Was it past there you saw them?" said the doctor.

"Yes, past there. Try again, Mr Bartlett."

"Oh yes, we'll try till we get one or two," replied the mate. "Mustn't go back without something to show."

The men, who seemed as eager as so many boys, let the bait go again, and once more drew it back without result, then a third time, but were no more fortunate.

"The tide's fallen since you were here," said the mate, after a few moments' thought. "Pull a few yards farther away from the shore, and let it go down to the right of the canoe, where the water's deeper, and jerk it about like a man swimming—at least as near it as you can," he added in a low voice to Jack and the doctor.

"Oh dear, I wish I was at that end of the boat," muttered Ned, as the bundle floated down again from the fresh place, and it had not more than reached the canoe when a thrill ran through Jack, for the calm water was suddenly disturbed as if by something shooting through it.

"Look out!" said the mate sharply; "don't let him have it—make him follow it up. See him, Mr Jack?"

"No! Yes, I can see that black thing sticking out of the water."

"Back fin," said the mate.—"Well done, my lad. Steady.—Make the poor victim swim for his life, Mr Jack, to escape the shark. Capital. Do you see he is following the dummy?"

"Yes, I see," said Jack in a husky whisper. "Shall I get the lance?"

"No, no, not yet. That's to kill him when he's harpooned. This is a good big chap, judging by the size of his fin. Look at it sailing along like a tiny lateen-rigged boat. Oh, he's coming on splendidly. Smells the meat. That's it; coax him well up astern, Lenny."

"Ay, ay, sir."

And there, as the man hauled upon the line, and the dummy answered to each jerk with a splash, the black triangular back fin of the shark came on behind, cutting the water steadily, till the fish was only about ten feet from where the mate stood in the stern, giving a sharp look to see that the rings of line he had drawn out of the tub would run clear.

"Don't move, either of you," he said sternly, as he balanced the harpoon pole in his hand, well above his head.

Jack could hardly keep in his place as he strained his eyes to watch for the shark, and the next minute he saw its white under-part as it turned on one side to make a snap at the dummy, now close astern; but at the same moment the mate darted the keen-bladed harpoon downward with so true an aim that he buried it deeply in the shark's sleek side. There was a tremendous swirl in the water as the dummy was dragged aboard; the rings of rope curled over the side, and others began to run out of the tub at a rapid rate, while the mate took a big leather glove out of his pocket and put it on.

"This is three times as big as the one that towed us before," he said quietly; "but we're better prepared this time."

"What are you going to do when the line's all out?" cried Jack excitedly. "Look! it will soon be gone."

"I'll show you," said the mate, and taking hold of a piece of the rope secured to a couple of hooks in the outside of the tub, he cast it loose, hauled a few yards out, and secured the end of the line to a ring-bolt astern. Then, raising his foot, he pressed it on the line where it ran over the boat's edge, slowly increasing the pressure so as to make his boot act as a brake, with the result that the boat began to follow the shark, at first slowly, then faster, and at last, when the line was all out, quite rapidly, farther and farther from the yacht.

"Not a wise shark this," said the mate. "He is going against the tide. Make it all the better, though, for us. Does not disturb the water where the rest are."

The shark took them for some distance, but at last began to show signs of being tired, and then made a curve round toward the sands, but, finding the water too shallow, made a tremendous leap right out, and came down with a heavy splash, to begin swimming back nearly over the same ground. "Cannot be better, eh?" said the doctor. "It's splendid!" cried Jack.

"Haul upon him now, my lads," said the mate. "Take the tub forward."

This was done, the tub placed right in the bows, and as two men hauled, another laid the line back in rings, till, about a couple of hundred yards above the sunken canoe, the motion in the water, and the occasional appearance of the harpoon pole and shark's back fin, showed that the end was getting near.

"Now, gentlemen, it's your turn," said the mate. "I'll get out of your way. Hold your lances ready; wait till you get a good chance, and then thrust hard just behind the head. Into the white if you can."

"Strikes me it only takes one to kill a shark," said the doctor quietly. "Your lance there, Jack."

"No, no, doctor—you," cried Jack excitedly.

"Don't lose the chance, Mr Jack. Be ready, sir. Haul, my lads. Put your foot on the thwart, sir. Now then! Let him have it."

Jack stood there flushing with excitement, and with his eyes dilated, following out his instructor's orders to the letter, till, startled at the aspect of the monster being brought close up astern, he was ready to shrink from his task.

But he did not. As the mate spoke he thrust the lance down with excellent aim, feeling the keen blade pierce into the great fish's side, and then seeming to dart out again.

"Give it him once more. Well done, sir. Bravo! Now another."

Jack, in his excitement, thrust twice to the mate's orders, and each time the dangerous brute made a feeble rush, but the harpoon held firm, and the last thrusts were fatal. The water was dyed with blood, and the shark turned up, showing all white in the ruddy surface; its tail quivered a little, and its career was over.

A cheer, headed by Edward, rang out, and the beast was examined before being cast loose, a clever cut or two from Lenny's knife setting the harpoon at liberty.

Then, as the dead fish floated away, a good ten feet in length, the tub was replaced astern, and the dummy brought into requisition for a repetition of the novel fishing.

"My turn now," said the doctor.

"To harpoon?" said the mate.

"No, no, you do that; I'll lance. And I flatter myself that if I have as good a chance as Jack here, I can perform that feat more artistically, and kill the monster at the first stroke."

"Let's see," said Jack, laughing.

The opportunity soon came, for the blood in the water seemed to have excited the other sharks, one of which, on the same tactics being carried out, soon became fast on to the line; the harpoon held, and after it had towed them about a bit it was brought alongside.

"Now's your time, sir," cried the mate, and the doctor delivered a quick thrust, and, to Jack's great delight, missed entirely.

"Well, that's curious," said the doctor; "I thought I had him."

"Try again, sir."

"Will you let me take my time, Bartlett," said the doctor tetchily. "I want to strike in a particular place."

The mate remained silent, watching; while, after letting two or three chances go by, the doctor struck again and wounded the shark, but with a stroke that seemed to infuse vitality instead of destroying it.

"Lesson, Jack, my lad," he said, rubbing his ear. "Doesn't do to be cocksure about anything. Never mind, third time never fails. Here, you tell me when, Bartlett."

"Very well," said the mate; and as the shark was drawn close up, lashing about a good deal, he cried, "Now!"

The doctor thrust, and his stroke was this time so true that the creature gave a few sharp struggles and turned up dead.

"There, Jack," cried the doctor, "what do you say to that?"

Two more were killed in the course of the next hour, and then one of the men drew the mate's attention to different objects out toward the opening in the reef, and in turn the mate pointed them out to the doctor and Jack.

"I can count at least ten," he said.

"What! sharks?"

"Well, their back fins, and they're all heading up this way. Why, they must swarm on the outside of the reef. We might go on killing them all day."

"We didn't see any hardly before," said Jack.

"Seems as if the more we kill, the more they come to the funeral," cried the doctor.

"Oh, the reason is plain enough," said the mate; "they scent the blood, which is carried out by the tide, and the more we kill, the more will come."

"Signal from the yacht, sir," said Lenny, pointing to a little flag being run up.

"All right. Give way, my lads."

The boat's head was turned, and they were rowed rapidly back, this ending the sharking.

"Strikes me the captain sights the blacks again," said the mate, and in a few minutes they were alongside.

Chapter Twenty Four
A circumnavigation

But no canoes were in sight, for Sir John cried directly—

"Come, I thought you had had long enough for one day. Up with you, we are anxious to be off. Captain Bradleigh says we're wasting steam."

"Beg pardon, coals," said the captain, smiling; and giving his orders, the cutter was hoisted up, the screw began to revolve slowly, and with an easy motion the yacht glided on past the opening in the reef, and then to follow the course taken by the boats.

Two men were placed forward with leads to keep on sounding, but in a short time it was found that the deep water could easily be traced by its darker colour, and the mate ascended to the foremast-head to con the ship, the navigation proving in such perfectly smooth water free from all danger, so that a fair rate of speed was kept up.

The trip was glorious, and as the various points and indentations noted on the previous day were passed, they seemed to display fresh beauties, and Jack, full of animation, kept on calling his father's or the doctor's attention to the manifold points of interest.

"Oh!" he cried at last, "if people only knew what they would see if they travelled they would never care to stay at home."

"Yes," said Sir John dryly, "if they only knew."

They reached the beautiful glen at last, where the two springs—hot and cold—sent their waters into the shadowed pool, Jack being now forward with Edward, who, as an excuse for being well to the front in anything fresh which might arise, made a point of keeping close behind his young master with the glass, which he handed to him from time to time.

Now it was to sweep the sea beyond the glittering, misty edge of the reef, where a rainbow showed brilliantly from time to time; now to look up through a deep gash at the summit of the great volcano, which curved upward till its crater was lost in a cloud of vapour. Every now and then too a flock of birds had to be watched in some huge tree a little way back from the sands.

And still the yacht glided on in perfect safety hour after hour, with the reef nearer or more distant, but always affording an ample space of deep pellucid water full of the wonders of the tropics, and calling for a brief inspection.

"Here, look, sir," cried Ned suddenly, as they were passing a lovely park-like stretch which ran high up amongst the dense forest growth. "Catch hold, sir. It's just your focus."

"Pigs," said Jack contemptuously, "half-a-dozen."

"I never saw pigs like them, sir. Why, hark at 'em. They're barking."

"Well, pigs make a short, sharp, barking noise sometimes," said the doctor, whose attention had been taken by the man's words. "No, they're not pigs, Jack," he said, as he brought his glass to bear well upon the little cluster of animals running here and there among the trees, and ending by darting down upon the sands to stare at the yacht. "Dogs, by all that's wonderful. Here, Meadows, Bradleigh, what do you make of these?"

"Mongrel wild dogs," said the captain, after a glance; "descendants of some that have been left by a passing ship."

"Why, we may find cows, sheep, and goats yet," said the doctor.

"Very likely goats," replied the captain, "but I doubt whether we shall find the others."

Every mile they passed spread fresh beauties before them, the rugged nature of the mountain scenery precluding all sameness; and early in the afternoon, when, by the captain's calculation, they had arrived nearly at the opposite point to where they had lain at anchor, Jack had come to the conclusion that they need go no farther on their voyage, for they had hit upon the loveliest place in the world, where they ought to stay for good.

He said something of the kind to Sir John.

"And what about studies, books, and the realities of civilised life?" said his father.

"I feel now as if I don't care for them a bit," replied the lad dreamily. "I should like to stop here and do nothing."

"Do you mean that?"

"Well, not exactly nothing," replied the lad, "for I should want to shoot and fish and collect all the birds, insects, flowers, and shells."

"In other words, lead a very active life, my boy. But you would weary of it in time and want a change. Better do as we are doing now, visit an island like this and return home."

"Yes, that is perhaps the best, father; and of course there are the troubles here—the dangerous reptiles and poisonous insects."

"And the blacks," said the doctor, who had been leaning over the rail with his glass to his eyes, but had heard every word.

"Yes," said Jack with a shudder, "there are the blacks."

"I should like to know whether they are cannibals," continued the doctor. "The worst of it is, if we killed one we should be no wiser. You see, you couldn't tell whether he was carnivorous or herbivorous by his teeth.—Well, captain, no signs of any inhabitants."

"Not a bit; and we're quite half-way round. No signs either of another opening in the reef. Fine island to annex, Sir John. It's a regular fortification, a natural stronghold with an impregnable wall round it, and a full mile-wide moat inside. A fort at the point commanding the entrance would be sufficient."

"But we do not want it," said Sir John.

"No, sir, it's on the road to nowhere."

The captain went aloft, glass in hand, to have a good look ahead, and descended pretty well convinced that there would be nothing to hinder their progress round the island, the water of the lagoon being very calm, and deeper than on the other side of the island.

The gentlemen lunched and the men dined, and the afternoon was spent in gazing at the wonders of sea and shore. Shoals of silvery and golden fish, startled by the vessel, leaped out of the water and darted in all directions; a shark showed its back fin now and then, and twice over droves of pigs started up out of the hot sand to make for cover. But still there was no sign of inhabitant or opening in the reef, while scores of tempting places were passed, all inviting to a naturalist, and above all to Jack; vistas among the trees took his attention, and valleys rising upward toward the higher parts of the mountain.

Upon one of these occasions, when he was sitting back in a deck-chair, sweeping the side of the mountain with his glass, the doctor came up behind him.

"Looking at the mountain?" he said.

"Yes; couldn't we get up there?"

"I vote we try," said the doctor. "Will you come?"

"Yes," cried Jack eagerly; "but we couldn't land and start now."

"Hardly," said the doctor, laughing. "We should have to start at daybreak."

"What, to get up a little way like that?"

"Yes, to get up that little way," said the doctor, with a queer twinkle of the eye. "Well, we don't seem to see anything likely to hinder our landing to-morrow and having a good time at collecting. We must soon get round to our starting-place. Let's ask the captain how far we have come."

"Roughly speaking, nearly fifty knots," said the captain. "It's getting well on toward six bells now, and we've been coming at a fair speed, and are going a bit faster. I want to reach the anchorage before dark."

At one time this seemed to be doubtful, but just as the captain announced his intention of dropping anchor for the night, Mr Bartlett hailed him from above.

"I can just see the opening in the reef over that low strip of sand."

"How far off?"

"About a mile," was the reply; and the speed being increased, they picked up the buoy they had left in the morning just as it was beginning to grow dark, having completely circumnavigated the island.

"I say, Mr Bartlett," cried Jack suddenly, as the mate approached him, and he pointed toward the shore. "Wasn't it just there that we killed the sharks?"

"Yes; just there. Can you see any back fins?"

"No; but where's the wrecked canoe?"

The mate clapped his glass to his eye, and swept the shore for some minutes.

"Could it have been carried out to sea?" said Jack excitedly.

"No; hardly possible."

"Then has it sunk?"

"No; it could not sink."

"Then what does it mean? We left it there."

"It means that the blacks have been and fetched it while we were away," said the mate, drawing a deep breath. "Just as Captain Bradleigh prophesied."

"What's that?" said the captain sharply.

"I don't think there is any question about it. She might have drifted a little way, but that is doubtful, for one end was well aground. We must have had visitors while we were away. I thought they would not give up that canoe without a struggle."

"Yes," said the captain, "they must have been. That canoe was too valuable to be lost. I said so."

"Then they may come again at any moment?" said Sir John.

"Yes, sir," replied the captain; "and they must find us well prepared."

"Mr Jack, sir," whispered Ned at the first chance, "we're going to have some fighting after all."

Chapter Twenty Five
"A was an archer, who shot—"

No more was seen of the blacks, while a fortnight passed; and encouraged by the utter solitude of the place, the well-armed parties which left the yacht made longer and longer excursions, coming home with an abundance of specimens to preserve. The sailors took to the task with the greatest of gusto, and evidently thoroughly enjoyed the hunt for rare birds and butterflies, of which there proved to be an abundance. One day Jack would be helping his father collect the wonderfully painted insects which hovered or darted about in the sunny glades or in the moist shady openings over the streams, where they hung over the lovely blossoms of the orchids. At another time the doctor would claim his attention, and shouldering one gun, while Edward carried another and the cartridges, long tramps were taken over the mountain slopes and at the edge of the forest, to penetrate which, save in rare places, was impossible. Their sport was plentiful enough, for the birds were fresh to the gun, and when startled their flight was short, and they alighted again within reach. They were all new to the boy, who seemed never weary of examining the lovely plumage of the prizes, which one or other of the sailors carried afterwards, slung by their beaks from a stick, so that the feathers should not be damaged. Now it was a green paroquet, with long slender tail and head of the most delicate peach-colour or of a brilliant orange yellow. At another time, after a careful stalk, one or other of the pittas, the exquisitely-coloured ground thrushes, in their uniforms of pale fawn and blue, turquoise, sapphire, and amethyst. And perhaps the next shot would be at one of the soft feathery trogons, cuckoo-like birds in their habits, but instead of being pale slate-coloured, barred and flecked like a sparrowhawk, Jack's specimens would display a breast of the purest carmine, and a back glistening with metallic green. Something like cuckoos, Ned declared them to be, but not in aspect.

One morning, after several times hearing their calls in a clump of gigantic trees up one of the volcanic ravines, the doctor called the lad to be his companion to try and stalk what he believed to be birds of paradise; but they had evidently chosen the wrong time, for to their disappointment not a sound was heard, and they would have gone back to the yacht empty-handed if it had not been for Ned's sharp eyes.

"There they are!" he whispered, pointing across the ravine to where another little forest of tall trees feathered the steep sides of the slope.

"What are?" said Jack excitedly.

"The birds you are looking for, sir. Saw about a dozen, big as pheasants, fly across and settle there."

He pointed with the gun he carried to one tree which towered above the rest.

"They went down under there, sir. I could lead you straight to the place."

Jack took out his small glass, and after gazing through it attentively he suddenly said—

"I saw a big bird fly down. Yes, and another."

"They can't be those we want," said the doctor, "but they may be good specimens of something. What do you say, Jack, will you go down and across?"

"Oh yes," he replied.

"It's very steep, and will mean lowering ourselves cautiously."

"I don't mind," said the lad. "If it's very bad they will help me."

"Oh yes, sir, we'll help," said Lenny, turning to his companions; "won't us, lads?"

There was a chorus of "Ay, ays," and the steep descent from the great grove commenced, it being necessary to get to the bottom of what became low down a precipitous gully, along which one of the springs which had its source high up in the mountain dashed along. This had to be crossed, and then there was a similar climb on the other side.

The start was made, and proved difficult enough, for where the trees were not close and their roots interlaced, there were openings where masses of volcanic rock were tumbled-together in inextricable confusion, and the way over them was made more difficult by the bushy, shrubby growth and creepers which bound them together.

But the sailors were activity itself, and they slashed and trampled down and hauled and lowered till the whole party found themselves upon a broad stony shelf at the very edge of a sharply-cut rift, whose sides showed that it must have been split from the opposite side by some convulsion of Nature, so exactly was the shape repeated.

At the bottom of this crack—for it could be called little else—the water of the stream rushed foaming along some thirty feet beneath, the whole place looking black and forbidding enough to make any one hesitate before attempting to cross, though the distance to the other ledge was not above five feet, a trifling jump under ordinary circumstances. But here, with the deep black rift and the foaming water beneath, it looked startling to a lad accustomed to a quiet home life. He, however, put a bold face on the matter and stood looking on.

Jack was, however, conscious of the fact that the doctor was watching him in a side-long way, as if expecting to hear him make some objections. As, however, the boy was silent, the doctor spoke.

"Rather an ugly jump, Jack," he said. "Think you can manage it?"

"Oh, I think so. I shall try."

"Try? It must not be a try. It has to be done."

"Yes, I can do it," said the lad confidently.

"Oh yes, you can do that, Mr Jack," said Ned in a whisper, as the doctor turned off to speak to Lenny; "think it's only a ditch a foot deep."

The boy could not think that with the water roaring beneath him far below, and he could not help glancing back up the steep slope they had descended. This looked so forbidding and meant so much toilsome work, that he felt as if he would rather do the leap, though all the same there was the climb on the other side. Still there was an attraction there in the shape of the strange birds, which he was as eager to secure as the doctor.

"Who'll go first?" said the doctor. "Here, I will."

He handed his gun and satchel to Ned, walked a little way to select the broadest and clearest path, which happened to be a couple of feet higher than the opposite side, stepped back as far as he could, took a short run, and landed easily a couple of feet clear.

"There: nothing," he cried, "but I shouldn't like to try it back. Throw my satchel over, Ned."

This was done and deftly caught. Then the gun was carefully pitched across, the others followed, and the specimens shot that morning.

Then one by one the sailors leaped over, and Jack and Ned remained.

"Will you go next, Ned?"

"Me, sir, and leave you behind? 'Tisn't likely. Don't think about it, sir. It's easy enough. Off you go. The thinking's worse than the doing."

To an ordinary school-boy it would have been nothing. His legs, hardened by exercise, would have sent him across like a deer, but Jack's muscles only a short time before were flaccid and weak in the extreme. Still the voyage had done something; the strong will growing up within him did more, and without a moment's hesitation, feeling as if his reputation was at stake, he went sharply to the starting-point, took the short run, and leaped, but too hurriedly. If he had gone quietly to work it would have been different; as it was, he cleared the gulf and landed on the other side, but without throwing himself forward sufficiently to recover himself, and Ned uttered a cry of horror as he saw the lad apparently about to totter backward into the depths below.

Lenny saved him by a curiously awkward-looking act. He had been on the look-out on one side, the doctor on the other, to give the lad a hand as he landed, but instead of a hand he gave him an arm, delivering a sharp blow on the back, and driving him into safety just as he was hopelessly losing his balance, and the men gave a cheer.

"Thank you, Lenny," gasped the boy breathlessly, as he saved himself from falling forward by catching at the nearest sailor; "but don't hit quite so hard next time; it hurts."

A roar of laughter followed this, and the doctor took off his pith helmet to wipe his forehead.

"That's a nice sort of an example to set a fellow," muttered Ned as he stood on the other side, rather unnerved by what he had seen. "Makes a poor man feel as if he would rather be at home cleaning the plate."

Then in a fit of determination he flung up his arms, and in regular boyish fashion shouted—

"Clear the way, there. Here comes my ship full sail."

He cleared the gulf with a good foot to spare, and felt triumphant.

Each took his gun or rifle directly without a word of allusion to Jack's narrow escape, and with the doctor leading the way they began to climb the steep ascent in silence.

"I hope that fellow's shouting has not scared our birds," said the doctor after a time. "Quiet as you can, below there."

"They were so far off I don't think the birds could have heard him," replied Jack. "Perhaps the noise would not have gone out of the gully."

"Perhaps not," said the doctor. Then laconically: "Hurt?"

"Oh, not much," said Jack, smiling. "He did hit me a good bang though."

"Never mind, my lad; I like to see you bear it stoically. Shows me you're recovering tone. Phew! this is warm work. How much more of it is there?"

"Not half-way up yet," panted Jack.

"Take it coolly, men, or our hands will be all of a tremble, so that we can't shoot straight."

There was no need to advise an impossibility, for no one could have taken it coolly. The blocks of stone, the tangled creepers, and higher up the dense undergrowth, made it a slow, laborious task; but at last the huge trees of the upper slope were reached, and the work promised to be lighter.

The doctor made a sign, and they both sat down to rest for a few minutes, the men who came on smilingly following suit; but all at once a peculiarly hoarse cooing sound arose from not far away among the trees, and all the fatigue passed away as if by magic.

"Pigeons!" whispered the doctor excitedly. "Hark! more of them! They must be the big fruit birds, Jack, and we must have a pair or two of these. When you're ready we'll go on."

"I'm ready," whispered Jack.

"Then we'll go abreast. Don't you study me. Keep your eyes open, and the first moment you have a good chance you fire. Get one with each barrel if you can."

Jack nodded, and directly after they advanced among the trees, with Ned about a couple of yards behind, carrying a second gun for whichever needed it.

These were exciting moments, more exciting than they knew of, as they crept forward among the huge trunks, and gazing upward among the branches, expecting moment by moment to catch sight of the flock of great fruit-pigeons, whose cooing kept stopping and commencing again.

It had sounded to be so close that they felt puzzled, and wondered whether they had passed them, for the doctor argued that if they had taken fright the rustle of their wings would have been heard among the branches.

All at once Jack, who walked on the doctor's left, held his gun in his left hand only, and made a sign with his right.

His companion crept close to him, and the next moment a flock of enormous pigeons, which had been feeding on the fallen nuts of one of the biggest trees, rose with a tremendous rushing of wings, and four barrels were fired into them, with the result that three birds fell.

"Our dinner, Jack, and the men's too," cried the doctor; and the boy felt a chill of horror run through him, as from close behind there was a wild cry from Ned, followed by a shouting amongst the men a dozen yards below. Then *shot—shot—shot* followed one another quickly, and Lenny cried—

"Down, gentlemen, down!"

The doctor dropped instinctively, and began to creep to Ned, who had fallen heavily, when he heard Lenny cry—

"Down, Mr Jack—down!" and he saw the lad standing motionless, staring with horror at the ground.

The next instant something whizzed by his ear and struck quivering in the tree-trunk behind. Then he dropped into shelter, and began rapidly to reload.

"Fall back on us, my lads," said the doctor sharply, "and don't fire unless you have a good chance. Keep well under cover."

"The blacks?" panted Jack.

The doctor nodded. "Is Ned—hurt much?"

"Can't tell yet, my lad. How are you, Ned—much hurt?"

"Oh, it hurts, sir, horrid," said the man faintly; "but I shouldn't mind that. It's feeling so sea-sick and swimming I mind. Let's go back to the yacht."

"Yes, of course; but you can't walk."

"But I will walk, sir; must walk. 'Tain't my leg, it's my arm," cried the man, who was sick with agony, but full of spirit. "Who's going to carry a fellow in a place like this?"

"Much hurt, mate?" said Lenny, who now crept to them on all fours.

"What's the good o' asking stupid questions, old 'un?" cried Ned petulantly. "Course I'm much hurt. Can't you see it's gone right into my arm? Why look at this—gone right through. Going to cut the arrow-head out, sir?"

"No," replied the doctor sharply. "Kneel, and be a man. I won't hurt you more than I can help."

"All right, sir. No use hollering," cried Ned cheerily.

"Look out there!" cried one of the sailors from below. "They're going to rush us!"

"Never mind me, sir," said Ned, letting himself sink back. "You three has to fight. Nasty cowardly beggars—shooting a man behind his back! Let 'em have it, I say."

He had hardly spoken when the men below fired a little volley across the gully, and then there was a cheer.

"That's scut 'em to the right-about, sir. We've dropped two," cried one of the men, and they crept back under the dense cover to where Ned lay.

The doctor had seized his gun, but he laid it down again, and took out a keen-bladed knife.

"Thought you wasn't going to cut out the head, sir?" said Ned faintly.

"I am not," replied the doctor.

"Oh, don't you mind me, sir. I tell you I won't shout. You do what's right. I know it must come out; but I'd take it kindly, Mr Jack, sir, if you'd lay hold of my hand. Cheer a fellow up a bit. Go on, doctor; I'm game."

"That you are, my lad," said the doctor, and kneeling behind the sufferer he took hold of the long arrow, which had completely transfixed the fleshy part of the arm, and snapped it sharply in two on the side where it had entered, then in an instant he had drawn the head portion right out of the wound in the same way in which it was driven.

"That's the way, sir. Don't you be afraid to cut," said Ned sturdily, but with his eyes shut. "I'll bear it; but I didn't know you'd got a red-hot poker up here to dress the wound with.—What! have you got it out?"

"Yes. Take hold of these pieces, Lenny."

"Well, you have been quick, sir. My word, it was a stinger—just like as if twenty thousand wasps was at you. Eh! going to bind it up?"

"Yes, only lightly. It will be all the better for bleeding a bit. Now then! We must retreat as fast as we can. Can you get up, Ned?"

"Can I get up, sir! I should just think I can! I'm not going to make a regular how-de-do because I've got a prick from a bit of wood."

"Are the enemy coming on, men?" said the doctor sharply.

"Can't see any more of 'em, sir," sail one of the sailors. "I think that volley scared 'em a bit."

"Here, take my arm, Ned. Jack, you come next. Come on, my lads."

"All right, sir, we will," cried Lenny.

"Who has Ned's gun?" said Jack. "That must not be left behind."

"I've got it, sir; he's loaded too," said one of the sailors.

"Forward then," cried the doctor.

"I can get on without your arm, sir," grumbled Ned now sturdily. "No, I can't. Things turn round a bit somehow. Thank you, sir. I shall be better directly."

At that moment there was a heavy concussion, and a rolling echo which went reverberating up the gully toward the mountain top.

"One of the big guns," said Lenny. "That means a signal to come back."

"Then the black fellows are in sight there," cried Jack excitedly. "Come on."

The start was made, with Ned making a brave effort to keep his legs, and succeeding fairly well as they struggled on through the tangled growth, Jack springing to the front, hunting-knife in hand, to slash away at creepers and pendent vines which came in their way. But every now and then the poor fellow stopped short.

"Bit touched in the wind, gentlemen," he said cheerily. "Go on again directly. If there is a chance to get a mouthful of water I should like it. If there ain't, never mind.—Off we goes."

The doctor said nothing, but supported him all he could, and they started again, with Jack leading and the sailors forming their rear-guard, retiring in regular military fashion, dividing themselves in twos, one couple halting face to the enemy till the rest had gone on a hundred yards and halted, and then trotting or rather forcing their way along the track, to pass their companions and halt again.

Moment by moment an attack was expected, but it was not made, though from time to time those in the rear caught sight of a black face peering round the trunk of a tree, showing that they were followed.

At last as they descended they came to a spot where the stream in the ravine could be reached, and the wounded man drank of the cool clear water with feverish avidity, while the doctor frowned as Jack looked at him with questioning eyes.

"Does take the conceit out of you, Mr Jack," said Ned, as they continued their retreat. "I did think I was a better-plucked one than this. Talk about a weak 'un; I'm downright ashamed of myself."

"Don't talk so much, my man," said the doctor. "Keep your breath for the exertion."

"Cert'nly, sir. That's right," said the man in quick, excited tones. "Won't say another word, only this. I should like to have just one pop at the chap who shot me, and hit him in the same place. I'm ashamed to see you working so hard, Mr Jack, sir. How far is it down to the boat?"

"About a mile, Ned; but pray do as Doctor Instow says—keep quiet."

"Right, sir, I will," replied the man, setting his teeth hard, his drawn face showing the agony he was in; and they went on descending, to be startled by another heavy detonation.

"Another signal," said the doctor; but the words were hardly out of his lips when there was a fresh report running up the gully, and being multiplied in echoes which gradually died away.

"Those are not signals, Jack," said the doctor quietly. "It means an attack upon the yacht by the canoes."

"Oh! and we not there," cried the lad excitedly.

"*Well*, the more lucky for us, eh?"

"Doctor Instow!" cried Jack indignantly; "when these men are wanted to help defend the vessel. Pray, pray try and walk faster, Ned."

"Trying my best, sir, but I'm very shaky. Legs must be a regular pair of cowards, sir, for they won't hurry a bit. Ah!"

The poor fellow reeled and would have fallen but for the doctor's strong arm supporting him and letting him gently down.

Just then the regular short, sharp report of rifles reached their ears from below, announcing that there was no mistake about an attack being made upon their friends, and the anxiety of Jack and the doctor was increased as they trembled for the fate of the two men left as keepers of the boat in which they had come ashore.

"I hope they have escaped back to the yacht," said the doctor.

"They wouldn't do that," cried Jack indignantly. "But what is to be done? Can't we make a sort of stretcher with two of the guns?"

"No," said the doctor, "it would take time; and the wood is too thick. I'll carry him for a few hundred yards."

"Let me have first go, sir," cried Lenny. "You're tired. I'll take him. Help me get him on my back, so as not to hurt his arm."

This was done, poor Ned remaining quite insensible; and once more they began to descend through the solemn aisles of the forest, with the sunshine coming through the leaves in showers of rays, while the firing away below them kept rolling up to where they were.

After a time Lenny was relieved, and dropped into the rear-guard, and this evolution was performed again and again, Jack still leading the way, and hacking through some growing rope from time to time.

"Soon do it now, sir," said the man who was carrying. "Keep a good heart, sir. That's the best o' being mates. Chap goes down, and t'others 'll always carry him. Hullo! what, a'ready?" he continued, as one of his companions came to relieve him. "I've only just begun."

"Don't be greedy, matey," said the new-comer with a grin. "You allus was such a chap for wanting to have more 'n your share. Gently, let me get under the poor chap here without hauling him about so. That's your sort. Warm work, mate?"

"Tidy," said the man relieved with a grin. "Warmer where there's none."

On they went again with the relieved man taking his place ready for the defence if called upon, and the fresh bearer toiling on as if there was nothing to mind.

"Mustn't whistle, I suppose, Mr Jack?"

There was a shake of the head.

"S'pose not. Like letting the beggars know where we are. My word, how things seem to grow here. Take some muscle to cut a good road. Say, sir; think poor Ned here's much hurt?"

"Hurt a good deal, of course, but it can't be a dangerous wound."

"I dunno," said the man thoughtfully, after a few minutes' silence. "Is he onsensible like, sir?"

"Yes, quite," said Jack, after a look at Ned's face.

"Can't hear what I say then, sir? I'm a bit afeard for him."

"Why?"

"Chap wouldn't go like this after a hole being made in his arm. I had a bayonet through mine once, but it didn't turn me this way. Felt a bit sick at first, but it made me feel hot and savage after."

"What do you mean?" said Jack, baring his head for a moment.

"Arrows, sir; poison."

"Ah!" ejaculated Jack in horror. "Then that's what made Doctor Instow look so serious."

"That's it, sir. But don't you say anything. I dare say as soon as we get aboard the doctor 'll put some of his acquy miraculos on it, and set it right again. My word, they're having a good round with the niggers. I do wish we were aboard in the fun. I don't like this running away."

The bottom of the forest slope at last, and now an open park-like stretch lay between them and the patch of jungle which ran down to where they had left the boat. But upon this being neared they could see no sign of her.

Jack put a whistle to his lips and blew shrilly, but there was no sign still, and his heart sank as they hurried on across the open part toward the cover; and none too soon, for the party of blacks which had been following them from where the first attack was made suddenly appeared at the edge of the forest they had just left, and arrow after arrow came whizzing by to stick in the shrubs and dense grass around.

"Don't stop to fire till we are in cover," cried the doctor, and they kept on till they were once more hidden by the low jungle scrub, when at the doctor's order four shots were fired amongst the trees from whence the arrows kept coming.

These had their effect, and the missiles ceased falling, but a dark figure appeared from time to time, and it was evident that the enemy were running from cover to cover, so as to try and cut them off from the shore.

Just, however, as this danger was growing imminent, there was a loud hail from the part of the lagoon hidden from them by the low scrub. "Here they are, sir," cried Lenny. "Then now for it, my lads; a sharp run to the boat. Here, take my gun, some one. I'll carry him now."

"He's all right, sir," cried the man upon whose back Ned still hung, and the bearer rose from his knees. "Some one take care as they don't spear me, and I'll soon have him in the boat."

"Lead on, Jack," cried the doctor.

"All here?" said Jack.

"Yes. Forward."

The distance was short now, and in a few minutes they had put the low growth between them and their enemies, and were running toward where the boat, with its two keepers, was being backed on to the sand.

"Hooray!" panted Ned's bearer, as he waded in and let the poor fellow glide over the gunwale of the boat, following directly after.

The others, as soon as Jack and the doctor were aboard, dropped their rifles in, ran the boat out till they were waist deep, and then gave a final thrust and slipped over, to seize their rifles again and squat down ready to fire.

They were none too soon, for a party of about a dozen blacks, armed with spears and bows and arrows, came into sight, and began to shoot.

"Give them a volley," said the doctor sternly. "Six of us. We can't be merciful now."

The pieces were rested upon the sides of the boat, and the sharp rattle of gun and rifle followed, Jack and the doctor firing both barrels of their fowling-pieces, loaded with largish shot.

The effect was instantaneous. As the cloud of smoke rose, they could see that two of the blacks were down, and several running wildly about as if in terrible pain. Then the two fallen men were seized by the wrists and dragged under cover, from which arrow after arrow was discharged— fortunately without effect—till the vigorous strokes of the oars took them beyond their reach, and toward where a dense cloud of smoke hung over the lagoon, drifting slowly toward them in the soft sea-breeze, and completely hiding the yacht.

Chapter Twenty Six
A poisoned arrow

"Better run out toward the reef and approach from that side," said the doctor, after considering for a few moments the difficulties of their position.

For they were literally in the dark, and did not know but what they might be running into danger—that from the canoes which must be attacking the crew, or that of getting into their friends' line of fire.

As the doctor kept a sharp look-out, he helped to lay the wounded man in a more easy position, and bathed his head and face with the comparatively cool water; but the poor fellow showed no sign of revival, and Jack's face grew more anxious, the doctor's graver and more stern.

At the end of a few minutes they had passed out of the smoke cloud, which was still increasing from the firing going on and the fumes rolling out of the funnel, and they could now grasp the position of affairs.

The steamer still lay at anchor, and she was engaging half-a-dozen long canoes, whose occupants were raining arrows upon the deck, and every now and then, with terrible temerity, they were paddled rapidly near enough to hurl their spears at any one they could see.

"Well, we must risk it, and get on board somehow," said the doctor. "Give way, my lads, and pull for your lives. I'll steer as well under cover as I can. Jack, lad, keep on bathing the poor fellow's face."

The men began pulling with all their might, and the nearer they drew to the yacht, naturally the better cover they secured, though, as Jack sat dipping his handkerchief in the sea from time to time, and laying it upon Ned's burning head, he wondered that one or other of the canoes did not come round to meet them and cut them off.

Probably they were too much occupied by their own troubles, for, stung at last by the vicious attack into fierce reprisals, the yacht was giving the savages ample proof of her power.

"Don't fire at them with rifles," Sir John had said, "it is only slaughtering the poor ignorant wretches. Give them some good sharp lesson that shall teach them to respect an English vessel come upon a peaceful mission."

"There is only one, sir," said the captain quietly. "Sink two or three of the canoes with round-shot."

"You feel that it is absolutely necessary?" asked Sir John.

"So necessary, that if we do not do that they will for certain board us, and as they are about fifty to one, we shall not be here to-morrow to tell the tale."

Sir John hesitated no longer, and just as the boat was racing for the yacht, the firing had begun, the former shots having been with blank cartridge, in the vain hope of scaring the enemy away.

The boat was now sighted from the yacht's deck, and a faint cheer reached Jack's ears as they sped over the water. But while they were still some three hundred yards from the gangway, one of the great canoes suddenly started away from the others, and with the paddles making the water flash and foam, came round the yacht's bows and made a dash for the solitary little boat to cut her off.

"Cease rowing," cried the doctor; but every piece was already charged, and giving the order now for the rifles to be laid ready to seize at a moment's notice, they began pulling now for the yacht's bows.

"If they don't give us some help soon from the yacht, Jack," said the doctor rather despondently, "it will go rather badly with us."

"Oh, don't say that," cried the boy, whose face was flushed with excitement.

"I am compelled to, my lad. If anything happens to me, keep the men rowing for the yacht. They must send help soon."

"I don't see them lowering down a boat," replied Jack. "Oughtn't we to fire?"

"I'm afraid that it would be no good. But we must not let them master us without striking a blow to save our lives."

"Striking a blow to save our lives," thought Jack, as he glanced round him and saw their helpless position, for to have tried to escape by rowing, if they were cut off from the yacht, seemed to be folly.

But, as is often the case when things look blackest, a ray of light suddenly gleamed out. There had been no signs of help from the yacht, but all the same those on board had not been neglectful, and as soon as the danger the returning boat ran was seen, Sir John and the captain prepared the needed help.

All at once there was a white puff of smoke seen to dart from the yacht's bows. The water close to the middle of the great canoe was sent flying, and as the roar of a gun echoed from the mountain side, the canoe was seen to be cut right in two, and slowly settling down, with half her men in the water.

"That was a charge of grape-shot, I know," growled Lenny. "Round-shot wouldn't ha' done it."

"Hah!" ejaculated the doctor. "Pull, my lads, as you've never pulled before."

The crew gave a cheer, and the cutter almost leaped to their vigorous strokes, every man being now at the oars.

A minute or two later they were alongside, having nothing to fear from the half-sunken canoe, whose occupants were struggling to keep themselves afloat till they could urge the portions of the damaged vessel on to the sands.

"Quick, all of you," cried the captain, "and look out for the arrows. What! wounded man! Here, two of you."

A couple of the crew ran to him, and poor Ned was lifted over the side and borne down into the cabin.

"Keep in shelter, Jack, my boy," cried Sir John, as he caught his son's hand. "The arrows are coming in like hail. You are sure you are not wounded?"

"Quite, father; I'm all right," said Jack, as he stepped on deck.

"Is Edward much hurt?"

"Here's Doctor Instow, ask him," said the boy, as the doctor came up out of the boat, the last man but those who were hooking on the falls, to be run up.

"Ned? I can't say yet. Don't stop me. I'm not sneaking out of the fight, Meadows. I must go down to the poor lad."

"Speared?"

"An arrow. For goodness' sake keep in shelter, for I'm afraid they're poisoned."

"Glad to see you back safe," cried the captain, hurrying up to him. "I can talk to the miserable wretches now. Hi! there, forward. Come away from those guns. Capstan-bars, all of you. Keep in shelter, and down with every one who tries to get on board; but mind the spears."

A few more orders were given, a tub to buoy the cable thrown over the side, and the yacht began to glide steadily with the tide, as the engine clanked, and the motion of the shaft produced its regular vibration through the graceful vessel, with only two men visible to those in the canoes—the captain and the man at the wheel, and they both sheltering themselves from the black marksmen as well as they could, the sailor kneeling on the grating.

The savages in three canoes uttered a furious yelling, and plunged their paddles over the sides to attack in front and on both quarters, but one was a little late in crossing the yacht's bows, and the next minute, with full steam ahead, and in obedience to movements of the captain's hands, the sharp prow of the swift vessel struck the sluggish canoe full in the side about 'midships. Then a dull crashing sound, but no perceptible shock. The *Silver Star* cut the canoe cleanly in two, and the portions of the destroyed vessel floated by on either side, coming in collision with the others, which after closing in with a vain attempt to board, grated against the yacht and were then left far astern.

It was all the matter of a minute. A few black heads appeared above the bulwarks, as their owners leaped up and tried to climb on deck, but a sharp blow, rarely repeated, sent them back into the lagoon with a splash, to swim to the floating canoes, and the fight was over, save that an arrow or two came whizzing to stick in the white planks; but the enemy was too much engaged in picking up the swimming warriors to continue their assault.

"There," cried the captain, rubbing his hands. "Your men-of-war may carry the biggest guns they like, and their crews may be drilled to the greatest perfection, but to my mind nothing comes up to the management of the craft under a good head of steam. Now, Sir John, shall we give them a few rounds of grape-shot, or let the poor wretches study the lesson they have had?"

"No, no," cried Jack eagerly, "they're beaten; let them go."

Sir John nodded his approval, saying nothing, for he seemed eager to let his son come well to the front.

"Very good," said the captain. "Then I think we'll run outside and lie-to a mile or so beyond the reef, and see what they mean to do, for I suppose you don't want to give up the island to the enemy!"

"No, it would be a pity," said Sir John, "just when we are getting on so well. But what do you say, Bradleigh, will not this be a sufficient lesson for them?"

"It ought to be, sir; but we are dealing with savages, and I will not venture to say."

The steward came hurrying up at that moment, to give a sharp look-out for danger, but seeing the enemy far astern, and the yacht gliding swiftly along toward the open sea, he walked confidently to where the group stood by the wheel.

"Doctor Instow would be glad if you would come into the cabin, Sir John."

"It's about, Ned," cried Jack. "I'd forgotten him."

He ran to the cabin hatch, and Sir John followed quickly.

"Hah!" cried the doctor. "I'm glad you've come. He's very bad, Jack. Yes, very bad, Meadows, poor lad."

"But from a wound like that?" said Sir John, and he and his son bent over the poor fellow where he lay on one of the cabin settees, with his eyes wide open, and looking very fixed and strange.

"Yes, from a wound like that," replied the doctor. "It would be nothing in an ordinary way, but I saved the head of the arrow which passed through his arm, and it and the top of the shaft had been well smeared with some abominable preparation. The poison is affecting his system in a very peculiar manner."

"Can he hear what you say?" whispered Jack anxiously.

"No; he is quite insensible. He was talking wildly a few minutes ago, but he could not understand a word."

"Surely you don't think it will prove fatal?" said Sir John.

The doctor was silent.

"Oh, Doctor Instow," cried Jack in agony, "this is too terrible. The poor fellow came out for what he looked upon as a pleasure-trip, and now he is like this. Oh, pray do something."

"My boy," said the doctor gravely, "I have done everything possible."

"But try something else," cried Jack angrily. "I thought doctors could do anything with medicine."

"I wish they could," said his father's friend sadly; "but it is at times like this, Jack, we doctors and surgeons find out how small our powers are."

"But only this morning he was so happy and full of life and fun," cried Jack, as he sank on his knees by the couch to take the poor fellow's cold hand in his. "It seems too hard to believe. Ned! Ned! you can hear what I say?"

There was no reply, and the boy looked wildly from one to the other.

"Oh, father," he cried, as he saw their grave looks, "is he dying?"

Sir John was silent, and Jack caught at the doctor's hand.

"Tell me," he cried. "But it can't be so bad as that. It would be too dreadful for him to die."

"He is very bad," said the doctor slowly, "but I have not given up all hope. It is like this, Meadows. The poison is passing through his system, and in my ignorance of what that poison really is, I am so helpless in my attempts to neutralise it. Even if I knew it would be desperate work."

"Then you can do nothing?" cried Jack in agony.

"I can do little more, my lad, but help him in his struggle against it. The battle is going on between a strong healthy man and the insidious enemy sapping his life. Nature is the great physician here."

Jack uttered a piteous groan, and still knelt by the couch, holding the poor fellow's hand, watching every painful breath he drew, and noting the strange change in his countenance, and the peculiar spasms which convulsed him from time to time, but without his being conscious of the pain.

As Jack knelt there it seemed to him that it was in a kind of confused dream that he heard his father's questions and the doctor's replies, as, after some ministration or another, they walked to the end of the cabin.

Then the captain came down softly.

"The enemy's coming out to sea," he said, "and making north; they'll be in a fix if the wind rises, for they are clustering in their canoes like bees. How's the patient?"

"Bad," said Sir John.

"Tut—tut—tut!" ejaculated the captain. "I am sorry. But you'll pull him through, doctor?"

"If I can," said Doctor Instow coldly.

"That's right. I have been so full up with my work that I seem to have taken hardly any notice of him. Wound through his arm. You have well cleansed it, of course?"

"Of course, and injected things to neutralise the poison."

"Ah!" cried the captain, angrily, "it takes all one's sympathy with the miserable savages away when one finds that they fight in so cowardly, so fiendish a fashion. I was ready to be sorry for them when I was crushing their boat. But this makes me feel as if one ought to lose no opportunity for sweeping the venomous wretches off the face of the earth. They have no excuse, you see. It is our lives or theirs. We are inoffensive enough surely; and they would have gained by our presence if they had been friendly. But they're nearly all alike."

"Have you seen cases like this before?" asked the doctor.

"Oh yes, several."

"And after a few hours' struggle the strength of the poison dies out, and the sufferer recovers?"

The captain glanced in the direction of Jack, and seeing that his attention was apparently entirely taken up by the sufferer, he said in a low tone— "Yes, sir, the strength of the poison died out, but the wounded man died too;" and every word went through Jack like some keen blade, and for the moment he drew his breath with as much difficulty as the man before him.

"In the cases I saw there was no doctor near at hand, and we who attended the poor fellows could do no more than try to draw the poison from the wounds and burn them out. But it seemed to me that the poison acted like the bite, of a snake, and altered the blood, while at last the symptoms were like those I have heard of when the patient has lock-jaw."

"Tetanus," said the doctor gravely.

"But it can't be so hopeless here. You were with him and attended him from the first."

"Yes; I have done all I can for him, poor fellow, and with his fine physique he may fight through it."

"Would amputation have saved him?" asked Sir John.

"I do not believe it would have had any effect upon a wound like that, even if it had been performed ten minutes after the injury," said the doctor. "The circulation is so rapid that the poison is running through the system at once, and to proceed to such an extremity seems to be giving the patient another terrible shock to fight against when his state is bad enough without."

"Then you have done everything you can?"

"Everything. He is beyond human aid."

Chapter Twenty Seven
The crew have their own opinions

The utter exhaustion produced by the struggle on the mountain slope and through the forest died away with Jack in the light of the terrible trouble which had come upon him; and as the afternoon wore on he just partook of such food as his father brought to him, for he would not leave the wounded man's side; and at last sunset came as they lay about a couple of miles out softly rocking upon the calm sea. He had heard how the canoes had been watched till they disappeared below the horizon line, and that all danger from another attack had passed away, but that seemed nothing in the face of this great trouble.

The night was approaching fast, and Jack shuddered at the thought of the darkness, and what it would bring; and once more it seemed impossible that the strong, active fellow who had been his companion that morning should be passing away.

If he could only have done something besides kneel there, keeping the poor fellow's head cool—something that would have helped him in his terrible fight with death—he would not have suffered so much; but to be so completely impotent seemed more than he could bear.

"You will go to bed early, Jack," said his father that evening, when the cabin was almost dark from the lamp being turned low.

"No, father; I am going to stop here, please," he replied.

"I will take your place, my boy. I feel too that we owe a great duty to the faithful fellow who has served us so long. You are tired out."

"No, father, I don't feel a bit tired now. Don't ask me to leave him. It is so hard with no one who knows him here; and I feel as if he will come to his senses some time, and would like to speak to me. I never did anything for him, but he always seemed to like me."

"Very well, Jack," said Sir John quietly, "I will not press you to go. But you will take necessary refreshment from time to time?"

"I could not touch anything," said the boy with a shudder.

"If you do not you will break down."

"Tell the steward to bring me some tea, then, by and by. You will go to bed?"

"I? No, my boy. I could not sleep."

Jack was left alone with the patient save when every half-hour or so the doctor and Sir John came down from the deck to minister in some way, and the long-drawn-out night slowly passed, with poor Ned breathing painfully, and lying nearly motionless, till a faint light began to come through the cabin windows, and the distant cries of birds floated to him over the sea.

Another day was at hand, and the solemnity of the hour seemed appalling to the watcher as he rose and went to the open window. A sense of the terrible loneliness of the sea oppressed him, and, exhausted now, he felt how helpless he was, how awful and strange was the change from night to the coming of another day.

There was not a sound to be heard on deck, though he knew that there were watchers there too, but not a footfall nor a whisper could be heard.

He stood there looking at the paling stars and the faint streaks of soft light low down in the east, till the black water stretching out to the horizon grew to be of a dull leaden grey, which gradually became silvery with a peculiar sheen, and then all at once there was the tiny fiery spot high up to the right above where the reef encircled the island, which was too distant now, after the night's steady glide away upon the current, for the breakers to be heard.

"Will he live to see the sun rise once more?" thought the boy, as the silvery sheen grew brighter on the surface of the sea, and then he started, and a great dread came upon him, for he felt that the time had come, for a faint voice said—

"Is that you, Mr Jack?"

Jack's first thought was to call the doctor from the deck, but he did not, he stepped quickly to the couch.

"I thought it was your back, sir. I've been watching you ever so long. I say, hadn't you better have the lamp lit, and let some of 'em carry me to my berth?"

"The lamp lit, Ned?" faltered Jack, with his heart fluttering the while.

"Yes, sir; it'll be quite dark directly."

"Yes," thought the lad, with a pang of misery shooting through him as he realised that after all this man was a friend that he could not afford to lose, "it will be quite dark directly."

"I'd go and fetch one, sir, but I don't feel up to it. I should go down on my nose if I tried to stand; and," he continued, laughing weakly, "smash the glass shade."

"Ned!" cried Jack, catching his hand, which closed upon it tightly.

"Have I been lying here all the afternoon, sir?"

"Yes—yes," sighed Jack, and he tried to withdraw his hand so as to call for help; but Ned clung to it tightly.

"What a shame! Upsetting everybody, and turning the gentlemen out of their place. I say, you can't have had dinner here, sir."

"No, Ned."

"'Shamed of myself. I don't know how time's gone. Been asleep. Dreaming like mad, and—Heigho! ha—hum! Hark at that, sir, for a yawn. Never put my hand before my mouth. I say, what about the niggers?"

"We are far out at sea, Ned," whispered Jack.

"Good job. I don't know though. I hope we shall go and give 'em an awful thrashing. We didn't interfere with them. Coming and shotting their arrows at us behind our backs. I say, Mr Jack, don't you get one in you. My word, how it does make you dream—all the awfullest nonsense you could imagine. I should like to tell you, but it's all mixed up so. I say, I fainted, didn't I?"

"Yes."

"I remember; up there in the wood. I felt myself going like a great gal. Just as I did once when I was a boy. How rum! That was through an arrow. I used to make myself bows and arrows, and I was making a deal arrow, and smoothing it with a bit of glass, when the bit broke and I cut my finger awful, and turned sick, and down I went.—I say, Mr Jack."

"Yes, Ned," said the lad in a voice full of pity.

"I can't recollect a bit after that. How did you yet me down to the boat?"

"The men carried you."

"One to them. My turn next. Good lads. Then you rowed out to the yacht."

"Yes, Ned."

"Yacht! I wish I could spell yacht when I write a letter home ready for posting first chance. I always get the letters mixed up. But I say, Mr Jack, this won't do! I say, would you mind giving me a bit of a pull? I could walk to my berth. This is luxurious, this is. Me on the cabin couch, and you waiting on me. Here, I feel like a rich lord. Now pull."

"No, no, Ned; lie still."

"I say, don't you get taking on like that, Mr Jack, sir," said the man earnestly. "That is being chicken-'arted. I'm all right. These two holes in my arm don't burn so; don't burn at all. Feel as if I hadn't got no arm that side. But I say, what's the matter?"

"Oh, Ned, my poor fellow!"

"Here, I say, Mr Jack, sir! Don't—don't, please. I say, I have upset you; but— Here, what does that mean? am I a bit off my head?"

"No, Ned, you are quite sensible now."

"No, I ain't, sir; I can't be, because things seem to be going backward. 'Tain't the moon, is it? because it's getting light instead of dark."

"Yes, Ned, the sun will soon rise."

"What! Don't play— No, you wouldn't do that. Sun rise? Why, I ain't been lying here all night, sir?"

"Yes, Ned."

"Well, my lad, how are you?" said Doctor Instow. "I thought I heard you speaking."

"Morning, sir. You're up early, sir. Won't want calling."

"No, I shall not want calling this morning, Ned. How are you?"

"About all right, sir, only I don't seem to have no arm. Oh, Mr Jack— Sir John!" cried the man wildly as his master entered the cabin, and he turned his head with a shiver from his injured limb, "you ain't let him do that, have you, while I've been asleep?"

"Do what, Ned?" said Jack in a soothing voice.

"Take a fellow's arm off, sir."

"No, no, Ned, my lad," said the doctor, laying his hand upon his patient's forehead. "It feels numb and dead from the wound."

"Then—then it isn't off?" cried the poor fellow with a gasp. "Oh, thank goodness! It give me quite a turn, sir, and I was afraid to look."

"You're better, Ned, and coming round fast," said the doctor, as a warm glow of light began to illumine the cabin, driving away the shadows of that terrible night.

"Oh yes, sir, I'm all right," said the wounded man, speaking more strongly now. Then in quite an apologetic tone, "Not quite all right, Sir John; you see, there's my arm. Sorry to have give so much trouble, Sir John; but you see, it wasn't quite my fault."

"Ah, lie still, you rascal!" said the doctor, as the man made an attempt to rise.

"Yes, don't move, Edward," said Sir John warmly. "I am very very thankful to see you so much better."

"Thankye, Sir John. It's very good of you to say so. But I can't stop here in your way. Seems as if I was shamming ill like so as to get waited on: and if there's anything I hate it's that. Don't seem nat'ral, Mr Jack, sir."

"Now lie still and be silent," said the doctor sharply. "Your tongue's running nineteen to the dozen, and it will not do your arm any good."

"But really, sir," protested Ned, "if you'd put on a couple of good round pieces of sticking-plaster, and let me wear it in a sling for a day or two, it would be all right."

"Will you hold your tongue, sir, hang you!" cried the doctor sharply. "I'd better put a bit of sticking-plaster on that. Do you think I want you to teach me my profession as a surgeon?"

"No, sir; beg pardon, sir."

"Silence, sir!"

Ned screwed up his mouth and his eyes as well. "Now, Jack, my lad," said the doctor, "I can't afford to have you ill too. Go to your room, undress and get into bed."

"Doctor! Now?"

"Yes, my lad, now. You went through a terrible day of excitement yesterday, and you have not stirred from this poor fellow's side all night."

"Mr Jack, sir! Oh!" cried Ned in a voice full of reproach.

"Look here, Ned," said the doctor, "if you say another word I'll give you a draught that will send you to sleep for twelve hours.—Now, Jack, my lad, do as I advise. Believe it is for your good. Go and sleep as long as you can. Never mind about it's being daylight. Ned is quite out of danger, and in a few days, when the poison is quite eliminated, he will be himself again."

At the words "danger" and "poison" the man's eyes opened wonderingly, and he looked at Sir John and his young master in turn.

"Yes, Jack, my lad, go."

"But if—"

"There is no *if* in the case, my boy," said the doctor. "It was a battle between the poor fellow's strength and the poison on that wretched arrow, and Ned has won."

"Oh!" ejaculated the man softly.

At that moment the captain and Mr Bartlett entered the cabin.

"We have heard all you said," exclaimed the former, as he came to the side of the couch and took the patient's hand, to give it a firm grip. "Good lad: well done."

"And I am very glad, Ned," said the mate warmly.

"There, that will do," said the doctor sharply. "He is forbidden to speak, but he says through me, that he is very grateful to you all, and glad to find that his manly, straightforward, willing ways have won him so many friends. Nod your head to that, Ned."

The man gave him a comically pitiful look, which seemed to Jack to mean, "Oh, I say, doctor, you're pitching that last too strong," but he remained quiet after giving every one an attempt at a nod.

"Now then," said, the doctor, "I want this cabin cleared, for he is going to sleep for a few hours, to get cool and calm. Yes, you are," said the doctor, in answer to a look full of protest. "And as soon as you wake I'll have you carried to your own berth. There, behave yourself, and you'll be all right in a few days."

Half-an-hour later both patient and Jack were sleeping soundly, and that evening, thoroughly out of danger, Ned was resting again in his own berth, and Jack was dining with the rest in the cabin as if nothing whatever had occurred; the yacht many miles now from the island, which stood in the evening light like a blunted cone of perfect regularity resting upon the placid sea.

That night the regular watch was kept, and the sea was steadily swept in search of danger in the shape of canoes stealthily approaching to try and take the yacht by surprise. But no danger came near, and at last, after lying awake for some time, thinking of the account his father had given him of the attack made by the enemy, and the terrible anxiety about the little shooting party, Jack fell into a deep and dreamless sleep, to rise refreshed and find the doctor's prognostic was correct, the patient having also had a quiet night, with the steward and Lenny to keep watch by his pillow, and there was no sign of fever to check a rapid recovery.

That day, with his mind at ease, Jack sat listening to a discussion held under the awning, as the yacht softly rose and fell upon the long pulsations of the calm sunlit sea, with the island lying ten or a dozen miles away.

"Of course, gentlemen," said the captain, "it is for you to decide. We are your servants, and your wish is our law."

"Well," said Sir John, "I am ready to speak apologetically to you, Bradleigh, for you cannot feel the interest in the place that we as naturalists do."

"Don't apologise, Sir John. Speak out and say what you feel."

"It is Doctor Instow's feeling too. We think that now we have reached here—thanks to you—"

"Only done what you wished, sir," said the captain bluntly.

"Well then, now that we have reached a place which teems with objects of interest, and which we have not half explored, it is a pity to leave it. What do you say, Jack? Shall we give it up?"

"Because a pack of senseless savages come and attack us? No, it would be cowardly," cried the lad.

"Poisoned arrows, spears, war canoes," said the doctor, with a queer look at Jack.

"Of course they are horrible," said the lad, flushing; "but perhaps we shall see no more of the blacks. Don't give it up, father."

"I should regret to have to do so, my boy, but mine is a very responsible position. I feel that I have to study others. I have no right to keep the officers and crew of this vessel where they are likely to encounter great risks."

"For the matter of that, sir," said the captain dryly, "those who go to sea look upon risks as a matter of course, and are rather disposed to think you landsmen run the most; eh, Bartlett? What do you say?"

"What, about the risk of staying here? Oh, I don't see any particular risk if we keep our eyes open, and are not sparing of the coal."

"Thank you, Mr Bartlett; but there are the men to study."

"Oh, you need not study about the men, Sir John," said the captain bluffly. "What do you say to that, Bartlett?"

"Study them, sir, no. They like it. They thoroughly enjoy the bit of excitement. If you put it to them you'll soon find which way they go."

"I should like to put it to them," said Sir John quietly.

"Have the lads all on deck," said the captain.

The hands were piped aft, and the captain waited for Sir John to speak, but he remained silent and looked at his son.

"Ask the men which they would prefer to do—stay here, or sail farther on account of the risks from the blacks."

Jack flushed a little, but he acquitted himself pretty well, and a hurried conversation went on for a few moments, ending in Lenny being put forward to answer, amidst a burst of cheering, which kept on breaking out again and again whenever the man essayed to speak, and at last he turned round angrily.

"Lookye here, mates," he cried, "hadn't you better come and say it yourselves? You've about cheered it out o' me, and made me forget what I meant to say."

"All right, matey," cried one of the men merrily, "let 'em have it; we've done now."

"Well, gentlemen," said Lenny, taking off his straw hat and looking in it as if the lost words had come through his skull to get hidden in the lining. "We all on us feels like this—as it wouldn't be English to let a lot o' lubbers o' niggers, who arn't got half a trouser to a whole hunderd on 'em, lick us out of the place. 'Sides, we arn't half seen the island yet, and 'bout ten on us has got a sort o' wager on as to who shall get up atop o' the mountain first and look down into the fire."

"Hear, hear, hear!" cried the men, and encouraged by this, Lenny began to wave his arm about and behave like a semaphore signalling to distant crews in his excitement.

"You see, gentlemen, we say it seems foolishness to come all this way to find what you wants, and then let these black warmint scare us off; when we arn't scared a bit, are we, mates?"

"No," came in a roar.

"So that's about all, gentlemen. We like the place and we're very comfor'ble, and if it's all the same to you, we'd like to stop and go fishing and shooting and storing; and—and—and—that's all, arn't it, mates?"

"Hooray! Well done, Billy," shouted the man who had tried to be funny before.

"Thank you, my lads," said Sir John, "and I hope you will have to run no more risks."

"Don't you say that, sir," cried Lenny; "we likes a bit o' fun sometimes; it's like pickles and hot sauce to our reg'lar meat."

"Ay, ay, mate, that's so," cried another, and there was another cheer, followed by the joking man stepping out before his companions to say quite seriously—

"And some on us, sir, think as you might hoist the British colours atop o' the mountain, and when we go back for you to go and give the island to the Queen."

"We'll think about all that," said Sir John. "Then my son and I understand that you are quite willing to stay in spite of the risk?"

"O' course, sir," said Lenny. "We'll go with you anywheres; won't we, mates?"

A burst of cheers greeted this speech, and Sir John said that they would stay in spite of all the canoes which might come.

Chapter Twenty Eight
Taken by surprise

It was the next day, when the yacht was just beginning to glide over the water again to pass through the opening in the reef, that Jack was sitting by Ned's berth.

"Here, I call it foolishness, Mr Jack, sir, I do really. What is the good of my lying here?"

"To get strong and well. Doctor Instow knows best."

"Well, he thinks he knows best, sir; but he can't know so well as I do how I feel."

"You lie still and be patient."

"But I can't, sir. Here's Mr Bob Murray, who's a good enough steward, valeting you and Sir John, and of course he can't do it properly."

"Nonsense. He is very good and attentive."

"Pooh, sir! So could any chap in the ship be good and attentive, but what's the use of that if he don't understand his work?"

"Why, there's nothing to understand."

"Oho! Isn't there, sir! Don't you run away with that idea. There's a lot. It seems nothing to you because things go so easy with you and the guv'nor. You find your clean shirts and fresh socks all ready laid out at the proper time, and you put 'em on just as you do your clothes, and think it's nothing; but all the time there's some one been there thinking it out first. Cold and dull morning; these trousers and that silk shirt won't do, and warmer ones are there. Going to be a scorching hot day, and it's the thinnest things in the bunks. Then don't I manage the buttons the same? and when did you ever find a button off anywhere?"

"No, I never did, Ned."

"There! I suppose you think, sir, that when a button's knocked off another one comes up like a mushroom in the night; but you take my word for it, sir, buttons don't come up so how, and it's never having no troubles like that to a gentleman that means having a good valet. I don't say nothing about holes in socks or stockings, because when it gets to that a gentleman ought to give 'em away. No, sir, it won't do. Every man to his trade, and I'm fretting to get back to my work, for it wherrits me to have other people meddling with my jobs. I don't believe I shall find a thing in its place."

"Never mind all that, Ned. I've got something to tell you."

"Have you, sir? Let's have it."

"I don't know what you'll say to it."

"More do I, sir. Let's hear what it is."

Ned told him of what had passed on deck concerning the stay at the island.

"Glad of it, Mr Jack," said Ned excitedly. "I should have been wild if you'd give it up because of me getting that arrow in my arm. But look here, I ain't a grudger, but if I do get a chance at the chap as shot at me—well, I'm sorry for him, that's all."

"What would you do to him, Ned?" said Jack, smiling.

"What would I do to him, sir? What wouldn't I do to him, sir!"

"You don't mean to say you'd kill him?"

"Kill him, sir?" cried Ned, in a tone full of disgust; "now do I look the sort of chap to go killing any one?"

"Well, no, Ned, you do not."

"Of course not, sir. Murder ain't in my way. I ain't a madman. Of course if one's in a sort o' battle, and there's shooting and some of the enemy's killed, that's another thing. I don't call that murder; that's killing, no murder. But in a case like this: oh no, I wouldn't kill him, I'd civilise him."

"What, and forgive him?" said Jack, who felt amused.

"Not till I'd done with him."

"And what would you do?"

"Do, sir! Why, what I say, sir; I'd civilise him, and show him something different to hitting a man behind his back. There'd be no call for him to strip, he'd be all ready; but I'd just have off my jacket and weskit, and some of the lads to see fair, and I'd show him the way Englishmen fight. I'd give him such a civilising as should make him respect the British nation to the end of his days. That's what I'd do with him. Fists!"

"Very well, Ned, look sharp and get strong so as to do it."

"Strong, sir? Why, I could do it now if you'd let me get up instead of making me bask about like a pig in a sty. I just feel, sir, as we used to say at school, as if I could let him have it, though it would hardly be fair. He'd have the greatest advantage."

"Yes, I should say he would," said Jack, laughing.

"Ah, you mean about muscle, sir. I don't. I mean that if he managed to get home with his fists in my face—not as I think he would—he'd make me look disgraceful, and not fit to appear before the guvnor for a fortnight. And all the time I might pound away for an hour and make no difference in him. Whoever heard of a nigger with a black eye?"

"Well, no, Ned, I never did," said Jack, laughing. "Nature ain't been fair over that, sir. Black chaps' eyes ought to go white after a fight; but I suppose it's because they don't fight fair. Hitting a man in the back, and with a poisoned arrow too! It makes me feel wild; it's so cowardly. But there, they don't know any better. I say though, Mr Jack, I am glad we're going to stay, and it makes me feel proud of our crew. I'll shake hands with the lot as soon as I may go on deck."

"That's right enough, Ned, and as soon as you're fit Doctor Instow will let you go."

"Tell you I'm fit as a fiddle now, sir," said the mate testily. "Why, nothing would do me more good than to stretch myself by having a set-to with that nigger as shot me."

"With one hand," said Jack dryly.

"Eh? With one hand, sir?" said the man, beginning to feel his closely-bandaged arm.

"Yes; how could you fight with one hand?"

"I forgot all about that," said Ned thoughtfully. "Would be rather awkward, wouldn't it?"

"Yes, I should think it would."

"Like fighting with one hand tied behind you, same as you did at school."

"I never did have a fight at school," said Jack, quietly.

"No, of course not, sir; I remember you said so once before. Seems rum, though. I used to have lots. But you were different, sir. My word though, Mr Jack, how you have altered since we left home!"

"Think so, Ned? Have I?"

"Wonderful, sir. Don't you be offended, sir, at what I say."

"Not I, Ned."

"You would have been then, Mr Jack. Seems to me that you were quite an old gentleman then, and now you've got to be quite a boy."

"Then I'm going backwards, Ned?"

"Not you, sir. You make me feel quite proud of you. Why, Bob Murray told me yesterday that you'd been right up all three masts as high as the sailors can get."

"Yes, I went up with my glass to look out for canoes. What of that?"

"What of that, sir? Well, fancy you trying to do such a thing a few months ago!"

"Perhaps I am a little stronger now," said Jack thoughtfully.

"Stronger, sir! I should just think you are. But I say, Mr Jack."

"Yes?"

"About my arm. I should get licked now. Think it will ever come right again?"

"Doctor Instow says it will, only it must have time. Do you feel any sensation in it now?"

"Not a bit, sir. Doctor asked me if he hurt me when he altered the bandages this morning, but I had to tell him he might do anything and I should not feel it. Just as if it was quite dead. Rum, ain't it, sir?"

"It's very sad, Ned."

"Oh, I don't know, sir. It's a nuisance; but the doctor says it will come right in time, so one's got to wait. He says he'll get the wound healed up, and then we can talk to the nerves and muscles with some good friction. Treat it like a lucifer, sir; give it a sharp rub and make it go off. But I shall be glad when he'll let me come on deck. Might do a bit o' fishing, sir."

"You shall, Ned, as soon as you can."

There were no signs of the savages' visit when they passed inside the lagoon again, and, in the hope that they might remain now unmolested, the yacht steamed right away from the entrance and cast anchor nearly on the opposite side of the island, where the lagoon was at its widest, so as to give ample room for manoeuvring in case of attack, where the shore was more beautiful than in any part they had yet seen.

One of the tiny rivers ran down a precipitous gully in a series of fern-hung falls, to lose itself in the golden sands, and close at hand the sheltering trees were of the grandest in size and loveliness, overhung as they were with festoons of flowers, each tree affording ample study for Sir John and his friend; and the collecting went on apace from morn to eve, so that the boxes they had brought began to fill up and smell strongly of the aromatic gums and spices used to keep ants at a distance.

The sailors took the keenest delight in the birds, and were eager to learn to skin, and carefully laid them in the hot sunshine till they dried. They gloried too in the pickle-tub, as they called the spirit-cask, to which the abundant snakes and lizards were consigned. Then of an evening they were always waiting for Jack to give the word for fishing, partly as an interesting sport, but after the first few times, for the sake of what Lenny called the pot, though in almost every case the capture was fried.

It needed a good deal of care and discrimination though, and the doctor's natural history knowledge was often called upon to decide whether some gorgeously-armoured creature would be wholesome or no, some of the tropic fish being poisonous in the extreme.

Then in addition there were the handsome birds which were collected; these, especially the fruit-pigeons, being very toothsome, though the larger parrots and cockatoos were, as Wrensler the cook said, not to be sneezed at, though he declared that they would have been far better if plucked instead of skinned.

So beautiful was the shore by the stream that the temptation was very great to erect a tent and live on the land, but it was considered too risky.

"Only fancy, Jack," said the doctor with a queer look, "our meeting with the same trouble out in this solitary island as we should in London."

"What trouble?" said Jack, laughing. "You don't mean the noise?"

"No, but I mean the blacks," said the doctor.

"Oh, I see," cried Jack; "but it does seem such a pity. I should like to have a tent ashore."

"It would be delightful under one of those big trees, but canvas is a poor safeguard against the point of a spear. It wouldn't do."

"No," said Jack with a sigh, "it would not do."

Many excursions into the interior were made—the interior meaning a climb up the slope of the great mountain—and in all cases a grand selection of beautifully-plumaged birds was secured. Many of these were the tiny sun-birds, glittering in scales of ruby, amethyst, sapphire, and topaz; then too at the sides of the streams vivid blue-and-white kingfishers with orange bills were shot, many of them with two of the tail-feathers produced in a long shaft ending in a racket-like flat, giving the birds a most graceful aspect.

Then there were plenty of paroquets, rich in green, orange, and vermilion; rain-birds as the Malays call them, in claret and white, with blue and orange beaks; parrots without number, and finches, swallows, and starlings of lovely metallic hues; but the greatest prizes were the birds of paradise, of which several kinds were secured, from the grandly-plumaged great bird of paradise to the tiny king. Whenever one of these was shot in some great grove at daybreak, Jack hesitated to have it skinned for fear of injuring the lovely feathers, over which adornments Nature seemed to have done her best. Now it was one of the first-named, a largish bird, with its feathers standing out to curve over in a dry fountain of golden buff, ornamented with their beautifully flowing; wave-like shafts; and this would be of a prevailing tint of soft cinnamon red; while the smaller kinds were lavishly adorned with crests and tippets and sprays of feathers brighter than burnished metal.

"I don't know how it is," said Jack one day, "but every bird we find seems more beautiful than the last."

He had just picked up a fresh specimen which had fallen to the doctor's gun.

"Well, it is more novel than beautiful, Jack," said the doctor, as they turned over and re-arranged the dark purple, or dark-brown, or claret, or black, or green metallic plumage, for it might have been called either according to the angle at which it was viewed. "Come, this will help to make them believe that birds of paradise are of the crow family."

"No one ever saw a crow half as beautiful as that," cried the lad.

"At home—no. But look at the shape of this bird—its wings, claws, and build altogether; doesn't he look as if he could be a crow?"

"There is a slight resemblance, certainly," said Jack; "but this isn't a bird of paradise."

"It is next door to one, my lad, and I am surprised to find it here."

"You know what it is then?"

"I know there's a northern Australian bird almost like it, if not quite. I think it is the rifle bird. We'll have a good look when we get back. Take special care of that one, Lenny."

"Ay, ay, sir. I takes special care of all of 'em, when the bushes and thorns 'll let me."

They were well up the gully through which the stream off which the yacht was anchored ran, for, finding the place rich in specimens, they had toiled up higher and higher that morning.

Ned was for the first time of the party, on the condition that he would be very careful, for his arm was still stiff and numb, though otherwise he was much better; but he kept pretty close to his young master, and let the men with him carry the guns and ammunition, and in several ways made silent confession that he was not so strong as he was.

Jack noticed it, and made some allusion to the fact.

"Oh, don't you fidget about me, Mr Jack, I'm getting on glorious," said the man quietly. "I feel as if the sun and wind up here were doing me no end of good, drinking 'em in like. Doctor said I was to take it coolly; so coolly I take it, as the sun 'll let me, so as to get strong again as soon as I can. But, my word, what a place it is!"

"Lovely," said Jack. "It grows upon one."

"Ah, I should like to grow upon it," said Ned, grinning. "I don't feel as if I should like to go away again."

"There's no place like home, Ned," said Jack, who had stopped to watch a pair of vivid sun-birds probing the tiny trumpet blossoms of a white creeper with their beaks.

"They say so, sir; but I say there's no place like this. When are we going right up to the top?"

"When you are quite well, Ned. We should have started before now, but I asked my father to put it off till you were strong enough to carry my gun and wallet."

Ned said nothing, but he looked as if he thought a great deal, and when he next spoke as they went on mounting the gully, it was directly after the doctor had added a lovely kingfisher to the bag.

"I say, Mr Jack, sir, of course the doctor knows a deal, but do you think he is always right?"

"I suppose no one is always right, Ned. Why?"

"About that bird—bird he shot. He said it was a kingfisher."

"Well, so it is. You heard him explain about its habits?"

"Yes; and that's what bothers me. How can it be a kingfisher if it don't fish?"

"You might just as well say, how can it be a kingfisher if it don't fish for kings."

"No, I mightn't, sir," replied Ned, whose illness seemed to have developed a kind of argumentative obstinacy. "Nobody nor nothing does fish for kings, sir, so that's nonsense. But what I say is, how can that bird be a kingfisher if it don't fish?"

"But it does fish."

"No, it don't, sir; it flits about and catches butterflies, and moths, and beetles. Doctor said it never caught fish at all, and never dived down into the water. So what I say is, that it can't be a kingfisher."

"Well, but Doctor Instow says that far away back in the past its ancestors must have lived on fish; and then the land where they were changed, till perhaps it was one like this, with plenty of beautiful little rivers in it, but few fish, and so they had to take to living upon insects, which they capture on the wing, and they have gone on doing so ever since."

"Seems rum," said Ned thoughtfully. "Then I suppose if this island was to change, so that there were no more butterflies, moths, or beadles, and more fish took to living in the rivers—they'd take to fishing again?"

"Yes, I suppose so; all things adapt themselves to circumstances."

"Do they now, sir?"

"Yes; but you don't know what I mean."

"No, sir, I'm blessed if I do."

"How stupid! why don't you ask then?"

"'Cause I don't want to bother you, sir, when you're getting tired."

"What nonsense! Always ask if you don't understand me. I meant that I have read about plants and animals altering in time to suit the place where they are. If dogs are taken up into the arctic regions they get in time to have a very thick fur under the hair; and if they are taken into a hot country like this, they have a very fine silky coat."

"Do they now, sir?" said Ned. "Now I wouldn't have thought that a dog would have so much gumption. But I don't know, dogs are very knowing."

"I don't think the dog has anything to do with it, Ned; it is a natural law. Now, if a fir tree is in a sheltered place, where the soil is deep and sandy, it grows to a tremendous size; but if the seed falls in a rocky place, where it has to get its roots down cracks to find food, and cling tightly against the cold freezing winds, it keeps down close to the ground, and gets to be a poor scrubby bush a few feet high, or less."

"Then the trees have got gumption too, sir. That's better than being blown down."

"I don't know about gumption, Ned; but it's the same with flowers. They grow thin and poor on rocks and stones, and rich and luxuriant on good moist soils, and— Hallo! where are the others? we mustn't be left behind."

"Oh, we're all right, sir. They're only just ahead, and we can't lose ourselves, because all we've got to do is to go back along by the trickling water here. I'll shout if you like."

"Oh no; I could blow my whistle, but I don't want to, because it would startle the doctor. He'd think there was something wrong."

"Don't whistle him, sir. Here's a nice comfortable bit o' rock here; would you like to sit down?"

"You're tired, Ned," said Jack quickly.

"Am I, sir? Well, I dunno—p'r'aps you're right. I s'pose I am a bit fagged. Legs don't seem to go quite so well as they used. If you wouldn't mind, I think I should like just ten minutes' rest to freshen me up a bit."

"Sit down then."

"After you, sir."

"Very well: there. No, sit down—or, better still, lie down on your back."

"Make the things about puzzled, and want to know what I am. I shall be having snakes and lizards going for a walk up my arms and legs, sir. But I don't know as I mind for a bit—I'll risk it."

Jack had halted at the foot of a perpendicular wall of moss-grown rock, and set the example, after disturbing the grass and ferns at the foot, of sitting down, and Ned lay at full length.

"Lovely, sir," he said. "It's worth while to get regular tired so as to enjoy a rest like this. I don't s'pose they'll go much farther, and they must come back this way, I suppose."

"I think so, Ned. They couldn't come back through the forest, and they would not as soon as they missed us, they'd be sure to come this way so as to pick us up."

He was silent for a few moments, and then went on softly, as his eyes wandered over the trees and creepers about them—

"How lovely it all is, with the sun sprinkling light through the leaves. It looks just like silver rain. Look at that great flapping moth. That must be an Atlas, I suppose. I ought to try and catch it, but it seems such a pity to go out and destroy every beautiful thing one sees, so as to turn it into a specimen. Look at those orchid clusters growing out of the stump where the tree branches. Shall I pick it, Ned? Say yes, and I won't. I haven't forgotten the little snake which crept out on to my hand that time. Hallo! What bird's that? What a chance for a shot!"

As he sat there with a gun across his knees, first one and then half-a-dozen large birds, emboldened by the silence, came stalking out from beneath the bushes, looking something like so many farmyard hens as they began to peck and scratch about.

"What a chance!" thought Jack. "I might get a couple for roasting, but we've killed enough things for one day."

He sat perfectly still, watching the birds till they had crossed a little opening in front and slowly began to make their way up the slope in the direction taken by the doctor, Lenny, and the four men with them.

Then all at once one of the birds uttered a low clucking sound, and stood up with outstretched neck gazing in Jack's direction.

The bird was absolutely motionless for a few moments, then it ducked down its neck and ran off beneath the undergrowth.

"Birds are beginning to know that we're dangerous," he said aloud. "Did you see those, Ned?"

There was no answer, and Jack turned to gaze down at his companion, who was fast asleep and breathing heavily.

"Poor fellow, he is not so strong as he thinks," said Jack to himself, "or else he will not own to his weakness for fear of being a trouble to us. What a wonderful thing strength is! I suppose I'm a good deal sturdier than I was. Must help father to-night arranging and making notes of some of the insects we got yesterday. Why, we shall have a regular museum by the time we get back to England."

And as he sat there in the calm silence, with the huge trees towering above his head, as if to filter the light and let it fall in streams and drops, it seemed to him that the best way to observe Nature was to sit down perfectly still as he had, and watch. For in different directions he saw next how animal and even insect stole out now to pursue its ordinary courses, and he sat watching till the whole place seemed alive.

Twice over he heard shots, but they were faint and distant, and once there was a peculiar bump as if a large stone had fallen from far up the mountain side. Then all was still again, and the birds he had seen pause in alarm resumed their pecking and climbing about.

"How soundly he sleeps!" thought Jack; and at last, when a good hour had passed away, he began to wish for the return of the doctor and the men, but there was no rustle of leaves, no sound of breaking strand or twig, everything was perfectly still, and the lad shifted his position a little so as to find a place to rest his back, and as he did so a peculiar sensation came over him. It was as if a mental shadow crossed his mind, begetting a shock of dread. The next moment a heavy blow from behind fell upon his head, and all was blank.

Chapter Twenty Nine
The missing pair

"Here! Hi! Jack! Where are you, lad?" There was no reply, and the doctor called the nearest of the men, who were slowly making their way through the dense growth, putting up some strange bird from time to time.

"Where's Mr Jack, Lenny?"

"Mr Jack, sir? Arn't seen him lately. 'Long o' Ned, I think. See Mr Jack from where you are, mate?"

"No," came back, and the fresh speaker hailed his nearest companion, and he his. But no one had seen the boy lately. They had all been too much occupied in looking out for rare birds.

"Let's wait a bit," said the doctor. "Give them time to come up. Here, Lenny—and you—let's look at the sport."

He sat down on a block of lava, and became so interested in the specimens he had obtained that he did not notice the lapse of time.

"Here," he cried at last, "they must have knocked up, and are waiting for us to go back. Why, we must have come much farther than ever we came before."

"That's why we've got such good birds, sir," said Lenny.

"Perhaps so. Well, back again now.—Oughtn't to have left him behind like that," muttered the doctor to himself.

He was hot and weary from his exertions, but his anxiety made him hurry back nearly in the path they had made in ascending, but that soon proved to be too difficult, the growth having sprung back after they had passed, and as they had gone up the steep slope well separated, the tracks were feebly marked, and not as they would have been had they followed in each other's steps.

The consequence was that first one mark was found, then another, in the shape of a broken twig or crushed-down patch of grass, but the next minute the steps were lost, and everything looked so different in descent they in a short time found themselves ready to give up the laborious task of trying to follow in the steps taken when going up, and glad to go back wherever the way was easiest.

To make up for this the little party spread out as far as was reasonable, and at every few yards the doctor gave a loud whistle and waited for a reply.

None came, and they hurried on, rarely recognising anything to act as a guide, but steadily going down toward the shore; and as there was no reply to his calls, the doctor soon came to the conclusion that, tired of waiting, Jack had turned back, and in the full expectation of finding the missing ones down by the boat, the party was pressed on, but with their leader getting more annoyed at every step.

The boat was invisible till they were close upon it, lying in the mouth of the little river where the great trees spread their boughs right across, and at the first rustle of the bushes being heard the sailors in charge started up and began to draw her close in shore.

The doctor uttered an ejaculation full of annoyance, but began clinging directly after to the thought which struck him.

"How long have they gone on board?" he cried as soon as he was well within hearing.

Then his hopes were crushed, for the men addressed replied—

"Gone on board, sir? Who gone on board?"

"Mr Jack and his man."

"Haven't been down here, sir. Arn't lost 'em, have you?"

The doctor made no reply.

"Here," he cried, "take these birds, and you two who have been resting come back with me. Lenny, I want you, and you come too," he continued to another of the men.

The other two who had come down from the mountain slope were eager to return, but the doctor ordered them to take charge of the boat, and without pausing a minute shouldered his gun and turned to follow the path they had taken that morning, with better hope of success.

"I dare say we came close by them somewhere," he said to Lenny. "I hardly see though how we could have missed them."

"Strikes me, sir, as I know how it was," said the man.

"You think you know?"

"Yes, sir, but it's only thinking, and mayn't be right."

"Tell me what you think," cried the doctor impatiently.

"It was hot, sir, steamy hot under the trees, and Mr Jack is young and none too strong, and Ned arn't quite got over his trouble."

"Yes, of course. Well, go on."

"Well, sir, they must have trudged after us till they were tired out, and then sat down to wait for us, and went to sleep."

"I hope that's it, Lenny," said the doctor as they struggled on, up and up, amongst tree, bush, and rock, while, to add to their difficulty, a complete change came on with tropic rapidity, a black curtain of clouds swept across the sky, and in an incredibly short time the lightning flickered for a few minutes through the trees, and then came in blinding flashes, accompanied more than followed by peal upon peal of thunder which seemed to shake the island to its foundation.

Worse still was to follow. Just as the lightning was flashing and quivering among the trees, and the thunder was at its loudest, the rain came down. It had approached from the sea with, a dull hissing sound which grew louder and louder, till with startling force the wind which bore it on its wings flung it as it were with a tremendous force upon the mountain slope, whipping the boughs and tearing the leaves from the twigs, pouring away with terrific violence, and rushing downward into the gully, which soon became filled with a roaring torrent which swept all before it.

This was the first example the doctor had encountered of the power of a tropical storm, and he was glad to shelter himself and his four companions beneath an overhanging ledge of lava rock—a poor protection, but such as it was it saved them from much of the force of the storm.

The downpour ceased as suddenly as it had commenced, the tempest sweeping over the island to pass on to the ocean and be dissipated there, so that in little more than an hour the sun was shining down through the trees again, where the drenched earth was spangled as it were with jewels.

But the task of continuing the search was now made excessively difficult. The ground was slippery in the extreme, save where the lava had been washed bare, and at almost every step the water-laden boughs poured down a fresh shower upon them. The labour was terrible, for now it was as if they were forcing their way through a bath of hot vapour which was enervating in the extreme.

But they struggled on hour after hour, vainly seeking for some trace of the missing ones—a task which would have baffled the keenest-eyed

Red Indian, for the rain had swept away every footprint, and when at rare intervals a broken branch or torn-off leaf-covered twig was found, it was as likely to have been the work of the storm as of any one passing through.

Faint with an exhaustion he would not own to, the doctor was still urging or cheering his men on, when the dull concussion of a gun and the following echoes announced that those on the yacht were impatient for their return.

"Signal to come back, sir," said Lenny despondently.

"Yes, but we can't go back without finding them first," said the doctor angrily. "Who is to face Sir John Meadows and tell him we have failed in our duty of protecting his son?"

No one answered, and the silence was broken by the dull thud of another gun.

"It is of no use, I can't return while it is light, but the summons must be answered. Here, Lenny, go back and tell Sir John what has happened, and that we are searching in every direction."

"Me, sir?" cried the man with a look of horror; "I couldn't do it, sir."

"You must. You have been out all day, and must be done up."

"Me, sir! My mate's ever so much worse nor me. Send him."

"G'orn with you," cried the other sailor who had been with them since the first start; "why I arn't half so done as he is, sir."

"I want you to go, Lenny," said the doctor sternly. "I dare say you will find another boat waiting. Send the men up to help the search. But there is no need to send that message, Sir John is sure to have come himself."

"Mean it, sir? I'm to go?" said Lenny.

"Yes, of course."

"Well, sir, I'd sooner keep on hunting for the poor lad all night than face Sir John; but if you say I am to do it, why do it I must."

"Go then," said the doctor, "and mind, you are not to attempt to return."

"Arks your pardon, sir, but it'll be 'bout two hours 'fore I get down to the boat."

"No, no; not half that time," cried the doctor.

"We've come a long way, sir. What do you say, mates?"

"All two hours," was the reply.

"Yes, sir, you've been so anxious 'bout it you arn't noticed how the time goes, and as I was going to say, by the time I get down to the boat it will be black as the inside o' one o' the coal-bunkers."

The doctor stood gazing at the man wildly.

"There won't be no more searching then."

"You're right, you're right," groaned the doctor. "There, stop with us. Come what may the poor fellows must be found."

Bang! went a signal gun again, and the echoes rolled away up the mountain, growing fainter and fainter, while the lovely grove, full of dazzling light and darkest shade, resplendent in its beauty, and with the air fragrant with the freshened odour of leaf and flower, seemed to Doctor Instow the most horrible solitude to which man had ever been condemned.

"There they go again," said one of the men, as once more a gun was fired.

"Forward," cried the doctor, rousing himself from his utter despondency.

"Which way, sir?" asked Lenny.

"Any way, my lads. System is of no use here. We must trust to chance."

"Think he can have got over into the next gully, sir?" said Lenny.

"No, no, impossible. It would take a party of strong men to cut a way through, and they would not make the clearance in a week. Forward! Open out and keep on giving a hail from time to time."

Another signal gun for their recall was fired.

"We can't help it," said the doctor. "Forward, my lads. We must find them now."

It was not until the occasional glimpses of the sky they caught told him by their altered colour that the night was close at hand, that the doctor once more halted, and then gave the order for the party to return as well as they could upon their tracks.

And now as they staggered more than walked wearily back a shot was fired every few minutes, and a short halt made to listen for a response.

But none came, and they struggled on through the darkness, the rapidness of the descent of the ground and the roar of the torrent at their side being their only guides, for the darkness beneath the trees was now intense.

How long they had been going downward no one could have said, as they kept now in line, following each other closely, with Lenny first, when after stumble and fall at every few yards, as the doctor's gun flashed and the report rang out, it was at length answered from higher up on their left.

"At last!" cried the doctor, rousing himself from the feeling of exhaustion which seemed to have deadened all his energies. "Bear to the left, Lenny, for a few minutes, and then I'll fire again."

"Ay, ay, sir!" said the man huskily, and in a very short time he stumbled and fell, rolling down a precipitous part.

"Hurt?" cried the doctor.

"Dunno, sir," said the man with a groan. "Feels like it; but don't you mind me, you fire again."

The doctor cocked his piece and raised it to fire in the air, when a shot rang out again, apparently about a hundred yards away, the flash before the report being plainly seen.

"Ahoy!" yelled Lenny hoarsely, and this was answered faintly.

"That's Ned," growled Lenny. "No, no; not his voice," cried the doctor. "Mind how you go down there."

The words were useless, for the men were too much worn out to study anything, and they let themselves slide down, only too glad to get to the bottom.

"Ahoy!" came now, and as they answered there was a breaking and rustling heard among the trees, shouts and sharp orders could be heard, and in a few minutes the two parties encountered.

"Have you found him?" cried the doctor, for he had known for some moments that he was wrong.

"Found him!" came back in the voice of Sir John, full of agony. "Is not Jack with you?"

The doctor's answer was a groan before he announced what had happened.

A few minutes' conversation followed between Sir John and the mate, before the former said sharply, in a tone which cut the doctor to the heart—

"Can you give me no idea where you missed them first?"

"Not the slightest," said the doctor bitterly. "We are completely lost."

There was silence for a few moments before Sir John spoke again.

"Go on down to the mouth of the gully," he said sharply, "and make the best of your way on board."

"What are you going to do?" said the doctor.

"Stop here till daylight, and then continue the search. Better make a fire, my lads."

"Yes," cried the mate. "It may guide them to us."

"I must stay," said the doctor.

"I do not want you," said Sir John coldly, "and you are too tired to be of any use."

"I suppose so," said the doctor bitterly, "but I must stay all the same."

"Then back with you, my men," said Sir John.

"Keep on downward near the stream, and you must come upon the boat."

There was a dead silence.

"Well," said the mate sharply, "why don't you go?"

"Dunno 'bout the others," said Lenny softly. "I'm ready to make a start, but I can't. It's my legs won't go."

"That's about it with me," said another of the men; and the result was that the mate told them to sit by the fire that was made, and rest for an hour before starting back. But when the hour had elapsed the poor fellows were plunged in a stupor-like sleep from which they could not be aroused.

Chapter Thirty
The reverse of circumstances

"The worst headache I ever had," said Jack Meadows to himself, as he lay with his eyes close shut, and in terrible pain; and then, with his brow throbbing, and a miserable sensation of sickness making his head confused, he began thinking, as a lad who has been brought in contact a good deal with a medical man would think, of the causes of his ailment, and what he had eaten that so disagreed with him, while he mentally resolved that, however good it was, he would never be tempted into tasting it again.

He might have added—till next time, but he did not. For just then in his weariness, pain, and mental confusion it seemed to him that some one else was suffering too, and in a similar way, for he heard a low, dismal groan, and a voice muttered—"Oh, my poor nut." Jack's eyes sprang open, and apparently let light into his brain, for in one glance he saw more than he had ever seen before in so short a glimpse.

For he had a full comprehension of his position, while the details thereof fixed themselves like an instantaneous photograph upon his mind. The mental agony chased away the physical, and he gasped as he realised that he was bound hand and foot with green rotan cane; that Ned was in a similar condition lying alongside, but with his face away; that they were in an opening on the mountain side shut in by rocks and trees; and worst of all, that a few yards away a party of about twenty blacks of fierce aspect, and their hair mopped out with gum till each savage's coiffure was bigger than a grenadier's cap, were seated chattering together and feasting upon some kind of food which they had been roasting at a fire made among the stones.

The peculiar odour of burnt flesh sent a thrill of horror through him, and made a heavy dew of perspiration break out upon his brow at the thought of what probably was to follow, and for a time he felt as if he must shriek aloud. But he remained silent, though he did struggle fiercely to free his hands and feet from their bonds.

How these people had come there was a puzzle, but he was bound to confess that it was no dream. They had evidently landed on the island, prepared a fire, and cooked their food, which certainly was not fish, and they had surprised him and Ned, coming behind and stunning them by blows of the war-club each savage carried stuck through the band he wore about his waist.

One of Jack's first thoughts was, Had they surprised the doctor and the four men with him as well?

As this thought occurred to him he searched the group eagerly, but there was no sign of any plunder, and certainly he and Ned were the only two prisoners, so there was some hope of their being rescued as soon as they were missed. They were five, and Doctor Instow would not hesitate a moment about attacking—how many were there?

He counted twice over, and then, with his head still sufficiently confused to make the task difficult, he counted again, to find that there were more than he had thought at first, several being flat on chest or back, while two, like the Irishman's little pig, would not lie still to be counted.

His further thoughts were put an end to by a low groan from his companion in misfortune, who suddenly made an effort and rolled himself over so that he lay face to face with his young master.

"Oh, I say, sir," he whispered, with a look of horror in his eyes, "ain't this awful!"

Jack nodded.

"My wristies and ankles are nearly cut through."

"So are mine."

"Have they got your gun as well as mine?"

Jack nodded, keeping his eyes on the lithe, shiny bodies of the hungry blacks the while, but they were too much intent upon feasting to take any notice of their prisoners.

"They must have fetched me an awful crack on the head, sir. Did they hit you too?"

"Yes, my head aches horribly, Ned. Look, there are our guns standing up against the rock with their spears."

"And bows and arrows too, sir. Ugh! gives me the shivers. Poisoned!"

"Ned, do you think we could get at our guns and make a dash to escape?"

"What, and risk the arrows?"

"Yes. Once we could get amongst the trees we should have as good a chance of getting away as they would of catching us."

"Don't know so much about that, sir. They ain't got no clothes to catch in the thorns and creepers."

"But you'll try?"

"Try, sir! I should think I would; only I'd wait till it got dark first."

"By that time we may not be alive, Ned."

"Oh yes, we shall, sir. If they'd been going to kill us they wouldn't have taken the trouble to tie us like this."

"You are saying that to cheer me up, Ned," whispered Jack.

"No, sir, 'strue as goodness I ain't. It's just what I mean. But I'm ready to do anything you do if I can. Legs hurt you, sir, where they're tied?"

"Horribly, Ned."

"So do mine, sir, and so does one hand and wrist. T'other don't seem of any consequence at all. It's ever so much number than it was before, so that it don't ache a bit."

They lay there for some time watching the blacks, who kept on eating as if they would never leave off. Every now and then one went round to the back of the stones which formed their rough fire-place, and helped himself to more, returning to sit down and go on eating with the customary result. Thoroughly glutted at last, first one and then another sank back and went to sleep where he had sat eating, till not one seemed to be on the watch, and Jack looked full in the eyes of his companion in misfortune, questioning him.

"I'd wait just a bit longer to let 'em get off sound, sir," said Ned softly; and seeing the wisdom of the advice, Jack waited with every nerve on the strain. But there was no sound to be heard, and he took it for granted that the blacks had dragged or carried them for some distance, right away from the track taken by the doctor. As he examined the place more attentively, it seemed as if this was a spot which had been used as a camp before, for the bushes and trees were disfigured by flame and smoke, and the stones and rock which rose up like a wall were utterly bare of grass, lichen, and creeper.

Then as he lay he began to reason out matters a little more, till, right or wrong, he came to the conclusion that this must be a hunting party landed on the island to pursue the droves of pigs, one of which they had killed, cooked, and eaten.

He felt lighter-hearted as he thought this, for ugly ideas had crept into his mind and made him shudder with horror.

That this was the true reason for the blacks being there he felt more and more convinced, and this meant that there must be another opening through the reef somewhere unnoticed during their cruise round the island, so that if an examination had been made then, a canoe would be found run up on the sands waiting for their return.

This point reached, Jack whispered suddenly to Ned—

"Do you think they have tied us up like this so as to take us down to a canoe?"

"Yes, they've made us prisoners to take us away somewhere. That's what I think, sir."

"Yes, and that's what I think, Ned. Now look carefully all round, and see if you can make out whether any one is watching."

"Can't get my head up, sir," whispered the man after a pause, "but as far as I can make out they're all fast asleep."

"Then let's try to get away."

"Yes, sir; but how?"

"Do as I do. I'm outside, and the ground slopes down from here. I'll start and you follow."

"But I'm tied wrists and ankles, sir. I can't stir."

"Yes, you can. Don't whisper so loud. I am going to roll myself over slowly, and keep on down that slope till I'm a little way off. Then I think we can get our knives out. I can get yours, or you can get mine. Or did they take yours?"

"No, sir. It's in my pocket all right; I can feel it against me."

"Then, ready. It's of no use to wait longer. I'll start, and you lie still and watch. If they don't notice my moving, then you can come."

"No, sir, we go together or we don't go at all. I'm not going to lie still and let you be caught and knocked about perhaps."

"There's no time for arguing, Ned. Do as I tell you. There, I'm off."

Ned drew his breath hard, and raised his head a little to note whether his young master's movements were heard, but though the growth rustled and crackled a little not a savage stirred, and Jack went on rolling himself over and over, suffering pretty sharp pain from his bonds, but setting it at nought, and struggling on till well down out of sight of the rough camp.

Then he stopped and waited for Ned during what seemed to be quite an age before the man joined him, breathing laboriously, and then they lay listening, but all was still.

"Easy enough to escape, sir, if you make up your mind to it."

"But we have not escaped yet, Ned," whispered Jack. "We ought to have waited till it was dark. Now then, I'll creep close to you. Try and put your hand in my pocket and take out the little knife I have there."

It was harder to do than either of them had anticipated, and Ned suffered agony in one wrist as he strained to get at the knife with one hand, while the other was always in the way and kept it back. At last though he was successful and held it in triumph, but there was something more to do, for a closed blade was as bad as nothing.

Still they say "where there's a will there's a way." Certainly there was will enough here, and by degrees Ned worked himself along so that he could hold the little clasp-knife to Jack's lips. These parted directly, so did his firm white teeth, and closed upon the blade, while Ned drew at the handle, with the result that the blade was opened a little. Then it was drawn from between Jack's teeth, and closed with a snap, when the work had to be gone over again.

This time, trembling with excitement and dread lest at any moment the blacks might miss them, Jack closed his teeth with all his might upon the narrow portion of the blade awkwardly offered to him, held on at the risk of the ivory breaking, and Ned drew the handle away slowly, with the result that the strength of the spring was mastered, the knife half opened, and this done the rest was easy.

Ned paused for a few moments to wrench his head round and gaze up the slope toward the savages' camp, then turning to Jack he laid the blade flat upon the back of his hand, and forced it under the thin cane which bound his wrists, having hard work to do it in his hampered position without cutting his companion's hands.

"Now, sir," he whispered, "I'll turn the blade edge outwards, and you must work yourself up and down against it. Try now."

Jack made an effort, which hurt his wrist horribly without doing the slightest good.

"That won't do, sir," whispered Ned. "I can't help you half so much as by holding still. Now try again, not jigging as you did before, but giving yourself a regular see-saw sort of swing. Now then 'fore they wake. Off you go."

It was agony. The back of the knife-blade seemed to be cutting bluntly down upon his wrist-bones, but setting his teeth hard, Jack forced himself downward and drew back.

"That's the sort, sir. Don't do much, but it's doing something. If I had my hands free I could soon cut the withes. Keep it up."

Setting his teeth harder, Jack kept on the sawing movement, apparently without avail, but the pain grew less as the edge of the blade cut into the cane.

"It's of no use, Ned," whispered the lad. "Let's try to undo the knots with our teeth. I'll try on yours first."

"You keep on sawing," said the man in a low growl, and the words came so fiercely that Jack involuntarily obeyed, and the next minute, to his great surprise, there was a faint cracking sound; one strand of the cane band was through, and the rest uncurled like a freed spring.

"Hah! I thought so," said Ned with a low chuckle of satisfaction. "Now catch hold of the knife and cut the band round your ankles."

"I can hardly feel the handle," muttered Jack.

"You will directly. Look sharp, sir, sharp as your knife."

"Yes," said Jack, "but I'm going to cut your wrists free first."

"No, no, sir; your legs."

Jack set his teeth again as hard as when he was holding the back of the knife-blade, and in response he took hold of Ned's hand with his left and applied the edge across the cane which held the poor fellow's wrists, and in a clumsy fumbling way began to saw downward.

"Mr Jack, Mr Jack!" whispered the man excitedly, "you shouldn't, you shouldn't! I wanted to get you cut loose first."

"You hold your tongue and keep still," said the lad. "I don't want to cut your wrist. Steady. Oh, how numb and helpless my hands feel."

"They cut well enough, sir," said Ned with a laugh, as the outer turn of the cane band was divided, and once more the tough vegetable cord opened like a spiral string.

"That's your sort, Mr Jack, sir. Give me hold of the knife. My turn now."

"No, no, my hands are getting better. Rub your wrists while I cut your ankles free."

For answer Ned made a dash at the knife, but Jack avoided him, and forgetting everything in his desire to set his companion at liberty, he began sawing away at his ankles, while Ned thrust his hand into his own pocket and drew out his knife, to begin operating directly after upon Jack's bonds, with so much success that he was able to free him first.

His own were at liberty though directly after, and then they lay panting and perfectly still.

Jack was the first to speak.

"Now then," he said, "shall we crawl up and try and get our guns?"

"And make one of them wake and tap us both again on the head. No, sir, that won't do. Soon as you feel that you can move, crawl right away in among the bushes, and I'll follow. Have you got any hands and feet? because I feel as if I hadn't."

"Mine are terribly numb, Ned, but we'll start at once. It will do me more good to work them than to rest them. Which way?"

"Downwards, because it's more easy. Then go into that hollow ditch-like bit."

"But it goes upward."

"Never mind, take it, and we shall be out of sight. It will be best. They're sure to think we've made for the sea. Why, how dark it's growing. Didn't know it was so late."

Jack said nothing, but began to crawl away as fast as his tingling, helpless limbs would allow, feeling that so long as they got away from their captors it did not so much matter which direction they took. He turned his head from time to time to see if Ned was all right, and found that he was lamely struggling on after him, but always gave him a cheery look.

Jack followed the rugged little ditch-like place, which had evidently been carved out by one of the rivulets which ran down from the mountain, but after following it some time and turning to look back at Ned, he suddenly dropped flat on his face and began to crawl out of it, and toward the shelter of the forest, which came close up.

"What's the matter?" said Ned.

"Don't lift your head; creep as flat as you can, and let's get among the bushes."

"That's right enough; but why? It won't be such good going."

"We've been crawling higher and higher," said Jack, "and when I turned to see how you were getting on, I looked down over your shoulder, on to the smoke of the fire, and the blacks were lying about it, and just at that moment one of them jumped up, and then all the rest followed, and they must have missed us!"

"Shall we get up and run then?"

"No, no, they may not come this way. Hark! what's that?"

"Wind. Why, I didn't see it coming, only thought it was evening. We're in for a storm."

"Never mind, if it will only keep them from following us, Ned."

They struggled on, finding their limbs less helpless. Minute by minute, and just before plunging into the darkness beneath the trees, Jack turned to raise his head slightly, and to his great delight saw ten or twelve of the blacks far below the smoke of their camp, and evidently descending the mountain slope, but the next instant his hopes were crushed, for there in full pursuit, coming along the stony hollow up which they had crawled, was another party of the enemy.

"In with you, Ned," he whispered, as he dropped down again to creep into the dense growth which swallowed him like a verdant sea, while before they had penetrated many yards the gloom beneath the spreading branches was lit up by a flash of lightning. The next minute the flashes came so quickly that the forest seemed turned into one vast temple, whose black pillars supported a ceiling of flame, and as the deafening detonations shook the earth around them, they were glad to crouch as quickly as they could in a recess formed at the foot of a gigantic tree which sent out flat buttresses on every side, more buttresses passing down into roots.

They were none too soon, for the storm was, brief as the time had been, now in full force; the rain dashed and swept in amongst the groaning trees, and the noise and confusion were deafening, and made the more awe-inspiring by the lashing of the branches as they were driven here and there by the wind.

"What's that, sir?" cried Ned, with his lips to his companion's ear, for a tremendous crash had succeeded a roar of thunder.

"Tree gone down."

"Oh!" said Ned, pressing Jack close up into the recess. "Well, so long as it ain't this one I suppose we mustn't grumble. But I'd rather have undressed myself before I took my bath, sir, wouldn't you?"

"Oh, how can you talk like that!" shouted Jack.

"'Cause I feel so jolly and satisfied," said Ned, with his lips again to Jack's ear. "A bit ago it was all over with us, going to be took and tied up again, sir. P'r'aps to be taken away and fatted and eaten. Now there's nothing the matter, only it's a bit dark. Don't seem, sir, as if I'm doing any good in trying to be your umbrella. You are a little moist, I suppose, sir?"

"Moist, Ned! I'm soaking; I can feel the water running down into my boots."

"Oh, never mind, sir. We'll have a good wring out as soon as the storm's over. But my word, I never saw lightning like this before, and never felt it rain so hard."

"Nor thunder so loud," cried Jack. "It is terrible. Hush! hark at that!"

"Water, sir, running down this way."

"Shan't be washed away from here, shall we, Ned?"

"No, sir, I think not. Seems to me that it's coming down that bit of a ditch we crawled up."

It was: the dry, stony bed having been filled in a few minutes six feet deep by a raging torrent, which was constantly being augmented by scores of furious rills, the upper portions of the mountain having been struck by what resembled a swirling water-spout.

"I say, Mr Jack, I hope the yacht won't get washed away. Which side of that stony ditch were the niggers when you saw 'em last?"

"The other side."

"Then they won't come this. Now if they'd only take to thinking that we'd been washed down the side and out to sea, what a blessing it would be for us! They wouldn't come and hunt for us any more."

"Don't—pray don't talk," cried Jack. Then to himself,—"Oh, if the storm would only keep on."

But, as has been shown, it did not. Its violence on their side of the mountain was soon exhausted, and it swept on and out to sea, leaving the fugitives standing where hundreds of rills came amongst the foot of the trees on their way toward the stream overflowing the stony channel, while the leaves and boughs poured down a constant shower of heavy drops.

By degrees the force of the water abated, the slope being too steep for it to continue long within the regular channels which scored the mountain side; and leaving their temporary asylum, the fugitives pressed on in the hope of reaching the ravine up which they had been making their way that morning when they hung back and were left behind.

But it was in a bewildered way that they pushed on, till hours must have passed, feeling that there was nothing for them but to try and find a refuge in some rude shelter such as they had several times encountered by the side of one of the lava-streams, where in cooling the volcanic matter had split up and broken, and formed wildly curious, cavernous places, any one of which would have been welcome.

Night was coming on fast; they dare not attempt to descend, and it began to be plain that they would have to be content with a resting-place on some stony patch from which the water had drained, when, as they staggered along, just within the sheltering gloom of the huge forest trees, they stumbled upon one of the ancient lava-streams, which stopped their progress like some mountainous wall, and a very few minutes' search was sufficient to find the shelter they required, a dark, cavernous place whose flooring was of volcanic sand.

"It's dry as a bone, Mr Jack, sir," said Ned, after stooping down, "and as warm as warm. Well, sir, if this ain't sunshine after storm I should like to know what is!"

Jack was too much exhausted to reply, and directly after he began to follow his companion's example by stripping off and wringing his clothes.

"Black sunshine this, Ned," he said.

"Well, sir, it is certainly; but you can't say it ain't warm. You put your hand down on the sand."

"Yes; it's quite warm, Ned."

"Why, is this only the back-door into the burning mountain, sir? Because if so, will it be safe?"

"Ned, I'm too tired to talk. Pray be quiet and let me think. We must be safer than out upon the mountain side. Let's lie down and rest."

Chapter Thirty One
A bi-startler

"What's that?" cried Jack, starting up into a sitting position, to face Ned, who rubbed his eyes and stared.

"I dunno, sir; sounded to me like a horrid shriek."

"Yes; that was what woke me, Ned," said Jack in an awestricken whisper. "It sounded like some one being killed."

"There it is again!" cried Ned, as a harsh, shrill sound arose from close at hand, to be followed by a chorus of discordant cries, which seemed to run in by them to be echoed and made more hollow and strange.

"Talk about sharpening saws," said Ned, as he hurriedly began to dress, "why that's lovely to it. Cockatoos, that's what it is. Good job it's daylight, or I should have been thinking that we'd come to sleep in an awful place."

"I couldn't make out where we were, Ned, for some time. Did you sleep well?"

"I dunno, sir. Don't know nothing about it, only that I lay down and snuggled the sand over me a bit. Next thing I heard was those birds. How did you get on, sir?"

"Slept! oh, so soundly!"

"And feel all the better for it, sir?"

"Yes—no, my head aches and feels sore from the blow."

"Ah, I should like to have a turn at those chaps, Mr Jack, sir; I owe 'em one, and you owe 'em one too. Perhaps we shall get a chance to pay 'em some day."

"I hope not," said Jack, who was hurrying on his clothes.

"You hope not, sir?"

"Yes, of course. I hope we may never see or hear anything of them again. And perhaps they're waiting on the mountain side to seize us as soon as we go out of this cave."

"Then we mustn't go out till they're gone, sir. Clothes pretty dry, sir?"

"Yes, Ned, they seem quite dry; but I want to bathe."

"What, again, sir? I got washed enough last night to last me for a bit. Fine place this would be to bring a cargo of umbrellas, if there was any one to buy 'em. I never saw it rain like that."

"Oh, Ned—Ned, do try and talk sensibly," cried Jack. "How can you make jokes when we are in such danger?"

"I dunno about being in danger now, sir. We're pretty safe at present. I say, sir, this must be the way down into the kitchen," continued Ned, as he went on dressing, and trying to peer into the darkness of the cavernous place. "My word, can't you smell the black beadles?"

"I do smell something," replied Jack thoughtfully. "It must be volcanic."

"Beadly, sir. There, it's quite strong." At that moment from farther in a fluttering and squealing sound was heard, and Ned started back. "There, sir, I said so. Mice and rats too."

"Nonsense; it is the great fruit bats."

"What, those we see of a night, sir, bigger than pigeons?"

"Yes; this is one of their roosting-places."

"And do they smell like beadles, sir?"

"Yes; very much like. But now, Ned, what shall we do next?"

"Well, sir, if I did what I liked I should choose a good breakfast; but as I can't, what do you say to going a bit farther in here to see what it's like?"

"Not now. I want to make out whereabouts we are, and whether the blacks are on the look-out for us still; and then I want to communicate with my father; he must be horribly anxious about us, Ned."

"Yes; I expect he thinks we've gone down some hole, sir, and it strikes me he'll be saying something to the doctor for going and leaving us behind."

"I'm afraid that it was our fault, Ned, for not keeping up."

"Well, sir, we can't help it now. Next best thing is to get back to the yacht, so as soon as you're ready we'll make a start; but I'm afraid it will be a long walk before breakfast."

"Terribly long, I'm afraid."

"But there's always a good side to everything, sir, even if it's a looking-glass," continued Ned philosophically. "We're better off than you might think."

"I can't see it, Ned."

"Why, we've got no guns, nor wallets, nor cartridges to carry, sir. Now then, will you lead?"

"Yes; be cautious. We don't know but what some of the blacks may be near."

"That's true, sir. First thing I s'pose is to get what old Lenny calls our bearings."

"Yes; we must find out where we face," said Jack, and he advanced cautiously to the cavern's entrance, and began to peer round warily for danger.

But there was no sign of any. They were very high up, the morning was clear, the sun was gilding the vapours which rose from the rifts and valleys, and the sea glittered gloriously. Far below they obtained glimpses of the reef with its fringe of foam; but not a murmur of the beating waves reached them, while overhead, partially hidden in clouds, the crater of the volcano showed some of its craggy slopes, and the forest beneath seemed to be less dense.

"I can't make out where we are, Ned," said Jack at last. "Yes, I can; we have worked round more to the south, and must have done nothing but get farther and farther away from the yacht."

"Think so, sir? Let's see; we anchored east side first, then we went round and anchored west, and you say we've been travelling south. Well, I dare say you're right, and that means we must keep to the west again. Why, those black fellows must have taken us out of that little valley and put us in another one. I must say it's rather puzzling, sir. But you lead, and I'll follow, for it's of no use for me to pretend to be able to steer."

Jack made no reply, but stood looking downward, seeing nothing of the glorious prospect below, his mind being taken up with thoughts of trying to hit the head of the ravine up which they had travelled, for he knew the difficulties attendant upon going down another, to be led right to the edge of the lagoon, with the puzzle before him of not knowing whether to travel to right or left.

"There's that flock of shriekers coming along below there, Mr Jack, sir," said the man, breaking in upon the lad's reverie. "No, it ain't: it's pigs. I can see 'em, sir; there they go. My word, I wish I had a gun, and they came within reach; I'd have a shot at one of 'em, and before long it would be roast pork for breakfast. See 'em, sir? There they go."

They were plain enough to see at times, a drove of twenty or so, of all sizes, down to quite small porkers, as they raced along over the open patches, and then disappeared in amongst the trees, to re-appear once more as they made for the denser portions of the forest.

"Why, there's one left behind, Ned," said Jack suddenly. "It looks as if it was lame."

"Why, it has broken down. Look, sir, how it keeps limping. I say, we must have him. We can't let a chance like that go when we're starving. Keep your eye on the spot, sir, while I try and hit off some mark to know him by."

Jack's response, as Ned moved to get into a better position for observation, was to leap upon the man and drag him back into the entrance of the cavern.

"What did you do that for, sir?" he cried angrily.

"Couldn't you see what was coming?"

"No, sir," cried Ned surlily; "could you?"

"Go down on hands and knees to that block of stone lying there, and peep over cautiously."

Ned obeyed in an ill-used fashion, and dropped down again to crawl back into the cavern.

"Oh, I say, Mr Jack, seven or eight of them."

"I only saw two."

"Quite what I said, sir. They must have been hunting the drove, and speared the one that hung behind. Now, then, they'll be stopping to cook and have another feast. Suppose they come in here to make this their kitchen? Hadn't we better slip out at once and make a run for it?"

"Run for it?" cried Jack. "How can we up here, where it is all slow climb? No, we must keep in hiding."

"But suppose they choose this place and come here?"

"Not likely, Ned. If they do we must go farther into its depths."

"Ugh!" cried the man with a shudder. "I want to get out of the hole. It's hot and steamy, and unnatural. I believe some of the melted stuff came out this way."

"What, the molten lava? Of course," said Jack coolly. "I don't understand much about it, but it's plain enough that this was all liquid molten matter once, and that it ran out along here."

"What, this rock, Mr Jack? Do you mean melted like lead and running down?"

"Of course."

"Oh, I say, Mr Jack, is this a time, with black Indians close at hand, to go stuffing a fellow with cranky tales?"

"I am only telling you the simple truth, Ned."

"But hard stone can't melt."

"Yes, it can, if the heat is great enough. This was all running like molten metal once, this part under our feet."

"And what about this where we are, sir?"

"It seems to me, Ned, as if it were the cindery froth on the top, that was full of gas and steam, so that when it cooled it left all these holes and cracks and crevices. Look at that piece lying there; only that it's of a beautiful silvery grey, it looks just like one of the pieces of cinder which pop out of the fire."

"Want a pretty good-sized fire for a piece like that to pop out of, sir," said the man scornfully.

"Well, it must have been a good-sized fire when this great mountain was in eruption, and the red-hot lava boiling over the sides of the crater and running down."

"But do you really think it ever did, sir?"

"I have no doubt about it whatever. Look at that piece lying half buried in the black sand. What is that?"

"Looks like black glass, sir," said Ned, kicking a piece of obsidian.

"Well, it is volcanic glass. How could that have been made without heat?"

"I dunno, sir. It caps me."

"You said the place was hot."

"No need to say it, sir. I'm as hot as hot. Brings me out in a prespiration."

"St! don't talk so loudly, Ned. The place echoes so."

At that moment the man laid his hand upon Jack's arm and pointed downward.

The lad followed the direction of the pointing hand, to see that a group of the blacks were coming in their direction, and for the moment Jack felt that they must be seen, until he saw that they were standing well in the shadow.

His first impulse was to catch Ned's arm, stoop down and hurry away to reach the shelter of the trees, but Ned stopped him.

"No good, sir. We should be seen. Let's go right in here."

"What, to be trapped?"

"They mightn't come in here, sir, and if they did, perhaps they couldn't find us. Anyhow they're sure to see us and come after us if we go outside."

The wisdom of the words was evident enough, and with a sigh Jack drew back with his companion, startling some birds from a shelf where they seemed to be nesting within reach of his hand, and sending them rushing out uttering their alarm notes.

"Are we in far enough, Mr Jack?" said Ned.

"No: any one could see us here. Come along."

They went on inward for another twenty yards, the mouth of the entrance still being in full view. It was awkward travelling, the black sand having given place to loose pieces of scoria and obsidian, some pieces of which crackled under their boots, and took revenge by entering into the soles. As they went in the place widened out, but remained much about the same height overhead, the highest portions of the roof being nearly within touch of Ned's hand.

Here the latter stopped again.

"Don't let's go any farther, sir," he said nervously. "Don't you feel a bit frightened?"

"Of course I do. It would be horrible if they caught us again. They would kill us."

"Yes, sir; most likely," said Ned. "Be awkward, wouldn't it? But don't you feel scared-like about this great black hole?"

"Scared? No; I like it, Ned."

"Oh, no, you don't, sir. You can't. Don't say that. There! There it is again. Just over your head."

He shrank back with his fist doubled as if prepared to strike.

"What is it?" cried Jack, startled now.

"I dunno, sir. Let's go back," cried the man in an agitated whisper. "It's very horrid though. There's lots of 'em shuffling and scrambling about in the cracks and holes, staring at you with their wicked-looking eyes, and more 'n once I've seen 'em flapping their wings. I don't like it. Let's go back."

"Go back to be taken? Impossible. Look, they are only bats."

"Bats with wings a yard across, sir? Oh, come, I know better than that."

"What are they then?" said Jack angrily.

"Oh, I dunno, sir. Something horrid as lives in this dreadful place. They make me feel creepy all down my back. I'd rather have a set-to with one of the ugliest blacks yonder."

"I tell you they are bats—the great fruit bats. Why, Captain Bradleigh pointed them out to me the other night, flying overhead in the darkness just like big crows."

"Are you sure, sir? There, look at that thing staring down at you and making noises. Mind, pray, Mr Jack, sir, or he'll have you. Perhaps their bite's poison."

"They will not bite if we leave them alone. They are flying foxes."

"Flying wolves, I think, sir. I say, hadn't we better go back?"

"No," said Jack firmly. "Why, Ned, are you going to turn coward?"

"Hope not, sir; and that's what worries me—me being a man and feeling as I do, while you're only a boy and don't seem to mind a bit. I wouldn't care so much if you were frightened too."

"Well, I am frightened, Ned—horribly frightened, but not of the flying foxes."

"But you don't seem to mind what might be farther in, sir," said Ned, staring wildly into the darkness ahead.

"Oh yes, I do," replied Jack. "I'm afraid we might slip down into some horrible black pit; but we need not if we're careful."

"Ah, you don't seem to understand me, sir, and I don't quite understand myself. I suppose it's from only being half myself again, for one of my arms is no good at all. That's what makes me feel a bit cowardly like."

"Yes, of course, it makes you nervous," said Jack quietly.

"There! Feel that, sir?" whispered Ned in a horror-stricken voice.

"That hot puff of air? Yes, it's curious. I suppose it would grow warmer the farther we went in."

"And you taking it as cool as can be, sir," said Ned in a voice full of reproach.

"Well, why not? We've only got to be careful, just as we should have to be if we were climbing up to the crater. There would be hot steamy puffs of air there, and— Quick, don't speak. Take hold of my hand, and let's go softly right in."

Ned did not hesitate, but obeyed at once, and they walked softly on into the darkness ahead, for from apparently close behind them—though the speakers had not yet reached the mouth of the low cavern—there came the confused angry gabble of many voices, and on looking back Ned saw the mouth of the place darkened, and it seemed as if the enemy were about to come in; but some were apparently hesitating, and protesting against its being done.

Ned's dread of the unseen departed at sight of the seen, and he walked firmly onward, gripping Jack's hand tightly.

"Come on in, sir," he whispered; "they're after us. Let's get into a dark corner, and let 'em have it with stones—some of these sharp bits."

Everything seemed to point to the fact that they must either get right into the depths of the cavern and trust to finding a place of concealment, or stand on their defence as Ned suggested, and meet their enemies with stones.

They must have retreated quite fifty yards over the sharp cracking fragments, when the light which shone in upon them from the mouth suddenly ceased, and looking round for the cause, they found that the passage had made a sudden turn, so that they had to go back three or four yards before they could catch sight of the enemy.

That which they saw was enough to startle them, showing as it did the imminence of their danger, and that the blacks were probably coming in search of them, under the belief that they were in hiding. For one, evidently the leader, was in advance, with bow and arrow in hand ready to shoot, and his companions held their spears prepared for action as they came on in a stooping attitude.

"Shall we shoot at 'em?" whispered Ned, feeling now in the presence of danger.

"No. Let's get a little heap of stones and be ready to throw when they are well in reach."

"Oh, if I could only use my other arm!" muttered Ned. "Come on then, sir. They can't see us now. Perhaps there's a narrower place farther in, and the darker it is the better for us and the worse for them."

The change in the poor fellow was wonderful. He did not seem like the same. It struck Jack for the moment, but he had something else to think about, and he followed his companion quickly, at the risk of slipping into some precipitous place.

It was too dark to see much when they stopped again, but they could feel plenty of rough pieces of stone beneath their feet, and the place was narrow enough to make the chances of a successful defence greater.

"It's an ugly job, Mr Jack, sir," said Ned, "and I feel precious shaky about my throwing, though there was a time when I'd hurl a cricket-ball with any man I knew. If they think they're coming nobbling us about with their war-clubs and getting nothing back, they're precious well mistaken, so scuffle up all you can, and— Oh! Murder!"

Ned dropped down on his face, and Jack crawled against the wall, for at the first attempt made to pull a stone from a heap there was a sharp rustling sound, a little avalanche of fragments was set in motion, and they fell with a tremendous splash into some subterranean natural reservoir; a loud reverberation followed, and instantaneously, as the echoes went bellowing out through the passage by which the fugitives had entered, there was a strange rushing fluttering, and the sound as of a roaring mighty wind unchained from some vast chasm where it had lain at rest.

Jack felt the wind touching him as it passed. Then in a flash he knew that it was caused by the beating of thousands of wings, and then, with his heart beating heavily, he was listening to an outburst of shrieks and yells, and lastly nothing was to be heard but Ned groaning and muttering:

"Oh dear! oh dear! it 'd frighten any man, let alone a poor chap who's been wounded mortal bad!"

A few minutes of time only were occupied by the whole of what took place, from the first rattle of the stones to Ned's piteous ejaculations, and Jack crouched there listening till the poor fellow exclaimed—

"Mr Jack, sir, where are you? Don't say you're dead."

"No, Ned, I won't."

"Oh, my dear lad, where are you then?" gasped the poor fellow wildly.

"Here, quite safe; but don't move, there must be a terrible gulf close beside you."

"Yes, sir, and I thought it had swallowed you. I say, is it all over with us?"

"I hope not," said Jack quietly. "But listen, Ned; can you hear the blacks?"

"Hear 'em! No, sir. My ears seem full of the shrieks and cries of those things as they tore out of the place, and you would stick out that they were bats. Phew, can't you smell 'em?"

"Yes, plainly enough; but it was not the bats made those noises, it must have been the blacks."

"No, no, sir, it was those horrid things. I felt 'em hitting me with their wings as they swooped by."

"Nonsense, nonsense. They were scared by the noise of the stones falling, and the echoes, and it seems to me that they scared the blacks as well as us, and they have run out again."

"What!" cried Ned. "You don't mean that, Mr Jack?"

"But I do. Ned, they've gone."

"Well! and I was only just before thinking that I was getting over being so shaky and nervous, and not so queer about myself, and then for me to break down like that. Of all the cowardly cranks I ever did come across! Oh, I say, Mr Jack, sir, ain't you ashamed of me?"

"I'm quite as ashamed of myself, Ned. I don't know who could help being frightened; my heart's beating tremendously still. But they've gone, Ned, I feel sure."

"Well, I believe they have, sir, 'pon my word. But I say, Mr Jack, sir, don't be offended at what I say."

"Of course not. Say it quick."

"It's on'y this, sir; are you the same young gent as sailed with us from Dartmouth a short time ago? because you cap me."

"Here, give me your hand," cried Jack. "No; stop. Don't move. You might slip. Can't we get a light?"

"Light, sir? Yes; of course. I've got a little box of wax matches in my pocket."

There was a faint rustling sound in the darkness, and then Ned uttered a groan.

"Lost them?"

"No, sir; here they are, but I forgot about the rain last night. They must be all soaked and spoiled."

"Try one."

"Yes, sir, I'll try. But I say, Mr Jack, this is like being in a mine, and it must be fiery, as they call it, being so hot. Will there be any danger of an explosion from gas?"

"Oh, surely not. This isn't a coal-mine, but a sort of grotto under a flow of lava. Try if one of them will light."

"All right, sir. I say, they rattle all right, as if they were hard."

The box clicked as Ned opened it; he took out a match, rubbed it sharply, and there was a faint line of phosphorescent light.

"No go, sir; just like one of them fishy things we get alongside."

"Try another."

Whisk—crick—crick—crack—and a flash of light.

"Hooray!" cried Ned, as the tiny taper blazed up and burned steadily, showing that the holder was close to the edge of a huge chasm, down which a couple of strides would have taken him, and as the light burned lower Jack crept quickly to where Ned still crouched by the side of the passage.

"Why, Ned, I could not see much, but this opens out here into a vast place."

"Yes, sir; I got a glimpse of it. Shall I light another match?"

"No, no, save them."

"But we ought to get out of here as soon as we can, sir."

"Of course, but we shall see a faint gleam from the entrance directly our eyes have grown used to the change."

"Shall we, sir?"

"Of course."

"Well, I don't want to show the white feather again, but I can't help feeling that we ought to be out of this."

"Wait and listen."

"Can't hear nothing, sir," said the man after a minute's pause.

"No, and I can see the faint dawn of light there gleaming against the wall yonder. Let's begin to go back very quietly in case the blacks are still there."

"I'm more than ready, sir."

"Then lead on, Ned."

"Mean it, sir?"

"Yes, go on."

Ned rose, and Jack followed suit, to begin stepping cautiously on, till by slow degrees they reached the sharp angle in the passage, and could look straight out to the entrance and see that all was clear, while there before them was the bright sunny sky, and away in the distance the gleaming sea.

"I say, who's afraid?" cried Ned excitedly. "But, Mr Jack, sir, what a rum thing darkness is! I felt twice as much scared over that as I did about the niggers, and— Oh, I say, look at that!"

Before the lad could grasp what he was about to do, Ned ran forward toward the light till he was half-way to the mouth of the cavern, when Jack saw the dark silhouette-like figure stoop down again and again, to pick up something each time, and he returned laughing, bearing quite a bundle of spears, bows, and arrows.

"There, I was right," cried Jack; "they were frightened—so scared that they dropped their weapons and ran."

"Yes, sir, and set us up with some tools. Oh, if it had only been our guns!"

Chapter Thirty Two
The evil of not being used to it

But the blacks had not left the guns, and utterly unused as these two were to the use of such savage weapons, they felt a thrill of satisfaction run through them as they grasped the means of making one stroke in defence of their lives.

"It's a many years since I used to go into the copses to cut myself a good hazel and make myself a bow, Mr Jack, and get reeds out of the edge of the long lake, to tie nails in the ends and use for arrows. I used to bind the nails in with whitey-brown thread well beeswaxed, and then dress the notch at the other end to keep the bowstring from splitting it up. I've hit rabbits with an arrow before now, though they always run into their holes. You can shoot with a bow and arrow at a target of course?"

"I? No, Ned," said the boy sadly. "I can't do anything but read."

"Oh, I say, sir! Why, I've seen you knock over things with a gun. Look how you finished that sea snake."

"I suppose I'd better try though, Ned."

"Why of course, sir. You take the one you like. Here's three of them. Wish they hadn't been so stingy with the arrows—only five between two of us. Never mind. Hadn't got any ten minutes ago. We'll keep a pair apiece and have one to spare, and a spear each. We'll leave the others in here, and let 'em fetch 'em if they dare."

"Yes," said Jack, selecting his weapons; "but we must not go out yet."

"Well, sir, I don't want to interfere, but I haven't had anything to eat since lunch yesterday, and if I don't soon do some stoking my engine won't go."

"But you don't expect that you are going to kill anything with these things?" cried Jack.

"I'm going to try, sir. Savages can, and have a feast of roast pig after, so we ought to be able to. Don't you think we might risk starting, and get higher up the mountain, and then round somehow, and make for the shore?"

"It will be very risky by daylight."

"But we can't go in the dark, sir."

"Come on then," cried Jack. "The blacks may have been scared right away, so let's chance it."

He led the way to the entrance, where, to the great delight of both, they found another bow lying, and close by one of the melon-headed war-clubs and a bundle of arrows, upon which Ned pounced regardless of danger, while Jack crept to the stones outside and took a long look round, over gully, rock, and patch of forest. But there was nothing living within sight but a couple of flocks of birds, one green, the others milky white, and showing plainly as they flew over against the green trees.

"See anything of that lame pig, sir?" said Ned, handing him the arrows to take what he liked.

"No; nor the blacks neither."

"They're hiding somewhere, sir, and I dare say on the look-out, or I'd be for going to have a look below there."

"That would be too risky, Ned. Let's creep to where we can get cover, and then do as you say, keep along the more open part under the trees, and see if we can get round somewhere by the sands."

"On you go then, sir, and whatever you do, don't lose a chance of a shot. We must have something to eat, or we can never get back. Oh yes, you're a very beautiful island, no doubt—very well to look at, but I don't think much of a place where you can't find the very fruit as would be a blessing to us now."

"And what fruit's that, Ned?" said Jack, as they reached the shelter of the trees about a couple of hundred yards from the mouth of the cave.

"Well, sir, I'm not an Irishman, for as far back as I know we all came from Surrey; but I'd give something if I could find a patch of 'em going off at the haulm, ready to be grubbed up and shoved in the ashes of a fire to roast."

"What, potatoes?"

"Yes, sir, a good big round 'tater would just about fit me now, and I shouldn't fiddle about any nonsense as to trying it on."

"There'll be no potatoes for you, Ned, but we may find some wild bananas lower down."

"That's a nice comforting way of talking to a poor hungry chap who is going up, Mr Jack; but you keep a good look-out, and we must have a shot at the first thing we see, and then light a fire and cook it, and if that first thing we see happens to be a nigger, sir—well, I'm sorry for him, and I hope he won't be tough!"

Ned directed a comical look at his young master as he began to try the bow, holding it in his injured, nerveless grasp, and pulling at the string.

"Is it hard, Ned?"

"Pretty tidy, sir. Takes a good pull, but I can manage it, and—Hullo! Look at that."

He threw the bow, arrows, and spear down, stretched out his left arm to the full extent; drew it in so as to raise the biceps, and then stretched it out again, and began to move it round like the sail of a windmill.

"What's the matter with you?" cried Jack. "Are you going mad?"

"Pretty nigh, sir. Look at that—and that—and that!"

The three "thats" were so many imaginary blows in the air, delivered sharply and with all the man's force.

"But I don't understand you, Ned. What do you mean?"

"Why, can't you see, sir? That arm's been as dead as a stick ever since I got that arrow, now it has come to life again, and is stronger than ever. I know what's done it!"

"Being obliged to try and use it," cried Jack quickly.

"That's got something to do with it perhaps, sir, but that isn't everything. It was that soaking last night, and then the stewing in that hot sand. It took all the rest of the trouble away. Now then, only let me get a chance at one of these chaps, and I'll try how he likes arrow. I'll 'arrow his feelings a bit."

"But are you sure your arm is quite strong again?" cried Jack joyfully.

For answer Ned swung his left round the speaker's waist, lifted him from the ground, and held him up with ease.

"What do you say to that, sir? But there, come along, I want to get something to eat. I feel horrid, and begin to understand how it is that some of the people out here eat one another."

"Don't keep on talking such absurd stuff, Ned," cried Jack, half angrily, half amused; for in the early stages of suffering from hunger there are symptoms of a weak hysterical disposition to laugh.

"But I'm so hungry, sir!"

"Well, push on, and we may get a chance at a big bird of some kind. But suppose we should shoot one—we might—these arrows may be poisoned."

"Wouldn't matter, sir. They say cooking kills the poison. Which way now?"

"Keep bearing to the right up the mountain, but always well within shelter. We must not be taken again."

"Good-bye to the wild bananas that grow below," muttered Ned; and he pressed on eagerly, but keeping a sharp look-out all the while, and whenever an opening had to be crossed, setting the example of going down on all fours.

"Won't do though to keep like this, sir," he said; "why, they'd shoot at us at once for wild beasts of some kind. But do look here, sir! Ain't it wonderful—ain't it grand? My arm feels as if it had been bottling up all its strength, and to be readier than ever now. Oh, if we could only see something to shoot at."

But saving small brightly-plumaged birds, they encountered nothing to tempt the venture of an arrow, and at the end of what must have been quite two hours, when the cave of the lava flow was left far behind, and several hundred feet lower, Jack dropped upon his knees beside a lovely little pool, into which trickled through the rocks and stones a thread-like stream of the clearest water.

"No, no, sir, don't drink—it's bad. Cold water when you're hot, and on an empty stomach."

"But I'm so thirsty, Ned, and it looks so tempting."

"I'm ever so much thirstier, sir. Look here, let's do what they do with horses. Just wash our mouths out, but don't let's swallow any."

As he spoke he went to the other side of the little rock pool, which was not above a foot deep and about four across, lying close up to the foot of one of the great rock walls which grew more frequent the higher they ascended. Then together they dipped a hand in the soft, cool, limpid fluid, and raised it to their lips.

"Poof!" ejaculated Ned, spluttering the water away. "Oh, what a shame! There ought to be a notice up—Beware of the water. Why, it's like poison, sir. Ten times worse than that horrid stuff by the falls. Oh, come on. Only fancy for there to be water like that. Physic's nothing to it."

Jack's disappointment was a little softened by his amusement, and they resumed their tramp, rising higher and higher as they kept up a diagonal course along the mountain slope; but the difficulties in the way, and the caution requisite in passing through what they felt to be a dangerous enemy's land, made the progress slow, and after a time they seated themselves for a rest upon one of the many moss-grown masses of lava rock they passed, beneath an umbrageous tree, in which a flock of tiny finch-like birds were twittering, and once more looked around.

The prospect was not wide, for they were surrounded by trees, and it was only by keeping close to one or other of the many lava rivers, where the growth of the forest was scanty, that they were able to progress as they did.

"Nothing to eat, nothing to drink," groaned Ned. "I say, Mr Jack, this is getting serious. What's to be done?"

"Rest a bit, and then at the first opportunity, say as soon as we have passed over that knoll there, let's begin to descend toward the shore. I hope we shall miss the blacks then."

"And come across some one looking for us, sir, and carrying a basket. If it was only a bit of hard ship's biscuit now, I wouldn't care."

"Hark! What's that?"

"Cockatoo, sir," whispered Ned. "I know their screech. I'll go and try and get a shot at him."

"Better sit still and rest, and chance the flock coming near. If you follow them they'll hear you, and lead you farther and farther away."

"Yes, I know that, sir, but I'm so hungry, and I'm afraid to begin chewing leaves for fear of poison. Hullo! Don't move, sir. Hear that? You're right, this is the best way and the easiest."

"What shall we do, Ned, shoot, or try to get at them with the spears?"

"Let's see 'em first, sir," said Ned wisely, "and wait our chance, and then do both."

The objects which had excited their attention by sundry familiar sounding grunts were not long in showing themselves in the shape of a little herd of pigs, three old ones and about a dozen half-grown; and as they came down a slope to their left, and began rooting about under the trees a couple of hundred yards away, Ned softly smacked his lips, looked at Jack, took out his brass matchbox, and said the expressive word "crackling."

The formation of the mountain side was mostly that of shallow stony gullies opening one into the other, but all with the general tendency up and down, and it was on the slope of one of these that the fugitives were resting, while the herd had entered it from its highest part.

Ned's fingers played tremblingly about the bow he held. Then he felt his arm, and a look of joy and pride came into his eyes.

"It's all right," he whispered. "I say, sir, wasn't it a grand idea to leave some pigs here to breed? You stop quiet and wait your chance."

"Why? What are you going to do?" whispered Jack.

"Creep round by the back of this tree, sir, and as they feed down I'll go up the side, and by and by you'll see me dodging softly along toward you over yonder beyond them. Then we shall have 'em between us, and if they take fright they must either go up or down, and pass one of us. It's our chance, and we must not let it go. Look here, sir, you choose one of the little ones, and wait till you think you can hit him. Then hold up your hand and we'll fire together. Then run at 'em with your spear. We must get one or else starve."

It was the best way of approaching success, as Jack saw, and whispering that he would do as his companion suggested, he sat there watching Ned's movements as he crept away up the slope and disappeared. Then fitting an arrow to the bowstring, after laying his spear ready by his side, he rested the bow across his knees, and sat on his mossy stone, watching the movements of the little herd, and expecting, moment by moment, to see one of the watchful elders take alarm, give warning, and the whole party dash back up the gully.

But they kept rooting and hunting about, evidently for some kind of fruit which fell from the trees, and Jack felt as if he were far back in the past, a hunter on that beautiful, wild mountain slope, dependent upon his bow for his existence. The sun poured down its hot rays, making the leaves glisten like metal, and the air was so clear that the pigs' eyes and every movement were as plain as if close at hand.

"Seems treacherous lying in wait like this," he thought. "Poor wretches! they all look as playful and contented as can be."

But he knew that he and Ned must eat if they were ever to escape from that mountain, and the sentiment of pity died out as the time went on.

The pigs were slow in coming down, for under the trees at the other side of the gully the fruit they sought seemed to be plentiful, and he could see the younger ones hunting one another as a lucky find was made, this resulting in a good deal of squealing, while above it the deep grunts of the elders were plainly heard.

But there was no sight of Ned, and half-an-hour must have passed, with the pigs still out of reach for a good shot.

"If they do come this way," thought the lad, "I can't study about picking one; I must shoot into the thickest part and chance it. But where is Ned? Why don't he show?"

At last there was the appearance far up of a large pig coming down toward the herd, but the next moment, as it glided among the leaves, Jack saw that it was a pig with clothes on, and that it carried a bow and arrow.

The time had come for a shot, and softly and slowly the lad edged himself back till he could drop on his knees behind the stone, rest the bow upon it horizontally, and wait for the critical moment to draw and launch his arrow.

He could watch Ned the while as well as the herd, and by slow degrees he saw his companion creep from tree-trunk to tree-trunk, slowly diminishing the distance, while, having probably cleared off the fallen fruit, the herd broke into a trot as if to pass within twenty yards of where he waited.

But the next minute they had stopped fifty yards away, and Ned had soon reduced his distance till he was about as much above them. Then all at once he disappeared.

The minutes seemed to be terribly long drawn out now, but the herd came lower and lower, till fully half of them were rambling about just in front; and feeling that he would never have a better chance, the lad singled out one half-grown fellow in the midst of three more, all feeding, and he held up his hand for a moment or two in the hope that Ned might see it, though where he hid it was impossible to say.

Slight as was the movement of the raised hand it was seen, for the biggest pig, a rough, bristly-necked animal, suddenly raised its head and gazed sharply, with eyes that looked fiery in the brilliant sunshine, straight in his direction.

Twang! twang! went two bowstrings, the arrows whizzed through the air, and in the midst of a rush, away tore the herd down the valley, just as Ned leaped up, made a bound or two, and plunged his spear down amidst the bushes.

Jack dropped his bow, caught up his own spear, and dashed forward to help finish the wounded pigs, and Ned was up before him, panting and dripping with perspiration.

"Got one?" cried Jack.

"Got one!" cried Ned bitterly. "Course we ain't. Just like my luck."

"Oh!" groaned Jack, as a pang of hunger shot through him.

"I never saw such arrows," cried Ned passionately. "I could smash the lot. They don't go straight."

"Is it any use to follow them?" said Jack.

"No, sir; it ain't," cried the man angrily. "And what's more, you know it ain't. What's the good of aggravating a poor fellow? And," he added pathetically, "I did mean to have such a roast."

Chapter Thirty Three
In the face of peril

"Come on," said Jack, after they had stood listening for a few minutes, and gazing in the direction taken by the pigs. "Is it any use looking for the arrows?"

"Not a bit, sir. Here, only let me find one lying asleep in the mud somewhere. I dare say there's, dozens doing it now, with their eyes shut, and their curly tails pretending to whisk away the flies. Come on, sir, we must keep going, hot as it is. Never mind, we shall do it yet, but next time I'm not going to trust to bows and arrows. You shall hunt them down to where I'm hiding, and I'll skewer one somehow or another."

But in the next two hours' weary struggle among trees, rocks, and waving creepers they only heard pigs once, and then it was as they dashed off unseen, grunting and squealing wildly. Birds were scarcer and very small, while they felt no temptation to try the esculent qualities of the lizards they saw glancing about over the hot lava, or of the snakes which hurriedly crawled away.

They were successful though in finding a trickling stream of pure cold water, and a tree bearing a kind of fruit something like a poor, small apricot with a very large stone. It was bitter and sour, but it did, as Ned said, to clean your teeth.

Three more arrows were lost in shooting at birds, but without success, and Ned shook his head.

"I don't know how it is with you, sir," he said, "but my arm has had such a long rest that the muscles now seem to be too strong, and they must have jerked the bow just when I let go the string."

"I can soon tell you how it is with me, Ned," said Jack. "I never could use a bow and arrow, so of course I can't now."

They struggled on, growing less cautious in their eagerness to get down to the shore.

"Shall get some cocoanuts there, if we can't get anything else, sir," said Ned; "but I do hope it will be somewhere near the yacht."

"But how are we to signal them if we don't get there before dark?"

"Light a fire on the sands, sir. Oh, don't you be afraid of that. It's the getting there is the difficulty."

It was growing well on in the afternoon when this was said, and, so weak and exhausted that they could hardly struggle on, they welcomed an open slope covered with some creeping kind of plant, as it seemed, for it offered the prospect of getting along better for a couple of hundred yards. Here, too, they could see down a ravine to the reef, which seemed to be wonderfully close at hand, though they knew that they had miles to struggle over before they could reach the sands—and such miles.

"Let's make for that valley, Ned, and try to go down there."

"Very well, sir; just which way you like. Seems all the same; but let's get close up to the trees, though it's furthest, for we may find some kind of fruit. What a country! Not so much as an apple, let alone a pear, or— Mr Jack, sir! Oh!"

"What is it?" cried Jack, startled by his companion's excitement. "What have you found?"

For Ned had thrown himself upon his knees, and with one end of the bow was tearing away at the straggling plants which covered the ground wherever it was not rocky or smothered by bush.

"Can't you see, sir? Here, come and help. *'Taters!'*"

"What?" cried Jack.

"Yes, 'taters, sir; only little 'uns. Not so big as noo potaties at home, but 'taters they are. Look!"

"Fingers were made before forks," says the old proverb, so under the circumstances it was not surprising that Ned began to use his hands as if they were gardener's potato forks, and with such success that in a short time quite a little heap of the yellow tubers were dug out of the loose sandy soil, the average size being that of walnuts.

Jack set to work at once to help, but he had hardly dragged away a couple of handfuls of haulm when he started up with a cry of alarm.

Ned leaped up too and seized his spear, expecting to have to face the blacks; but the enemy was a good-sized snake which had been nestling beneath the thick stalks of the plants, and now stood up fully three feet above the tops of the growth, with head drawn back, moving to and fro as if about to launch itself forward and strike at the first who approached it.

"Stand back, Mr Jack," cried the man, and with one mower-like sweep of his spear-handle he caught the serpent a few inches below its threatening head, and it dropped writhing at once, with its vertebras broken.

"Can't stand any nonsense from things like that, sir," cried Ned, as he took his spear now as if it had been a pitchfork, raised the twining reptile from among the haulms, and after carrying it a few yards, threw it cleverly right away among the bushes at the side.

"Take care, perhaps there are more," said Jack. "So much the worse for them if there are, sir. I want the 'taters, and I'd have 'em if the place was full of boa-constrictors as big as they grow. Come on."

In a very short time they had their pockets and handkerchiefs full, the tubers coming out of the hot, dry, sandy soil perfectly clean; and thus furnished, they made for a spot where the lava rock was piled up, selected a niche, and scraped out a sandy hollow about a couple of feet across, laid the potatoes down singly and close together, covered them again with the sand, and then turned to the edge of the nearest patch of trees to gather dead boughs, leaves, everything they could which seemed likely to burn, and carried it to their improvised oven.

"Suppose the blacks see the smoke of the fire?" said Jack, as they piled up the smaller twigs and leaves over the potatoes, and Ned brought out his box of matches.

"I can't suppose anything, sir, only that we must eat. If they do come on for a fair fight, I'm ready. Fight I will for these 'taters, come what may."

The leaves and twigs caught readily, and the smoke began to curl up in the clear sunny air, as bigger and bigger pieces of wood were thrown on. Then as they went to the foot of the trees for more of that which lay in abundance, they glanced in all directions, but all was silent and solitary, with the beautifully-shaped mountain curving up above them, and a faint mist as of heat just visible in transparent wreaths above its summit.

"Don't let's take too much, Mr Jack—only a little at a time, so as to have to come again and again."

"Why not take as much as we can carry now?"

"Because if we do we can't put it all on at once, and we only want a nice gentle fire, and to keep on mending it till there are plenty of ashes."

"Well, we need not put it all on if we've got it there."

"But we must have something to do, sir."

"Well, lie down and rest till the potatoes are done."

"You don't know what you're talking about, sir. You can't think of what agony it will be. They must have half-an-hour, and it will seem like a week. You take my advice, sir. I'm sure it's right."

"Very well," said Jack, and they kept on going to and fro, breaking enough to keep on feeding the fire, and trying hard not to think about what was cooking, as they still piled on the twigs and branches of dead wood, Ned busying himself in breaking them up, far more than was necessary in his desperate determination not to be tempted to draw out a single tuber before they were done.

"I know what 'taters are, sir," he said between his teeth, "and as bad as can be really raw, but the gloriousest things as ever were for a hungry man when he has got nothing else. But what a pity it is! If we'd had our guns we could soon have brought down a skewerful or two of those green and scarlet parrots to roast, and— Oh, don't talk about it. Makes my mouth water horribly."

"Think they're done now, Ned?" said Jack, after three or four journeys to and fro.

"No, sir, nor yet half. The sand underneath has to get hot. I tell you what, we'll dig up some more and put them in the hot ashes after these are done, to cook and take away with us. They'll do all right while we're eating our dinner."

"Very well," said Jack, as he tried hard to curb his impatience, "but it's terrible, this waiting."

"Try not to think about it, please, sir. There, let's make up the fire once more, and then go and dig."

The wood was fetched and thrown on, both standing a little back afterward, and having a hard struggle to keep from raking out two or three of the potatoes to try if they were done, but they mastered themselves bravely, and hurried to the spot where they had dug before, to find it taken possession of by a larger and thicker snake than the one that had been killed. It was coiled up on the dry sand which they had cleared of leaves, and rose up menacingly at their approach.

"What shall we do—go somewhere else?" said Jack.

"No, sir, that we won't," cried Ned fiercely. "If that long eely thing chooses to play dog in the manger over the potatoes, it must take the consequences. I'll soon finish him. Think he's poisonous?"

"I feel sure of it, Ned," said Jack anxiously. "Look at the swollen poison glands."

"That settles it. Seems to me like a duty to kill poisonous things. I know what it is to be poisoned, sir."

He gave his shoulder a twist, and advanced toward the serpent with his spear-handle ready.

"You keep back, sir, and let me have room to swing my spear round."

"No; I want to kill this one, Ned."

"Better not, sir. It's risky. You might miss."

"You be ready to strike him if I do."

"Very well then, sir; only be careful. A good swish round will do it, but snakes are quick as lightning, and we've had trouble enough without you getting bitten."

The snake rose higher, and prepared to strike as Jack advanced, holding his spear in both hands, and waiting his opportunity, he brought it round with all his force, but the end passed, through his miscalculation of the distance, a couple of inches short of the reptile's head, and before the lad could recover himself to make another blow, the creature struck back, and would have fastened upon him but for Ned's quick interposition of his own spear-handle, against which the serpent struck instead.

The next moment Ned struck again, full on the creature's back, and it was helpless now for attack, writhing in amongst the growth till Jack obtained another fine cut at it, and the battle was at an end.

Ned picked it, up upon the end of his spear.

"They say that things are good if roasted, sir. What do you say—shall we cook him?"

"Ugh! No. Throw the horrible thing away."

"Yes, sir; off it goes. One wants another day's starving to eat roast snake."

He sent the nearly dead creature whirling through the air with a sudden jerk of his spear-handle, and then turned to Jack.

"Now, sir," he said, "as quick as you can, and then—"

He did not finish his sentence, but threw himself upon his knees again. Jack followed his example, and for about ten minutes they busied themselves getting another load, and then ran to the fireside and emptied all they had into a heap.

"Now then," cried Ned; "but be careful, sir; they'll be horribly hot."

Jack said nothing, but looked on while his companion thrust the still burning wood aside with his spear, then swept off the thick bed of glowing embers, and lastly the hot sand, before turning the potatoes out into a heap on the other side, and spreading them to cool.

"Let 'em be, sir, till we've charged the oven again," cried Ned, and the fight now was harder than ever as they began to throw the fresh batch into the hot pit. But it was done, and the sand swept over them. The glowing embers followed, the wood was piled on, to begin crackling and blazing, and then, and then only, did they fall to.

Only a meal of little hot roasted potatoes, without butter, pepper, or salt, but no banquet of the choicest luxuries could have tasted half so good. They were done to a turn, and though very small, of the most desirable flavour, and satisfying to a degree.

"Try another, sir, try another," Ned kept on saying; but Jack needed no urging, and as he sat there eating one after another, the sun seemed to be less hot, the place around more beautiful, the shore less distant, and the possibility of their reaching the yacht that night more and more of a certainty. But that certainty began to grow into doubt when, well satisfied by their meal, the pair lay back to rest a little before making a fresh start.

"Must give the second batch time to get well done, sir, and to cool a bit, before we toddle, and then we ought to be on the look-out for water. A good drink wouldn't come amiss."

"No," replied Jack slowly; "but hadn't we better get some more wood to put on? The fire's getting very low."

"No, sir, it's just right. There's a good heap of embers now, and by the time the wood's all burned the potatoes will be about done. Think any one planted them here first?"

"I should say they were planted by the captain who left the pigs."

"Then I say he ought to have a monument, sir, for it was the finest thing he ever did in his life—much finer than anything I shall ever do. My, how different everything looks after you've had a good feed!"

Jack made no reply to that, but said, a minute or so later—

"Think the savages have seen our fire, Ned?"

There was no reply.

"'Sleep, Ned?" said Jack, looking toward him.

There was still no reply.

"Poor fellow! Let him rest a bit," thought the boy; and then he began to think of what news it would be when he got back to the yacht, to announce that the arm was restored. The yacht brought up the thought of sailing right away over the blue waters, gliding easily on, with the warm sun upon his cheek and the soft breeze fanning his brows, and Jack Meadows went on sailing away, but it was only in fancy, for he too, utterly worn out by the morning's exertions, was fast asleep, without a thought that danger might be near.

Chapter Thirty Four
Cookery under queer circumstances

"Ah–e! Ah–e! Ah–e!"

A loud peculiar call, followed by a repetition from a distance, too long after to be a reverberation, though strange echoes had been heard from far up the mountain when a shot was fired well down in one or other of the ravines which scored the slopes of the volcano.

There was a pause of a few minutes, another cry came again, and was answered or echoed.

The first time it had no effect whatever upon Jack, who lay upon his back fast asleep, in the deep slumber which comes to the hungry after that hunger has been appeased.

But there was the strange instinct of self-preservation awake in the lad, and that had started into watchfulness, though the body remained inert, and when the cry was repeated the body was warned, and Jack aroused into wakefulness, feeling, he knew not why, that something was wrong.

It was close upon sunset, and the cap of the mountain glowed once more as if it had burst into eruption, but all was perfectly still save the whistling and shrieking of birds at a distance.

He did not move, but turned his eyes toward where Ned lay snoring softly; then he cast his eyes toward the fire, which was apparently quite out, but the next moment the soft sea-breeze came with a gentle puff, and the embers glowed faintly, showing that with a little tending there was enough left to revive the blaze again.

The silence in face of that wondrous glow overhead was oppressive, and the feeling of danger at hand seemed to grow, and then began to die out, for there was nothing visible, till all at once a peculiarity close up by the glowing wood ashes took the lad's attention, and then he shuddered slightly, for there, evidently attracted by the warmth, toward which they had crawled, were several snakes, with the possibility of there being more which he could not see. For the most part they were small, but a part of the coil of one showed that its owner must be as thick as his arm, and beyond lay in a kind of double S one that was far larger.

Then all at once there came the peculiar cry which had awakened him, and it had hardly died out when it was answered from the edge of the forest beyond the opening, at one side of which they lay.

"All right, Mr Jack, sir," said Ned in a muttering, ill-used tone. "We'll toddle on now. Needn't be so hard on a fellow. Only just closed my eyes."

Jack turned his head to the speaker, but Ned had not stirred, and after a momentary glance in the direction from which the call had come—evidently the ravine leading down to the sea—he rolled over three times, and brought himself close enough to touch his companion. But in the act of turning he felt something move, there was a sharp struggling, and a snake glided from beneath him hissing angrily, and he turned cold at the thought that another of the dangerous creatures had been sleeping coiled up closely to him for warmth.

Worse still, the hissing and rustling had startled those by the fire. Two malignant heads suddenly started up a few inches, and there was that peculiar gliding of coils in which the same serpent seems to be going in several directions at once.

For a few minutes Jack lay perfectly still, feeling as if he were yielding to that peculiar fear which paralyses in the presence of a serpent. But he closed his eyes, set his teeth hard, and remained motionless, mentally combating the sensation of horror and mastered it. While upon unclosing his eyes and looking in the direction of the fire, he saw that the coiling and uncoiling had ceased, and the raised heads had been lowered as if to resume the interrupted sleep.

Jack felt that action was the best safeguard against the horrible, paralysing sensation, and softly passing his hand along till he could touch Ned's face, he tapped his cheek sharply.

"Don't!"

He tapped again.

"I'm awake, I tell you. Guv'nors' call?"

"Ned!—Ned!"

"Eh? yes!—all right. That you, Mr Jack?"

"Yes. Hush!" whispered the lad. "Don't move; don't raise a hand. Listen. Are you quite awake?"

"Yes, sir. What's the matter?"

"We're in danger, Ned."

"Yes, sir, I knew that before I shut my eyes; but it was no use to holloa about it. What is it now?"

The call was repeated and answered before Jack spoke.

"Oh, that's it, is it, sir?" said Ned quietly. "Pretty creatures. After us again, eh? Well, if we lie still they won't see us, and—yes—shadow's rising on the mountain, it will be dark directly. All we've got to do is to make out which way they go, and then go the other, so the sooner they show the better for us—I mean before it gets dark. Such a stupid place too; there ain't no evening, it's dark directly."

"There's more danger, Ned," whispered Jack.

"Eh? what, ain't that enough, sir? Well, what is it?"

"Turn your head very gently, so that you can look at the fire."

"Yes, sir.—Well, it's out."

"Don't you see anything there?"

"Whoo!" ejaculated the man in a tone full of horror, "snakes, hundreds of 'em! Oh, we mustn't stand that, sir; they're waiting till it's cool enough, so as to get our 'taters."

"Nonsense: after the warmth. Now you see, Ned. What's to be done?"

The man was silent for a few moments. Then softly—

"This is nice, Mr Jack; we can't get up and run away because of the niggers, and we can't stop here because of the snakes. Yes; what's to be done?"

Jack was silent in turn for a few moments.

"Let's crawl a little way off, Ned."

Jack set the example, and it was very willingly followed, till they were a dozen yards farther from the fire; but before half the distance was covered, the shouting of the blacks was heard again.

"I say, Mr Jack," whispered Ned, as they subsided, "you're a very clever fellow over your books."

"Am I, Ned?" said Jack sadly.

"Oh, yes, I've often heard the guv'nor and Doctor Instow say so. Well then, there's me. I'm sharp enough over my work—sort of handy chap."

"Yes; but what's the good of talking about that now?"

"I was only thinking, sir. Here's you and me making no end of a fuss, and starving, and all the rest of it, and getting into a state o' melancholy, because we've lost our way, while these poor ignorant savages go about without any clothes, and regularly enjoy themselves in the same place."

"Yes, Ned, they are a deal cleverer than we are after all."

"That they ain't, sir. We've only got to use our brains more, and we can beat 'em hollow. I ain't going to dump it any more. It's like saying a nigger's a better man than a white; and he ain't. Now then, as the boy in the book I once read used to say, take it coolly, and let's see if we haven't got more brains than they have."

"Very well, Ned; but now, if we don't mind, they'll kill us."

"Then we will mind, sir. I should like to catch 'em at it. First thing is we must now be cool. Well, we've got enough for to-morrow, only those snakes are watching it. Well, while we're waiting for those niggers to go by, let's give the snakes notice to quit."

"How? Pelt 'em?"

"There; look at him!" said Ned. "Only wants a bit of thinking. Come on, sir, we can do it as we lie here; they'll soon scatter."

"But suppose they come this way?"

"Throw at 'em again, sir. Ready?"

There were plenty of loose fragments of lava lying about in the sandy soil, stones which had doubtless been ejected by the volcano, to fall upon its slopes, and which had in course of time been washed lower and lower, and armed with these, they began to pelt the sides of the fire, the effect being wonderfully speedy. As the first stones fell there was a strange rustling and hissing, heads were raised menacingly up, and as a second couple fell the reptiles began to move off rapidly.

"Two biggest coming this way, Ned," said Jack excitedly, and gathering a half-dozen or so smaller stones in his right hand, he hurled them catapult fashion right at the advancing heads, with the result that the two reptiles turned sharply, and went off at full speed in beneath the abundant growth of plants, while at the end of a few minutes the missiles thrown in their track produced no effect.

"That's done, sir," said Ned coolly, "and our to-morrow's dinner's safe, and it'll be very hard if I don't dodge something better to go with it. Hist! hear that!"

The call had been uttered evidently much nearer, and Jack grasped his spear.

"That's right, sir," whispered Ned, "but this is a big place, and it ain't likely that they'll come right over us. Let's lie still and listen. We can't see them, and they can't see us."

At that moment Jack pinched the speaker's arm, and pointed over him.

"Something to see that way? All right, sir."

He softly wrenched himself round, and gazed in the indicated direction, to see a black figure standing in bold relief against the orange slope of the mountain. He was nearby a hundred feet higher than where they lay, having mounted upon a ridge which was probably one of the hardened lava-streams which had flowed down, and as they watched him, one by one seven more joined him.

He stood looking round for a few moments, and then uttered the cry they had heard before, and turned to descend, making straight for the bend of the ravine which seemed to lead to the shore.

The call was responded to, and a few minutes after another party came into sight away to the left, making apparently for the same place, and if they kept on, it was evident that they would pass about a hundred yards from Jack and his companion, so that their policy was to lie quite still.

"Be too dark to see us in ten minutes, sir," whispered Ned.

"Yes; and then we can't do better than make our way up that ridge till we come upon another valley running down to the shore."

"That's the way, sir," said Ned. "Only wants a little thinking about. A set o' naked niggers beat you at scheming? Why, it ain't likely."

But they had a scare a quarter of an hour later, the second party of blacks coming into sight suddenly, not twenty yards away, tramping in Indian file, with their spears over their shoulders, and for the moment Jack's heart seemed to stand still, and he grasped his weapon, ready to make one blow for his life.

For it seemed impossible that the men could pass by—men of such a keen, observant nature—without seeing the pair lying there amongst the trailing growth of the potatoes.

Worse still, they came nearer, so as to avoid a block of stone in their way, and one of the number leaped upon it, and after a look round, uttered the call of his tribe, just as one of a flock of running birds does to keep the rest together.

"Now for it," thought Jack, as the black looked straight in his direction, and he prepared to spring up as the man leaped down, and seemed about to run at him, spear in hand.

But just when an encounter for life or death seemed inevitable, the savage trotted on, and the others followed, seeming to grow shorter, till one by one they disappeared, shoulders, heads, tops of the spears, dissolving into the coming gloom of evening.

"Oh, scissors!" whispered Ned. "I say, Mr Jack, sir, if I'd held my breath much longer, I'm sure all the works would have stopped."

"I thought it was all over, Ned."

"Yes, sir, so did I; but I meant to have a dig at one or two of 'em first. Talk about as near as a toucher, that was nearer. How do you feel now?"

"Heart beats horribly."

"So does mine, sir. It's going like a steam-pump with too much to do. But who's afraid?"

"I am, Ned."

"That you are not, sir. I'm just the same as you, but it's only excitement, and what any one would feel. Now then they've gone down and blocked our road, so we must go up another way. Just give 'em another five minutes, and then we'll go and get our 'taters."

The ashes were soon being raked aside, and the invaluable potatoes about to be uncovered, when Ned sniffed.

"I say, Mr Jack, sir, they smell good."

"Why, what's that, Ned?" cried Jack, pointing through the gloom at something long and stiff curled up into a knot.

"That, sir? Well, I am stunned. Why, it's one of they snakes, sir, got closer in to get warm, and he overdid it. He's cooked; and just you smell, sir."

"Ugh! throw it away."

"But it smells 'licious, sir. It does really."

"It makes me feel sick, Ned—the idea's horrible. Why it will have spoiled all the potatoes."

"Don't make me feel sick, sir; makes me feel hungry. You've no idea how good it smells."

"What! a horrible reptile?"

"So's a turtle, sir; and you won't say turtle-soup isn't good."

"But a snake, and perhaps poisonous, Ned?"

"We shouldn't eat his head, sir. Don't see why you might not just as well eat a snake as an eel, sir."

"Throw it away!" cried Jack sharply.

"All right, sir, you're master.—Good-bye, good victuals!" Ned added in an undertone.—"Won't have hurt the taters, sir, there was all this thick layer of ashes between."

"Are they burnt up?"

"No, sir, just right, and floury as can be. Look at that."

It was getting too dark to see much; but Jack made out that the little round vegetable was all floury where it was broken.

The whole cooking was raked out, the ashes scattered away, and Ned proceeded to take out his knife and hand it to his young master, with instructions to cut out his shirt-sleeves just at the shoulder.

"I shall be warm enough without them, sir," he said. "There: now we'll just tie up the ends, and here we have a good bag apiece to carry the taters in. Nothing like having a bit of string in your pocket, sir. I wonder whether Robinson Crusoe had a bit o' string when he was wrecked; I 'spose he would have, because he could have twisted up a bit out of the old ropes. It's always useful, sir. There you are, now. I'll tie the bags together, and swing 'em over my shoulder, one on each side."

"I'll carry one."

"You shall have 'em both, sir, when I'm tired and want a bit of a rest. Now then, ready, sir?"

"Yes."

"Then shoulder arms: march!" They made for the ridge of lava, climbed upon it without much difficulty, and began to ascend the gradual slope it formed, till they were shut in by the trees rising on either side, when the darkness became so intense that their progress was very slow, and they had to depend a good deal upon their spears used as alpenstocks. But one great need urged them on, and it chased away the thoughts of pursuit, and of the risks they were running. This need acted as a spur, which kept them crawling up the solidified river for fully a couple of hours, which were diversified by slips and falls more or less serious.

At last, as the lava flood took a bend round toward the north, they became aware of a bright glow high above their heads, where the summit of the volcano must be, and after a remark from Ned that it looked as if a bit of the sunset was still there, Jack grasped its meaning.

"It's the reflection of the fire that must be burning up at the top of the mountain."

"Think so, sir? Well, I suppose it's too far off to hurt us. That's miles away."

"Yes; but we are walking on one of the rivers which ran down, and these stones we keep kicking against were once thrown out."

"Ah, you've read a lot about such things, sir; I haven't. Then you say it's all fire up there?"

"Yes, Ned; look, it's getting brighter."

"Then what's the good of our expecting to find water?"

"Because so many springs rise in mountains, and so much water condenses there. Hark! what's that?"

Ned listened.

"Can't hear anything, sir."

"Not that?" cried Jack, whose senses seemed to be sharpened by his needs.

"No, sir, nothing at all."

Jack made no remark, but pressed on with more spirit than he had before displayed. Then he stopped short in the darkest part they had encountered, a place where the trees encroached so much from the forest on either side that they seemed to be completely shut in.

"Now can you hear it, Ned?" cried the boy triumphantly.

"Yes, sir, I can hear it now—water, and a lot of it falling down the rocks. It must be there just below."

Ten minutes after they had lowered themselves down amongst the trees, to where in the darkness they could lie flat at the edge of a rocky basin, scooping cool, sweet water with one hand, and drinking with a sense of satisfaction and delight such as they had never experienced before.

"There, Mr Jack," said Ned joyously, "I don't know what you think, but I say that it's worth going through all the trouble we've had for a drink like that. Here goes again."

He bent down over the stone basin, scooping up the water with his hand.

"Have another, Mr Jack, sir," he cried. "That first one was nothing. It's coming down over the fall sweeter and fresher than ever."

Jack, nothing loth, went on drinking again, but in a more leisurely manner.

"That's it, sir; have a good one. We shall be wanting it to-morrow, when perhaps we can't get any. Fellow ought to be a camel in a place like this, and able to drink enough to last him a week. Go on, sir; I feel as if it's trickling into all kinds of little holes and corners that had got dried-up. Think it goes into your veins, because I'm getting cosy now, right to the tips of my toes, where I was all hard and dry."

"I've had enough now, Ned," said Jack with a sigh, as if he were sorry to make the announcement.

"Don't say that, sir. We've got no bottles, so we must take what we want inside. Have another drink, sir, so as to get yourself well soaked, then you'll be able to stand a lot. I didn't like to howl about it, so as to put you out of heart when you were as bad as me; but my mouth was all furred inside like a tea-kettle, and as for my throat, it was just as if it was growing up, and all hard and dry."

"That was just as I felt, Ned."

"I thought so, sir. Hah!" with a loud smack of the lips. "I've tasted almost every kind of wine, sir, from ginger up to champagne, and I've drunk tea and coffee, and beer, and curds and whey, thin gruel, and cider, and perry, but the whole lot ain't worth a snap compared to a drink of water like this; only," he added with a laugh, "you want to be thirsty as we were first. Done, sir?"

"Yes, quite, Ned."

"Then I tell you what, Mr Jack, sir; we'll try and hunt out a snug place somewhere close handy and have a good sleep."

"I don't feel sleepy, Ned. I want to get back and end my father's terrible suspense."

"So do I, sir; but I put it to you—can we do anything in the dark to-night?"

"No. There is only the satisfaction of trying."

"Yes, sir; but you have to pay a lot for it. Say we try for home now—that's all we can do,—shan't we be less fit to-morrow?"

"I'm afraid so."

"Very well then, sir; it's a lovely night, let's have a good sleep. Then as soon as it's light we'll set to work and eat one of these sleeves of potatoes, come down here again, and take in water enough to last us for the day, or till we find some more, and try all we can to get down to the shore somehow or another. By this time to-morrow night, if I don't find some way of showing that a white man can manage to live where a black can, my name's not what it is."

It was rough work searching for a resting-place, and the best they could find was upon some rough, shrubby growth, not unlike heather, in a recess among several mighty blocks of stone. But if it had been a spring bed, with the finest of linen, they could not have slept better, or awoke more refreshed, when the forest was being made melodious by the songs of birds. The mountain top was beginning to glow, and just below there came the soft tinkling splash of the falling water.

"Morning, sir," cried Ned, springing up. "Your shower-bath's waiting, sir. Come along, sir. Do us no end of good to have a dip. We shall take in a lot of water that way, and get rid of the dust that choked us yesterday."

Jack needed no farther invitation, and upon descending the sides of the stone river, there was the natural bath ready to send a thrill of strength through them, for the rivulet came down in a series of little falls each having its well-filled basin.

There was the drawback that there were no towels to use, and Jack said so.

"What, sir?" cried his man. "You don't mean to say that you would have used a towel if you had had one!"

"Why, of course. Why not?" "Been waste of so much water. Let it soak in gradual, sir. You'll want every drop by and by. You wait till we get out in the sun. Just think of how we were yesterday."

Ten minutes after they were seated beneath a tree, discussing their potatoes, eating away with a glorious appetite till about half of one sleeve-full had been demolished, when Jack cried, "Hold!"

"Why, you ain't had enough yet, sir?"

"No, but we will keep these till by and by when we are hungry again."

"But I'm hungry now, sir," cried Ned; "and they'll be so much easier to carry after we've eat 'em—we shall have got rid of the skins."

"Never mind, don't let's be improvident."

"But I'm pretty sure to spear or shoot a pig to-day for supper, sir."

"Then the potatoes will come in all the more useful as we have no bread," said Jack, smiling. "Let's go now, and climb to that little basin, to have a good draught of water."

"All right, sir; what you say's best, but it's hard work leaving those beautiful little 'taters. They make you feel as if you could go on browsing like all day long."

But the rest were carefully tied up in the sleeve, a good hearty draught of the cool refreshing water taken, and they descended once more to the natural road.

"The breakfast makes one feel different, Ned. I am not nearly so low-spirited this morning."

"Low-spirited, sir? Why, I could run and shout *Hooray*, I feel so well. Look at that arm, sir! Who's going to feel mis'rable when he's got his strength back like that. Ready, sir?"

"Ready? Yes," cried Jack. "Now then, we must make up our minds to get back to the yacht to-day."

"That's it, sir; but if you see me run mad-like, and go off with my spear, you come and help me, for it means pig."

They started once more, following the course of the lava-stream, with its steady ascent, and at every turn Jack looked back longingly, feeling as he did that they were going away, but knowing that the longest might prove in the end the shortest road. They kept on, waiting for the time when they found that the great flow of fiery molten stone had encountered an inequality which had made it divide into two streams, the further of which might lead them down to the sands somewhere far from the yacht.

But mid-day with its burning sun had come, and the intense heat compelled them to stop and rest beneath a clump of trees, which struck them both as being more dwarfed in appearance, though their growth was luxuriant and beautiful. The forest, too, had become more open, there were glades here and there, and it was possible, if they had been so disposed, to have left the stony road and threaded their way among the bushes.

"Why, if we are forced to keep on like this much longer, Ned, we shall reach the crater."

"Well, why not do it, sir? Once up there we can look all over the island, and choose our way down straight to the yacht."

"I should like to do it now we are so high," said Jack; "but we must only think of getting back."

"And getting our suppers, sir," whispered Ned, as he pointed toward a rocky ridge high up above the lava-stream to the left, where seen against the sky-line, as they browsed on the herbage among the rocks, there was a group of about half-a-dozen goats, two of which were evidently kids, while one was a patriarch with enormous curved horns.

"Now, Mr Jack," whispered Ned; "we had some practice with our bows and arrows yesterday; this time we must do it at any cost."

"Yes, Ned," whispered back the lad excitedly. "It may mean the strength to escape."

The next minute, bow and arrow in one hand, spear in the other, they were carefully stalking the herd by creeping upward among the trees and blocks of tumbled-together volcanic stone, which gave them the opportunity of climbing up within easy shot unseen.

Chapter Thirty Five
In spite of all

They were too close to the goats to venture upon much whispering, and the decision was soon arrived at that they were to divide, and each make the best of his way up the ridge till there was an opportunity for a close easy shot; then without waiting that shot was to be sent whizzing from the bow, the probability being that as there was no report, the goats would not be much alarmed, and another chance might be afforded.

"Think we must have one this time, Mr Jack," whispered Ned, and they started from behind the great block which now sheltered them, each taking his own side.

From that moment Jack had no eyes for his companion, his attention was centred upon the great father of the herd, to the left of which the two half-grown kids were browsing upon the tender young shoots of the bush-like growth.

It was nervous work, for every now and then the old goat raised his head on high to take a long careful look round, and when he did, Jack remained motionless where he had crawled. Directly he saw the tips of the horns lowered he began to creep again, taking advantage of every tree-trunk, stone, or bush, and always getting nearer, though still far too distant to risk a shot. His hands trembled and were wet with perspiration, and again and again he felt that he must be seen, and expected to hear the beating of the animals' hoofs as they dashed off, but the great curved horns, sweeping back like those of an ibex, were still visible, and he crawled slowly on, forgetting all about Ned and his progress.

At last, after many minutes devoted to the struggle upward, he reached a spot sufficiently elevated to give him a view of the volcano whose crater rose above the ridge, and forming; a background for the big goat, which stood out plainly about forty yards away even now, and offering itself for a shot, easy enough with a rifle, but very doubtful with a bow and arrow. The lad was in a capital position, but unfortunately the slope beyond offered no cover, and to have moved from it meant to be seen at once, while, more unfortunately still, the two kids, which should have shown themselves nearer, were now completely hidden by a clump of dense growth twenty yards from where he lay.

"If I could only have got there," thought Jack, "how easy it would be." But to have moved would have been to send the whole herd careering away, and all he could do was to wait and see if the kids would at last come from behind the shrubs.

"They may come nearer," he thought, and he softly fitted an arrow to the bowstring, and waited for his opportunity, for he could do no more.

There he rested, bow and arrow held ready, in a very awkward position for shooting, but he dared not move, for at the slightest movement even of his companions, the goat raised his head, and several times gave an angry stamp with one of his fore-feet.

"I wonder where Ned is now," thought the boy, and he hoped that he was having better fortune, and he glanced cautiously in the direction where he must be, but all was still; butterflies were flitting about, birds darted by, and the old goat, the only one of the herd now visible, still browsed or watched.

Jack glanced away to his left to see if he could take and creep round to a better position, but there was less cover than where he was; and after waiting impatiently for what seemed to be over a quarter of an hour, the lad determined to risk all, and creep to the clump in front, if only a few inches at a time, bearing to his left in the hope of getting it between him and the old goat, and bearing still more off till he could get his shot at the young.

All at once, in the midst of the soft hum of insects and the cropping sound made by the invisible goats, Jack heard a peculiar bleating noise away to his right.

Jack looked quickly round, expecting to see an easy shot, and the big goat looked too, and took a step or two forward. Then the bleating began again and ended suddenly in a peculiar smothered way, as if the creature which uttered it had been suddenly strangled.

The big goat looked puzzled, raised his head higher, and stared in the direction of the sound, stamped angrily, and uttered an angry, defiant *ba–a–a–a–a!*

At the cry Jack's heart leaped, for a kid that he had not previously seen sprang into sight, and stood within thirty yards of the watcher, side on, offering an easy shot, while the rest of the herd trotted hurriedly up to their leader.

Twang! Jack's arrow had sped after he had drawn it to the head, and as he was in the act of springing up to see if the shaft had taken effect, something heavy pitched on to his shoulders, throwing him face forward among the thick growth, and a pair of black hands clasped his neck and throat.

It was all done so suddenly that he was half stunned. The stalker had been stalked, and as he was twisted round by the man who had leaped upon him, and who now sat upon his chest, half-a-dozen more black faces appeared, their owners grinning with triumph. Jack yelled with all his might—

"Run for it, Ned. Savages. Run!"

The warning was all in vain, for the next minute four more blacks appeared, dragging the man after them bound hand and foot, and looking purple in the face, and scratched as if he had been engaged in a severe struggle.

"There you are, Mr Jack," he panted. "They've 'most killed me. Jumped upon me just as I had a splendid chance. On my back. Five to one, the cowards. And then they come behind you, and can't hit fair. Are you hurt?"

"Not much. Oh, Ned, and I thought we had got away from them."

"Yes, but they must have been on the look-out, sir."

The blacks were standing round them, spear in hand, ready to strike if an attempt was made to escape, and Jack said so.

"Oh yes, sir, they'd let go at us if we tried to run, but it's of no use to do that, for they'd bring us down at once. There, we may as well look it straight in the face and make the best of it."

"We can't, Ned," said Jack dismally; "there is no best to it. I only wish I knew what they were going to do with us. Only fancy, after us taking all that trouble to get away!"

The bewailings were brought to an end by a stalwart black clapping him on the shoulder and saying something as he pointed over the ridge.

"Ugh! you ugly, mop-headed Day and Martin dummy," cried Ned. "If I hadn't a better language than that I'd hold my tongue. No use to kick, Mr Jack; suppose we must go on."

Jack was already stepping forward, urged by another powerfully-built fellow, who showed his teeth and pricked him forward with the point of the spear he carried.

It was a blunt, clumsy weapon, the point being merely the wood of which it was formed, hardened by thrusting in the fire, but the hand which held it was powerful, and the prod received severe, though the skin was not pierced. Jack uttered no cry, neither did he shrink, but turned round so fiercely upon the black that the fellow started back.

"Well done, Mr Jack, sir," cried Ned excitedly; "that did me good. I like that, sir. Let 'em see that you're Briton to the backbone, and though they've tied me up again with these bits of cane, Britons never shall be slaves. Here, ugly: come and stand in front and I'll kick you."

It was waste of words, but the blacks understood that it was meant defiantly, and they lowered their spears and signed to their prisoners to go on.

"Oh yes," cried Ned proudly, "we'll go on. Can't help ourselves, can we, Mr Jack? But don't be down-hearted, sir. They haven't killed us, and perhaps after all they may take us where we want to go down to the shore."

But as they tramped on, with one of their captors leading the way, and the rest behind, keeping an eye upon the cane bonds which now held both prisoners' wrists behind, their way proved to be diagonally up the slope of the volcano, and the tramp was kept up for hours beneath the broiling heat of the sun, while it seemed to Jack that every now and then hot sulphurous puffs of wind escaped from the stony ground over which they passed. The trees grew rapidly fewer and less in size, till there were only scattered bushes, and higher still these were dwarfed into wiry grasses and tufts of a heather-like growth, with lichens and dried-up mosses.

"Try and hold up, Mr Jack sir, they must halt soon to eat and drink. My word, if we weren't prisoners, I'd say what a view we get from up here. See anything of the yacht?"

"No, Ned; she's inside the reef, and we can't see that."

"No, sir, you're right. 'Britons never shall be slaves,' but all the same I feel just as if I was being driven to market. That's it, they're taking us somewhere to sell us, I know; wonder how many cocoanuts we shall fetch, or p'r'aps it'll be shells. Thirsty, sir?"

"I don't know, Ned, I haven't thought about it. I suppose I am, and hungry and very tired; but I've been thinking about whether we shall ever see the yacht again."

"Oh yes, sir. Never say die. Life's all ups and downs. Sir John ain't forsaking us, you may be sure, and any moment we may see him and a lot of our jolly Jack Tars coming round the corner, and the doctor with 'em, ready to give these black brutes a dose of leaden pills. Ah! and they'll have to take 'em too, whether they like 'em or no. Don't you be down."

"I'm not, Ned. I keep trying to think that it's all adventure and experience."

"That's it, sir. Do to talk about when we get back to old England."

Twice over, as the diagonal ascent grew steeper, the blacks halted for about half-an-hour, and the prisoners were glad to lie down in the shelter of one of the lava blocks with which the slope was strewn, the cool air which came from the sea being fresh and invigorating; and the second time Ned suddenly exclaimed—

"Not going to take us up to the top, are they, and pitch us into the fire?"

"Not likely, Ned," replied Jack; "but we little expected to make the ascent like this."

"With our hands tied behind us, sir."

"I believe they are going this way so as to avoid the forest, and as soon as we get a little farther round they will begin to descend on the other side."

Jack's idea proved to be correct, for upon reaching a spot where nothing but a friable slope of fine ashes kept them from the summit, the leader suddenly leaped down into a hollow which was scored into the mountain side, and began to descend, followed by the rest.

"Due west," said Jack thoughtfully. "Why, Ned, we shall reach the shore far from where we left the yacht."

"If it goes straight down, sir; but is it west?"

"Yes, we are going straight for the sun now, and this gash in the mountain grows deeper. Look."

"Yes, that's right, sir; but I do wish we could get to some water now. It's a dry journey from here to the shore, and you're beginning to be done up."

"Yes, Ned," said Jack wearily; "I am beginning to be done up now."

Chapter Thirty Six
Running the reef

The whole of that journey down the rugged gash in the mountain side was a prolonged agony to Jack, but he fought like a hero to keep his feet, and at last, satisfied that he could not escape, the man who had surprised him and treated him as his own prize caught him by the shoulder as he was tottering down the descent, with the stones every here and there giving way beneath his feet, and about to fall heavily. The next minute his numbed and swollen hands were set at liberty, so that he could better preserve his balance, and the first use he made of them was to point to Ned's bonds, with the result that the man's captor entered into a short colloquy with Jack's; and the savage fitted an arrow to his bow and took aim, half drawing the arrow to the head, while he jabbered away and scowled menacingly, showing his white teeth the while.

"What does he mean by that, Mr Jack? going to shoot me—a coward?"

"No, no; he means he will untie your hands, but that if you attempt to escape an arrow will go faster than you can run, and he will bring you down."

"And very kind of him too, sir. But I shan't run away without you, sir. Here, undo 'em then, blackie."

He bent forward so as to raise his tied hands, and the black began to unfasten the cane.

"I always knew you were a big scholar, Mr Jack, sir," continued Ned, "but I didn't think you were up to this jibber-jabber.—Thankye, old chap. Nice state you've got my hands in though. Why, I don't believe the size gloves I should want are made. Look, Mr Jack, about four-and-twenty they'd take, wouldn't they? How's yours?"

"They ache horribly, Ned."

"Oh, mine don't. I shouldn't know I'd got any if I couldn't see 'em. Plain enough though, ain't they?"

Ned had no time to say more, for his captor urged him on.

"Just like driving a donkey, sir, ain't it?—All right, blackie, I'll go."

The party descended as rapidly as they could till just after the great orange sun had descended over the rim of the sea, and then, as if perfectly familiar with the place, they turned suddenly off to the left, down a second ravine much steeper than the larger one they had left, and after going down about a quarter of a mile to where dwarf trees were beginning to grow thickly again, they stopped short in a natural shelter close by a rock pool, into which a clear thread of water trickled.

Jack's captor pointed to the pool, and the lad lay down and drank deeply, Ned following his example without orders, and upon being satisfied they rose, to find the men busily preparing a fire.—Then one of the party rubbed a couple of pieces of wood together till the friction produced sparks, which began to glow in the wood dust fanned by the fire-maker's breath, and soon after the fire was burning merrily.

Jack did not see it dug out, but a quantity of closely-packed green leaves were lying about, and a rough hollow was close at hand where it had evidently been buried—*it* proving to be the hind-quarters of a small pig, which as the fire burned up well was put to roast, and soon began to send out a pleasant odour.

The prisoners had taken the place pointed out to them, and found that they were well guarded, Ned drawing Jack's attention to this fact.

"And that means, sir," he said, "that it's of no use to try and run unless they go sound off to sleep again as soon as they've had a feast. We might perhaps steal off then, but not if we're watched. I don't want any more arrows in me, and I'm sure you feel the same. I say, sir, I hope they mean to ask us to dinner. Only fancy niggers dining at quality hours in black soots!"

"Don't talk about eating, Ned; the idea makes me feel sick."

"Fight it down then, sir. You must eat, or you can't try to get away, and if you can't try to get away, I can't."

"I'll try, Ned," said Jack abruptly.

"That's right, sir; only let's wait and see if they give us any first. Shame on 'em if they don't." ·

The pig extracted from the blacks' hiding-place began to smell tempting enough to excite any one's appetite, and as a good-sized piece was handed to each by their captors—

"Don't mean to kill us yet, Mr Jack," said Ned merrily. "Hope they don't mean any of that nonsense later on."

But Jack was too weary and low-spirited to reply to his companion's jokes, and he lay back after a time, watching the soft glow over the volcano far above their heads, then the brilliant stars, which looked larger than at home, and glided suddenly into a deep sleep, from which he was awakened by a rough prod from the butt end of a spear.

The lad flushed angrily, but tried to curb his resentment, and turned away as he rose, to find Ned standing watching him in the early morning light.

"Never mind, Mr Jack," he said softly. "It's hard to bear; but this isn't the time to show fight. That black brute kicked me to wake me, and it made me as savage as a bear. If he'd had boots on I should have hit him, I know I should, I couldn't have helped it even if he'd killed me for it; but then you see he hadn't boots on, though the sole of his foot's almost like hoof."

"They're going on directly, Ned."

"Are they, sir? Well, I must have a drink of water first."

He took a step toward the pool; but a spear was presented at his breast, and it was not until Jack had made a sign of drinking that they were allowed to bend down over it.

Directly after they started back up the side gorge to where it joined the greater, and then began to descend again by what proved to be a very precipitous but direct way down toward the sea, water soon after making its appearance in a mere thread, which suddenly leaped down from a crack in the side and found its way to the bottom: while as they were hurried on by their more nimble captors, the stream kept on increasing in volume by the help of the many tiny tributaries which joined it.

Under different auspices the walk would have been glorious. Sir John and the doctor would have found it one grand preserve for birds and insects; but the prisoners had hard work to keep up with their sure-footed captors, and any hesitation on arriving at a difficult bit of the descent was looked upon as an attempt to escape.

The blacks were evidently quite at home in this one of the many ravines which carried the water condensed upon the mountain down to the sea, and consequently made pretty good speed; but this came hard upon their prisoners, who occupied so much time in descending the worst parts that they became at last menacing, and Jack trembled for the consequences of Ned retaliating with a blow.

"It would do no good, Ned," he said earnestly. "But it makes us seem so cowardly to let them poke at us with their spears, sir, and never do anything."

"Never mind how it seems, Ned. You are not cowardly."

"Well, I'd punch any fellow's head who said I was, sir, or who said the same about you."

"They can't say it so that we can understand, and let them think what they like. We'd fight if there was anything to be got by it; but there isn't, Ned. Let's pretend to be beaten now, and then they will not be so watchful. To-night they will sleep somewhere down near the shore, and we may get a chance to escape."

"Then I'm not to hit out, no matter what they do to me?"

"Certainly not."

"But suppose I see 'em hitting or prodding you, sir? Must do something then."

"Nothing whatever, Ned; I'll bear it patiently in the hope of getting a chance to escape later on."

"All right, sir; but I'm getting very hungry for a bit of revenge."

"Wait, Ned, and perhaps it will come."

The difficulties of the descent detained them so that it was fast nearing sunset when the ravine began to widen out and pass beneath the branches of the huge forest monarchs which clothed the lower slopes of the mountain, and wearied out with the day's exertion, Jack began to look out eagerly for the green, park-like expanse which followed the dense jungle, to be succeeded in turn by the sands that ran down into the lagoon.

The more open part appeared sooner than he expected, and with it the river widened into a good-sized pool of open water, where, to the prisoners' surprise, they suddenly found themselves face to face with another party of blacks, who welcomed the new-comers with an eager jabbering as they closed round and examined their captives curiously.

"Our chance of escape cut shorter, Mr Jack," said Ned.

"Yes, I'm afraid so, Ned. They must have been camping here; and I suppose we shall have to stop in this place for the night?"

"Dunno. P'r'aps," said Ned. "See that, Mr Jack?"

He glanced down beneath the trees, where the water lay dark and deep; but for a few moments Jack saw nothing unusual. The next moment though he uttered a little cry of surprise.

"Yes," he said, "I see it now, the boat—drawn right up beneath the boughs."

It was impossible to comprehend the words of the reunited parties of the blacks, but easy to grasp the meaning of their gestures, and as Jack's attention was caught by the eager conversation going on, he pretty well saw that those who had been waiting had seen danger, for they kept on pointing and making other signs, the end being that the prisoners were hurried down to the edge of the water, and pushed toward the great canoe.

"All right!" cried Ned angrily. "I ain't a sack of oats: I can get in. Don't chuck a fellow into the tub."

Expostulation was useless, and the two were thrust down in the bottom; the blacks hurried in and took their places, each man seizing his paddle, and in perfect silence they began to dip their blades into the smooth water, the huge canoe began to move very slowly, and then by degrees faster, the men paddling almost without a splash.

"The *Star* must be pretty close at hand, Mr Jack," said Ned, as they glided at last out of the little dark river into the bright, golden waters of the lagoon, "and they know it; that's how I take all their play-acting jigging about to mean."

"Yes, Ned, that's it. Oh, if we could only see her, or one of the boats! Which way are they going?"

"Well, Mr Jack," said Ned grimly, "I don't like to tell you; but it seems to me that we're off on a voyage to nigger-land, and yet the newspapers say that slavery's nearly done away with now."

"Slavery?" said Jack, and his heart sank within him. "Oh, Ned, that would be awful."

"Better than being made beef and mutton of, Mr Jack. But don't you be down-hearted; p'r'aps we may be together after all, and if we are, there ain't nothing I won't do to make it easier for you, sir, and we'll cut and run, as the sailors say, some day. Ups and downs in life we see; right-tooral-looral-looral-lee. There's only heads and tails to a penny, and if you spin it up in the air, it sometimes comes down one side, and sometimes the other. Well, it's come down wrong way for us this time, next time p'r'aps it may come down right. If it don't, well, you've got too much pluck in you to howl about it: so have I. Here, I don't care; let's look at the bright side of things."

"Oh, Ned, how can we at a time like this?" groaned Jack.

"Easy, sir. It's all adventures, and it might be a jolly deal worse."

"How?"

"Why, this might be a poor old leaky canoe as wasn't safe, and all the time it's a fizzer. See how it goes. Then we might have had a shabby, common-looking crew; but I will say it for them, spite of all the love I don't bear for 'em, they're the blackest and shiniest set of fellows I ever did see. Look at their backs in the warm light; why, you might see to shave in 'em—well, I might; you're lucky enough not to have any beard yet."

"It don't seem as if I shall live to have one, Ned."

"Tchah! nonsense. You'll live to a hundred now. This voyage has made a man of you, my lad. All you've got to do is to keep up your pluck. I say, look at 'em, Mr Jack; they paddle splendid. Talk about our boat-races; why look here, I'd back these chaps. What's that old song? You know; voices keep toon and our oars keep time—only it's paddles. Row, brothers, row. Keep it up, niggers. Slaves indeed! why they're the slaves, not us; we're sitting here as jolly as two lords in a 'lectric launch, going down to Richmond to eat whitebait and drink champagne. Let's see though, I don't mean Richmond, I mean Blackwall. Let's think we've got a crew of blacks taking us to Blackwall."

"Why, Ned!" cried Jack excitedly, "they're paddling straight across the lagoon for the reef."

"That's right, Mr Jack; so they are," said Ned recklessly. "Hooray! who cares! Go it, you black beggars. I say, Mr Jack, sir, look; did you ever see such lovely heads of hair? They'd make splendid grenadiers, and be an advantage to Government to 'list a lot of 'em. They'd come so cheap. They wouldn't want any clothes, and there they are with their busbies a-growing already on their heads. Might call 'em the Blackguards, and that's what they are."

"But, Ned, this long low canoe can never weather the waves on the reef."

"It can, sir, or they wouldn't go for it. Tend upon it they know a place where they can get over, and that's how they came. What do it matter to them if she fills with water? they only pop out over both sides, and hold on and slop it out again, and then jump in. Water runs off them like it does off ducks' backs. I believe they oil themselves all over instead of using a bit of honest soap. Don't matter though; the dirt can't show. My word, we are going it. Straight for the reef."

Ned was right; the long canoe with its fifty men paddling glided over the calm lagoon straight for where the great billows came curving over on to the coral reef with a deep boom, and it was now not above a quarter of a mile away.

"Take tightly hold of the side, Ned," said Jack excitedly. "You are right, they will manage it, I suppose, or they would not attempt it."

"Trust 'em for that, sir. I'll stick to the canoe like one of those limpet things; mind you do too. I say, I'm beginning to like it, ain't you?"

"It is exciting, Ned, and I don't think I mind."

"That's your style, sir. That's the true British boy speaking. Ah, it's no wonder we carry all before us when we don't get licked. There now, you look every inch of you like Sir John, and he'd be proud of you. Hooray! who cares! Go it, you black rascals. We shall go over that reef like a flash. One of our boats with a big crew dare not attempt it, and— Oh, I say, look, Mr Jack, look. You were wishing for it, and there it is, half-a-mile away—one of our boats coming to save us, and—"

"She'll be too late, Ned," groaned Jack, and, unseen by their captors, every man of whom had his back to them, and was working away with his paddle, the lad rose softly in his place and waved his hand above his head.

"Sit down, sir," whispered Ned excitedly. "It means a topper if they catch you at it. But look, look, there's some one waving his helmet."

"Yes, yes," whispered back Jack, "it's father."

"Hooray!" said Ned softly. "But what are they firing for?"

"Signal that they see us, Ned," whispered back Jack hoarsely, as there were two faint puffs of smoke seen and the reports followed.

"Too far off to try and swim to 'em, sir?"

"Yes, Ned," said Jack sadly, "and there are the sharks."

"Ugh! yes, sir. That won't do. Never mind, let's sit still. They've seen us, and they'll have us now."

"But our boat can't follow through the surf."

"Can't!" cried Ned; "it has to. Never know what you can do till you try."

The rush through the water had been exciting before; it was tenfold more so now, and the prisoners looked wildly over the lagoon at the cutter, which was being pulled after them evidently with all the rowers' might, the oars dipping and the water flashing in the last rays of the sun as it dipped swiftly down. But Jack's heart sank again as he saw that they would be crossing the reef while the rescue party were still half-a-mile away.

Ned felt with him, and said softly—

"Oh, why don't they go back to the yacht and signal to 'em to get under weigh and go out in chase of us—cut us off on the other side?"

"But where is the yacht, Ned?" cried Jack. "She may be the other way."

"Ah, that's what we don't know, sir. There, we can't do anything but sit fast. You get your arm over that side, I'll hold on this."

There was little talking now, the two prisoners' attention being turned to the reef in front, which the paddlers were now straining every nerve to reach at full speed. Suddenly a couple of the blacks sprung up, came aft past where Jack and Ned sat, and thrust a long paddle over the stern to help in the steering, which so far had been managed by the paddlers themselves, one side easing when it was necessary.

The two men said something as they passed, but took no more notice of them, and after looking sharply ahead for a few moments, Jack turned to gaze at the pursuing boat, coming on steadily now. But the next minute it looked dim, then it died out of sight, for the canoe had entered into the mist of fine spray raised by the billows on the reef, and directly after they were in a thick fog, as they rushed into the tremendous race of waters leaping and surging about them. The long canoe quivered, the men behind them yelled, and were answered by a fierce shout as the crew frantically plunged their paddles into the yielding foam water, while the spray blinded, the canoe bumped again and again, and then all at once began to rise, till she seemed as if she were going to fall backward prow over stern.

"It's all over with us," thought Jack; but the next moment she began to sink toward the horizontal, hung for a second or two level, and then glided down after a tremendous pitch, rose again, and then began to race along on the top of a huge billow which foamed and raved hungrily by their side.

This was repeated again and again, but the canoe shipped very little water, and before Jack could realise that they were in safety, the wild excitement and confusion of the tumbling water was at an end, and they were being paddled away out to the open sea in the fast-coming transparent darkness of the brief evening, with a wall of white waters behind.

Chapter Thirty Seven
A stern chase—very

"Ah!" ejaculated Ned, as he sat wiping the salt spray out of his eyes; "can't say as I should like to go through that again, Mr Jack, but now we have done it I like it. My word, how I can brag now to our chaps on board!"

"Do you think they will try and follow us, Ned?" panted Jack, who spoke as if he had been running hard.

"Surely not, sir. Never be so mad."

"But I'm afraid they will. My father would never sit there and make no effort to save us."

Ned was silent for some minutes, and the foam of the breakers on the reef began to soften as the blacks paddled hard straight out to sea.

A few minutes later it was night, with the stars beginning to shine out clearly from the purpling sky, and the paddles making the water flash into phosphorescent foam.

"You're right, Mr Jack," said Ned at last; "Sir John wouldn't mind running any risk to save us, but he might see that it was only throwing away a chance to get the boat capsized, and he may have to row back to the yacht so as to get her out of the lagoon and after us to cut us off before these black ruffians can get home to where they came from."

"It means slavery after all, Ned," said Jack bitterly. "Why didn't we jump overboard and—and try to swim to the boat?"

"What the doctor calls 'law of self-preservation,' sir," said Ned quietly. "We'd seen too much in that lagoon, very pretty to look at, but too many ugly things about in the blue waters. Been just about as mad as for them to try and follow the canoe. What do you say to making ourselves comfortable, sir, and having a nap?"

"What, now? At a time like this?" cried Jack.

"Yes, sir, that's what I was thinking, so as to be ready for work to-morrow."

"I could not sleep," said Jack sadly, as he sat gazing back in the direction of the reef.

"Very well, sir; then you take the first watch while I go below, only there ain't no below. It's of no use for you to look back at the reef, sir, for they couldn't have got through, and if they could this canoe goes two miles to their one. What we've got to do is to wait for to-morrow morning, and hope for the best."

Jack said nothing, but he knew that all his companion said was right, and he sat there silent, while Ned stretched himself in the bottom and was off soundly to sleep. Almost directly after about half the blacks withdrew the paddles from the water and lay down in the bottom, leaving the rest to urge the boat along.

It was hard work in the solitude of that night to keep from giving way to despair, and to cling to the hope that those in the boat had not attempted the daring feat performed with the canoe, but had turned back to the yacht to get her under weigh and come in chase. For always there came the thought that by morning the canoe would be out of sight, and he and Ned still on the way to some state of captivity, preserved for Heaven only knew what terrible fate.

From time to time the resting half of the savages sprung up, summoned by a thump given with the handle of a paddle, each rower awakening the man who was to relieve him after about an hour's spell; and Jack watched all this in a dull, apathetic way again and again, till somehow the long weary night sluggishly drew near its end. Over and over again an angry feeling of resentment attacked the watcher, and when the sleeping savages were aroused he felt disposed to kick Ned and make him wake up and talk.

But a better feeling soon prevailed. "Poor fellow!" he said to himself; "why shouldn't he rest and forget all his troubles for a few hours? It is only selfishness to rouse him."

It was still dark when Ned suddenly sat up. "Morning, sir," he said; "been to sleep?"

"I? No, Ned, I couldn't sleep."

"That's a pity. I could, like a top. It's done me a lot of good, and I'm ready now for anything, fighting, swimming, or breakfast, specially the last. Hot coffee, toast, fried ham, or a bit of fish. Not particular. Don't do to be when you're at sea."

"You don't seem to trouble much about our position, Ned," said Jack bitterly.

"Not a bit, sir. What's the good? Don't make it any better to go on the dump. It can't last. It's like the weather—either gets better or it gets worse. My word, what a fine thing a bit o' sleep is! Bit cool though. Always is just before sunrise. Seen anything of the yacht, sir?"

"Bah! Impossible! How could I?"

Ned said nothing, but glanced at the dimly-seen paddlers working away, and at the sleeping party who were in the bottom of the canoe, and then turned his attention astern.

"Wonder where they are taking us, sir," he said. "There must be a big island somewhere out in this direction, and—"

He became silent so suddenly that Jack turned to him in surprise, and saw that he was gazing fixedly over the stern of the canoe into the black darkness, for there was no sign of the coming day.

"What are you thinking?" said Jack at last.

"That I shall have to report you to the captain, sir, for not keeping better watch. I didn't set you to it. You volunteered."

"What do you mean, Ned?" cried Jack excitedly.

"You said, when I asked you whether you had seen anything of the yacht, 'Bah! Impossible! How could I?'"

"Well, how could I in the dark?"

"By keeping a bright look-out, sir. There's her light."

"What!" cried Jack.

"Steady, sir, steady. Don't jump out of the boat."

"But you don't mean—"

"Oh yes, I do, sir. Look yonder."

"Oh, nonsense!" cried Jack bitterly; "that must be a star setting in the west."

"Well, it may be, sir, and if it is, it's so close down that in another five minutes it'll be one; but it strikes me that there's a little lighter look yonder, and that it's the east. Of course I don't know for certain like, and I've been asleep. Let's watch for a bit. I believe it's our star as the guv'nor's had lit up to let us know he's coming after us—that's what I think, sir."

"It is too much to hope," said Jack despondently.

"Not a bit, sir. You can't say but what it's as likely as likely. But there, we shall soon know. I wonder whether the niggers have seen it yet."

Evidently they had not, and this, knowing how sharp-eyed they were, strengthened Jack's belief that it was only a star, and he said so.

"All right, sir," said Ned, after a long watching, "pr'a'ps you're right; but it's a new kind if it is, for it don't come up nor it don't go down. Anyhow that's the east, for the sun means to come up there, or I'm a Dutchman."

They sat watching for about a quarter of an hour longer, and then Jack exclaimed softly—

"You were wrong, Ned, it was a star, and it has sank out of sight."

"Down in the east, sir?"

"It cannot be the east, Ned, it must be the west."

"Then it's last night again, sir, and that's a speck left up to show where the sun went down."

As Ned spoke he pointed to where there was a faint flush of light, which grew warmer and warmer as Jack sat trying to keep from being too sanguine. Then he turned away and feared to gaze aft any more, oh account of the blacks, who were paddling steadily away, for against a pale streak of light in the east, there, plainly enough to be seen, were the hull and spars of the *Silver Star*, while like a pennon there floated out behind her a long dark cloud of smoke, telling that her engine fires were roaring away and her propeller hard at work.

"I was afraid to hope, Ned," whispered Jack. "Think they see us?"

"Think they see us, sir! Why, of course. Mr Bartlett's up in the main-top with his glass to his eye, you may be sure, and the lads below are shovelling in the coals as if they cost nothing. Look at the smoke. I say, see how the niggers are at it. They know. Shouldn't be surprised if we catch sight of the place we're going to when the sun's up. All I hope is that it's so far away that they can't reach it."

The sun rose at last, and the mountain became glorified once more, but it was a long time before a glimpse could be caught of their destination, and then, like a faint cloud extending right and left for miles, there was land— dim, low-lying misty land, without a sign of elevation or peak.

"That's it sure enough, Mr Jack, sir," said Ned, shading his eyes from the glare of the sea; "and now it's a question of paddles against screw."

"Yes. Which will win, Ned?"

"Screw, sir. If it was wind and sails in this changeable sort of place I should be a bit doubtful, but I ain't the least."

A stern chase is always a long one, they say, and to the prisoners it seemed to be here, and Hope and Doubt alternately held sway, while to Jack's agony the dim, distant flat land, which by degrees began to assume the aspect of a long range of extremely flat islands, appeared to come steadily nearer, while the yacht hardly seemed to stir.

"She will never catch us, Ned," said Jack despondently.

"Go along with you, sir. She'll do it before we get near. Not but what these fellows paddle splendidly. Hallo! what are they going to do?"

The answer came in the quick hoisting of a couple of low masts and the same number of matting sails, for the water was beginning to be flecked by a coming breeze. In addition, the men rapidly rigged out a couple of bamboos on one side, and lashed their ends to another which lay along the bottom of the boat, so as to form an outrigger to counteract the pressure of the sails.

A few minutes later the paddles were laid in, for the great canoe was gliding through the water faster than the men could propel her.

At last, though, hope began to grow stronger in the prisoners' breasts, for it was plain now that with full steam on the yacht was rapidly coming up.

"They'd got no pressure on at first, sir, only enough to send her along a bit. What do you say to it now?"

"It's in doubt, Ned. They may run us into shallow water where the yacht dare not come."

"But she dare send her boats, sir. Oh, we're all right now.—If they don't knock us on the head when they find they're beaten," Ned added to himself.

The faces of those on board the yacht began now to grow plain as the mountain seemed to be steadily sinking in the distance, and figures could be made out on the low shore in front.

"Ned, Ned, look," whispered Jack excitedly. "It's all over with us."

"Why, what for?"

"Can't you see they are getting out two more canoes?"

"You've got better eyes than I have, sir; I can't see anything."

Jack proved to be right, for soon after a couple of great canoes came through an opening in a line of breakers, and made straight for the one which bore the prisoners.

"It's going to be a close shave, Mr Jack," said Ned at last. "If they get near enough to the land they'll win, because the *Star* won't dare to follow, but I don't give up yet. Only look here, sir, if matters come to the worst they'll try and kill us, so be on the look-out. You can swim now after those lessons I gave you."

"Oh, Ned, only a few strokes. I cannot trust myself," groaned Jack.

"Oh dear! and you a gent, and your education neglected like that. Why, to be able to swim now, sir, is worth all the Latin and Greek in the world. But never mind, I can, though all the Greek I know is *quantum stuff*, and p'r'aps that's Latin. You do as I tell you; the moment you see that one of the niggers means mischief, over you go; I shall be there, and I'll help you swim, sir, and the yacht's sure to have a boat ready to drop and pick us up."

On they went, with the wind sending the canoe rapidly along, and the blacks sat on the edge to keep her well down, and on the outrigger. The speed now was wonderful, the long elastic vessel bent and glided like some live creature over the swell, and had the blacks had another mile to go, the fate of the two prisoners would have been sealed; but at full speed now the yacht, with sail after sail shaken out to the help of the propeller, came up hand over hand, and when pretty close swayed off to windward, curved round as she glided by, and was once more answering her helm in the other direction, racing for the canoe's bows, the steering being so true that the fore-part was forced under water while the stern rose slowly in the air. "Now for it," said Ned sharply. Jack hesitated for a moment or two, and then tried to plant one foot upon the side and leap after his companion; but his momentary hesitation was nearly fatal, for one of the blacks made a dash at him, caught him by the shoulder, and struck at him with his raised club.

In his despair the lad forced himself forward, and instead of the head of the heavy club, it was the man's arm which struck him across the shoulder, and the next moment they were thrown by the rising of the stern headlong amongst the struggling crowd as the canoe filled. Then all was darkness and confusion as the lad felt himself dragged down lower and lower, till it seemed as if he would never rise again.

Moments are changed to minutes at such times as these, but prolonged as the agony seemed, he was soon at the surface once more, panting for breath and beating the water like a drowning dog.

But coolness came with the strong desire for life, and he now struck out bravely as he saw the water about dotted with the black heads of his enemies, one and all swimming for the floating wreck of their canoe, whilst the yacht was far away, and Jack's courage became despair as he kept on swimming slowly, better than he could have believed, so as to keep himself afloat.

"That's the way, Mr Jack, sir," came from behind him; "and you said you couldn't swim."

"Ned," gasped the boy, turning in the direction of the sound, and his slow, steady strokes became on the instant fast and wild.

"Ah, don't do that!" cried Ned, swimming alongside. "Slow and steady, sir. Don't wind yourself. There, it's all right; I could keep you up, but I want you to try yourself. Strike out as I told you last time we bathed. Slow and steady. Let your legs go down as far as they like. Never mind if the water comes right up to your mouth; lay your head sideways and screwed round so that you can look over your right shoulder, and rest the back of it on the water. That's the way. Think you're having a lesson in swimming, and do just as I do. See? We only want to keep afloat till a boat comes from the yacht to pick us up. Well done, sir. This is the best lesson in swimming you ever had."

Jack took stroke for stroke feebly enough, and kept well afloat, but he felt all the time that if Ned were not at his side he would have begun to strike out again in frantic despairing haste, wearied himself in a very short time, and gone down.

"Man never knows what he can do till he tries, sir," said Ned cheerily. "It's all right. Just keep your mouth above water while you take a good long breath, and then shut it again. Lower you are the easier you float. When you're tired you shall turn on your back, and I'll guide you."

"Shall we be drowned, Ned?" panted the lad. "We'll talk about that by and by, sir. We can go on like this easy in the sea for an hour, if you do as I tell you. Now then, we're not running a race. Just try to think you're standing in the water, and to move your hands as slowly as you can. It's all right, Mr Jack, sir. We've escaped. Here's the yacht coming back to pick us up, and they've got one of the cutters ready to drop with the men in her. Don't you say nothing. You just attend to your swimming lesson: I'll do all the talking. I learnt to swim when I was a little bit of a nipper and went with the boys at school. They used to pitch me in, so that I was obliged to swim, I can tell you. That was only fresh water. It's ever so much easier to swim in the sea—when it's smooth. Mind you, I don't know nothing about it when it's rough."

"Is the yacht near, Ned?" said Jack huskily. "What's that to you?" cried the man fiercely. "You mind your lesson. Ought to know better than that. I want to see you swim well, and you were doing beautiful before you began to talk. No, you ain't getting tired. If you was, as I told you, I'd make you float. Ur–r–r!"

Ned uttered a sound like a savage dog, for a panting and splashing had made him turn his head to see, not six yards behind him, a fierce-looking black face, with grinning teeth and flashing eyes, looking the more savage from the fact that, to leave his arms both at liberty, the black was holding his war-club in his grinning teeth.

The partly submerged canoe, burdened with its clinging crew, was a hundred yards away, the two which had been launched to her assistance quite three, and the yacht still two, but cutting the water fast.

Ned set his teeth; and for a brief instant thought of getting out his knife, but he knew it would be madness to attempt it, and he prepared with desperate energy for the worst.

"Don't you take any notice of me," he growled fiercely to his young master. "You keep on swimming. Do you hear?"

In utter ignorance of the peril behind, and influenced in his weakness and helplessness as a swimmer by one whom he instinctively felt to be at home in the water, and his master, Jack obeyed, keeping to the slow stroke with his arms, while his action with his legs was that of the well-known treading water.

All this was but brief.

After savagely shouting at Jack, Ned drew a deep breath and turned to meet the black, whose eyes glowed with race hatred as he raised one hand from the water, took the short melon-headed nulla-nulla club from his teeth, rose a little higher, and struck at his fellow-swimmer with all his might.

But it was for dear life. Ned threw himself sidewise, the head of the club grazed his shoulder as it splashed the water. Then, quick as thought, Ned retaliated by dashing out his left fist, and struck his enemy full on the cheek.

But it was a feeble blow, and did no more than make him fiercer as he turned to renew the attack.

"It's all over!" groaned the poor fellow. "If they'll only pick up the poor young governor in time!"

A hoarse sob of despair escaped from Ned's breast, as he prepared to dodge the next blow from the club, meaning not to strike another nerveless, helpless blow from the water, but to grapple with the black.

"And then it's who can hold his breath longest," he thought. "Oh, why did I come on a trip like this?"

Thought comes quickly at a time like this.

The club was once more raised and held suspended in the air for a few moments, the wily black feinting twice over, and making Ned dodge. The third time he made another quick feint, and was in the act then of delivering a tremendous blow, when Jack uttered a wild cry, for he had turned his head to appeal to his companion for help.

At that moment Ned heard a whizz, as if some beetle had suddenly passed his ear; there was instantaneously a sharp pat, and the moment after the report of a rifle. The club fell into the water with a splash.

"Hah!" ejaculated Ned, turning on his side, and in a dozen side strokes he was alongside of Jack once more, as he was making a brave effort to come to his companion's aid.

"Back, my lad, back!" cried Ned as he swam. "No, no; you're not beaten yet. Hooray! the boat! They're close here, and—Mr Jack, sir—it's—it's too much—I—I— Swim, sir, swim—don't—don't mind me!"

The poor fellow's look seemed fixed and staring, his arms refused their office, and Jack caught at him to try and support him. Then struggling vainly the water closed over his head, as his starting eyes saw the flashing of the water thrown up by six oars, and a figure standing leaning toward him, boat-hook in hand.

Chapter Thirty Eight
Not beaten yet

"How are you, boy?"

The voice seemed to come from a great distance, and the face of the speaker looked far away, and yet his hand was being held in his father's firm palm.

"Ah!" sighed Jack in answer. Then quickly, "Ned! Ned! Where's Ned?"

"Safe here," said Sir John. "In the boat. We were only just in time."

"He's coming to," said another familiar voice. "Pull away, my lads. Well, Jack, old fellow, you've been carrying on a nice game. How are you? Glad to see you. No, no, lie back for a bit. We'll soon have you on board."

Jack said nothing for a few moments. Then quickly—

"Who was it fired that shot?"

"Oh, never mind about who fired it," said the doctor gruffly; but he picked up a double rifle lying against one of the thwarts, and mechanically opened the breech, drew out a spent cartridge, and thrust in another.

"Have your pieces ready, my lads. Half at the word cease rowing, aim, and fire. Are you ready, gentlemen? They're coming on very fast."

"Yes; all right," said the doctor; and Sir John rose in the boat, rifle in hand, and gave the mate, who had spoken, a nod, and then he smiled as Jack rose up quickly and picked up one of the loaded pieces at his side.

But no one fired at the rapidly advancing canoes, which were crowded with men; for suddenly there was a deep roar from the yacht, a heavy charge of grape-shot ploughed up the water in front of the first canoe, and the paddling in both ceased.

Another shot sent the water flying over the second canoe, and as if animated by one brain, the paddles began to work again, not to send the vessels forward, but back toward the island; and five minutes later the boat was alongside the yacht.

The men sent up a hearty cheer as Captain Bradleigh held out his hand to assist Jack on board, and his words were almost drowned in the welcoming cries; but Jack heard him, as the warm grip retained his hand, and another pressed his shoulder.

"The best day's work, my lad, we ever did. God bless you, and thank Him for giving you safely back."

Five minutes later the boat was swinging to the davits.

"Don't want to punish them any more, Sir John, I suppose?" cried the captain.

"No, no, let the miserable wretches go," said Jack's father.

"Then we'll go back to the old anchorage, sir, for there's a look about the sky I don't like."

The signal was given, and the yacht began to glide rapidly through the water, back toward where the volcano rose up glowing with colour in the morning light, while Jack was at Ned's side as he lay coming to on the deck.

He stared about him for a few moments, and then fixed his eyes on those of Jack, breaking out half hysterically —

"I couldn't help it, Mr Jack, sir; don't set me down for a cowardly cur."

"Help what?" said the lad wonderingly.

"Turning like a woman, and fainting away that how. Oh, do give me a dose o' something, doctor, I feel sick as a dog."

"No, no; lie still for a minute or two, and you'll be all right," said the doctor, patting his shoulder, and Ned uttered a cry.

"Don't, don't, sir. It's agony — my bad shoulder — the arrow — and he hit me there with his club."

"Ned, Ned," said Jack softly, as he bent over the poor fellow and held his hand, "who could think you a coward for saving my life?"

The men began to cheer again when Ned was helped by the doctor and Jack down to his berth, wincing at the slightest touch, for his arm had received a nasty jar, but a smile came into his drawn face as he heard the hearty welcome.

"Thankye, lads, thankye kindly," he kept on saying till he got below, where the steward helped him to change his clothes, and Jack went to his cabin for the same purpose.

"Ever so much better, sir," cried Ned half-an-hour later, when Jack went to see him, and found him dressed and ready to go on deck. "That crack was just like one on the funny-bone, sir, but it's all gone off now. My eye, though! suppose it had been where he meant it! What a headache I should have had!"

By the time Jack reached the deck, the islands from whence the blacks came were hidden by a peculiar-looking haze, and the *Star* was racing through the sea to gain the shelter of the lagoon.

"A hurricane, my lad," said the captain, "and we shall get into shelter none too soon."

"A nice hunt you gave us, Jack," said his father. "Here have we been with half the crew hard at work every day looking for you two. Well, thank Heaven you are both back safe and sound."

"We did our best to get back, father," said the lad, looking at Sir John wistfully.

"Of course, I know that, my boy, and I hope you think we did our best to find you. The doctor here pretty well lamed himself with walking."

"Of course I did," said that gentleman. "Doctors don't like to lose their patients, do they?"

Go where he would during their run back to the harbour, Jack found the men ready to smile and salute him with a hearty "Glad to see you back, sir," till it set him wondering, and finding Ned forward alone, he went to him and said something about it.

"Yes, sir, ain't it queer? I was thinking the same. I ain't done nothing but be civil to the chaps since we come aboard, but they're as pleased as Punch to see us back again. They're a bit disappointed though that Sir John didn't go in for giving the black beggars an out-and-out good thrashing."

"My father says he came for a pleasure-trip," said Jack quietly, "and he does not wish to go back home feeling that it was obtained at the cost of killing a number of fellow-creatures."

"No, no, of course not," said Ned quickly; "only you must draw the line somewhere, and I want to know whether black fellows who shoot poisoned arrows into you, and when you're swimming for your life, and ain't never interfered with them, and they come and try to knock your brains out with clubs, is fellow-creatures. Why, if it was me, I'd rather try to make friends with a respectable set o' wild beasts. They wouldn't eat you unless they was hungry. Strikes me that if I hadn't dodged that gentleman when he hit at me, I shouldn't have been here; nor I shouldn't neither if some one hadn't fired that shot. I say, Mr Jack, sir; it was Sir John, wasn't it?"

"No, Ned, it was Doctor Instow."

"Then that's two I owe him. I always used to think that Sir John was best man with a gun, but after that—well, I'm done. All I can say is, I hope my turn 'll come to do something for the doctor, and till it does I'll take anything he likes to give me, even if it's jollop, and won't make a face."

Jack laughed.

"Oh yes, it's easy to smile a grin, sir," said Ned, "but if you'd tasted some of the stuff he gave me you wouldn't."

"Ah, well, you will not want any physic now, Ned."

"Hah! it seems more natural on board now," said the mate, coming up smiling. "You two have given us an anxious time. We must have it all over as soon as we're safe from the hurricane."

"Hurricane?" said Ned, staring. "What hurricane? Where?"

The mate pointed astern, and Ned stared out to sea as the yacht raced along.

"Well, I can't see anything," he said.

"Can't you see that thick, hazy look astern?"

"What, that bit o' fog?"

"Yes; it is chasing us pretty sharply; I'm afraid we shall not get into harbour before it's down upon us. Ah, there's the skipper."

The speaker walked quickly aft, and found Captain Bradleigh, who had just come on deck from the cabin, and after a look round there was a brief consultation, and all hands were piped on deck. Then for the next hour there was a busy scene. The tops were sent down, the sails doubly secured, boats swung inboard and lashed, and every possible precaution taken to make all that could be caught by a furious tempest thoroughly secure.

"Well, I suppose they know what they're about, Mr Jack, sir," said Ned; "but it looks to me like taking a lot of trouble because the sky's getting a bit dark, and a shower's coming."

But Ned's knowledge of the typhoon of the eastern tropical seas was naturally not very extensive, and he altered his opinion an hour later, when, in spite of the speed with which the yacht had rushed away before the terrible storm sweeping after them, the sea was white, and half the heavens black as night. It was at half-speed the yacht ran in through the gates of the reef into smooth water, and then turning round at full speed again, went on and on, till she was well under the lee of the great volcano, which did its part when anchors were down, and head to the wind they lay facing the quarter from which the awful hurricane blew.

There was no narrative of adventure given by the seekers or the sought that night, nor any thought of sleep, for officers and men never left the deck, but passed a terrible time of anxiety in the expectation that one of the terrific blasts would tear the little vessel from her moorings and cast her upon the inner side of the reef. But the steam was kept up, and the propeller gently turning, sufficient to ease the strain upon the cables, and the anchors held fast.

"She's a splendid craft, gentlemen," said the captain, when they had assembled for refreshment in the cabin, during one of the brief lulls of the furious blast; "but I'm afraid we should none of us have seen another day if we had been caught outside. A man feels very small at a time like this. The worst hurricane I was ever in. Didn't think the wind could blow so fiercely, Mr Jack, eh?"

Jack shook his head.

"It feels," he said slowly, "as if the world had broke away, and was rushing on through space faster and faster, and never to stop again."

"Yes, sir," said the captain quietly, as he gazed at the thoughtful lad. "You're a scholar, and have read and studied these things. So have I, sir, but not from books, and it seems to me that these things work by their wonderful laws for reasons far beyond our little minds to grasp, and all are working for some great end."

No one answered, and the wind began to increase in violence again, the noise almost stifling the captain's next words:—

"But we have not broken away, sir, and the sun will rise to a minute in the morning, just as if this hurricane had not come, and please God everything around us will be calm; but be sure yonder you will hardly know the island, it will be such a wreck."

The captain's words were true enough as to the calm, for just before daylight the intense blackness which had covered the heavens passed away, leaving the stars glittering with a most wondrous brilliancy; there was a deep murmur dying away in the distance, and, utterly exhausted, Jack laid himself down on one of the cabin lounges, to drop off into the deep sleep of utter exhaustion, one from which he awoke to find the warm glow of evening shining in at the open window, and his father watching him with an anxious expression upon his face.

Captain Bradleigh was quite right. The hurricane had passed, and the aspect of the island from where Jack stood with his glass on deck, sweeping the mountain slopes, in places a terrible wreck. The hollows and deep ravines had naturally escaped, but the higher portions, even on that side, were swept bare, and every now and then the lad gazed through his binocular at piled-up masses of tangled bough and branch shattered and splintered as if they had been straws.

"Yes, my lad, it looks a terrible ruin here and there," said the captain, as Jack handed him the glass to try; "but changes take place quickly out here, and the sun's hard at work already repairing damages. Those heaps will soon rot away, and fresh growth cover the bare patches. It's bad enough, but an eruption from the mountain there would have done more mischief than this."

Over a late meal there was a discussion about their future proceedings, and the elders went into the pros and cons of their position.

"You could find us another island, captain, couldn't you?" said Sir John.

"Oh yes, sir; several that I dare say would answer your purpose, but I'm afraid that we shall have the native difficulty go where we may, for these sanguinary blacks are a restless lot, and wherever there is a beautiful spot they generally take possession of it."

"Of course," said the doctor gruffly. "We should do the same."

"We have done the same all the world round," said Sir John, laughing.

"Of course. 'It is their nature to,'" quoted the doctor. "For my part it seems a sin to go away when we have not secured half the grand specimens of birds to be found."

"And my cases of insects not half filled," said Sir John.

"But after his rough experience," said the captain dryly, "I cannot wonder at Mr Jack here feeling anxious to be homeward bound."

"I?" cried Jack, turning upon the captain excitedly. "I anxious to go back? Why, what made you think that, Captain Bradleigh?"

"Oh, I thought you must be, sir, after what you have gone through. Nobody could like that."

"Of course I did not," said the lad, flushing. "It was terrible and risky while it lasted, but I don't mind it all now, and we might stay here for months and never see the blacks again."

"That means you would like to stay a little longer?"

"Yes, father," cried the lad excitedly. "It would be dreadfully disappointing to go away and not climb right to the crater now I have been so near, and know the way."

An hour later Jack was on deck watching the stars, and listening to the deep, heavy boom of the surf on the reef, thinking of how wonderful the contrast was, and mentally going over the horrors of the past night, when he heard a familiar air being whistled forward, one he had often heard coming from the pantry at home, and he walked ahead, to find Ned leaning over the side.

"Ah, Mr Jack! here you are then. I say, I'm not going to have any more of this nonsense. Doctor's all very well, but it's a strange thing if a man don't know best how he is."

"Why, what's the matter?"

"Doctor Instow's the matter, sir; and after all he ain't my master. If the guv'nor says I ain't to do a thing, or you, my young guv'nor, says it, why that's enough; but Doctor Instow don't pay me my wages."

"What has he been saying to you?"

"Put his foot down, and wouldn't let me wait dinner, sir. But I mean to go on as usual to-morrow morning."

"Oh, very well; go on, then. But what do you think of our starting for home to-morrow morning, Ned?"

"What, sir? Start for home—to-morrow morning?"

"Yes, aren't you glad?"

"Glad, sir? Will you excuse me asking you a question?"

"Of course. What is it?"

"Would you be good enough to tell me why we come out here, if, as soon as we find a place like this, we want to start back?"

"The place is dangerous. These blacks—"

"Bother the blacks! Who cares for the blacks, sir? Why, haven't we licked 'em over and over again? Oh, well, sir, I'm not master. All I've got to say, sir, is, I'm jolly sorry we came."

"Then you are glad we are going back?"

"That I ain't, sir. I say it's a shame. Why, the fun has only just begun."

"Ah, well, we're not going yet. I said I should like to stay and see more, and do more collecting, and ascend the mountain by the way we came down."

"There, I beg your pardon, Mr Jack, sir, I do indeed, for I was all wrong. Thought you were saying that because of the niggers; and I did hope you were too English for that."

"Well, Ned, I hope I am."

Chapter Thirty Nine
The last adventure

From that day the collecting went on merrily, for it seemed as if, to use Ned's words, "the niggers" had had "a regular sickener," excursion after excursion being made with careful precautions, which as the weeks rolled on were more and more relaxed.

Naturally at every landing traces of the terrible havoc made by the hurricane were seen; but, as Captain Bradleigh said, the sun was hard at work repairing damages, and there were endless lovely places which had completely escaped.

The men were never happier than when they were forming guards or porters for the various expeditions, and the naturalists' cases grew fuller and fuller of gorgeously-painted or armoured birds. The display of butterflies and wondrously-shaped flies and beetles was extensive, and as Jack and his henchman handled gun, butterfly-net, dredge, or fishing-line, the very existence of inimical natives not many miles away began to be forgotten, just as Jack's life before he was roused from his dreaming existence into that of a strong, manly English lad seemed to be a thing of the past.

Many months had elapsed since they left England, and in spite of the way in which the provender was supplemented by fish and fresh meat in the shape of pork, kid, and a small kind of deer discovered in one valley, as the captain said, stores would not last for ever, and they must soon either turn homeward, or run to one of the ports where supplies could be obtained.

Sir John said that another fortnight must end their stay at the island, and then they would sail for Hong Kong, take in stores, and start for their journey homeward round the world.

One thing had been kept for the last, and that was an ascent of the volcano, and three days before the fortnight had elapsed, the yacht was run round to the foot of the valley where the canoe had lain and from here a strong party was to start at daybreak, carrying provisions and canvas for a couple of tents, so that they could sleep somewhere up the mountain, and descend on the other side, where the yacht was to meet them.

Full of excitement over this, which he looked upon as the great event of the voyage, Jack was awake before Ned came to summon him, and headed by Sir John and the doctor, the captain remaining on board, the expedition, which included ten well-armed men from the crew, who were provided with axes, ropes, and light tent-poles, started in the highest of spirits.

No collecting was to be done, but every effort directed to scaling the mountain, which had several times shown a brighter light from its top, and in anticipation of strange sights and the discovering of fresh wonders, Jack stepped to the front with Ned, their experience being sufficient to warrant their acting as guides.

It proved to be a stiff climb, but at sunset they had reached a sheltered hollow where there was a sufficiency of scrubby dwarfed trees to supply them with wood and a screen to keep off the keen wind which blew pretty hard at five thousand feet above sea level, and after watching the sun set from the grand elevation supper was eaten, and a watch set, the rest lying down eager for morning and their ascent of the final slope of some hundred feet to the crater.

These long tramps and climbs in the open air had the effect generally of making the night's rest seem astoundingly brief to Jack, who lay down, be the bed hard or soft, took a few deep breaths, and then all was oblivion till it was time to rise. And it was so here high up on the mountain slope, upon a bed of soft grey ashes, with a thin canvas loosely hung tent fashion. One minute he was awake, thinking of the coolness of the wind at that height, the next fast asleep, and then, so it appeared, directly after staring at Ned, who had shaken him to announce breakfast, while a scent of newly-made coffee floated in through the opening in the canvas.

In half-an-hour they were climbing the yielding slope of ashes diagonally, with the sun just appearing at the edge of the sea, glorifying the mists and the island below in a way that forced them to halt and gaze in wonderment at the beauty of the scene. Then up and up once more, but so slowly that a good two hours were spent over what had seemed to be to Jack the work of a few minutes. For the sides were deep in cindery stones which gave at every step, and ran down in little avalanches, leaving beneath a bed of fine silvery ash into which their feet sank deeply.

To have gone straight up would have been impossible, but by a side movement the way was slowly won, and at last Jack paused for a few moments to get his breath, then hurried up the rest of the way, reached the top first, and was seen by those below to pass over what seemed to be a sharp edge and disappear.

Ned shouted in alarm and rushed up after him, Sir John and the doctor next, for there was no reply to the shouts, and as just then a puff of smoke suddenly shot into the air, a horrible dread assailed the little group. But when they reached the edge they saw that their alarm was needless, for Jack had dropped into a sitting position upon the soft ashes, and was gazing down into a great cup-like depression about half-a-mile across, and gradually dipping down till the centre of the hollow was about five hundred feet below the top.

"Not much to see, Ned," said Jack as the man joined him. "That must be where the bright glow comes from at night."

He pointed down over the dark silvery grey waste, dotted with stones of all sizes, to where a pool lay on one side, apparently of water, for a shimmering light played over it, and a faint mist was rising slowly into the air.

"Couldn't come from water, sir," said Ned. "I didn't expect to see a pond up here; but I suppose it's hot, and that's steam."

"Oh yes, that's hot enough," said the doctor, who was panting with his exertions. "Liquid fire, eh, Jack?"

"Wouldn't it be molten metal of some kind, father?" cried the boy.

"No, my lad, it is molten stone—rock. Lava."

"But it puzzles me," cried Jack, "how stone can melt. You said something to me one day about a flux."

"Yes, of course. People who smelt metals found that out long enough ago, and it is the same with making glass. If you expose some minerals separately to great heat they merely become powder; but if you combine them—say flinty sand with soda or potash—they run together and become like molten metal. I believe if ironstone and limestone are mixed, the ironstone becomes fluid, so that it can be cast like a metal—in fact becomes the metal itself."

"Then that pool down there, if emptied out, would run like the volcanic glass we have found below?"

"Most likely."

"Let's go down this slope so as to see the pool from nearer."

"Rather a risky proceeding, my boy," said Sir John; "suppose we were to break through."

"Break through? Why, you don't think it is hollow under here?"

"I should rather believe that there was a stony crust hardened by cooling, and that a very short distance beneath us the rocks are all molten."

"But all these great stones lying about don't break through. Let's go a little way down."

"Don't be rash then. Will you come, Instow?"

"Oh yes, if it's safe. Let's go cautiously."

Just then the sailors, who had had to pack up and carry the camping-out necessaries, appeared at the edge, and waited there watching the little party as they slowly descended toward the shimmering pool, threading their way in and out among the blocks of lava and pumice which lay in their road.

Sir John led, with Jack close beside him, and the doctor and Ned followed a little way behind, to their right. But they had not descended a hundred yards before Sir John stopped short.

"No farther!" he said. "The heat is getting intense, and overpowering gases are escaping from the ashes. We must go back, Jack."

"I suppose so," said the lad unwillingly. "We don't see the pool any the better for being here either. Oh, look at that!"

There was no need to call attention, for all were startled by a sudden report, and a glow of heat swept past their faces as a huge fountain of fire suddenly played up some sixty or seventy feet like a geyser, and fell back with a heavy splash, lower and lower, still playing till there was only a slight eminence, as if bubbling in the middle of the pool. Then it was perfectly level again, and a cloud of white smoke floated away.

"That would have been grand by night," shouted the doctor.

"It was grand now," replied Sir John.

"Well, I think we had better turn back," said the doctor. "There is no doubt about its being molten fire below here, for the heat gets fiercer. Look."

He had been resting on the climbing pole he brought up with him, and found that the end had gone down a couple of feet, while as he drew it out the point was charred and smoking.

This induced Sir John and Jack to do the same, and theirs were burnt as well.

"Yes, get back at once!" shouted Sir John in startled tones. "Quick, all of you; our weight is acting upon the ashes, and they are gliding down with us."

"Hi! look out below, gen'lemen," shouted Lenny from the edge, "that there's bending like thin ice."

The warnings were none too soon, for as the pair turned sharply and began to climb back, it was quite plain that though the blocks of stone about lay or half floated upon the ash-covered surface, any further weight was sufficient to produce a change, and before they had taken many steps, one huge mass not twenty yards from Sir John was seen to be sinking slowly, then faster and faster, and disappeared through the ashes, which changed rapidly to a shimmering fluid, and sent forth a terrible heat.

"Don't hurry—open out slowly so as to spread the weight!" cried Sir John; and the doctor and Ned obeyed; but Jack saw that at every step his father's feet sank lower, and that his alpen-stick gave him no support, but went right in.

"Do you hear me, Jack?" shouted Sir John.

"Yes, father, but I can't leave you," cried the lad. "Here, give me your hand, or take hold of the end of my staff."

"Go on! Obey me, boy, or you will destroy us both," cried Sir John sternly, and Jack continued to climb up the slope, finding it more and more yielding, and as if below the ashes and stones there was a quivering or bubbling going on.

"That's right! go on, Jack; go on," cried Sir John. "It isn't far now."

They pressed on with a horrible feeling of panic attacking them now, for the quivering beneath them increased, the surface over which they toiled was trembling, and several of the blocks they passed began to settle slowly down.

"Only another fifty feet!" shouted the doctor. "Come on."

But at that moment a yell of warning came from the sailors, and Jack looked round to see that the ashes where his father climbed up were changing colour; then he noted that the slope was growing steeper and steeper; and to his horror his father threw himself at full length and began to crawl.

"Below there!" yelled Lenny. "Look out, Sir John."

"Below there! look out, Mr Jack," cried another sailor; and a couple of ropes flew down the slope in rapidly opening rings, and so accurately pitched that Jack caught his just as he felt that he was sliding downward.

Before he could turn to look at his father the rope tightened, and he was rapidly drawn up out of a heat that was terrible; but as he reached the edge of the crater he wrenched himself round in time to see that Sir John was nearly up; and the next minute he too was well over the side, the doctor and Ned, who had reached the top unaided, coming up white and trembling.

It was none too soon, for a minute later the slope down toward the pool, which had been easy, had now become, from the sinking of the centre, tremendously steep, and the pool itself suddenly began to spread out more and more, till half the expanse below was covered with the shimmering molten lava, and the heat became so intense that they were all glad to retreat down the side.

"What an escape, my boy!" panted Sir John, as he grasped his son's arm.

"It was dreadful," whispered Jack. "But are you hurt?"

"Nothing much; a little scorched."

Sir John held up one of his feet, and Jack could see that the leather of the boots was crushed up and drawn out of shape, while this drawing his attention to his own feet, which he now felt were uncomfortable and strange, he saw that his heavy boots were wrinkled up in the same way.

But they had to hurry their steps down the mountain side, for an earthquake-like quivering made the earth feel as if a wave was running beneath them, while in quick succession two thunderous explosions came from below; huge stones were thrown high in the air, and could be heard falling back into the crater with an awe-inspiring sound.

There was no temptation to pause and watch what was evidently the commencement of an eruption, and which might at any moment grow in force, so every effort was made to reach the shore, as nearly as they could judge about the part of the island off which the yacht was expected to lie.

They were fortunate on hitting upon one of the ravines which scored the mountain side some time before noon, and after a brief halt for refreshment, pushed on down its precipitous sides hour after hour, for the explosions from the crater grew more frequent, and all felt that they might culminate in some terrible cataclysm that would overwhelm them all.

Darkness did not overtake them that night, for long before it was sundown they were conscious of a peculiar glow above them, and the final part of their descent was illuminated by an intense light, which as night fell was reflected from the clouds which had gathered, and helped them to reach the shore not above half-a-mile from where the yacht lay with her lights burning.

A shot or two brought a boat to where they were waiting, and weary though they all were, they sat for hours gazing up at a great glowing stream of fire, which was plainly enough the beginning of one of the lava-streams which flowed down the mountain's sides.

"Notice to quit, I think, sir," said the captain quietly.

"Yes," said Sir John, "it would be foolhardy to stay here longer now."

"Then by your leave, sir, I'll take the yacht outside at once, for one never knows what may happen when a volcano begins to work. There! look at that! We'll get out while we can."

A terrific explosion reached their ears as he spoke, and without a moment's delay orders were given for steam to be got up, and before morning the yacht glided out through the reef, and past a flotilla of canoes which looked as if on their way to the island, but were lying-to as if startled from landing by the explosions which kept coming from the crater.

"Quite time our adventures ceased, Jack," said Sir John, "when they were becoming as dangerous as this. It seems that we have just had another escape."

"Yes, father," said Jack quietly. "I am sorry to leave the place; but, as you say, it was quite time to go."

Peaceful sea voyages in fine weather, from one of the well-known ports to the other for coal and other supplies, have been described too often for Jack Meadows' quiet journey to China, from thence to Japan, Australia, New Zealand, and then round the Horn to Rio, Barbadoes, and then homeward, to need recapitulation here. Let it suffice that it was within six weeks of two years from starting that Sir John's yacht steamed into Dartmouth harbour once more.

Two years—from sixteen to eighteen—work strange alterations in some lads; they had done wonders here, and Sir John and the doctor exchanged glances as Jack stepped down into the boat amid the cheers of the men, after he had shaken hands all round.

"Good-bye!" he shouted. "Remember that in six months we start on another cruise."

A deafening cheer was the answer to this, and the men sprang up into the rigging, to stand waving their caps to the lad—the young man who had been almost carried on board.

That evening as the express steamed into Paddington, and Ned met his master on the platform to say that the luggage was all right, the man seized the opportunity to whisper to Jack—

"Home again, sir! I say, what will they think of you there? They won't know you!"

"Not know me, Ned? Am I so much changed?"

"Changed, sir? What, don't you know it?"

"I—I think I'm stronger, Ned, and grown a little."

"Why, sir, you're as strong and as big as me."

"My cure, Jack!" said the doctor, shaking hands with him as they reached the old home. "I say, Meadows, what am I to charge for this?—No: I'm paid already in the sight of my old friend's son."

It's rather a hard thing to do, but it is to be done. I mean for three people to shake hands at once. These three—Sir John, the doctor, and Jack Meadows—did in self-congratulation at being safe and sound at home.

It is done like this— No, you can find that out yourselves.